AETERNUS

THE IMMORTALLE SERIES BOOK ONE

D.M. SHANE

Edited by
TELLTAIL EDITING

Cover by
PARADISE COVER DESIGN

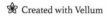

CONTENTS

Warning   vii

Prologue   1
1. Aislin   3
2. Aislin   11
3. Arkkadian   26
4. Aislin   37
5. Arkkadian   42
6. Aislin   49
7. Arkkadian   54
8. Aislin   60
9. Arkkadian   64
10. Arkkadian   79
11. Aislin   84
12. Aislin   88
13. Arkkadian   97
14. Aislin   101
15. Arkkadian   110
16. Arkkadian   119
17. Aislin   122
18. Arkkadian   130
19. Aislin   133
20. Arkkadian   138
21. Aislin   140
22. Arkkadian   144
23. Aislin   148
24. Arkkadian   161
25. Aislin   166
26. Arkkadian   172
27. Aislin   179
28. Arkkadian   182
29. Arkkadian   188
30. Arkkadian   192
31. Aislin   196
32. Arkkadian   198
33. Aislin   203
34. Arkkadian   206

35. Aislin	209
36. Arkkadian	211
37. Aislin	219
38. Arkkadian	222
39. Aislin	224
40. Arkkadian	228
41. Aislin	235
42. Aislin	240
43. Arkkadian	245
44. Aislin	251
45. Arkkadian	259
46. Arkkadian	262
47. Aislin	270
Acknowledgments	279
About the Author	281
Coming Soon	283

For my husband

For twenty years, you've sailed the world. You've experienced things you'll never forget. Like Greece and Borneo. Spain. Italy. France. Malaysia. Even the North Pole. You've also sacrificed. Missed milestones and many a birthday, anniversary, or holiday just to keep us safe. But through it all, you never stopped being my anchor and have always been my biggest cheerleader throughout this crazy awesome life. I love you deeper than maximum operating depth.

P.S. You start up my reactor.

For L.B.

You, my dear friend, whom I often wish lived closer, are amazing. You are one of the kindest, sweetest, caring, and compassionate women I know, and I am both lucky and grateful to call you friend. Even with all the struggles you have endured, your spirit never gives up. Your light shines bright. Never forget it.

For T.B.

I know I've told you many times, but I will say it one more time because it's true. You inspire me. You gave me advice. You encouraged me. If it wasn't for you, I'm not sure I'd have ever had the courage to sit down and tell the story. Thank you for being the kick in the pants I needed to find my courage and my confidence. I know you'll find your Man Bear, and when you do, the journey will have been well worth the wait.

WARNING

Aeternus is a paranormal romance containing mature themes that might make some readers uncomfortable. Please be advised that this book contains strong language, graphic violence, spanking, and scenes of sexual assault/abuse that may be triggering.

PROLOGUE

Whitewater, Montana. A tiny little town on the western outskirts of Glacier National Park. The first place in a long time where I fit in. Where I had friends I could call family. I hadn't had that in so long, I'd almost forgotten what it felt like. All the moving from town to town, working my tail off to make ends meet, and never knowing where life might take me had made it difficult to find a home, but when I came to Whitewater, I knew it was the place for me right away.

For three years, I was happy. I finally had a home, and people I loved and who loved me back. I was finally settling in. Finding a life for myself.

And then one terrifying night, everything changed.

That was the night a date with Kane West went horribly wrong. Little did I know, the events of that one night would change my life forever. Little did I know, those events would later thrust me into the arms of a man called Arkkadian Rime and a whole new world I never knew existed.

My name is Aislin Barrington, and this is my story. I won't lie and tell you it's all sunshine and rainbows because it's not. No, mine is a story of fear. Anger. Monsters. But it's not just those things—it's also a story of finding courage and love.

1

AISLIN

I backed up against the wall, my heart pounding against my ribs like a jackhammer on hard pavement. Fear slithered through me, snaking icy tendrils around my spine. Kane's hands slapped the wall on either side of my head and his hot breath blew in my face as he tried to force his tongue in my mouth. He smelled of chewing tobacco, and the sickly-sweet scent turned my stomach. I tried to shove him away, but he was so much stronger. Feeling trapped and helpless, my anxiety slipped into overdrive.

"Come on, baby, you know you want this. Give me some sugar, Ash... lynn." Kane leaned forward, pushing my body into the wall, and inhaled deeply. I loathed the way he spoke my name. "Mm... you smell... divine. It's been a long time since I came across a scent as delectable as yours. Too bad you're not mine. Not that I care."

Not his? What did that mean? Why was he sniffing me like that? A shudder racked through my body. I tried to squirm free of his grasp, but he pushed me harder up against the wall and forced a leg between mine.

"Get off me!" I begged. "I said no!"

I placed both of my hands on his chest and shoved him again, but it was futile, like trying to shove a boulder back up a steep mountainside. I was trapped.

Kane gripped both of my wrists and spun me around to face the wall, pinning my hands painfully behind me. I shouted for him to stop again, but the side of my head being shoved against the wall prevented me from speaking. I whimpered in pain when Kane gripped a handful of my hair and yanked, forcing my head back.

"I took you out for a nice dinner. I fed you. I bought you drinks. And you think you can repay me by denying me? Well, you thought wrong! I've waited ages for this. You will give me what I want and you'll like it. You don't get to tell me no," he ground out, lukewarm spittle landing on my skin and making me gag.

"Taking me on a few dates does *not* entitle you to sex! Get off!" I tried to push off the wall, but with my arms pinned so painfully behind me, it was physically impossible. "Let me go!"

"You'll give me what I want. You don't get nice things without giving something back." Kane let go of my hair and snaked a hand around the front of my blouse while the other kept my arms restrained behind me. He gave a yank on the fabric. Little white buttons flew, bouncing off the wall, plinking as they hit the hard-wood floor.

Suddenly, he released my arms and reached around with the other hand to rip the cups of my bra down, exposing my breasts. Tears streaked down my face. My breathing was rushed and heavy, and my chest felt tight. Kane leaned his head over my shoulder and moaned at the sight of my bare breasts. His rough, calloused hands pinched hard at my nipples, and I cried out at the pain.

"Look at those tits. Baby, I'm gonna have so much fun tonight!" He buried his face in my neck and inhaled again. I cringed as he ran his tongue up the side of my neck, leaving a disgustingly wet trail along the way. My stomach flipped. I wanted to throw up.

"No!"

It was now or never. I had to fight.

I crashed my head sideways into Kane's face, but it didn't have the intended effect. At that angle, I only succeeded in smashing my head against his cheek. Kane raged. He picked me up, threw me over his shoulder, and stormed down the hall. I screamed and kicked, raining my fists down on his back as he carried me toward a dark room near the back of the house.

"You've done it now, bitch! I'm not playing nice anymore," he growled.

That was playing nice?

He hit the light switch and tossed me onto a king-sized bed. I tried to scramble away, but Kane grabbed my ankle and yanked me back. "Yell all you want. Nobody's gonna hear you. These walls are soundproof."

My heart sunk, and I feared the worst. Tears continued to pour down my cheeks. Kane crawled on top of me, his legs straddling my hips. He leaned forward, pushed my head to the side, and took another sniff just below my ear. I tried to slap him away, but he grabbed my wrists and squeezed so hard, I thought my bones would snap. I struggled to pull myself free, but his grip was inescapable.

"Why do you keep smelling me?" Keep him talking. Maybe if I could do that, it would give me time to think.

"As if you don't know." Kane hovered directly above me, nose to nose, his foul breath hot on my face. His long brown hair swept over me, making my skin crawl. "You know damn well why. I knew the first time I saw you." When I stared back, utterly confused, a creepy grin crossed his face. "Wait. You really don't know, do you?"

"What are you talking about?" I didn't understand. I just knew I needed to find a way out before he hurt me.

Kane barked an obnoxious laugh at my question. The moment his grip lessened, I yanked my arms free and tried to shove him off again. His eyes flared bright green, and I found myself pinned to the bed in a flash. What the fuck was wrong with his eyes?

The distraction only lasted a moment before I remembered to fight, and I tried again to pry myself free of his grasp.

"That's it! Fight! I love it when women fight. It makes me that... much... harder," he growled above me. He actually growled. Like a beast.

I turned my head and screamed as loud as I could in his ear. Kane jerked away just before he slammed his fist down on my cheek.

"Shut up!" he snarled.

My head jerked to the side with the blow. Dazed, I lay there as rough hands groped me everywhere, fingers digging painfully into me, bruising my flesh. He pulled my torn shirt and bra off before making short work of removing my pants. The sound of tearing fabric filled my ears as my panties gave way. I tried to sit up, but the room spun in circles around me, and I fell back onto the bed, still dizzy. I scrunched my eyes shut to stop the room from spinning, but it didn't help.

Kane climbed off and stripped. His muscles bulged. Veins popped out of his neck. An ominous tattoo of a snarling wolf covered the entirety of his chest. His face was as red as the devil himself.

I sobered quickly when I noticed his eyes still emanated a sinister green glow. Something wasn't right. Eyes didn't glow!

Kane pulled his pants off, and his erection stood at attention. He was huge. I tried to scoot backward off the bed, but Kane grabbed my ankle and yanked me back again. In an instant, he was back on top of me, pinning me down. His dick twitched where it lay across my bare stomach. Oh, God. This couldn't be happening. I continued to struggle, doing everything in my power to shove him off, but Kane only growled in response.

"Get off me! Please stop! Let me go!" I screamed through the tears as I pushed at his chest.

He ran a hand down the jagged scars on the left side of my body, moaning as he touched them, before suddenly flipping me onto my belly. "Well, what do we have here? It looks like someone already left his handiwork on you already, girl. He even left his signature. Look at that. Huh."

When I tried to pull away, he jerked my left arm behind me and wrenched my shoulder. I wailed as the pain stabbed through me like a knife. Any harder and he would probably dislocate it. Kane placed his other hand in the middle of my back and forced me back down onto the bed.

"Just where did you get these scars? Hm? They make me so hard."

"Fuck off!"

"Oh, I fully intend to fuck you. You know, I just wanted a piece of ass, but you've pissed me off. I think I'm gonna take you and make you mine. Forever. It's not every day a rogue comes along. Oh, the things I can do to you once you're mine for all eternity. And there's nothing you can do about it."

His? Forever? What the hell was a rogue? I still didn't have a clue what he was referring to, but I knew I was in danger.

Kane pushed his knee between my legs and forced them open. In the next instant, his hand was on my backside, spreading my cheeks. The second I realized what he was doing, another wave of panic hit me. A low growl issued from his throat as he leaned forward to sniff at my neck again. Then I felt it. Something hard rubbing against my back entrance. No! This couldn't be happening!

"Please, no! Please stop! Not that. Anything but that," I begged through wrenching sobs, only to be met with dark laughter.

Kane let go of my arm and more pain seared through my shoulder as I pulled it around and tucked it under me, trying to catch my breath. His fingers dug into my flesh again. Tears of humiliation ran down my face at knowing what he was about to do and that there was little I could do to stop it.

"I'm gonna tear your virgin ass up and I'm gonna love every minute. You won't be able to sit for a month when I'm through with you."

My head felt fuzzy, and I suddenly wanted to puke. I tried to push the feeling down. I needed to find a way out of here. I needed to fight.

"Well, isn't that interesting? What's going on in that head of yours?"

I couldn't respond to anything with my shoulder screaming, but with both hands free, I reached for the lamp on the night-stand. Grabbing hold of it, I swung the lamp as hard as I could and slammed it into the side of Kane's head. The ceramic base shattered and sliced his face. A few shards lodged in his skin. He reared back onto the bed, an angry snarl ripping out of his throat. His eyes raged, the emerald glow intensifying. It was terrifying.

"You fucking bitch!" Kane violently roared.

Freed from his grip, I rolled over onto my back just as he leaned above me, his face an angry scarlet, blood pouring from the cuts. I pulled my leg back and kicked straight at his groin. My foot connected with its target, and he screamed in agony. Kane cupped himself and rolled to the floor, muttering profanities as he curled into the fetal position.

I jumped from the bed, grabbed my torn clothes, and fled down the hallway. I stopped in the living room and pulled on my pants, but before I could put my blouse on, a loud crash sounded from the bedroom. The door flew open and slammed against the wall. Kane launched himself through the opening and crashed into the opposite wall of the hallway. The force of his body punched a giant hole through the drywall. His face boiled with rage, and furious snarls rumbled from his throat. He sounded more like a beast than a man. Blood poured down the side of his face where the lamp shards had been and dripped onto his bare chest. Kane stood stock-still and glared. I couldn't look away from his glowing eyes.

"You are mine, you fucking whore! Binding you to me will be so much fun. Then I'll punish you for what you've done." Kane spoke so quietly, I wasn't sure if I'd heard him right, but I wasn't sticking around to find out. He slunk toward me, stalking me from down the hall like a hungry predator honed in on weak prey.

I scrambled for the front door and yanked it open. Covering myself as best I could with my torn shirt, I ran for dear life. I ran down the street screaming for help, with only fear driving me forward. I didn't look to see if he followed.

A light flicked on up the road. The front door swung open, and a man stepped out onto his front porch. I ran straight for him.

"Help! Please help! I need help!" I shouted as I ran up the steps and straight into the man's arms. Hot tears of fear and relief streamed down my face. The man ushered me inside and then shut and locked the door behind him.

I pulled free of his arms and ran to a corner, where I had a visual of the whole room. Wrapping my arms around me, I sunk to the floor and curled up into a ball.

"Let me call the police," he said, disappearing into the next room.

The moment he left, I pulled my ripped-up blouse on as fast as I could and curled into a ball again, making myself as small as possible. I wrapped my arms around my legs and rocked back and forth as I watched the front door. I was nearly hysterical by the time he came back into the room, still on his phone.

"Yes, that's right, ma'am. Sycamore Lane, not Drive. Thank you." The man hung up and took a seat on the end of the sofa furthest from me and didn't move any closer. "Miss, the police are on their way. Is there anything I can do? Can I get you anything? Water?"

I shrunk in on myself, unable to look at him. I flinched when he stood up, but he only walked to the window and peeked out through the curtain.

A few minutes later, a knock sounded, and he opened the door, letting a policeman and a pair of EMTs inside. Deep voices. All men. I didn't want them to touch me. I didn't want them to look at me. I didn't want them to know I existed.

The officer turned to the man and asked him some questions as one of the EMT's knelt down beside me. I tried to scoot back, but the wall blocked my path.

"I won't hurt you, miss. I'm a medic," he said, speaking quietly. "Can you tell me your name?"

"Ais... Aislin," I whispered.

"Okay, Aislin. My name is David. I just need to make sure you're okay. Can you tell me how you got that mark on the side of your face?"

I peeked up at him. My eyes felt swollen, and snot gathered on my upper lip. My cheek pounded with pain. He was young, maybe a few years older than me, with a gentle demeanor. The soft waves of his blond hair brushed over his brown eyes. He smiled gently at me, and the fear in my belly eased a little.

"My date attacked me. He seemed so nice. He'd asked if I wanted to join him at his place for a movie, but when we got there, he... he...." A shudder rocked through me.

Panic parked in my chest, weighing me down. I couldn't get in enough air. I felt like I was suffocating. Why couldn't I get in enough air? Oh, God—

His quiet voice cut through my panic. "It's okay. Let's take a deep breath and slow your breathing down. Just listen to my voice. Try to take a slow breath in. Good. Now breathe out slowly. There you go. Another. In and out, just like that."

I did as David asked, breathing in and out slowly. Surprisingly, it helped a little, the tight band in my chest easing some.

"Are you hurt anywhere? Are there any injuries besides the bruise on your face?" he questioned carefully.

"My... my shoulder. He wrenched my arm behind me when he pinned me down. I... he tried to..." I stuttered and looked away. I couldn't bring myself to say it. It was bad enough I had to remember it, let alone talk about it.

"That's okay. You don't have to say anything. Can you stand up? I'd like to take you to the hospital to have that shoulder checked. You may have a concussion." He reached for my elbow, but quickly stopped when I cowered away. "I'm sorry, I didn't mean to frighten you."

He backed away, giving me some space. Slowly, I crawled from the corner and stood up. I took two steps forward and then collapsed.

2

AISLIN

ix months later

Tall. Dark. Handsome. Mysterious. Formidable. He watched me as I watched him stride gracefully around the edge of the dance floor and head my direction. He grabbed a stool at the end of the bar and sat down. I finished drying a glass as I took in his features.

His hair was black as night, close-cropped, with bangs sweeping gently across his forehead. His goatee was perfect, not a whisker out of place. Muscles bulged under a black t-shirt and blue jeans that hugged every ounce of deliciously tanned skin. The man oozed power, and I couldn't look away.

A strange sense of familiarity swept over me, almost like I knew him somehow, though I'd never seen him before. I'd felt him the moment he'd walked in the door. I didn't realize I was staring until Paige, my best friend and roommate, tapped on my shoulder. A hot flush of embarrassment crept up my face.

"You gonna stand there and stare all night or are you going to fix Mr. Sex on Two Legs a drink? Wipe the drool off your chin," Paige whispered in my ear. "Damn, he's hot!"

"Paige!"

"What? It's true!" She laughed as she sauntered away.

Embarrassed, I walked down to the end of the bar to take the man's drink order. His beautiful sapphire eyes were hard as steel as they tracked my every move. I shivered, and the hair on the back of my neck stood up. I couldn't decide if I wanted to stare into those eyes forever or run the other way. The hypnotic pull between us was terrifying, yet captivatingly seductive.

Normally, I avoided men. I didn't like them. Not after... that. But something about this man drew me in like a moth to a flame. The connection was undeniable, like two magnets joined by an invisible force.

Suddenly, his eyes widened a tiny fraction and then he appeared to sniff the air as I approached. Did he just sniff me? I could have sworn he did. Or maybe my mind was just playing tricks. He wasn't Kane. I buried the memory quickly, sure I was imagining things.

"Good evening, sir. What can I get for you?" I asked. That same familiar feeling nagged at me, but I just couldn't place it. How could I know someone I'd never met?

"Arkkadian," he stated, hard eyes assessing me.

"Excuse me, sir?" I asked.

"My name is Arkkadian Rime. You don't have to call me sir," he remarked as he rested his elbows on the bar. His blue eyes bored into me, making me slightly uncomfortable while reeling me in at the same time.

"I'm sorry, sir. Um, Mr. Rime. May I get you something to drink?" I barely stuttered the words out. I felt like a nervous fool, and my cheeks grew hot. The raw power emanating off this man crashed into me. And that deep voice? It was like smooth velvet caressing every inch of my skin. From out of nowhere, desire pooled down low. Oh, my God! What was wrong with me?

"Just Arkkadian. Jack and Coke, please." The corner of his lips twitched before he smiled. He was playing it cool, but he knew what kind of effect he had on me. And he knew I knew because my poker face sucked. It always had.

"Very well, I'll be right back." I could have sworn his eyes twinkled when I'd called him sir. I turned on my heel and headed straight for the bottle of Jack.

Paige threw me a thumbs up, and I stuck my tongue out. Could she be any more obvious? Gah! I glanced back at Arkkadian as I mixed his drink. His eyes were still on me. Watching.

Waiting. Waiting for what, I didn't know. Goosebumps prickled my skin. It was unnerving, yet intensely arousing the way he watched me. I warred with the contradiction of feelings he spurred inside me.

"Oh... my... stars! Is he sexy or what?" Paige swooned, pretending to faint.

For fuck's sake! I rolled my eyes at her display of dramatics.

"Oh, come on, Ash! Admit it. You think he's hot! I know you do!" She let slip a giggle. My best friend had a naughty streak, and she wasn't afraid to show it. I wished I could be that confident.

"I'm not interested." I downplayed it, hoping she'd cool it. I wasn't interested in a man and hadn't been since that night.

"Hopeless! You are hopeless! You need a man in your life!" Paige laughed.

I ignored her and went back to mixing the man's drink. No. The last thing I needed or wanted was a man in my life. I was still dealing with the aftermath of what happened with that asshole, Kane West, a few months ago. I couldn't fault my best friend, though, because she didn't know. I hadn't seen him since that night, either. The investigation had gone nowhere, and Kane had disappeared. It devastated me when the detective had closed the case. I still worried every day that Kane would waltz right back into my life. The thought was terrifying.

Just as I set Arkkadian's drink down, a wave of nausea hit me so hard, I stumbled into the bar top, barely catching myself before I tumbled over. My head felt all fuzzy, almost like it was full of cobwebs.

When I looked up, Arkkadian's eyes were dead set on me, his head cocked to the side like he had something he wanted to say but dared not. I took a moment to close my eyes and catch my breath. When I opened them again, his face was unreadable—as if it hid a multitude of secrets behind that smooth façade—but his steel-blue eyes devoured me, betraying his hunger. Those eyes gave away a secret. Just one.

He wanted me.

I quickly tried to stifle my fraying nerves as they amped up under his piercing gaze. "Will that be all, sir?" I asked, grabbing the cash he'd laid down.

"Yes. And please, call me Arkkadian. May I ask your name?" His eyes twinkled again.

"Aislin. I'll be back to check on you, Arkkadian. Enjoy your drink." I smiled and quickly walked away.

I wanted to disappear. I couldn't shake the foreboding feeling in the pit of my stomach that I knew him somehow. And for whatever reason, his presence not only made me anxious but highly aroused. And confused. I needed a distraction before my anxiety got the better of me. The last thing I needed was a panic attack at work because I couldn't get a handle on my warring emotions.

Music. That's what I needed. Good music always made me feel better. I made my way to the DJ booth and added a few songs to Jimmy's request list. I watched as couples two-stepped around the outside of the dance floor. I would have loved to get out on the floor for a few dances, but the Black Horse Saloon was swamped tonight. Paige and I were too busy behind the bar. Sheryl was out sick, and Ginny was out of town for two days. That left Paige and me to run the bar. At least I got to listen to good country music while I worked.

Carter, my boss, grabbed me by the elbow as I passed him on the way back to the bar. "You okay, Ash?"

Carter not only owned the Black Horse, but he was also my landlord and friend. Paige and I rented the apartment above the bar from him. He was sharp as a tack. Never missed a thing.

Three years ago, I'd moved to the small town of Whitewater, Montana, and when I'd gotten the job at the Black Horse, Paige had offered me the extra room in the apartment upstairs. We'd become instant best friends. Carter and his wife, Ann, had become like family, but she'd succumbed to cancer a year ago. I missed her every day.

"Yeah, I'm good. Thanks. I think I just moved too fast or something," I fibbed. Carter raised an eyebrow. That excuse wouldn't get me far. He knew me too well. Truth was, I didn't know what it was. I'd never been sick a day in my life.

"Why don't you go take ten? Have a snack. You've been on your feet all evening and I know you didn't get a break earlier. Go on. I'll help Paige 'til you come back."

"But..."

"No buts. Go!" Carter grabbed my shoulders, spun me around, and pushed me toward the office in the back.

I thought about how good he had always been to me. Carter was the only real father figure I'd ever known in my life. I have no memory of my biological parents, and growing up, I'd bounced from foster home to foster home until I'd aged out of the system. I left Seattle as soon as I'd turned eighteen, bouncing around from small town to small town before settling in Whitewater three years ago. It was the first place that had ever felt like home. The first place where I felt like I fit in. Carter had hired me on the spot, and then Paige had offered me the extra room. They were the only family I had. I'd be lost without them.

In the office, I grabbed a granola bar from my purse and sat down in Carter's chair behind the desk. It felt good to get off my feet for a moment. While I snacked, I thought about the man at the bar with the steel-blue eyes. They were like bright sapphires, drawing me into their crystalline depths. Arkkadian was hot, but I wasn't interested in a man right now. I was still healing, and I'd been avoiding men ever since that night. I still had nightmares. Men scared me, and nothing about this man made much sense. I couldn't shake that nagging feeling either. The way he watched me at the bar felt like he knew the way to my soul. The thought startled me.

He exuded raw power, and it radiated off him in droves even as it reeled me in. He was attractive. Alluring. Dangerous. I couldn't deny the very thought of him shook me to my core.

Alpha. I didn't know where the sudden thought had come from, but it fit. He was in charge. And he knew it.

I finished my snack and headed back, hoping Arkkadian wouldn't be there. Much to my chagrin, he was still sitting there. I spotted Carter behind the DJ booth, which meant Jimmy must have been on a smoke break. Our eyes met, and recognition sparked inside of me. *Mine.* The thought sent butterflies zipping around my stomach.

On my path back to the bar, an arm snaked around my waist unexpectedly, pulling me back and making me gasp. Stiff whiskers and hot breath nuzzled my neck from behind, and I tried to shrug away. The sickly sweet smell of chewing tobacco assaulted my senses, and I froze, knowing exactly who it was.

No. No. No.

Bile rose up the back of my throat, and I could taste its acrid flavor. Shit! Kane. Panic sprung forth from my chest, but before I could speak, Kane's callused hand slid over my mouth. He inhaled before releasing his hot breath on my neck and rubbing his nose behind my ear.

Stiff with icy fear, I couldn't move. This couldn't be happening! Not here. This wasn't real. It couldn't be real. But it was. Kane was back. I couldn't breathe.

I scrunched my eyes shut with a whimper and willed him to let me go, but his grasp only tightened around me. The boulder of terror sitting atop my chest prevented me from taking in the air I so desperately needed. His hand wandered down my left side, along my scars, and firmly planted upon my hip before giving a harsh squeeze. Right where the R branded my skin.

"Hey, Ash, how are you? It's been a while," Kane crooned in my ear. "I missed you, babe. I've been looking forward to seeing you again. God, you smell so divine." He took another whiff.

Words froze in my throat. I squirmed in his arms, gasping for breath as tears poured down my face. I tried to be quiet to avoid drawing attention from the crowd. It would only fuel the panic ripping through me.

Kane squeezed me tighter. "Come on, Ash, why the tears? Didn't you miss me? I'm just here to show you how much I still like you. The boys and I want to have a little fun tonight, so maybe you can come back to my place after you get off work. You know, you still owe me for that little stunt you pulled."

The two men standing beside him laughed.

"I bet she's got a fine pussy, man!" The one with the scruffy dark hair laughed. His teeth were jagged and yellow.

"I wonder how tight her ass is," the other crowed. I couldn't see him. "I love a tight ass."

I cringed at the thought of either man touching me.

"Get off me. Please, Kane, let me go," I pleaded, struggling to pull away from him, but it was futile. My innate fear of the monster that was Kane coiled around me, squeezing me in its vice-like grip. I was on the verge of a full-blown panic attack.

"Let her go, Kane." Arkkadian's command filled the air.

I couldn't bring myself to open my eyes and look up at the beautiful stranger with the steel-blue eyes. I was mortified at the thought of him seeing me in such a state. The more I struggled to breathe, the more light-headed I became, and I felt like I was about to pass out.

Another wave of nausea hit me like a ton of bricks when I realized what Arkkadian had said. They knew each other. He'd called Kane by name. What the fuck?

"Well, well, well, if it isn't Arkkadian Rime. Get lost, Alpha. She's mine. Go find your own," Kane challenged. I feared the threat in his voice and wondered at their shared history. He'd also called Arkkadian "Alpha." I'd had that same thought only minutes ago.

"I said... Let. Her. Go," Arkkadian demanded.

"Or what?" Kane's grip tightened again, his chin digging into my shoulder. I could smell alcohol on his breath, mixed in with the tobacco. It made me gag. He still had a hand on my hip, the other splayed across my belly, clutching me against him as he continued to nuzzle behind my ear.

Judging by the smell, Kane had been drinking heavily. Last time I saw Kane, he'd been clean-cut, and now he reeked. His beard was greasy, his skin sweaty, and his hair unkempt. Had it all been an act before?

I was fully hyperventilating now. Tears poured uncontrollably down my face as I tried to suck in more air. Images of that night flashed through my mind. The smell of his breath. The fear. His fist hitting my face. Being pinned to the bed. The eyes. Shit, the glowing eyes!

"Let her go. Or, we can take this outside. We've already been down that road, you and I, and you know how that ends. Though I'm sure the lovely young lady behind the bar would call the police if I gave the word." Arkkadian's voice grew more forceful as he spoke, an air of authority present. *Dominant.* The thought quickly came and went. But the feel of it? It was instinctive. I felt it in my bones where it stayed. If I hadn't been so scared, I would have found it thrilling.

Paige had her hand on the phone, looking at me with uncertainty. She didn't know about the assault a few months ago, let alone that Kane was responsible. I never told my best friend. I never told her the reason for the increase in my hellish nightmares every night. I had refused to speak about any of it. It wasn't just that I hated what happened, I worried what others would think, and I didn't want them to see me any different. I didn't want them to pity me. Or think I was dirty. I felt dirty enough as it was.

While I silently pleaded with Paige to make the call, Kane grabbed my throat forcefully, cutting off my air entirely. "You and I aren't through, bitch. You owe me a punishment, and I will collect." And then I was suddenly shoved forward into Arkkadian's arms. "Get fucked, Rime."

I was still gasping for air when Arkkadian's warm hands enveloped me and pulled me in. I froze in his grasp, absolutely petrified. I didn't want to be touched, but I was too frightened to move. Still too scared of Kane and frightened by the peace and familiarity I suddenly felt in Arkkadian's arms. I didn't understand any of it. Arkkadian may have saved me from Kane tonight, but I didn't exactly feel safe around him either, though I wanted to.

Time slowed down as he guided me over to the corner of the bar and onto a stool. As I struggled to breathe, those same warm arms wrapped around me again, and I let them despite my fear. Arkkadian stood behind me, guarding me from the rest of the crowd while he held me. I turned to see Carter barrel over toward Kane and his buddies.

"Get the fuck out of my bar and don't come back!" Carter shouted.

"All right, all right. We're going, old man. This isn't over, Ash." He clicked his tongue and winked at me before walking out the door. I knew then that Kane wouldn't stop until he got what he wanted.

Paige placed the phone back on the receiver and came over. With Kane gone, there was no longer a need for the police.

"Ash, are you okay?" Carter asked, sitting down on the stool beside me. I still struggled to breathe, and I couldn't answer. "Thank you," he told Arkkadian, shaking his hand.

I stared at the counter, barely able to focus on anything but my struggle to draw in oxygen. I couldn't look at anyone, least of all the man holding me like he never wanted to let me go. I tried to slow my breathing, but horrible memories just kept flashing through my head. I scrunched my eyes as tightly as I could, willing the images to stop.

Arkkadian let go of me and sat down next to me. Oddly, I wanted him to keep holding me. I'd felt a sense of loss when he'd let go, almost like a part of me had suddenly gone missing. Weird.

"What the fuck was that about?" Arkkadian's anger wrapped around me like a cloak, and instantly, I knew it for what it was. Vigilance. Protectiveness. He was now my sentinel. My protector, whether I wanted it or not. And want it, I did.

"Not a clue. He used to be a regular, but I haven't seen him in months. He never caused trouble before," Carter mused. When he looked at me, I caught the change in his expression. He knew about the assault as my emergency contact, but I'd just never told him who it was.

I eyed him, hoping he'd understand my silent plea to stay quiet, but then the room spun. I almost slid off the stool before Arkkadian caught me.

"Aislin, listen to me," Arkkadian soothed. His voice was deep and rich. Smooth, like slow-aged whiskey as it slid down my throat. He turned me to face him and placed a hand on each of my knees. I flinched but didn't pull away. I couldn't, even if I wanted to.

I was at war with myself over this beautiful stranger. Don't freak out. Get control of yourself. Don't touch me. Please don't stop touching me.

"You're hyperventilating. You'll pass out if you don't stop. I need you to listen to my voice." He spoke in a slow, rhythmic manner, and I felt my body giving in to his request. Recognizing. Trusting. "Try to slow your breathing down. Breathe in and count to three. That's it. Now breathe out and count. Just like that. In... out... Good. You're doing great."

His voice was calming, and his eyes never wavered from mine. The intimidating feeling I'd felt earlier had disappeared. Instead, I found my attraction to him growing. The familiar pull was back, rippling through me like a plucked guitar string.

Warmth enveloped my body. It seemed to radiate from where his hands rested on my knees and spread outward, blanketing me from head to toe. My breathing slowed, but my tears refused to cooperate. My whole body shook with sobs as the fear I'd felt while imprisoned in Kane's grasp rippled to the surface again.

Once again, Arkkadian pulled me in close, and with gentle hands, he wiped my tears. When I opened my eyes, I found myself up close and personal with Arkkadian as he hugged me to him. He was so much taller than I realized. Lean and muscular. Firm, but gentle. Black rims circled around his sapphire irises. Like mine, only mine were silver edged in black. I'd never met anyone with eyes like mine before. How strange.

Despite his gentleness, I tried to pull away, but Arkkadian just held me there, murmuring quietly about me being safe. Deep down, I believed him. More waves of warmth radiated through my body. The sensation felt odd, yet familiar. It felt like it was being pushed through me by an unseen force. Every muscle relaxed as all the tension left my body. I pondered what that was as Arkkadian soothed, his hand rubbing up and down my back in slow circles. The urge to pull away from him subsided. I leaned into him, breathing him in, feeling comforted, yet confused about my mixed reactions. None of this made any sense.

"You're okay. Nothing will happen to you," Arkkadian said, his voice remaining low and calm. Then he gently wiped away more tears as I came back to myself.

"Ash, why don't you go home early tonight? Paige and I can handle the bar. You go rest. Take tomorrow and Friday off," Carter said, concern showing in his eyes. "We can talk about all of this later when you're feeling better."

"But I need the hours." I was still working my ass off to pay down the credit cards I'd maxed out with all the moving around I'd done over the past three years.

"Don't you worry, I'll take care of it. You get some rest. I'll call Ginny to fill in; she said she was coming home early tomorrow, anyway. I'll check on you in the morning." Carter hugged me and kissed my forehead, gave Arkkadian a nod, and walked away.

As I watched him retreat behind the bar, Paige sat down and took my hands. "You okay, Ash?" she asked, giving me the once over.

She handed me more tissues. I wasn't sure if Paige had figured it all out yet or not, but I knew when she came home later, I'd face the inquisition and there were things I wasn't ready to explain.

"Yeah, I'm good. Just shaken up." I eyed Arkkadian before telling my friend to go back to work. I knew nothing about the man who had his arms wrapped protectively around me, other than he'd stood up to Kane and that they apparently had a history together. I was thankful he'd stood up for me, but I wasn't ready to trust him, even if he saved me. Even if my body wanted to trust him, I didn't know him. The way he'd watched me earlier, though, as if he could see to the center of my soul, still unnerved me.

"You know I'm here for you, right?"

"I know."

"Good. Go rest. I'll be home in a couple of hours." With that, Paige hugged me and drifted back behind the counter. Soon, customers on the dance floor would leave for the night.

I pulled out of Arkkadian's embrace.

"Is there anything I can do to help? Do you need a ride home or anything? I can see you home safely," he asked.

I bristled. No. Full stop. There was no way I was letting him take me home. I didn't want him knowing where I lived, even if it was just upstairs. It didn't matter how safe he made me feel. How much I wanted him to protect me.

"Thank you, but no. I'll be okay. I don't live far. Thanks for standing up to Kane, though. This is embarrassing."

"There's nothing to be embarrassed about. The guy is an asshole. He has no respect for women. It's not your fault," Arkkadian stated. An angry expression flicked so quickly across his face, I almost didn't catch it before it disappeared.

"Speaking of, why were you watching me so intently all evening? And why are you being so nice to me? We barely know each other." I pulled further away from him. "And how do you know Kane? You called him by his name and I never said his name."

I didn't know where all of that had come from; I'd just blurted it all out. I wasn't usually so blunt.

"I apologize. Truly. It's just that you're beautiful, and I was drawn to you. I didn't mean to scare you. As for Kane, we grew up together. We've never gotten along and he's always been a trouble-maker. He's not someone to mess with. In fact, he's dangerous."

I looked down at my lap where I sat twisting my hands together. Did he really think I was beautiful? It wasn't often someone complimented me, but then, I'd never taken a compliment easily, anyway. My insecurities always took the forefront.

I've only ever thought of myself as a small-town girl. I wore boots and jeans. T-shirts and ponytails. A nerd. Damaged. Much of that stemmed from my years in foster homes, never feeling worthy. Or from the ugly scars I hid from the world. The homes weren't bad, but they weren't great. And they never felt like home or like I fit in. And then there were the nightmares from some unknown childhood trauma. And the anxiety. The panic attacks. I'd had them my whole life and never understood why. I only knew the dreams related to my scars somehow.

"Um, thanks," I told him, my cheeks flushing with heat.

"You don't take a compliment well, do you?" He laughed a little.

Hearing his laugh made me relax a little more. "No. I just... I don't know. Anyway, thank you again, but I really need to go."

"My pleasure. Truly." Arkkadian released me and backed up, giving me some space.

I hopped off the barstool, thanked him again, and hightailed it to the back. I didn't look back, but I swore I could feel his eyes on me the whole way. I punched out, grabbed my purse, and bolted out the back door and up the stairs to my apartment above the bar.

At the top of the stairs, I felt the hair on the back of my neck stand up. Something didn't feel right, but when I looked around the alley, I saw nothing. I chalked it up to nerves and rushed inside, locking the deadbolt behind me.

A hot bath and a glass of wine before bed sounded wonderful.

Ten minutes later, I sank down into the blissful heat, letting the water envelop my naked body. I didn't care that I'd dripped a trail of clothes down the hall and through my room to the tub. All

I wanted to do was forget about the world, if only for a little while.

I lay there in the silence, staring at the wall and trying unsuccessfully to clear my head. Thoughts of both Kane and Arkkadian muddled through my mind. The asshole... no... the rapist—call him what he really is—and the what? I didn't know what to think about Arkkadian. Kane was dangerous. No question. But what about Arkkadian? Was he a friend or foe?

Images of that night filled my head. All the things I tried to forget. Being pinned against the wall. Kane forcing his tongue in my mouth. Pinning me to the bed and trying to hurt me. His bloody face with the shards of ceramic sticking out. Running for my life. His eyes. I'd forgotten about his glowing eyes.

Tears came unbidden again, and I just cried. No panic. No freak-out. Just tears. I cried and cried until I couldn't cry anymore and my fingers were pruned and the water chilled; I climbed out and went to bed, where I sank into a fitful sleep.

Sometime in the night, I jolted awake with a scream. I'd been crying in my sleep. I'd dreamed about the fire again. A child screaming. Searing pain down the side of my body. It was the same nightmare I'd relived in my dreams since I was seven. They were the only thing I had left from my old life. I had no memories from before then. Was I ever going to get over this?

I'd gone to therapy for years, eventually giving up when it didn't help. The nightmares never stopped. The anxiety and panic attacks only got worse. And since the last attack, my nightmares had become more frequent than ever.

A quiet knock sounded on the door. Paige peeked her head in as I clicked on the bedside lamp.

"Hey. Bad dreams again?" she asked, padding over to my bed and climbing in beside me. She wrapped her arms around me, and I lost it. All the emotions I'd been holding in poured out of me in a teary river of misery. "Let it all out, babe. I'm here."

We sat together for what felt like forever, Paige hugging me as I cried. Deep down, I knew I needed to confide in her. She'd known about the nightmares since the day we'd become roommates, but she didn't know about Kane. I knew she had questions.

Releasing a sigh, I let it all out. Every single detail of that night.

"I'm so sorry. Why didn't you tell me?" she asked. There wasn't an ounce of accusation in her tone. There was no pity. No, all I felt from my best friend was love and understanding.

"Honestly, I just didn't want to think about it. I didn't want to remember it. I don't want people looking at me with pity. I just want to forget, but I can't."

Her voice was soft and kind. "Ash, I'm not sure that's something anyone else could forget either. But it can get better. It just takes time. You know it's not your fault, right?"

I squeezed my eyes shut. "I know. I just... I want it out of my head and I can't stop thinking about it. Tonight brought everything back."

"Was it him? The guy from tonight? Didn't he used to come to the bar and sweet-talk you all the time? He used to be so nice. And clean."

"Yeah."

"Oh honey, I am so sorry. If I had known, I'd have been on the phone faster." My friend surprised me. I'd expected a full-on interrogation, but she kept the questions to a minimum, showing me nothing but compassion. Then she wrapped her arms around me and held me close, comforting me as I drifted back to sleep.

A FEW SHORT HOURS LATER, the morning sun streamed through the blinds. I sat bolt upright out of bed, jarred by a flash of memory. Arkkadian's eyes. When Kane had shoved me into his arms, I'd caught a quick glance of his face before burying my face in his chest. His eyes were glowing a bright, brilliant sapphire. I'd been so frightened, it hadn't registered. Surely, I had imagined it. Eyes didn't glow. And earlier, when I'd taken his drink order, I swear I'd caught him sniffing the air. Just like Kane. And they knew each other? What the actual fuck?

This was too weird. I couldn't deny that Arkkadian emitted a magnetizing allure. He was both handsome and terrifying. Sexy, yet intimidating. However, I wasn't drawn to Kane in the same way. Arkkadian felt familiar. Like I could sense him. Kane most definitely did not. I couldn't put my finger on it what it was exactly, but I'd almost felt enthralled in Arkkadian's presence. It scared the shit out of me, but I wouldn't think about it. I'd probably never see him again, anyway. Kane, however, was a different story.

Shaking my head to clear it of all thoughts, I hopped out of bed and padded down the hall to the kitchen in my pajamas. Breakfast was already on the table, and Paige was pouring a fresh mug of Joe. Today was a new day, and I planned to make the best of it.

3

ARKKADIAN

eternus. Mate. Mine, I thought to myself as I lay in bed. I knew the moment I smelled the beauty in the bar last night that she was my Aeternus. The connection was instant, the wolf inside me howling for freedom the second her scent washed over me, the need to bond with her all-consuming.

The Black Horse Saloon was a usual stop on my way back to Eagle Ridge after visiting a few of the smaller outlying Lycan villages hidden among the mountains. There were some shifters who avoided the larger population at our Eagle Ridge compound, preferring solitude, and once every few weeks, I checked in on them. As the Alpha, it was my duty to make sure I met their needs.

Upon a recent visit to the bar, I recognized the lingering scent of an Aeternus immediately, but it hadn't belonged to any of the women there that evening. So, I'd been going back every few days over the past weeks to find her, and last night, there she was.

I'd smelled her as soon as I'd walked in the door. Her essence was everywhere, overwhelming my senses. She was mine, my wolf laying claim with no shadow of a doubt. I could hardly contain my excitement. I'd finally found my Aeternus. I'd finally found my soulmate after four hundred years. What I didn't understand was why she was working in a bar. She sure wasn't part of the outlying shifter villages.

What's more? She didn't know what she was. I'd attempted to pry into her mind, but I found no memories regarding who or what she was, or who her parents were. In fact, there were no memories before the age of seven, give or take. What I had found, however, was a memory block. My attempt to bypass the block had been short-lived as she'd quickly dizzied under my mental probing, and I'd had to back out of her mind before she passed out.

I needed to know what lay hidden behind that block. Something was amiss, and my wolf's gut instinct to protect her had heightened tenfold. If someone had blocked her memories, there was a reason for it. She carried a secret, and in my world, secrets were dangerous.

She belonged to me. I could feel it in my bones. My wolf knew it, and he would stop at nothing to claim her. It was pure instinct. My Aeternus. My mate. Fate had finally smiled at me.

Her scent called to me, made my body ache, told me everything I needed to know about her. She was my life mate. My heart pounded, the beast inside ready to burst through my skin and claim what was ours. My arousal had tried to spear its way out of my pants last night, and it had taken everything in my power to tamp it down while I watched her work.

I'd wanted to take her right there at the bar, to bend her over and slam home, to claim my mate. The urge was relentless and excruciating to deny, but I wouldn't dare jeopardize our existence. Unleashing the beast in public was expressly forbidden. Humans knew nothing of our supernatural existence.

Then that bastard rogue Lycan piece of trash had shown up and groped my mate, manhandling and frightening her to the point of a panic attack.

The bitter stench of her fear enraged my wolf, and I'd nearly shifted. The compulsion to protect her had almost been my undoing, and my beast wanted to rip the bastard's head off for threatening her. I'd battled my wolf's ire as it burned me from within, pushing the fire back down so I could take charge of the situation and get rid of the asshole who dared to put his hands all over my mate. Meanwhile, his cronies had ogled and made crude remarks about things they wanted to do. I still wanted to rip them all to shreds even now.

Such vulgar treatment of a woman was never tolerated in the Pack, and neither was the disrespect they'd shown an Alpha. Kane had to have known Aislin was an Aeternus. How could he not? Her scent alone was a dead giveaway. If he knew, then his friends knew. Guaranteed. That meant trouble.

If Kane got a hold of her again, he could force a bond and there was only one way to do so. Bonds were created during sex, but a forced bond was exactly what it sounded like. Forced. Bonds were for life, but a forced bond was like a prison sentence for an Aeternus. Pure pain and misery. Death, forcing a new bond, or a Soul Shadow shattering the bond were the only ways to break a bond. The latter was rare and just as difficult. Only a handful of Soul Shadows in history had ever been successful at breaking a bond.

Judging by her reaction, it was possible Kane had already tried to hurt her, and it didn't surprise me in the least knowing his history. Fortunately, I'd reined in my wolf quickly and got rid of him. And now I knew what I needed to do. I needed to save her. Protect her. Love her. But first, I had to convince her of who and what she was.

As a rogue Lycan, Kane didn't have a lot of power, especially without the backing of a Pack. He was young, seventy-five to my four hundred years, and he was no match for me in a brawl. I'd banished the son of a bitch nearly thirty years ago. Kane was a hothead, always in trouble, always challenging authority. Most of all, he was a fucking creep.

Kane had become infatuated with a young teenage girl in the Pack, and one evening, he took her against her will. Her parents had reported her missing when she didn't come home for dinner. We'd tracked her scent into the woods, half an hour east of Pack lands, near the edge of Glacier National Park lands. She had been stripped of her clothing and tied to stakes in the ground. Kane had been poised above her, ready to strike, when we found them. He'd planned to force a bond. Thankfully, we'd caught him before he'd hurt the girl any further.

Kane was whipped publicly in the commons, and after the lashing, he'd challenged me for Alpha and lost, resulting in permanent banishment. No Pack anywhere in North America would ever offer him sanctuary again. He would forever be rogue.

I needed to find out more about Aislin if I wanted to keep her safe. Many Vamphyre and Lycan alike often lived decades or even centuries before finding their Aeternus. Some never did, and others opted not to wait and bonded with someone they loved. I knew that better than most at four hundred, and yet, there she'd been last night, right in front of me. It was a damned miracle, and I was still in shock.

Aislin was damaged. Fragile. That much I knew. So, I needed to tread carefully. If I scared her, I could lose her, and I couldn't let that happen. Time was of the essence if I wanted to make this work. The downside? I was a brute. Dominant. A Lycan Alpha, and not just any Alpha. I was Arkkadian Rime, Alpha of the entire Lycan Nine. I was fierce and protective of what was mine, with zero tolerance for disrespect. I could be intimidating and downright scary when the time called for it. I had to be to control the packs of the Lycan Nine and to have lived as long as I had.

The last thing I wanted to do was frighten such a broken soul, but time was limited if I wanted to save her before anyone else found out about her. Kane was a problem, and as an Aeternus with memory loss, Aislin's life was in jeopardy.

After she left the bar, I'd made my way around the side of the building to the alley so I could follow her and make sure she made it home safely. As I watched her silently from behind a parked truck, she exited the building and jogged up the stairs to a second-floor apartment above the bar.

At the top, Aislin stiffened, as though spooked. She must have sensed me, but having been raised human, she wouldn't have recognized the feeling for what it was. Once she disappeared inside, I waited for the click of the deadbolt before leaving. On the walk back to my SUV, I'd scented Kane in the alley. Even though the scent had waned, my hackles stayed up. He'd been there after the scuffle inside, but I couldn't sense him in the immediate vicinity any longer. If my instincts were correct, then Kane was stalking her, and if he was stalking her....

No, I wouldn't let that happen again.

For the entire four-hour drive back to Eagle Ridge, I'd not been able to get the alluring, yet fragile woman out of my mind. I didn't sleep a wink after I'd arrived home, and I'd had a raging hard on all night. Aislin was a beauty. Tall. Slender. A little too thin to be honest, maybe from running herself ragged at work, but she was still gorgeous. Her long, wavy auburn locks were pulled up into a ponytail, and her soft silver eyes were edged in black, much like my blue. She wore no makeup to cover her smooth alabaster skin. High cheekbones accentuated her delicate features.

Those hips, though, they were luscious. Those were hips for making babies. Perfect for holding when making love. Perfect for grasping during a hard fuck. Despite clothes that were long past well-worn, she'd looked damned sexy in that t-shirt, denim jeans torn at the knee, and worn-out cowboy boots.

Aislin had smelled of cinnamon and spice, with hints of vanilla and citrus. The heady scent was a compliment to my own cinnamon, clove, and musk, another sign that she was my Aeternus.

All night long, I'd tried to avoid touching myself, but by morning's first light, I couldn't deny it any longer. The scent of my Aeternus excited the beast within, rendering my wolf unable to think of anything else except ravishing what was ours and forming the bond. The magnetism was impossible to ignore. From this point forward, I would have to do everything in my power to harness my wolf because it would be hell-bent on forging that bond.

I kicked the covers off and wrapped a hand around my hardened cock, sliding my hand up and down its length, fingers grazing across the sensitive tip of my shaft. Precum soaked my hand as images of Aislin flashed through my head, spurring the urge onward.

Up... down... up... down.... I gripped myself firmly, imagining her naked body splayed before me upon my bed, with legs wide open and her center glistening with need. The more I fantasized, the faster I stroked. I quickly reached a feverish pace when I imagined tasting and licking her soft center until I drove her over the edge.

A hot shiver raced through me as my orgasm drew closer. I slammed my fist up and down with reckless abandon. The tingling sensation in my spine spiked higher, possessing my body with a ferocious fire, the embers burning hot within. With one final stroke, every muscle in my body clenched, and I shuddered with the last aftershocks of my release.

Damn, I thought to myself as I climbed out of bed and headed for the shower. I'd barely met the woman and already, I was scorching hot.

"Fuck."

I knew the only thing that would sate my wolf was to claim my mate, or the beast would consume me and never let me rest. Neither of us would be satisfied until she was ours. In all of my life and all the women I'd had, I'd never felt anything like this blazing desire burning inside of me now.

How I'd break the news to Aislin, I didn't know. She would think I was insane, just like that bastard, Kane West. How would I convince this beautiful but broken angel that she was my mate? I could try all I wanted, but she had to come to terms with everything in her own time.

While in the shower, I ran every detail I could think of through my head. Lycan. Violent. Protective. Alpha. That alone would be enough to scare the woman. And how did I explain our immortality? Or that she was my Aeternus? We were fated mates. Destined. Aeternus were for life, and there would be no other mate for either of us as long as we were both alive.

What about the Pack? Lycan Nine? Or that she'd have to leave her whole life behind? Nine packs of shifters and she would rule by my side as Alpha. She was immortal royalty and didn't even know it.

Lastly... the rules. Rules kept the order. There were Pack rules, and there were my rules. I thrived on control. I thrived on submission. I thrived on respect. The Alpha beast inside required my mate to submit, to trust in me. It was essential to our immortal life. It meant protection. Safety. In all things. Follow the rules, and everything was well. Break the rules, and suffer the consequences.

I stood under the hot stream of water, thinking back to the night before when I'd scented her in the bar. It had been all I could do to stride carefully across that hardwood floor without rushing the young woman. I couldn't take my eyes off her.

Scenting her again only assured what my wolf had known all along, that she was mine. The beast beneath had nearly exploded forth at recognizing her essence. Given half a chance, the wolf would have taken her right there, its desire to bond that desperate.

I'd nearly dropped the leash keeping the beast at bay. In public, no less.

Any sort of scene would have exposed the existence of our kind. To humans, supernatural beings were things of legend. Myths. Scary stories you told children to keep them in line. Lies those in power used to keep populations from rising up. As much as we hated the myths, we preferred to keep it that way. Myths kept us safe.

Upon realizing Aislin hadn't recognized me as a shifter, I'd grown curious and attempted to shadow her memories. Only I'd been shocked to discover some things, like the fact that she had bounced from foster home to foster home for most of her childhood. There were no memories of her biological parents, but a single moment stood out, that of a woman explaining they had been killed in an accident. She was maybe six or seven. Everything before that time was blank.

I knew without a doubt that the accident was a lie. Memories didn't just go missing. Her parents were dead. Else why would an Aeternus not know what she was? How else would she have landed in foster care? If whoever had killed her parents had known about her, they either would have taken her or killed her. Or they'd tried to kill her and failed. You didn't put a memory block in someone's mind unless you needed to hide something. The block left me with more questions than answers. If the girl's parents had been killed, then it could only mean one thing. They were rogue, living outside of Coven or Pack. But why?

The memory block had prevented all attempts to dig further into her mind. I wanted to know what secrets were hiding there, but she had dizzied too quickly. I'd had to pull out of her mind before I made her pass out.

Once again, my thoughts drifted back to the young woman while the water streamed down my body. She'd felt so soft when I'd held her against me. I pictured her kneeling in front of me, her lithe body naked and wanting. Hands on her knees, legs spread slightly, her bare center silky smooth and slick with desire. Oh, the things I wanted to do.

With one hand against the shower wall, head bent and eyes closed as I fantasized, I grasped myself with the other and slowly stroked again. It had only been minutes since I'd last sated my hunger, but I was already rock hard again. I'd never been this aroused before, and I desperately wanted to stoke the fire again. I moved slowly and deliberately at first, but the more I thought about what honeyed rewards lay between her legs, the faster I stroked.

I wanted to kiss her in all the right places. I wanted to taste her. I wanted to fuck her mouth and see how much of my length she could take with my hands tangled in her hair. I wanted to bend her over the bed, ass in the air, and slide my cock into her sweet, succulent heat.

Faster and faster, my hand slid up and down my hot length. Like a roller coaster, I climbed up and up, all the way to the top of the track. And then, just as I tilted over the crest, the track gave way, taking my breath with it. I erupted with a growl, and my legs nearly gave out from the force of my climax.

With this last release, I knew that the longer I waited to claim her, the more profound my need for her would become. I needed to claim her soon, but I needed to know even more about that block in her mind. Knowing she wouldn't return to work until Saturday evening, I did a little research first to see what I could dredge up. Done with my shower, I donned my usual black t-shirt and my favorite pair of faded blue jeans before wandering downstairs barefoot.

I didn't know Aislin's last name, but I'd guessed her approximate age to be about twenty-three, give or take a year. Normally, birth and death records, passports, and various other identifying documents were forged to hide our immortal existence. Aislin, however, was raised in foster care among humans. If her parents were rogue, they would have hidden among humans anyway, so foster care wouldn't have been a far stretch if they were dead. Being rogue would have given them limited access to anyone among the Pack or Coven who could have provided them the proper documentation to disappear. That meant there was a record of the girl somewhere in the human system.

I searched for local birth records and came up empty. Then I tried the entire state. Zilch. Nothing that stood out anyway. One last search in a national database found a few dozen results for baby girls born with similar names... Ashley, Ashleigh, and Aislin.

I narrowed the list down to surrounding states and picked through them one by one until I'd eliminated all but three. Bingo! One of them had passed at birth, and a second was alive and well and living in New York State.

My jaw fell when I saw the third record. What the fuck? Shocked, I leaned back in my chair and stared at the name on the computer screen. You've got to be kidding me. She couldn't be. I pictured her again. Long auburn hair, silver eyes edged in black. Minus the raven locks, she was the spitting image of her mother, but she had her father's silver eyes. I'd only met Wren and Alaric once, years ago, but I never forgot a face. How did I not see it before? And how did Aislin hide for so long under her real name? Dammit. This was a clusterfuck of epic proportions.

Twenty-four years had passed since the daughter of Arden Vane, the Vamphyre leader, and her Lycan mate had gone rogue, and now it seemed as if a child no one knew existed, their child, had dropped right into my lap. This was dangerous knowledge. It could destroy lives. One word to the wrong person and the fire of a thousand hells would rain down upon the Pack. This could endanger the entire Lycan Nine if I wasn't careful. Arden Vane would go to war. He would kill everything in his path to find his granddaughter and destroy her.

I wouldn't put it past Vane to come for Aislin himself while trying to keep her existence quiet so he could save face. That was always a possibility. Everyone knew he wasn't exactly stable and had become a lot more paranoid and psychotic over the years. If the truth of Aislin's existence was ever revealed, it would make Vane look weak, and he wouldn't want that.

I pondered over the information I'd just learned about the young woman destined to become my Aeternus. I couldn't stop thinking about her. If I didn't tamp down the beast, there would be trouble. A shift and a long run were in swift order. It was the best way to calm the wolf when sex wasn't an option, and sex definitely wouldn't be an option for a while.

What were the odds the very woman I was fated to spend eternity with would also turn out to be the granddaughter of Arden

Vane? From here on out, I needed to remain rational and steadfast, but I worried I wouldn't be able to. One wrong move could mean death. A lot of death. I ran a hand through my hair and chuffed in frustration before continuing with my research. My run would have to wait.

Another search resulted in a birth record and an old article about a seven-year-old girl abandoned in an ER waiting room in Seattle. The article correlated with the date of the fire that destroyed Wren and Alaric's home. The child's clothes were bloody and torn, and she cowered away from everyone. A nurse had found her with a note and a birth certificate pinned to her shirt. The note said to find her a safe home and that her parents had died in a fire. No one had seen who had left the child there, and she'd burst into screaming fits upon the nurse's approach. For privacy's sake, the article had not named the child or her parents. I suspected the child was Aislin.

The doctors and nurses had had to sedate the distraught child to examine her for any wounds. The left side of her torso was sliced up and stitched from neck to hip, dredging up thoughts of a long forgotten foe, but I immediately dismissed the possibility. The cuts were fresh, and the wounds were stitched with near surgical precision. The girl had no memory of how the wounds had happened, how she'd gotten to the hospital, or who she was. She only knew her name and shouted hysterically about a fire. She was clearly traumatized.

They admitted her for a few days until they deemed her stable enough to be placed with a foster home. Social services had been called when no next of kin could be found.

All the records were sealed, however, so I couldn't trace where she'd gone or how many homes she'd been in after the hospital. The memory block had to have been put in place before leaving her in the hospital. Smart thinking, considering memories could be read as far back as infancy if one had the skill. Those of us who did, like me, were known as Soul Shadows and very few Lycan or Vamphyre had this skill. That explained the block. Whoever had left her at the hospital had needed to conceal sensitive information, including her identity. They knew who and what she was, and whoever they were, they had saved Aislin's life.

The little girl in the hospital had to be Aislin. The timeline fit. If the scar I'd noticed peeking out of her shirt collar was any sign, I'd know for sure when I saw her naked. Scars like that would take years to fade on their own, but a bond could drastically increase the speed with which they'd heal. The hospital story definitely explained her penchant for panic if any of this were true. I had plenty of time over the next couple of days to plan, but first, I needed to talk to my Beta.

4

AISLIN

"**G**olly, girlfriend, you look like a raccoon. You need coffee," Paige said.

"Har har." I rolled my eyes at my best friend. I hadn't slept well, so the bags under my eyes were darker than usual this morning. "This smells divine. I'm starving."

I piled eggs, bacon, and fried potatoes on my plate. As usual, Paige had put her magical culinary skills to good use, and I was glad for it. I hated cooking, but Paige loved it.

"Eat up. I figured you could use a little comfort food this morning," she said as she handed me a steaming mug of freshly brewed coffee. Then she set the frother full of steamed milk and a jar of honey in front of me. Paige knew exactly how I took my morning caffeine fix. A little milk, a little honey. It was my version of a poor man's latte.

I moaned when the first bite of eggs crossed my lips. "Oh, my God, these are so good. I swear you make the best eggs."

Paige grabbed my hand, her expression suddenly serious. "So... are you okay this morning?"

"Way to kill the mood, sunshine. I'm barely two bites into my breakfast." I sighed. It was too early in the morning for that ish.

"I'm sorry, sweets. You're my best friend. I worry."

"I know, but I don't want to dwell on it. I want to enjoy my breakfast. Change of subject. What are you doing today?"

"The gym and shopping. I've got to replace some of my clothing. Some of my pants are getting holes. You should come with," Paige declared. "Fresh air and sunshine will do you good."

I smiled at my best friend. She loved to shop, something I wasn't fond of doing. "Thanks, but Marcy asked me to cover for Gina for a few hours today at the diner and I said yes." I needed all the hours I could get if I would ever pay off my maxed-out cards.

"Well, if you change your mind, let me know. We're overdue for some girl time," Paige muttered. "Way overdue."

"I know." I laughed. "Let's try for next weekend. We'll do lunch and go see a movie or something. I haven't been to a movie in ages."

We continued the rest of our breakfast, making small talk and savoring the delicious meal. When we finished, I hustled to get ready for my shift at the diner. The pay at the Black Horse was good, but I had bills to pay and working extra shifts at the diner helped.

Thankfully, the diner was busy, which made for great tips. I'd arrived just in time for the brunch crowd and spent the next few hours making sure all my tables were taken care of. The crowds dwindled by four o'clock, so Marcy thanked me and sent me on my way as soon as my shift was over. By then, I'd cleared almost two hundred dollars.

I hadn't been home for more than a few minutes when Paige walked in, both arms laden with bags. She wore skinny jeans, a pink-flowered tunic, and black heels. Her pixie cut was styled perfectly, her raven hair contrasting beautifully with her creamy skin and emerald eyes. Hoop earrings dangled from each ear and candy apple-red lipstick graced her plump lips. My roommate was nothing short of stunning.

I shut the refrigerator, snack forgotten, and rushed to help her set the bags down before she dropped them.

"Jeez, did you buy the stores out? And damn, girl, you look sexy!" I whistled. One thing about Paige, she never left home unless she was dressed to the nines. It was one thing I loved about her. She knew what she liked.

"Girl, you know it!" Paige giggled. "They had awesome sales today, you missed out. I scored most of it for seventy percent off!"

She was ecstatic. She loved sales as much as she loved shopping. I loved sales, too, but I detested shopping as much as cooking. Paige had driven the half-hour drive south to Crater Falls; there were a few cute clothing stores in the small mall she liked to visit. Lord knew Whitewater was too small to do much other than grocery shopping or go to the bar. Or camp and hike if you were into that sort of thing. I much preferred the small, quiet life Whitewater offered than the busyness of Crater Falls.

As Paige unpacked her bags, she babbled happily about all the great deals she'd scored. I listened silently, smiling to myself. Her enthusiasm was contagious, and by now, I'd completely forgotten about last night.

"Here, this bag is for you!" Paige expressed with delight. She handed me a large brown paper bag that easily weighed several pounds. When I contested, she cut me off. "That's for you. No arguments!"

She knew me too well. I disliked when others spent money on me since it only reminded me of how poor I was and how much harder I had to work for things. Not that Paige could afford much either, but she wasn't thousands of dollars in debt.

In the bag were four new pairs of my favorite boot cut denim jeans, several cute shirts and blouses, two camisoles, and a fuzzy sweater, all in my size. My heart pitter-pattered in my chest with excitement. I desperately needed new clothes. I knew Paige couldn't afford much, just like myself, but that she had thought of me while she was out shopping made me feel wonderful. It also made me feel guilty. My heart sunk thinking about how much everything must have cost. There was easily three or four hundred dollars' worth of clothes here, and neither of us had anywhere near that kind of cash to spare.

"Paige, you didn't have to do this," I stammered. Tears stung my eyes. That was a lot of money.

"I didn't. Well, not all of it. Okay, very little." She laughed. "Carter gave me some extra cash last night when I told him I'd planned to shop for new work clothes. He handed me a stack of bills and told me to grab some things for you if I couldn't convince you to join me. He knows you hate to shop, and we both wanted to do something nice. Plus, your wardrobe desperately needs a makeover. I mean... how many holes does that shirt have?"

I laughed. She was right. I looked down, plucking at the shirt, noting the loose threads and thinning fabric. Being poor sucked. Royally.

"Thank you. Very much." I picked up the navy-blue sweater out of the bag and snuggled it to me with a smile. It was so soft. I rubbed the fabric on my cheek, enjoying the plush texture. The tag caught my eye, and I was stunned. Cashmere. My eyes bugged at the price. "Paige, please tell me you did not pay that much for this!"

"Relax. Sales, remember? Seventy percent off," she said, smiling. "I promise. Scout's honor!"

She began pulling more clothes out of her bags and laid them all out to admire. I continued staring at the tag, finding it hard to believe she scored a hundred-dollar sweater for thirty bucks.

"O-okay. Thank you. Really. This was very sweet of you and Carter. I appreciate it more than you know." I snuggled the sweater once again, elated I'd have some new outfits to wear to work. My clothing was becoming a little too threadbare. It had been ages since I'd shopped for myself. I couldn't afford it, not with all the credit card bills. I packed all of my new clothes back into the bag and took it to my room to unpack later.

"What are you doing tonight?" Paige hollered from the other room. "You should come down to the bar and dance. You haven't danced in forever."

I plopped down at the kitchen table when I returned. "I was thinking of hitting the gym, actually. Besides, I don't think Carter would appreciate me hanging out in the bar when I should be working."

"Stop making excuses. You know him better than that. I believe his words were, 'She needs to cut loose a little. She works too much.' He's not wrong. And honestly, we'd both feel better knowing you aren't alone right now. Plus, when I came home last night, I got this creepy feeling that someone was watching me. Maybe I'm being paranoid, but it skeeved me out. I don't think you should be up here alone tonight."

At that, I perked up. "I had the same feeling. I was unlocking the door and all the hair on my neck and arms stood on end."

"See? All the more reason for you to come downstairs. We'll

tell Carter. I know he'll feel a lot better; he worries about you as much as I do. And you know he'll check the alley for us before we leave if we ask," Paige said.

"Okay," I agreed. "I suppose we should get ready then. You have to be there in an hour. I think I'm going back down to the diner first, though, and grab a bite to eat."

"All right. But you better show up, or I'll come looking for you. Capiche?"

"Capiche." Bless the woman. She was my best friend, and I was so undeniably lucky to have her in my life. Without Paige by my side these past couple years, I didn't know where I'd be. Probably in some other Podunk town struggling just as much, if not more, to make ends meet.

5

ARKKADIAN

I dialed the number and my brother's gruff voice answered. "Gideon," I barked. "My place. Now. We need to talk. Don't bring Sara."

"Well, good morning to you, too." Gideon snarked. "What's going on?"

"I'll tell you when you get here. And keep your mouth shut," I snapped before disconnecting. All the information I'd discovered worried my wolf, making it hard to control the agitation pooling in my chest.

I paced around the den, impatiently waiting. I itched to get my mate to safety as fast as I could, and I had to do it without scaring her. A knock sounded just before Gideon entered and slammed the front door behind him.

"What in the bloody hell is going on, Arkken?" he hollered from the front room, using my childhood nickname.

Besides his mate, Sara, no one else used it. Gideon was my brother and only sibling, Beta of our own Glacier Mountain pack and the Lycan Nine. He was nearly as old as me, born just three years after me. The two of us have been thick as thieves our entire lives. There was no one I trusted more with my life than my brother. And there was absolutely no one I could trust more than him with the information I was about to impart. I shouldn't have been so snappy, but I couldn't help it.

"What's so bloody important that you couldn't tell me on the phone?"

"Who pissed in your eggs this morning?" I countered, though I knew damn well it was me.

"You did. Barking orders and not even a single hello. What's going on?" His voice dripped with sarcasm as he plopped himself down in the leather chair behind my desk and casually propped his feet up. Dried mud flaked off his boots onto my desktop.

"Get your mucked-up boots off my fucking desk," I growled. Fucking hell. My emotions were dancing on the edge of a cliff, about to tumble straight over into the abyss.

"All right, all right. Damn. I'm just screwing with you, bro. What's got you so worked up this morning? And this better be good. Sara and I were about to get a little…" He waggled his eyebrows. Under less stressful circumstances, I would have found my brother amusing. Not today.

"Sorry. I found something last night. My wolf is going crazy and I haven't put my hackles down since I returned home." I paused and looked my brother in the eyes. "I found her," I said, pacing across the floor once more.

Gideon sat up and drummed a couple of pens on my desk, an instant smile on his face. "You found your Aeternus? Hot damn. This is good news. Correction, it's great news. Who is she? Where is she?"

"A problem. That's who. Her existence puts all of the Lycan Nine in extreme danger." I stopped pacing the floor and glared at my brother.

The smile on his face fell. "What do you mean? Why would an Aeternus be dangerous to us?" I waited for the switch to flip and make the connection. Suddenly, his jaw dropped. "Wait, wait, wait. She's Vamphyre, isn't she? Dammit."

Bingo, little brother. Well, close enough, anyway.

Gideon paled at the recognition of what he'd just said and jumped up out of the chair. "What did you do, Arkken? Please tell me you didn't violate Vane's First Law. You know what he'll do."

And just like that, his mood shifted from amused to angry.

"I violated nothing. And I know full well what he'll do." I sighed. "She's not just of the Vamphyre line. Her father was a shifter." I'd hoped that last little detail would at least trigger something, but confusion still marked Gideon's face.

"Whoever she is, you can't touch her. You know that, right? This will get people killed."

"Tell my wolf that," I scoffed. "You know as well as I that we have no control. That we can't fight the instinct once our wolves discover our fated mates."

"Dammit, Arkken."

"There's more."

"What?" he asked, temper short. "End of story, you can't touch a Vamphyre Aeternus. You'll start a war, Arkkadian." His full use of my name meant he finally realized the seriousness of the situation.

I continued pacing back and forth across the room for several minutes in silence before finally stopping in front of the fireplace. I leaned on the mantle and ran my hand through my hair in desperation. I could feel the veins in my neck pulsing with every frustrated beat of my heart, ready to burst like an over-inflated balloon. The room brightened, and my vision sharpened as my eyes lit up.

"Spit it out," Gideon said, but I didn't move. I just stood staring into the empty fireplace. "Dammit, turn around and look at me. And shut the beast down, your eyes are glowing."

"We're fucked, Gid," I said, turning to look at him finally. I dragged my hand down my face. My wolf was keening for a run, needing to burn off the anxious energy I couldn't seem to dispel. I took a moment to push it back down. As I calmed myself, the brightness in my vision faded and my eyes returned to their normal blue. "I already said it. She's my Aeternus."

"Yeah, you said that. Stop dragging this out any longer. Tell me everything." He strolled over and placed a hand on my shoulder. "Tell me."

Fuck. Avoiding the truth wouldn't make this any less real. Sitting down at my desk, I filled my brother in on everything from my search to find her to Kane's attack the night before. Then I pulled a file from the drawer and tossed it across the desk. Gideon stared at it but didn't pick it up.

"Open it."

He picked up the file and opened the flap to the old newspaper article about a seven-year-old girl left in the emergency room. "I don't understand, Arkken, what is this?"

"Turn the page. Keep reading."

He flipped it over to find a copy of a birth record dated seven years before the article. He scanned the page and cursed, letting the paper fall back onto the desk. "Barrington. As in Alaric Barrington? Rain wolves? That Barrington?"

"The very same."

Everyone, Lycan and Vamphyre alike, knew the story. If Aislin was the daughter of Wren Vane and Alaric Barrington, then she had to be the granddaughter of Arden Vane, the infamous Vamphyre King and leader of the Covenant. He'd been the one to order Wren and Alaric's deaths for violating First Law.

Vane ruled the Covenant with fear. He was a psychotic, sadistic tyrant. He'd committed countless unspeakable acts during his reign of terror. To Vane, First Law was absolute. No exceptions. It had come about as the result of an old feud between Vamphyre and Lycans centuries ago that led to a war between the two factions. Many lives were lost.

Under Vane's rule, all members of the Covenant were forbidden under all circumstances to mate with any immortal not born of Vamphyre descent. Transgressors were imprisoned and sentenced to death. So were their offspring. Vane considered them an abomination. A taint of pure bloodlines. This would explain why Wren and Alaric had gone rogue. Vane's daughter had dared to mate with a Lycan, and to Vane, that would have been the ultimate betrayal. Especially if they'd produced a child.

Alaric was the eldest son of Mathias Barrington, the Alpha of the Pacific Rim pack and one of my Betas. Wren was the only daughter and youngest child of Arden Vane. The Covenant was the most powerful Vamphyre coven in the nation. Wren's father had imprisoned her when he'd found her and Alaric together in bed. He'd sentenced her to death, but Alaric and a few of his friends had rescued her, and the two had gone on the run.

Vane went mad with rage and ordered them found and put to death. For seven years, their whereabouts remained unknown, driving Vane further into madness. When efforts to find them repeatedly failed, he sent his right hand, Ryker Slade, to find and execute them. Slade was a sadistic fuck who loved to cut up and torture his victims before he killed them.

Wren and Alaric's home burned to the ground. They found only two bodies in the rubble, both identified as theirs. They were both decapitated and dismembered. The news of their deaths had shaken our immortal world to the core.

Strangely, no one ever saw Ryker Slade again. With Slade's disappearance, Arden Vane had gone on a rampage, killing several of his soldiers when they failed to produce his whereabouts. It was widely believed he'd either died in the fire, despite no evidence, or he ran off. Neither scenario made sense, especially since Slade worshipped the ground Vane walked on. When all was said and done, he forbade anyone from ever speaking his daughter's name again. She no longer existed in his eyes.

I stood up and started pacing the room again, wolf on edge. "I think Wren was pregnant when she and Alaric ran off. I think Ryker Slade tortured the girl, but she somehow survived. The child in that article would be about twenty-three now, the same age as the woman in the bar. The birth certificate says Seattle. Wren and Alaric were there when they died. The timelines fit."

Gideon quietly contemplated the information. "The timing, the name, they fit. But this could just be a coincidence. The woman in the bar could be anyone," he challenged.

"I don't think so. I shadowed her last night. I couldn't glean much. She became dizzy too quickly. But what I found was a memory block. She has no memory before the age of six or seven, and she has recurring nightmares of a fire. Her first name is also Aislin, same as the birth certificate."

Gideon's eyes widened a fraction. "Fuck. Are you sure? You've been looking for your Aeternus for nearly four centuries. What are the chances that the granddaughter of Arden Vane exists in the first place, let alone that she's alive and she's yours? After all this time?"

I closed my eyes and bowed my head. "Yes, I'm sure."

Those three words hung in the thick air. Gideon took a few steps backward to give the angry Alpha inside of me space. He didn't bare his neck, nor did I expect him to. In this moment, we were brothers, not Alpha and Beta.

"Fuck. Does anyone else know? What about Mathias, have you told him?"

I shook my head. "No, and I'm keeping it that way. If Arden Vane finds out he has a granddaughter, he won't stop until she's dead. You and I both know he's insane and he'll kill anyone who gets in his way. Vane will call in every single Covenant Guard from across the country to find her. People will die. The last thing we need is another war between the Coven and the Lycan Nine."

"Then we have to do everything we can to prevent a war," my brother stated.

"I know. The only way this ends is with death, and it won't be hers. I'll kill Vane myself if I have to."

"Mathias deserves to know he has a granddaughter. You can't hide this from him, he'll be furious," Gideon affirmed. "You need to tell him."

"Absolutely not. Not until we know more." I was tense. The room once again brightened around me, the telltale sign my eyes were glowing again. The mere thought of someone harming my mate sent my canines bursting through my gums as anger boiled beneath the surface of my skin.

"Brother, you've got to calm the fuck down. We need a plan, but first, you need to get this pent-up frustration out of your system. You're no good to anyone in that state. Let's go for a run."

I returned to the mantle and stared down into the empty fireplace. Closing my eyes, I took a few deep breaths to rein in the wolf. The more I learned about Aislin, the harder it would be for the wolf to remain calm, instinct be damned. A thought occurred to me, and I wondered if it might be possible.

"Gideon."

"What?"

"What if Aislin's an Immortalle? She is a product of both Vamphyre and Lycan lines."

Gideon let forth a string of expletives. "No. No way. There hasn't been an Immortalle in centuries. They died out."

"True. You're probably right, but I can't help but wonder."

"Shit. This is a clusterfuck. How the fuck do we handle this?" Gideon slapped the desk.

"I don't know, but we need to act fast. There's no way Kane

doesn't know what she is. We both know he won't hesitate to force a bond, and actually, I suspect he already tried. When he went after her in the bar last night, she had a panic attack. I sat with her afterward, but from her behavior," I paused, "there's a clear history there. She was petrified. Dammit! I should have shadowed her again, but I was too distracted. Kane still holds a grudge. If Kane figures out who she is, he could turn her over to her grandfather for revenge."

Gideon whistled. "We're in deep shit."

"I know. And she doesn't know who or what she is. Kane won't hesitate to take advantage of that, and there isn't a damn thing she could do about it. I have to break that memory block. Someone had to have known about her to save her. She's working again on Saturday evening. I'm going back, and I want you to join me."

"Of course, brother. In the meantime, let's go for a run. We'll stay out until morning." With that, Gideon dragged me out through the front door.

I stood a moment, taking in the fresh air and morning sun. I couldn't hide the worry on my face from Gideon, though.

"We'll figure this out. We're a team. Always have been a team. Come on, let's go." He was right. We were, and we would.

I stripped my clothes off and tossed them aside; they landed on the wooden floorboards of the porch. I leaped into the air, transforming mid-jump into my wolf, the air shimmering around me until the transformation was complete.

Gideon followed suit, landing beside me, his midnight-black wolf matching mine. The only difference between our wolves was the star-shaped patches of fur emblazoned on our chests, his a solid white and mine with a tinge of silver.

I let out a howl, and together, we bolted off at a blinding speed across the meadow and into the surrounding woods.

6

AISLIN

Sitting in my favorite booth, I picked at my sandwich and fries while I read. The book I'd picked out last month at the used bookstore lay open in front of me. Paranormal romances were my favorite, and the dark, sexy man with the gray eyes on the cover had caught my eye when I saw the book on the shelf. I devoured the pages, utterly engrossed, my meal completely forgotten as I read about the handsome, yet dominating wolf shifter and his beloved mate.

When the waitress asked if I'd wanted a to-go box, I looked at my watch and noticed an entire hour had passed. "Oh, I am so sorry! I got distracted. No, thank you, I'll finish quickly and be on my way."

I scarfed down my meal, paid the tab, and then hightailed it back to my apartment to grab my boots. I couldn't wait. I hadn't danced in way too long, and I missed it dearly. The dance floor was the one place I could escape. Where I could let go of all my worries. I could forget about all the bills I owed. I could forget about my nightmares. I could forget about Kane and enjoy just being me.

Upstairs, I checked my hair, and satisfied I looked presentable, I tugged my boots on. They were worn out and the loose threads barely held the worn leather soles on, but they were comfortable. Broken in and well-loved. Someday, I'd be able to afford a new pair, but for now, this tired, old, leather-scuffed pair worked just fine. If they lasted this long, they could last a while longer. With one final look in the mirror, I grabbed my keys and locked up.

Carter ambled into the office just as I dropped my purse in my locker and greeted me with a smile and a hug. I held on a little longer than usual, needing the comfort he offered.

"Thank you for the new clothes. I appreciate it." Carter had been more of a father figure to me in the last couple of years than any of the foster parents I'd lived with. Most of them were just in it for the paycheck and paid little attention to me. Some were bullies. None of them were home. Carter, though, he listened. He cared. For the first time in my life, he made me feel like I belonged. Like I mattered.

"You should have gone with her. You need to get out more, you work too hard."

"I know, but I'd already promised Marcy I'd fill in at the diner for a few hours today. She was short with Gina out sick, and I need the money, anyway." With a stack of mounting debt to pay down, it wasn't like I had a choice in working a second job. My bills wouldn't pay themselves. I knew Carter would help if I asked, it was just his way, but I was stubborn and determined to do things on my own, so he wouldn't push.

Carter pulled me close and hugged me one more time. "Listen. I'm sorry. I'm sorry for all the things that happened to you. If I could turn back the clock and fix any of it, I would. The least I can do is to be here for you. You may not be my daughter biologically, but I think of you as a daughter. I'm here if you need me."

My breath hitched, and my eyes watered. Carter was the kind of guy who would give the shirt off his back for anyone. He was the sweetest old man, but he often kept his emotions hidden. So it was rare seeing this side of him, especially after his wife's passing. Her death had been hard on all of us, Carter most of all. He'd thrown himself into work after her death, never taking the time to grieve. Or maybe he grieved so hard that work was his only escape. I supposed we all grieved in our own ways.

"Please don't apologize. It's not your fault."

"It's not your fault either. You're special, Ash. I hope you know that. You know I'm always here if you need an ear or a shoulder. Okay?" I nodded, and he continued. "I let the bouncers know that

Kane and his friends are no longer welcome on the premises. They'll make sure he never steps foot in the bar again."

"Thank you." I hugged him one last time and headed toward the dance floor, feeling much lighter.

Out front, Jimmy was in the DJ booth, so I made my way over and added a few of my favorite songs to the request list. Jimmy leaned over and looked at the requests with a grin, just like he always did.

"The usual, I see?"

I laughed. "You know it."

I could always count on Jimmy for a smile. The man was perpetually happy, and he always played all of my requests.

"You got it, doll. You okay?"

"Yeah, I'm good. Thanks." I really wished everyone would stop asking me. I knew he meant well, but I was tired of everyone worrying over me. I just wanted to dance and be free, if only for a few hours.

"Okay. You need anything, you just ask."

"I will, Jimmy. I promise." I gave him a hug and wandered back to the bar to claim my favorite stool at the end of the bar top. It was made from redwood slabs, polished until they shined, giving the bar a rustic look. Carter had recently renovated, and it was one of my favorite features. Paige brought me two bottles of water, setting one in front of me and the other under the bar top for later. I tossed her a couple of dollar bills to cover the water.

"It's about time you showed up. I was about to send Jimmy over to find you, figured you got lost in that new book with the sexy man-beast on the cover." She winked, fanning herself and pretending to be all hot and bothered. She loved to tease me about my book choices, but I knew she secretly read them, too.

I laughed. "You know me too well."

"Need anything else?" she asked.

"Just water. Besides, you know I'm a lightweight anyway, and if that asshole returns, I want a clear head." I turned and scanned the crowd. I knew they banned Kane from the bar, but I still worried. "Anyway, tonight's about dancing, not assholes."

"Good. Go get your boot scoot on. Make sure you hide your water under the counter when you go dance. Don't want anyone messing with it," Paige said as she turned to help the couple next to me.

I turned on my stool, facing the dance floor. I didn't know the current dance; it was relatively new, but I was good at picking up the steps just by watching.

Out of the corner of my eye, I caught Jimmy giving me a wave. That was my cue he was about to play one of my requests. Alan Jackson's "Chattahoochee" came over the speakers and I jumped off my seat. The Tush Push was one of my all-time favorite dances. It was an oldie, but a goodie, and still popular. I let myself get lost in the music and movements. This was exactly what I needed, and I felt much better. Lighter. Relaxed. Happy.

Song after song, dance after dance, I ignored the world until, during a water break, I felt the hair on the back of my neck stand up.

Arkkadian was here.

How did I know that? Spooked, I sat down and faced the mirror behind the bar and used it to scan the crowd. The tables and dance floor were full of people. He could be anywhere in the crowd.

On the first pass, I saw nothing out of the ordinary. Maybe I had imagined things, but when I turned back toward the dance floor, he was there. Arkkadian. The man who'd saved me from that asshole. The man with eyes as hard as steel and the color of warm cerulean waters. Eyes that said if I looked deep enough, I could see primal oceans and savage, hypnotic waves crashing onto rocky shores. He looked directly at me like he wanted to devour me. All of me.

My breath hitched when our eyes met. I could almost feel that primal ocean surging around me, pulling me into a swift current of raw power. A power that came from the very essence of his life force. An irresistible life force that commanded full attention. My very soul had been summoned, and I suddenly felt the need to be dominated. My skin flushed with hot desire, and for a moment, I hungered fiercely for this mysterious stranger.

Then just like that, I snapped back into reality, the spell broken. Embarrassed at having been caught gawking, my cheeks grew hot, and I quickly averted my gaze. Maybe if I pretended I hadn't seen him, maybe if I ignored him, he'd go away. Wait, no. I wanted him to join me. Wait. No, I didn't. Oh, my God, I was so confused! Between my brain and my body, I couldn't reconcile the mixed signals.

Fear. Attraction. Desire. My anxiety suddenly kicked into high gear. Did I stay, or did I run? This handsome man with the cerulean eyes intrigued me, yet part of me was frightened of the inexplicable magnetism pulling us together.

A man of similar age sat in the chair next to him. They could have been identical had it not been for the shock of blond locks upon the other man's head. Were they brothers? I turned my gaze back to Arkkadian, and when our eyes met, he stood up and walked toward me.

I suddenly felt very hot and quickly turned back to the mirror. I glared at my water bottle, willing him to go away before suddenly wishing he would stay. The closer he came, the more I sensed that raw power tugging on the other end of the tether that somehow linked us together. Tingles raced up my spine, making me tremble as both fear and excitement coursed through me.

And then that deep, smooth-as-whiskey voice caressed my ear. He was so close I could feel his warm breath upon my skin, and I jumped in my seat.

"Hello, Aislin."

Two words. Two simple words were all it took for me to melt like warm butter.

7

ARKKADIAN

Several hours later, the tension I'd felt earlier this morning finally eased. My temper had disappeared, and I was feeling more like myself. Mostly. Gideon and I crested the ridge above the mountain lake located a mile north of Eagle Ridge. Thirsty, I loped quickly down the hillside, toward the water's edge and drank in long, slow gulps. Once sated, I shifted back into my human skin, and next to me, Gideon did the same.

I waded out into the cool, crisp mountain water and dipped under the surface before popping back up again. The normally refreshing chill of the water against my warm skin left me wanting, and a whisper of uncertainty tickled my senses before taking up residence in my gut. I suddenly feared for my mate, and all the tension I'd previously lost returned. The longer I stood there, the more it nagged at me.

"What's going on?" Gideon questioned from the shoreline, picking up on my distress.

"We need to go. Something's wrong. I feel it in my gut," I uttered.

"Now hold on. You can't go running off half-cocked. What's your plan when we get to town?" he asked me.

"I don't know yet, but we have time to come up with something. I suggest you follow me if you're coming with," I told my brother.

Wading out of the water, I shifted and took off at a dead run toward home. Gideon followed close on my heels, then veered off the main path toward his own cabin while I raced up the front steps into mine.

I quickly pulled on a black t-shirt, jeans, and heavy work boots. I filled a backpack with a few overnight necessities in case we didn't return right away. The plan was to return immediately to Eagle Ridge with my mate in hand, barring any emergencies. But this way, I'd at least have a change of clothes since they were usually shredded in the event of a fast shift. I didn't particularly care for the sweats we kept stashed in Pack vehicles.

Gideon greeted me on the porch as I locked up. I started the vehicle just as Gideon's mate, Sara, approached with a cooler. He rolled his window down, and she passed it through.

"I packed you both some sandwiches and drinks. Gideon said you've got a long drive, and knowing the both of you, you won't stop once you've set your mind to something. May as well eat on the way. I don't know what's going on, but please be safe," Sara said.

Gideon leaned through the window and kissed his mate. Then she waved as I reversed out of the driveway.

Mile by mile, snow-capped peaks passed us by as we traveled south down old, bumpy mountain roads. The normal drive back to Whitewater took about three hours on hidden winding roads since the average speed limit was fifteen miles per hour for the first two and a half hours of the trip. After that, it was another half an hour down the highway. We made the trip in half the time.

It was nearly eight o'clock by the time we arrived in town. Brilliant reds, pinks, and oranges painted the sky as the sun slowly sank toward the horizon. They said that a red sky at night meant a sailor's delight, but I had the feeling tonight would be anything but delightful. Neither my brother nor I had spoken much the entire drive. The worried churning of my gut made it difficult to think, let alone speak.

"Let's make a perimeter sweep. I don't want any surprises." I reached for the handle, but Gideon stopped me before I could open the door.

"Do you even have a plan? You've not said more than a dozen words to me since we left home," Gideon inquired.

I couldn't answer. I was strung out with worry. My wolf paced just below the surface, growling and snarling on the periphery of my mind. With every mile closer to Whitewater we traveled, my wolf became more and more agitated.

"I honestly don't know, Gid. I can't think straight. The closer we got to town, the more alarmed I became. Something's wrong." I jumped out of the vehicle and scented the air. I instantly recognized the pungent odor of sweat, musk, and sickly sweet tobacco wafting across the air currents. I'd know Kane's scent anywhere.

"Kane was here," Gideon added, having scented him.

"Within the last hour, give or take. I'm sure he'll be back. You take the right; I'll take the left and meet you in the alley. Aislin's apartment is above the bar. Once we've cleared the area, we'll go inside," I told him and disappeared around the corner before he could respond.

In the alley, I waited at the bottom of the stairs for my brother to join me. When he appeared at my side, I said, "Wait here," and bounded up the steps three at a time. The door was locked, so I leaned over the railing to peek through the window. Satisfied no one was home, I descended the steps, and we returned to the bar.

Notes of cinnamon, vanilla, and citrus wafted upon the air, making my dick jump in my pants. I didn't realize I was staring until Gideon tapped me on the shoulder and pointed to a table. I followed, not taking my eyes off the smiling young woman on the dance floor. The tether connecting us rippled with vibrant energy, her happiness as bright as the sun on a cloudless day.

"Is that her?" Gideon asked. "No wonder your wolf can't stop pacing. You're worse than a female dog in heat. Her scent... wow. She's definitely an Aeternus."

"Mm."

I continued to watch my mate. Like last night, she wore a simple blue t-shirt, holey jeans, and those same well-worn boots that had seen much better days. Guilt filled me at the sight of her worn clothing. She should be dressed better. How long had she done without? I would have to remedy that.

I couldn't take my eyes off her radiant smile as she danced. Her skin glistened under the lights. She was beautiful, and she looked so happy compared to the frightened woman she was last night.

When the song ended, she headed back toward the bar, seemingly oblivious to my arrival, at least until she suddenly stiffened. It was barely noticeable, but I'd caught the movement. Intuition was a funny thing, and as an Aeternus, she could sense when her mate was near now that she'd met him. Not that Aislin would recognize it yet, but the ability would continue to strengthen.

"She's stunning, Arkken."

"She is."

"Are you sure she's Vane's granddaughter?"

"Yes. Look there, just above her shirt collar. You can see the scars crisscrossing her skin." My reply was curt, and my beast bristled at the thought of my brother eyeballing my mate, even if it was purely innocent. Even if it was a mated male like my brother. Instincts were funny that way.

Aislin sat facing the mirror behind the bar, pretending to sip her water while scanning the crowd's reflection. She slowly turned around, eyes inspecting every individual in the room until they landed upon me. I dared to look straight at her.

That's right, darling, you feel me, don't you?

I quirked my lip, thinking about how she'd be able to hear me inside her head once we were bonded. Her breath hitched, and she quickly averted her gaze to my brother before returning to me again. I could feel her attraction from here, and it filled me with immense satisfaction to know the bond was working its magic so quickly.

I stalked across the floor with one glaring purpose. Her. My mate. Her face turned scarlet, and she turned back to the mirror. I saw her body shiver from across the room and felt the wave of mixed emotions rolling off her. It was adorable the way she pretended not to notice me. She was nervous. Afraid. Embarrassed. And... was that lust? I grinned, savoring the scent of her arousal.

"Hello, Aislin," I said, my voice husky as I leaned in behind her. She jumped when I reached around her, placing an arm on either side of her, hands on the bar, caging her in front of me. "I didn't mean to startle you."

"It's... it's okay," she mumbled, trembling, and my cock jumped.

Despite her nervousness, her arousal spiked even higher. I loved having that effect on her so soon.

"Do you mind if I join you?" I laced the question with demand as I crooned into her ear, purposely letting the warmth of my breath caress the delicate skin just below it. She quickly averted her gaze from mine in the mirror and stared down at her water bottle. I immediately picked up on her natural submissiveness.

"N-no... not at all. Please." The poor woman looked like her heart was about to beat out of her chest. Failing to mask her arousal, she licked her bottom lip and then pulled it into her mouth. "I didn't expect to see you back so soon."

"To be honest, I wanted to see you again. I hoped you'd be here again tonight." I reluctantly stepped back and sat down on the barstool next to her when I would have much rather wrapped my arms around her and kissed her.

"How are you doing? You looked like you were having fun out there," I said, tipping my head toward the dance floor.

"I'm okay. I think. And yes, I love to dance. I don't get to do it as often as I'd like, though."

"You... think?" I asked, quirking an eyebrow.

"I'm okay, really." She didn't convince me. Her scent alone gave her away, like a bright beacon of light, radiating a mixture of nerves and lust.

I pretended not to notice her friend grinning like a giddy schoolgirl at the other end of the bar.

"You look nervous." I laughed, trying to put her at ease. "I don't bite. I promise."

She finally looked at me, quirking her lips. Her breathing quickened slightly but remained steady. "Truth be told, I'm petrified."

"I'm sorry, I truly didn't mean to startle you. I just needed to know you were okay."

"Thank you. I just... I can't help it." She sighed. "There's a lot going on right now."

She turned away, trying to hide the tears forming in the corners of her eyes. I hadn't intended to upset her. I placed my hand over hers and gave a slight squeeze. To my delight, she didn't pull away.

"Do you want to talk about it?" I asked. I couldn't help myself and sent a gentle wave of warmth and calm through my hand into hers. I continued pushing until I felt her body relax beneath my touch. My ability to do so was a by-product of being a Soul Shadow. It wasn't just memories I could affect, but energy and emotions.

"I won't lie, Arkkadian. You scare me. Men scare me." She looked away, embarrassed.

I cupped her chin and turned her head to face me, surprised when she didn't fight me. "I promise you have nothing to fear."

She tried to turn away, but I held her chin firmly, so she averted her gaze instead. There was the resistance I'd previously expected.

"Aislin, I won't hurt you. Ever. Please look at me?" I gently coaxed. When she did, I let go of her chin and replaced my hand over hers. "There, that's better."

8

AISLIN

I was giving him too much information! I didn't know Arkkadian from Adam, and yet I couldn't help talking to this beautiful man. His presence completely captivated me. Despite the emotions he called up inside me, I couldn't deny the words that flew from my mouth when he asked if I wanted to talk. When he'd placed his hand on mine, I could have sworn I'd felt a tingle of heat spread out, soaking into me like warm sunlight. I had to be imagining things. Talk about a mind fuck.

For a man who exuded so much dominance and power, he seemed genuinely concerned about me. I peered into his cerulean eyes, instantly riveted by the ocean of blue I saw in their steely depths. I wanted to get lost in them. I wanted to sail away in them. I wanted to sink down into their inky depths and let him pull me back to the surface again, where he would revive me with but a single breath.

Breaking the stare, Arkkadian turned and flagged Paige down for a drink. I shook myself, taking the moment to look for the other man who had come here with Arkkadian. He was still sitting at the same table, watchful and alone. A petite blond woman in a denim skirt and flowery blouse asked him to dance, but he politely declined, and she shuffled away in disappointment.

"Who is that man over there? He looks like you."

"That's Gideon. My younger brother."

As if he'd heard us, Gideon turned in our direction. He smiled, and I smiled back. Just then, my favorite two-step song came over the speakers, and I perked up.

Arkkadian held out a hand and grinned. "Would you like to dance, Aislin?"

"You dance?"

He laughed, his eyes twinkling. "Yes, I dance. And very well, I might add."

I noticed several women scowling as he led me out onto the hardwood, their faces failing to hide their jealousy. When Arkkadian placed his arm around my waist, the word *mine* flashed through my mind unexpectedly. Where did that come from?

"Two-step?" he asked.

"I'd like that very much." I nodded with glee. I so rarely ever got the chance, especially since I'd been avoiding men for the last several months. I hadn't even trusted my regular dance partners after that night. But somehow, I trusted Arkkadian.

Waylon and Willy sang about a town called Luckenbach, Texas, and I easily followed Arkkadian's lead as he gracefully and expertly led me around the dance floor. We moved together so naturally, like two pieces of a perfectly matching puzzle. I soon became giddy, smiling and singing along with the music.

After the song ended, I gladly let him lead me through several more songs. Before long, we'd become the center of attention as the crowd gathered. Arkkadian held me firmly without caging me. He was strong but gentle, knowing when to give and when to take. He was the perfect blend of dominant and sweet.

When the latest song ended, he thanked me for the dances and escorted me back to the bar, hand in hand. Arkkadian interlaced his fingers in mine, and I smiled. His hand in mine strangely felt right.

"That was fun. It's been a while since I've done that myself. I'd love to do it again sometime."

I felt the heat in my cheeks rise. "I would as well. You're an expert lead. I'm quite impressed," I admitted. The evening was drawing to an end, however, and soon the bar would close for the night. "Really, thank you so much. I had a wonderful time, but I think it's time for me to go. It's nearly midnight. I hope I'll see you again?"

"Of course, Aislin. Before you go, can I at least introduce you to my brother?"

"Sure."

Arkkadian didn't let go of my hand as he led me over to his brother's table. "Aislin, this is my brother, Gideon."

Gideon stood and shook my hand with a smile. His grip was strong, hands callused. Working hands. They were rough, yet gentle. I returned his smile and told him it was a pleasure.

"It was a pleasure to meet you also, miss," Gideon said, but then he took a step back, suddenly aloof, and I looked up to see Arkkadian glaring at him. What was that about? Was he possessive already? It should have scared me, but I found it incredibly sexy.

Arkkadian took my hand in his again. "I hope we can do this again."

It wasn't lost on me how quickly I became comfortable around him, and he sure seemed taken with me.

"Yes, I'd love that. Thank you."

Before I turned to go, he raised my hand to his lips and placed a sweet kiss across my knuckles. A warmth passed from his hand into mine. The sensation sent shivers through me, and I welcomed the sensation. What was that? Was he doing that or was his presence just naturally calming? I suddenly wished the night didn't have to end.

"Good night, Arkkadian. Goodnight, Gideon." I smiled one last time before leaving.

By the time I'd reached the back door, my heart was pounding and my breaths came in quick, excited bursts. Holy crap, I was aroused. My heart leaped into my chest at the memory of his scent. Cinnamon and cloves. Two of my favorites. I loved them because they were warm and inviting. Cozy. Just like Arkkadian. Once you got over all the dominance. And I wanted to get to know him better. For whatever reason, it went against my better judgment, but there was just something about him that pulled me in.

"Are you going home?"

I jumped at the sound of my best friend's voice. I hadn't heard Paige come up behind me. I turned to face her, my heart still bouncing around in my chest like an erratic ping-pong ball. "Jeez! Don't sneak up on someone like that!"

"Sorry!" Paige laughed. She could be such a brat, but I loved her.

"And yes, I'm heading back up."

Paige beamed. "You looked like you were having a lot of fun out there tonight. It's been a long time since I've seen you smile that much. You looked happy."

I blushed. I knew what she alluded to, but I refused to take the bait. I purposely avoided mentioning Mr. Tall, Dark, and Mysterious. "I am happy. There's just something about dancing that makes the world melt away."

I thought about his steely blue eyes, the ones I'd spent most of the evening staring into. Warmth radiated from my core, and my panties were drenched as liquid heat pooled down low.

"I'm not talking about dancing and you know it. Your face is redder than an apple right now. Be honest, Ash," Paige teased. "It was Mr. Sex on Two Legs, wasn't it?"

I groaned. Not this again! Heat moved from my core to my face, and my cheeks burned.

I was so embarrassed right now. I didn't know how to handle the mixed gamut of emotions I was experiencing, and Paige's teasing only made it worse. I was drawn to Arkkadian, excited by him, aroused by him, but I was still nervous around him. Why did he make my heart flutter so hard?

"Listen, I'm not sure what I feel. It's hard to explain. I just want to go soak in a nice hot bath with a good glass of wine. And maybe swoon a little." I winked.

"Swoon. Right. I have batteries if you need them." She laughed mischievously.

"Oh, my God! Paige!" I didn't even own a vibrator, and she knew it! In fact, I'd never even tried one....

9

ARKKADIAN

I watched Aislin walk away, eyes honed in on her delectable ass. What I wouldn't do to get my hands on it. If I didn't know any better, I'd say she strutted that way on purpose. Minx! I took a final swig of my beer as I watched her leave through the back door.

"Let's go. I want to make another sweep around the building," I told my brother.

"Arkken, you're being paranoid. We checked the building once. I've been watching the crowd all evening. There's nothing going on here," he said, clapping me on the shoulder. "Come on, let's go to the safe house. It's getting late. I doubt Kane will try something so soon with you in town."

He had a point, and the safe house was only a few blocks away.

I followed my brother toward the door, glancing over my shoulder for one last look, but my mate had already left. When I turned back, I smacked straight into the wall that was my brother's solid frame. His body was rigid with alarm and veins bulged in his neck. My hackles went up. I almost shoved him out of the way when the fresh stench of sweat and tobacco hit me. Son of a bitch!

"Move! Now!"

I raced off to the left, Gideon to the right, and we circled around the building. Peeking around the back corner, I spotted my mate climbing the steps. The alley was quiet. Almost too quiet. The only movement came from my Aeternus as she stuck a key in the deadbolt. Then I spotted Gideon poking his head around the opposite corner. The light in her window kicked on just as we met beneath the stairs.

"Kane's scent is everywhere," Gideon growled. "He's marking his territory, Arkken. He's challenging you. I'm sorry for not believing you."

"I know. I'll be damned if he gets a hold of her. She's mine! No more waiting. We've got to take her and go. She's no longer safe here."

Though still alert for threats, I didn't sense anyone else at the moment. That didn't mean they weren't there. Kane's scent could be masking others. The beast simmered just under my skin, keening for a fight. I was ready to tear Kane limb from limb, but Gideon stopped me before I could rush the stairs.

"I don't like this. His putrid scent has smothered everything. It's impossible to track where he's gone. Let's be smart about this, brother. I doubt Kane's alone."

I inhaled deeply, noting our surroundings. "You're right, it stinks back here, but I can't scent anyone but Kane. Circle the building again. Check all the vehicles. Text me if you find anything."

He quickly withdrew around the corner as I slunk back into a dark alcove across the alley. From this vantage point, I had a clear view of the apartment while remaining hidden in the shadows. Moonlight failed to penetrate the surrounding darkness.

Thirty minutes later, Gideon reappeared, and I waved him over.

"Have you come up with a plan yet?" Gideon asked, crouching down next to me.

"We're not leaving. Her friend hasn't left the bar yet, which means my mate is still alone." I sat on the ground, legs bent in front of me, fingers drumming impatiently on my knees. Gideon eyed me warily, sensing my agitation.

A few minutes later, Aislin's friend appeared, followed by their boss. He waited for Paige to enter the apartment before disappearing back inside the bar again.

A woman's shadow passed by the lit window just before a larger shadow appeared from behind and grabbed her. The woman flailed in the arms of her captor before being dragged out of sight. Then the light went out. Fuck! Aislin! I'd kill the motherfucker!

Gideon and I were instantly on our feet. I raged inside, the wolf barely contained below the surface.

A crash and a scream sent us running across the alley. Gideon took the stairs quietly while I climbed the fire escape to the side window. In the darkness, I could see nothing through the curtains. Gruff voices and the sounds of whimpering reverberated through the glass. Three men. I recognized the voices of Kane and those two Lycan creeps from the other night. The other two were wolves, but not dire wolves like Kane, my brother, and myself. They would be an easy takedown.

"We'll take them both, but the Aeternus is mine," Kane growled on the other side of the door. "I don't care what you two do with the human, but you won't touch the other one. She'll be mine. Permanently."

Dark laughter echoed. I nearly exploded into wolf form, pure fury painfully seething underneath my skin, every nerve ending on fire. My vision sharpened. Kane intended to force the fucking bond on my mate. Not if I had anything to say about it.

The instinct to protect raced through my veins, but I had to play this smart. We didn't need witnesses, and we didn't want the women getting hurt. An all-out brawl was out of the question.

Looking for another way inside, I noticed the window on the fire escape was unlocked and slightly ajar. I signaled my intention to enter through the window, and Gideon nodded. They would not hurt my mate. I would not allow it. I would kill for her if I had to.

Voices filtered through the open window.

"So, are we taking them back to the cabin to play?" one of them asked, his voice gravelly.

The other one laughed. "Damn right we're gonna play! How about a little tag team? A hole for you, a hole for me!"

More lascivious laughter followed, and it made my skin crawl. There were very few things that angered me as much as someone hurting a woman or child.

I was nearly foaming at the mouth by the time I opened the window the rest of the way. Gideon tried the doorknob. It was unlocked, but I waved him off. I stuck my head inside the darkened room and pushed the curtain aside. Aislin's bedroom. The room was dark and quiet, and her scent was everywhere. I let it soothe the wolf, cleansing my head enough to think. A framed photograph of her and her friend sat on the nightstand. The door was closed, giving me the opportunity to slide through the window.

Muffled sobs caught my attention. I carefully unlatched the door and peeked through the crack. Aislin and Paige sat bound and gagged, huddled side by side on the floor with their backs against the opposite wall. Aislin was hyperventilating, already having a full-blown panic attack. I could hear the men down the hall describing in vulgar detail the abhorrent things they were planning.

I tried to ignore them and focus on the task at hand. Squatting down, I opened the door enough to poke my hand out and grab their attention. Aislin's eyes widened in recognition. I placed a finger in front of my lips, signaling for them to stay quiet.

"Yes, we'll take them back to the cabin now that the holding cells are complete. Taggert, hit the bedrooms. Grab any lingerie you can find. Forget the clothes, they won't need them. Poe, go get the van," Kane ordered.

That sick fuck. I should have killed him instead of exiling him all those years ago. We didn't believe in killing just to kill, but damn if I didn't feel like I'd fucked up.

Back at the window, I watched the one they called Poe step out of the apartment. Gideon was gone, hidden somewhere in the dark recesses of the alley. I quickly shut the window, lest I give myself away when Poe returned. The door across the hall squeaked, its old hinges screaming for oil. Dresser drawers hit the floor as the other man rummaged around.

Spying through the crack, I watched angrily as Kane yanked Aislin up onto her tiptoes. He gripped her by the hair and tilted her face up to his. Fury raged through my core as I watched him lick the side of her face. It killed me to watch and do nothing, but I had to wait for Gideon to create a distraction. It was our best chance of keeping my mate from harm's way.

"I can't wait for you to see what I've got in store for you, baby.

We're long overdue for a lovely little chat. You still owe me." When she squirmed, Kane yanked her hair again, and she squealed in pain through the gag, squeezing her eyes shut. "Look at me, bitch!"

Instead, she turned her head away in straight defiance. The bastard jerked her head back and held her in place. "I said look at me, you stupid cunt. You either open your eyes or I will take you in that back bedroom right now," he growled.

She immediately did as she was bid. I could hear the distress in her ragged breathing and smell the acrid stench of her terror.

"There, that's better. I'm much nicer when you listen. You belong to me. Not that asshole, Arkkadian. If I see that mother-fucker again, I will fucking kill him. Do you understand?"

Aislin nodded quickly, nostrils flaring as she tried to suck in air through her nose. Between the hyperventilating and hysterical sobbing, she choked on the gag in her mouth. How she managed not to give my position away, I didn't know. Kane was so far lost in his own little world that he failed to scent me as he should have. Small miracles.

I silently waited, willing Gideon to hurry, when the front door clicked open. Kane whipped his head toward the sound and threw Aislin to the floor before taking off toward the kitchen. She stumbled on her way down, falling into the wall and smacking the side of her head on the panels.

"What the fu—?" A crash cut the asshole off.

Across the hall, the other shifter—still in human form—ran out of the bedroom and toward the fight. Glass shattered and snarls echoed down the hall. Gideon would keep them both busy. My brother was a formidable fighter. One of the best.

I had to get the women out quickly and safely. I opened the door and held my finger to my lips again. Paige froze at the sight of my glowing eyes. I was so distracted, I hadn't noticed the sparkling clarity in my vision, and I willed the glow away. Aislin watched me, the distress clear on her face. They were terrified, and I wanted nothing more than to comfort my mate, but that would have to wait.

I leaned in and whispered in her ear, "You're okay, love. We'll get you out of here. Gideon is buying us time, but we don't have long."

She whimpered, her body trembling. I tugged the gag from her mouth before carrying her back to her room, where I set her down on the bed.

"I need you to listen to me. My brother is keeping them busy. We have to get both of you out of here. It's no longer safe for you to stay here."

She shook her head no, eyes wide as saucers. Still breathing hard, she tried to stand up and nearly tripped over the ropes binding her ankles. I caught her and lowered her back down. With no time to spare, I put my hands on both arms and pushed small waves of calm into her. Not too much or I'd make her sick. A look of shock mixed with recognition crossed her face when she felt it pour through her.

"Stay here. I'll go get your friend."

"L-let me go!" she cried, struggling to sit closer to the edge of the bed.

"Shh!"

There was a crash down the hall and something large thudded against a wall. Growling ensued, and howls filled the air. Aislin froze. The woman in the hall screamed over and over through her gag. Then the wolves crashed into the other end of the hallway, tearing at each other, gnashing teeth and claw. Bits of fur floated down the hall, and the iron tang of blood drifted on the air.

Aislin's eyes shifted toward the door, but I continued to push calming waves through her body. I couldn't let her see them. Not yet. My mate was nowhere near the right frame of mind to see two giant wolves battling it out.

"Don't look out there. Look at me. You can trust me. I need you to listen to me. You need to slow your breathing down." I spoke as soothing as I could and she nodded.

"Deep breath in. There, that's good. Back out. Once more. I need you to keep your head about you. You've no idea how dangerous those men are. They will do terrible things to you. We have to go, but let me help your friend first, okay?"

She nodded without a word. The terror rolling off her set my teeth on edge, but I couldn't do anything about that at the moment. Before I could move, a shout from the hallway caught my attention.

"Where the fuck is the other girl?"

Fuck! I'd wasted too much time, and now the other woman was in trouble.

The sounds of furniture crashing and more glass shattering continued on in the living room as the wolves wrestled and tried to rip each other apart. Gideon was still fighting, buying us more time.

When I stepped back into the hallway, the other man stood there. He was naked and holding Aislin's friend in his arms with a knife to her throat. Paige was hysterical. Cold, raw fear leaked from her pores.

"Well, well, well. If it isn't the almighty Alpha himself," the man sneered.

He must be the one they called Taggert. I didn't know him, but he apparently knew me. His teeth were yellow, dirty blond hair unkempt, and he looked like he hadn't showered or shaved in days. The man reeked of unwashed sweat, wet dog, and stale smoke. Definitely rogue.

"Take your brother and fuck off. Leave now or I'll jam the knife in the bitch."

Paige whimpered and tried to pull away, but the man yanked her back and pressed the knife against her skin. A drop of blood welled just below her chin and ran down her neck. Her eyes pleaded with desperation for me to save her.

Just then, two massive wolves tore out of the living room, into the kitchen, and back into the living room. Paige screamed in terror. An old worn-out recliner toppled into the hallway, followed by a small glass table that shattered on impact and sent glass flying in all directions. The smell of urine permeated the hallway. She'd pissed herself.

Orange light flared from the living room. We all turned and saw flames rushing up a curtain where the lamp had fallen and sparked the fabric when it broke. Before I could move, Taggert jammed the knife through the bottom of the woman's jaw and up into her skull. In a blink, she was dead. I couldn't have reached her fast enough to save her if I tried.

I jumped forward and grabbed the hand that held the knife and yanked, and before the asshole could react, I jammed it sideways through his ear. He fell to the ground next to the woman with his hand still wrapped around the hilt. I turned at the shriek behind me and found Aislin staring at the lifeless body of her friend lying crumpled on the floor. Then the fire alarm blared, making my ears ring. Black smoke billowed into the hallway, swirling above us and drowning out the oxygen we needed to breathe. We were out of time.

"Stay there. Don't move. You can't help her now," I shouted above the ringing alarm.

My vision flashed brightly, and she stepped back at the sight of my glowing eyes. Aislin tripped and fell backward onto the floor. With her legs bound and arms still tied behind her, she wouldn't get far. I took off down the hall to find the living room engulfed in flames.

Kane stood naked in the center of the room, blood dripping from various wounds where teeth had pierced and torn through flesh. Gideon's black wolf, virtually unscathed, stood in the doorway blocking his escape. Flames licked across the ceiling, making the paint bubble and crack under the blistering heat. Wooden beams splintered, the sound echoing through the room and setting my teeth on edge.

"Gideon, we have to go. Now."

At my words, Gideon shifted back into human form, eyes blazing green. Suddenly, the ceiling collapsed, and I launched myself at my brother, knocking him back, our bodies rolling away from the debris. As we climbed to our feet, we both spotted Kane's foot sticking out from beneath a burning beam. We left him lying there as the inferno raged around us, bent on destruction.

Aislin was struggling to get up off the floor when we returned to her room. She stared at my brother's naked form, but her attention shot straight to me when I drew a knife out of my pocket. She screamed and scooted backward, bumping into her bed. Spinning her around, I quickly sliced through the ropes that bound her. With a sob, she tried to run toward her friend lying on the floor, but I scooped her up and hugged her to me. As Gideon shut the door, she pushed against me, screaming for me to let her go. To let her save her friend.

"Shh. There's nothing you can do for her now. I'm sorry. We

need to go now. The fire is moving too fast. Grab anything important you need. Go!"

I released her, expecting her to disobey, but she surprised me by doing what she'd been told. She raced into the closet first and grabbed a brown paper bag full of clothing. From the dresser, she pulled out a couple of sweaters, shorts, and intimates and then tugged on a pair of sneakers over bare feet. Last were a few items she pulled out of a drawer in her nightstand, including a photograph, a financial folder, a wallet, and a laptop, all of which she stuffed in a backpack.

Gideon waited impatiently on the landing outside. I took Aislin's bags and handed them to him through the window. Then he reached out his hand to help my mate through to the other side. I grabbed the framed photo of the two women off the nightstand and followed. I had a feeling it was something she'd want.

A windowless black van was parked in the alley when we climbed down the fire escape. We rounded the back of it and stumbled over Carter's body. He lay on the pavement, neck twisted at an odd angle, eyes staring unseeing at the stars above.

When she saw him, Aislin screamed and buried her face in my chest. I wrapped my arms around her, trying to shelter her from the grisly sight. Gideon checked for a pulse and shook his head. He was dead. My heart ached for my mate.

Scorching flames leaped through the kitchen window above us and licked up the side of the building, charring the brickwork. It wouldn't be long before the whole building went up in flames. Old buildings like that burned hard, and they burned fast. Too fast. The flames were already licking Aislin's bedroom door by the time we climbed out the window.

The other Lycan was nowhere to be found. He'd probably taken off when the fight broke out upstairs, fucking coward that he was. Carter must have come outside and interrupted him at some point.

The back door of the van hung open, a foul stench rolling out of it. An old dirty mattress lay on the floor, dark stains marring its filthy surface and filling my mind with troubling things. I turned the disgusting thoughts away as sirens blared in the distance. We needed to leave before the authorities arrived and get as far away as possible.

Gideon tossed Aislin's bags in the back of the SUV and then quickly pulled on a shirt and a pair of sweats while I helped her into the backseat. I pulled the seatbelt across her lap and buckled her in. The second I jumped in the back with her, Gideon pulled out of the lot and headed straight for the highway.

A few blocks away, a line of police cars and fire trucks passed us with sirens screaming. The flames had engulfed the entire top floor by the time we'd made it to the SUV, and by the time emergency services got there, there would be nothing left to save. Whether Kane made it out alive remained to be seen. We should have checked, but if we had taken the time to dig through the rubble, we may not have made it out of the apartment in time.

Aislin stared blankly out the window, not making a peep as we drove away. After several failed attempts to draw her attention, I backed off.

Half an hour later, we pulled over at a small rest area on the side of the highway. Thankfully, it was deserted at this time of night. Aislin still hadn't spoken a word, but she flinched when I touched her arm. I pulled my hand away, not wanting to frighten her any more than she already was.

"Aislin?"

She turned her head a little to the side but refused to look at me. A response was good, even if it wasn't the one I was looking for. She just sat there shivering with her arms wrapped around herself.

"Gideon, grab a blanket from the back, please. Aislin, listen to me. I need to make sure you're okay."

No response.

"Aislin? I need you to look at me, sweetie." Slowly, she turned, but her eyes were unfocused and glossy. "Good girl."

"Your eyes glowed," she whispered. The stench of fear rolled off her, tickling my nose. "They were bright blue. Like Kane's, but his were green. I thought I'd imagined it. Oh, God, you're gonna kill me, aren't you?" She slid across the seat, trembling as she leaned as far against the door as she could.

"I won't hurt you. I promise you're safe. And no, you didn't

73

imagine anything. I'm very sorry we scared you. Truly," I reassured, speaking as concisely as I could to allay some of her fear.

"Wh-what are you?" she stammered.

Just then, Gideon climbed back into the front seat and handed me a blanket. "Arkken, don't. She's not ready."

"Ready for what?" Aislin looked back and forth between my brother and me, and I glared at him. He took the hint and quickly pulled his phone out of his pocket and busied himself with a text to Sara.

"Can I check your wrists and ankles? Are you hurt anywhere else? What about when you hit your head?"

She shook her head no, but slowly raised her wrists and held them out for me. I turned them over, gently grazing the red marks with my thumbs. She hissed and tried to tug them away, but I held tight. I sighed, trying to calm my wolf as the beast within was still angry over this evening's events.

Gideon handed me the first aid kit before climbing over the console to the driver's seat. Aislin burst into tears when he started the engine and returned to the highway.

"Shh. It's okay. You're okay," I soothed.

I held her hands, and once again sent gentle waves of energy through her until she settled. Afterward, I took the healing salve from the first aid kit and applied it to the rope burns on her wrists. I did the same with her ankles and then wrapped the wounds with gauze. Aislin was barely aware of my ministrations.

"There. All done. Any other injuries?" I asked, but she didn't respond. "I'm very sorry."

She unexpectedly leaned into me, and I gently wrapped my arms around her while she cried. If I could do anything to take the hurt away, I would. It killed me I couldn't.

My beast still raged within, but for my mate's sake, I tamped it down. She was terrified. Eventually, the tears subsided, and she drifted off to sleep. I tucked the blanket around her to keep her warm while she slept.

We rode home in silence, though Aislin stirred a few times in her sleep. I stroked her hair lightly, soothing her back into slumber. By the time we made it back to Eagle Ridge, she was in a deep, relaxed sleep. She didn't even twitch when I carried her from the SUV to my bed.

The stench of Kane lay heavy on her clothing. Bringing that smell into my home only served to further enrage my wolf. Her clothes were also covered in spatters of vomit. I wasn't sure when that had happened. Most likely before Gideon and I had arrived. I wanted nothing in my home that reminded me of that sick bastard.

I removed her shoes first, and then with a pair of scissors, I gently cut away the torn, dirty fabric of her clothing piece by piece. I tossed the scraps into the fireplace on the opposite wall and then returned to the bed to cover her. She would probably be pissed when she woke, but I was willing to take the chance if it meant removing all traces of Kane.

Leaning over to grab the blankets, the sight of so much scarring down the side of her body sickened me. Nothing in the article I'd read could have truly prepared me for what I saw. Aislin was scarred from neck to hip, just as described, but it was so much worse than I'd imagined. Any doubt I had about her identity was gone. What kind of monster could torture a child this way? It was abhorrent.

My stomach lurched as I stared at the scars. When I couldn't take it anymore, I reached once again for the covers, but something caught my eye. Right there on her hip, a letter was carved into her skin. The son of a bitch had signed his work as if it were a piece of fucking art. R for Ryker Slade. Arden Vane's right-hand man had carved his signature mark right there on her skin. On a child!

Anger flowed like lava just under the surface of my skin, and I saw red. My fangs extended in my mouth as I fought the urge to shift. I couldn't remember the last time I had ever felt this enraged.

So help me, if I ever found the motherfucker who did this....

If I didn't calm down, I risked shifting right here and now. I couldn't let that happen or I could accidentally wake my mate, and she'd already experienced enough terror in her short life. With one last horrified look, I covered her up and stepped away from the bed. Then I turned to light the fire, hoping it would ward off the spring chill still left in the air.

And the sooner I could burn the soiled clothing, the better. I fell to my knees and watched with great satisfaction as the flames ate up the fabric, taking the fetid stench of Kane West with it. As I sat there, thoughts of Ryker Slade and his cruelty lodged in the forefront of my mind and my stomach roiled again. I'd long since suspected he was dead. But if I ever found out he wasn't....

I couldn't even fathom the pain and terror Aislin must have endured at that bastard's hands. She was a child! It was barbaric. No wonder she was so prone to panic. Surviving something so heinous would scar anyone for life. Even the best memory block couldn't wipe away everything entirely, especially something so traumatic. There were always residual bits and pieces floating around, popping up when least expected.

I shut the bedside lamp off, closed the blinds, and left her to rest. Gideon waited downstairs in the kitchen with a fresh mug of steaming coffee for me. It was nearly six in the morning, and Aislin would probably be up in just a few short hours. No sense in going back to sleep now. I couldn't stomach coffee, however, or anything else.

"What's wrong?" Gideon asked, noticing the distress on my face.

I paced over to the window and stared out at the pinks and purples crisscrossing the sky as the sun peeked over the horizon. On any other day, I'd marvel at the beautiful sight. Not today. I tried to gather my thoughts and regain some sense of composure before speaking.

"It's true, Gideon. All of it. Every bit."

"What makes you say that?"

"Scars. She's covered in them. Her clothing reeked of Kane, so I cut them off and tossed them in the fire. What I saw when I removed her clothes... fuck. I can't unsee that." I choked on my words, gagging on the lump lodged in my throat.

"What did you see?"

"Everything. Dammit. Scars from neck to hip down one side, just like the article described. Cut after cut. That son of a bitch, Slade, he tortured a little girl! A child!" I may have been one tough bastard, but there were just some things even I couldn't stomach. As immortals, we cherished children. Anyone who could do this to a child deserved a slow, painful death.

Gideon joined me at the window and placed a hand on my shoulder. "How do you know it was him?"

"The sadistic fuck signed his work. He carved an R right into her hip," I said through gritted teeth, and Gideon gasped in disgust. "You know the mark as well as I do. They don't call him the Blade for nothing. Jesus, Gideon. It's fucking barbaric!" I slapped my hands on the counter and leaned over the sink, feeling like I was about to vomit.

"Fuck." I could feel Gideon's ire as if it were my own, my wolf feeding upon his rage and becoming even more outraged with every second that passed.

"Yeah."

"Listen, Arkken, she's safe here. No one knows she's here, except maybe Kane if he survived. He won't be able to step one foot back in the compound. I already alerted security anyway. Let's hope he doesn't know who she is, but if he's seen the scars...." Gideon left that last bit unspoken. "There's not much we can do right now. Let her rest. You as well. Better yet, go for a run and blow off some of this steam pouring from your ears. I can send Sara to watch over her."

"No. I'm not leaving her. She'll need a familiar face when she wakes. Not that she trusts me anymore. I'm sure we ruined that last night." I slapped my brother on the back, dismissing him, and headed for the stairs.

"Her bags are in the den. I'm going home to see my mate, but we're not done talking about this," Gideon said as he walked toward the front door. "Call me later."

I hesitated at the bottom of the stairs. I couldn't make myself go back up yet. Instead, I went back to the kitchen, where I stared out the window, watching the children playing down in the commons. I bristled at the thought of anyone harming them the way Aislin had been hurt. I would kill anyone who dared try.

Back upstairs, I set water and painkillers on the nightstand and then took her bags to the closet. I pulled my boots off and tossed my soot-stained clothes in the hamper before donning a fresh outfit.

Aislin twitched on the bed, lost in the grip of a nightmare.

Words slipped incoherently from her lips and her fists gripped the sheets as they tangled around her. I sat carefully on the bed next to her and placed a hand on her forehead, letting my mind drift into hers, trying to see what she saw. I still couldn't bypass the memory block.

A vision of flames pierced by a child's scream filled my head. Willing the flames down, I sent soothing images of the tide cresting over the beach into her mind. Slowly, her body stilled under my touch, and the lines on her face relaxed.

Satisfied, I crossed the room to the soft leather chair by the fire and sat down. Leaving the lamp off, I sat in the darkened room with nothing but the warm glow of the fire for company. With the shades drawn, the room would remain dark even as the sun rose in the sky. Soon, my mate's easy breathing and the crackling of wood as it burned were the only sounds, giving the room a tranquil feel.

I wouldn't leave her. My wolf wouldn't let me even if I tried. It demanded I keep watch, so I did.

10

ARKKADIAN

I bolted out of my chair at the sound of Aislin's scream. I hadn't realized I'd dozed off. Aislin sat upright in my bed, eyes wide, fists clenched, screaming hysterically about glowing green eyes. Drenched in sweat, tears streamed down her face. I went quickly to her side, but when I touched her shoulder to soothe her, she erupted into more fits of terrified screaming.

"Get off me! Get off! I said no! Please!"

I jerked away, unsure how to help her. Then the realization she was having a night terror struck me. Her eyes were open, but she wasn't awake, so I backed away from the bed. Touching her would only make it worse. The only thing to do was ride it out and wait.

Aislin screamed for nearly an hour before finally slouching back down onto her pillow, sleep once again claiming her. I was nearly at my wit's end before the terrors finally ceased. Once she settled, I used a cool, damp cloth and gently wiped the sweat away from her body. She stirred slightly but didn't wake. When I finished, I carefully pulled the covers back up. She'd kicked them off with all her thrashing about on the bed. I did my best to avoid looking at the scars. Doing so would only stir up more anger.

Though exhausted, I knew sleep wouldn't come for me again. I put more logs in the dying fire and stoked it back to life. Even in the middle of May, it still got a little chilly up in the mountains.

Leaving Aislin to rest, I sought the comfort of a hot shower where I could wash off the rest of the fire's stench that still lingered upon my skin. My muscles ached from the stress of last night, and I welcomed the relaxing heat, letting it soak into me and soothe my weary soul until the water ran cold once more.

My heart hurt for my mate. All the things she'd endured in life, all the things she'd been deprived of... all because of a sadistic tyrant who murdered his own flesh and blood. Over a centuries-old fit of jealousy Aislin's parents had nothing to do with. The knowledge left my soul feeling bruised and tortured.

Pulling myself out of my thoughts, I toweled off and padded naked through the bedroom toward my closet without a second thought. Nudity was common among immortals. We thought nothing of stripping in front of others when shifting for a run or even walking naked through the compound on the way home. For us, it was just an everyday part of life.

Halfway across the room, a startled gasp caught my attention. Aislin sat upright in bed with a look of pure shock on her face. She quickly averted her gaze and yanked the covers up to her chin. Her cheeks pinked up, and she tried to hide her face.

"You're awake," I said with a smile, though she cowered away from me. "I'm sorry, please excuse me and I'll put on something more decent."

I wandered nonchalantly into my closet and donned the usual black t-shirt and jeans before walking barefoot back into the master bedroom. Aislin was shaking so I refrained from approaching her. Her embarrassment had quickly turned to fear. Couldn't say I blamed her. She was in a strange place with a strange man after witnessing her best friend's murder.

"Where am I?" Her voice was laced with alarm as she looked wildly around the room.

"Safe," I told her.

"Please tell me where I am! And where are my clothes? Why am I naked? Oh, God! Oh, God!" She lifted the covers and looked down and then back at me. "Did you—? Did we—?"

As the questions exploded forth, the look on her face changed from bewildered to terrified. She would think that. What woman wouldn't in her situation? It was plain to see Aislin had little control over her emotions. They were like a bright flashing beacon screaming, "Here I am!"

"No, we didn't. Please calm do—" I started, but she cut me off.

"Don't tell me to calm down! I want to know where I am!" Her face turned scarlet. She'd gone from afraid to angry as quickly as she'd gone from embarrassed to afraid. Her swiftly changing emotions were surely a product of all the trauma she had endured in her life, and she wasn't coping well with any of it.

"As I was trying to say, you are safe. You were asl—"

"Answer me! Where are my clothes? Did you fuck me?" she screamed.

"I told you we didn't. That's not my thi—"

"Tell me!"

I closed my eyes and pinched my nose in annoyance. Patience, Arkkadian, patience. She was afraid. Normally, I didn't tolerate such behavior, but I was willing to give her a pass considering the circumstances. Sometimes fear made one do or say things they normally wouldn't, and she carried that fear in spades. I let out a long sigh before I spoke again.

"Rule number one around here. Be respectful. Now, I would answer you if you would stop overreacting long enough to let me finish a sentence." My voice was dangerously calm as I let the Alpha side of my nature slowly seep into my tone.

"Fuck you! You took me from my home! Fucking asshole! Take me back! Take me back now!" The more she screamed, the shriller her voice became.

That's it. I finally had enough. I paced over to the side of the bed and leaned over her so we were nose to nose, eye to eye. Scowling at her, I made it a point to inhale deeply and let it out slowly, with emphasis. The muscles in my jaw ticked as I clenched my teeth. If she wanted to be childish, I was going to let the Alpha come out to play. She needed to know exactly who was in charge here.

"Stop." I spoke with deadly authority, and she stilled at my command. Her mouth opened and quickly shut again, words failing her. "Rule number two. I'm in charge. If you weren't so disrespectful, I would have gladly explained the situation. I know you're scared, but I will not tolerate that kind of behavior in my home or there will be consequences. I will not hesitate to take you over my knee. Do you understand?"

"But…" she stammered.

I let out a small growl, and the link between us resonated with brazen authority. I knew she felt it because I did, too. Her eyes widened and her body went rigid as it recognized its Alpha.

"Do you understand?" I repeated. I let the full power of the Alpha fill the room around us, and the air thickened with unbridled tension. I let it ferment until everything I'd said sank into her.

"Yes," she finally mumbled, instantly dropping her eyes, instinctively submitting to me and shrinking in on herself. I didn't think she was even aware she was even doing it.

"I burned your clothes. They were torn up, covered in vomit, and they reeked of that bastard who attacked you. Your belongings are in the closet, and there are fresh towels in the bathroom. I suggest you collect yourself and make use of them. I'll see you downstairs when you're ready to apologize and discuss things in a more civilized manner. This is a warning. Next time I won't be so lenient."

I left her sitting there with her mouth agape as I turned on my heel and walked out the door. I closed it firmly behind me before taking a deep, cleansing breath. I'd expected her to test me. I'd expected an outburst. I'd expected the anger. What I hadn't expected was how much it would affect me. How much it would make me yearn to punish her and make her submit to my authority. How much I wanted to kiss her. How much her defiance turned me on.

How hard it made me.

I THOUGHT about my mate as I leaned back against the bedroom door, and how I needed to tread carefully with her. Things would have been so much different if she'd been raised with the Pack. So much easier. She'd been dealt a hard life, and it had left her high-strung, prone to panic, and quick to anger. I'd say she was a clear case for post-traumatic stress disorder, honestly.

Such disrespectful behavior, however, was never tolerated from a Pack member, and anyone else would have received punishment for that outburst, but none of them had ever experienced the trauma she had either. The wolf inside me prowled, ready to bond.

The beast wouldn't be satisfied until it came to fruition, but it would just have to wait. Aislin's comfort and safety took precedence above all else.

The sound of her sobbing floated through the door, and the instinct to protect her surged forth again. But I couldn't walk back in there. She needed time to process, and I needed time to cool down.

I plopped down in my leather chair and propped my feet up on my desk as I turned on the news. According to the latest report, the building that housed the bar and Aislin's apartment burned completely to the ground, and only two unidentified bodies had been found within the charred debris. Over the next few hours, while I waited for Aislin to come out of hiding, the story played on an endless loop. They had found no other bodies, which meant Kane had likely survived. That didn't bode well for our current situation, and once again, I was angry with myself for not ending him. But had I done so, I very well could have endangered all of us.

My ears pricked when I heard the door upstairs finally open. I turned off the television and went out to greet her, stopping to lean against the doorframe of the den to wait. My breath caught in my throat as I watched her descend the stairs. She'd showered, and her damp hair hung loosely around her shoulders in waves. Her outfit hugged her curves in all the right places. She was a beautiful sight to behold. Hints of cinnamon and vanilla wafted down the stairs, causing an instant tent in my pants. I didn't even try to hide my attraction.

11

AISLIN

The sound of flowing water nudged me into an exhausted consciousness. My head felt like an angry woodpecker had taken up residence inside my skull. Pain came in bursts with every tap tap tap of his pointy little beak. My body ached. My wrists and ankles smarted under the bandages. I opened my eyes to a room I didn't recognize and hurriedly sat up.

Before I could take stock of my surroundings, the door to my left opened and Arkkadian walked out. Naked. Holy fuck! I barely registered the covers falling to my lap.

I was rewarded with a glorious view. The man had the body of a god. The heavenly scent of cinnamon and cloves filled the air and went straight to my core, turning my insides to liquid. Fire bloomed down low, and the slow burn of arousal took me by surprise. This wasn't right. I barely knew the man. This shouldn't be happening. My reaction mortified me. I wanted him, but I didn't want to want him. None of this made any sense.

In the seconds that followed, I took in every splendid ounce of tanned, bare skin from his six-pack abs and hard-toned muscles to his... Was that his...? He was huge. And hard. Rock fucking hard. I didn't realize I'd gasped out loud until he turned my way. His nakedness had caught me completely off guard. That slow-burning fire deep down in my core warmed my skin as lust wildly suffused every muscle fiber and nerve ending from my head to my toes.

My eyes slowly drifted upward to his gorgeous, hard-as-steel eyes. Did we...? No, no way. We hadn't, had we? Surely, I would remember fucking a god. With a body like that.... Embarrassed, I yanked the covers back up over my body. He disappeared into the closet with a smirk on his face, and then the events of last night came crashing back. Panic and anger returned, instantly drowning out the last moments as if they'd never happened.

When Arkkadian returned, I flung a barrage of questions at him and swiftly angered when he didn't answer me fast enough. My shouting at him only resulted in a harsh reprimand. And then he'd left the room. I was momentarily dumbfounded. I couldn't decide what angered me the most, being scolded or being dismissed like an errant child. Or maybe it was the fact that I'd become aroused by a complete stranger, my body's reaction traitorous. I barely knew the man, but that didn't stop my body from wanting something it shouldn't.

"Dammit!" I screamed out all of my frustration into the empty room.

Then suddenly remembering my nakedness, I yanked the covers off. I'd already checked once, but I wanted to be more thorough now that Arkkadian was no longer in the room. I couldn't remember anything after we'd left the apartment, so anything could have happened. He said we didn't, but... Oh, thank God! The sheets were clean, and I still had my panties on. Relief washed over me.

I took the proffered painkillers from the nightstand, hoped it would quell the throbbing in my head, and climbed out of bed. Both of my bags were on the floor of the closet, my boots and sneakers set neatly beside them. I sat down cross-legged on the plush carpet to inspect everything. I'd shoved whatever I could in my bags in my haste to pack last night.

When I pulled the navy-blue cashmere sweater out of the bag, the one that Paige had given me, I spotted the framed photo of her and I in the bag. I didn't remember grabbing it. Beneath it was the photo of Carter and I. Reality came crashing back as I stared at their faces, and I lost it. The two people I loved most in this world were no longer alive. Carter, lying dead on the filthy ground in the alley. Paige, crumpled on the floor, her blood pouring onto the hardwood. The thought of their bodies lying there cold and lifeless nearly made me wretch. They'd been tossed like pieces of trash with no regard for the beautiful lives being snuffed out.

Every single terrifying moment, it was all real. It hadn't been a dream. The only family I knew was gone forever, and now it seemed I was a captive in some strange man's home. I had no idea where I was. I could be anywhere. I didn't even know if I was still in Montana.

Hugging the pictures and the sweater to my chest, I cried and cried until eventually, the tears stopped, and I had nothing more to give. My life was now at the mercy of a man with glowing cerulean eyes that had seared their way into my very soul. He had done nothing to hurt me. In fact, he had saved my life last night, but that still didn't mean I could trust him. Even if my body wanted to.

Eventually, I pulled myself up off the floor and headed for the bathroom. I was thankful for the lock on the door. At least I'd have some privacy in case Arkkadian returned to his room.

Carefully laid out on the counter were a washcloth, hand towel, and a bath towel, along with a fresh bar of soap, shampoo, a new toothbrush, and a tube of toothpaste. Huh. Who was this man? He could have hurt me, yet he hadn't. He hadn't even slept in the bed with me, and here he'd laid everything out so nicely. I had way more questions than answers.

Arkkadian seemed like a walking, talking paradox. Alluring, yet intimidating. A stranger, yet familiar. Hard, yet gentle. Why was I so drawn to him? Why did I crave him so? Being in his presence was like a thirst I couldn't quench.

I let the hot water rush over my aching muscles, relishing in the warmth, but it didn't take long for the violent memories of last night to invade my mind. Bile rose in my throat. I could still feel Kane touching me. Grabbing me. Licking me. Breathing on me. I felt so dirty and disgusting. I was sure I'd never feel clean again. So I scrubbed and scrubbed and scrubbed. I scrubbed every square inch until my skin turned red and raw, and still, it wasn't enough. I didn't stop scrubbing until the water turned to ice.

Back in the bedroom, I studied my surroundings. The plush carpet, a deep blue that reminded me of Arkkadian's eyes, was soft between my toes. The king-sized, antique four-poster bed took front and center on my left, with its satin sheets and fluffy pillows. A closer look at the posts revealed an intricate design of hand-carved knots. I recognized the triple spiral of eternal life interwoven among the roots of the tree of life and wondered at its significance.

A large stone fireplace was built into the opposite wall on my right, framed by tall bookshelves and, next to it, the door. Two reading chairs faced the hearth. The master closet took up the space behind me, and the bathroom straight ahead. Other than that, the room was fairly sparse.

By now it was mid-afternoon, and I'd wasted much of the day. Curious, I padded across the floor to the window beside the bed and raised the blinds. Bright sunshine beamed in and blanketed me in its glorious warmth. A breathtaking view unfolded before me as I gazed out.

Situated on the edge of a large vale, Arkkadian's cabin was surrounded by vast forests and snow-capped mountains in every direction. Gravel pathways lined with colorful wildflowers intertwined between the surrounding cabins. I spied a handful of people working in a community garden while children laughed and raced, chasing each other on the large lawn. Everyone looked so happy.

I studied the scenery, letting the sun's warmth radiate through my body until my stomach rumbled. I was starving, but the last thing I wanted was a face-to-face with Arkkadian. Truthfully, though, I had behaved like an errant child, and he had done nothing except lecture me after I'd behaved so horribly. He'd saved my life, and I'd foolishly repaid him with a childish tantrum. No wonder he thought I was such an ungrateful brat.

I sighed and opened the bedroom door. I couldn't hide in here forever.

12

AISLIN

As I descended the stairs, Arkkadian appeared at the bottom. Even with the stoic expression on his face, he was still handsome. I froze halfway down the steps when I saw the obvious bulge in his pants, but I pretended not to notice. I was still embarrassed by my earlier behavior, but hiding upstairs would solve nothing.

"Hi," I whispered, eyes everywhere but on him.

"Hi." He raised his arm, showing the way to the kitchen. "After you." When my stomach grumbled impatiently, he inquired softly, "When was the last time you ate?"

That wasn't the response I expected. I'd come downstairs preparing to be lectured. Yelled at. Something. Anything but concern for my well-being. Maybe... maybe it was coming later.

"Not since dinner yesterday." When I hesitated, Arkkadian entered the kitchen, leaving me to follow awkwardly in his wake.

Arkkadian pulled various items from the refrigerator and set everything on the counter. Then he turned and handed me a plate, telling me to help myself to the sandwich fixings he'd laid out.

"Thank you." Why was he so calm? Shouldn't he still be angry with me? Glued to the spot, I watched him fix his own plate, wondering what his intentions were.

"I won't bite," Arkkadian offered. "Help yourself. Whatever you'd like. I've also got a couple of apples, but I'm afraid water and coffee are all I've got to drink."

His voice was low and smooth, no trace of the ire he'd displayed upstairs earlier. I didn't know what to make of it. If he was still upset with me, he hid it well. I wished I could hide my emotions as well as he could and not get so upset so quickly. I often felt like my inability to do so was a curse I'd never be rid of.

"This is fine, thank you," I said, still feeling contrite as I joined Arkkadian at the table.

"I'm sorry," I suddenly blurted. I stared at my lap and wrung my hands.

"Sorry for what?"

Was he really going to make me say it out loud? Apparently, I couldn't escape the conversation I'd been dreading after all.

"I'm sorry I yelled at you. It was rude." I wanted to crawl into a deep, dark hole and never come out again. "I just... so much has happened and I'm kind of..." Unable to finish the thought, my voice trailed off.

"Hey," Arkkadian said, reaching across the table to lift my chin. He spoke softly, a hard contrast from the authority that had previously laced his voice. "Look at me, please."

When I slowly raised my eyes to his, he continued. "I know you're frightened. A lot has happened. Despite the reprimand you received, you are safe and your safety will not be compromised. I mean that. But we have rules here, and there are punishments when the rules are disobeyed. You need to know that speaking to me in that manner is unacceptable, but because of the circumstances, I let it slide. I won't let it slide next time. Do you understand?"

A small bit of authority laced his words once again at that last bit. I nodded my understanding. Punishments? I didn't like the sound of that at all. My acknowledgment seemed to appease him, though, and we ate in relative silence for the rest of the meal. I kept my eyes downcast as I ate, though I could feel his on me the entire time.

When he took our dishes to the sink, I stared out the window and watched the people going about their day outside. When I turned back, Arkkadian was leaning against the counter, quietly assessing me. It should have made me uncomfortable, but it didn't, and I couldn't explain why. Minutes passed before he spoke again.

"I know you have some questions, but I have to meet with my security team. It'll take me an hour or two at the most. Come, I'll take you to my brother's, and you can meet Sara. She's his wife. I know she'd love to meet you."

"What do you have to do?" I really didn't care, but the last thing I wanted to do was visit with another stranger. What I wanted was answers.

What I wanted was a way out of here.

"I'm in charge here. My people look to me to make sure everything runs smoothly and safely," Arkkadian explained. "Come. Let's go meet Sara. I think you'll like her."

"Can't I stay here? I'm still tired. I could use another nap," I lied. A chance to search the cabin for clues to my whereabouts or a way to escape was the first thing on my agenda. Though no harm had come to me, I needed to find my bearings. I needed to get out of here.

Much to my disappointment, he shook his head. I couldn't be trusted. Not yet. It stung, but I couldn't very well expect Arkkadian to trust me if I couldn't fully trust him yet.

"I'm sorry, that's not an option. I can't leave you alone," he said with a knowing look. Dammit. A jolt of disappointment shot through me, knowing he'd seen right through my lie. I knew it wouldn't work anyway.

"How long do I have to stay? I want to go home." I faltered at the last, thinking about the fire that had taken everything from me. Who was I kidding? I no longer had a home. Where would I go? Where would I stay? I supposed that chintzy little motel across town would work for a few days, at least until I sorted some things out. Now that my home and family were gone, there was really nothing keeping me in Whitewater. I couldn't stay, anyway. Kane saw to that with his obsession with me. I sure didn't want to stay here either. Wherever this was.

"You can't leave," he stated.

My head jerked up at his response. "I don't understand. Am I a prisoner?"

"No, you're not."

"Then why can't I leave?" I asked. Anger and fear drowned out any bit of trust I might have had for Arkkadian. He reached for my arm, but I flinched away. "Don't. Touch. Me," I ground out, my last bit of patience gone like last week's trash.

"I'm sorry, you just can't. It isn't safe. Kane is still unaccounted for, as is his partner. As long as they're out there, you're in danger. Kane is a sick individual. You know this. If he got a hold of you…" Arkkadian let the sentence die, and he looked away, unable to meet my eyes. Even though I knew he told the truth, I refused to give up the argument. It was stupid, but I just couldn't help myself.

"I know exactly what kind of man Kane is, but I still want to go home," I demanded.

Arkkadian's face fell flat. "Need I remind you of your tone?"

Momentarily cowed, I shook my head. "No."

"There is no home to go back to. All that's left of the Black Horse and your apartment is a pile of cinder and ash. I'm sorry." Arkkadian ran a hand through his hair, and his dark locks fell across his forehead. I refrained from reaching out and smoothing it back. Despite his ire, it seemed like he genuinely cared, but why me?

"And, whatever you do, don't go wandering off with some half-baked idea that you can hike back home. It's a three-hour drive at best and a three- or four-day hike at worst through old winding roads and heavily wooded forest, and that's if you know where you're going. It's too easy to get lost out here. Not to mention the wildlife. The woods are full of apex predators. You'd never even see a mountain lion until it was too late."

I collapsed back down into the kitchen chair in despair. My breathing turned erratic, and my chest hurt. I covered my ears and scrunched my eyes shut. I struggled to breathe as the weight on my chest increased. I was drowning under the onslaught of emotions cutting straight through my heart like a knife. I didn't want any of this. I wanted my life back, but I couldn't have it. Any of it. My life as I knew it was over, and nothing would ever be the same.

"No. No, no, no, no, no, no. This isn't real. This isn't real," I cried, rocking back and forth in the chair. Paige and Carter were dead. My job at the bar was gone. My apartment was gone. My entire world had just disintegrated. The room tilted on its axis, and darkness swirled around the edges of my vision. I felt like all the oxygen had been sucked from the room.

Arkkadian caught me before I tumbled to the floor and helped me back into the chair. He crouched down in front of me and placed gentle hands upon my own. "Aislin, listen to me. Look at me. Look at me," he said, pointing to his eyes, not taking them off mine. "Take a deep breath. Can you do that? Good. Now breathe out. You're doing great. Just like that. Again. Just keep breathing, slowly."

Once again, the curious and familiar warmth I felt whenever Arkkadian touched me radiated through my body. Only this time, my body seemed to recognize it, grab ahold of it, and suck it in. The energy was soft, almost like tiny waves lapping at the shoreline.

Almost instantly, I relaxed into his touch. When his strong arms wrapped around me, I leaned into him and rested my head on his shoulder. My breathing stabilized, slowing down until it matched Arkkadian breath for breath. Whatever this was—how he could pull me out of such a state?—I didn't know, but whatever it was, it was a gift.

There were more pressing matters, though.

When I felt stable enough to speak, I pulled away from his embrace and faced him. "I want to see the news. I need to see it for myself."

I couldn't blindly trust him. Not yet. For all I knew, he could have been lying about the fire's destruction. I didn't want to believe it. I refused to believe it. I denied it even though I knew it to be true.

"All right, come on."

I followed him into the den, and the television screen flared to life. I watched in horror as images of the burned building flashed by. My home. The bar. They were nothing but a pile of charred debris, tar-black and ruined. Devoid of everything but memories.

"They've been replaying the same story all day. No new details have been released," Arkkadian told me. The sadness in his voice was tangible. I found his concern comforting, at least.

"Do the police know where I am?" I asked, fishing for information. Did they know I was there? Did they think I was missing? Dead? Various possibilities ran through my mind.

"Gideon took care of it. He called the police station in White-water this morning. He told them you were safe, and that you were away visiting friends. They said they'd let us know if they had questions," Arkkadian answered and then turned off the television.

"How did you know I needed help?" Of all the questions I had, that was the one that had nagged at me the most. The last thing I wanted was another man as obsessed with me as Kane had been.

"Call it a gut feeling. I didn't trust that Kane would stay away, and I wanted to make sure you made it home safe. So, Gideon and I watched for him, but it turned out he was already inside your apartment."

"That was some gut feeling," I huffed, but I still questioned his motive. "What now?"

I mean, I had nothing. Nothing but the clothes on my back and what I'd stuffed in those two bags upstairs in the closet. What little savings I had wouldn't last long.

"Come on, I'll take you to Sara's. It'll take your mind off things. I think you'll like her."

Just like that, the conversation was over, so I resigned myself to finishing it later. I still had questions that needed answers. Then Arkkadian took my hand and led me up a short path to another cabin close by. I stopped dead at the base of the steps when the memory of a giant black wolf resurfaced. I'd only seen it for a second, but I knew what I'd seen.

"You okay?" Arkkadian tried to tug me up the stairs, but I stood rooted to the spot at the bottom. I didn't know what Gideon was, and I wasn't sure I wanted to know.

"Please don't make me go in there. Can't I come with you?" I begged. If I mentioned the wolf, he'd probably think I was nuts.

Arkkadian looked down at me, compassion written on his face. "I'm sorry, but you can't. I promise you'll like Sara. Trust me?"

I didn't want to, but when he squeezed my hand gently in reassurance, I faltered on my earlier decision. "But what if he's here?"

"Gideon?"

"Yeah."

"He's not, but you're safe here. My brother is a good man."

Brother. Right. Screw it. I wasn't nuts. I had to say it.

"He's a werewolf, isn't he?" I whispered, staring at the front door. Now that I'd voiced it out loud, it sounded ludicrous. Men didn't turn into wolves. Or did they? Arkkadian's face didn't even twitch. Nor did he deny it.

The fuck? He knew. I'm wasn't crazy, was I?

"We have some things to discuss. When I get back, we'll talk. But, you need to trust me. Sara is wonderful, and you're in good hands. Now scoot," he said, placing a hand on my back and ushering me up the steps.

It didn't escape me that he never answered my question.

A petite blond answered the door. She was pretty, with joyful green eyes and a gentle smile. She wore a cute, flowery blouse and blue jeans, and her honey-colored hair was styled in a French braid. The rounded curve of her belly peeked over the waistline of her pants. She was pregnant. Several months along, if I had any guess. The smell of fresh chocolate chip cookies drew me in, making the home feel cozy and welcoming.

"Hi! I'm Sara. Please come in! Gideon mentioned his brother had a guest," she said, wrapping me in a warm embrace. "I almost didn't believe him. This big lug is a perpetual bachelor." Her laugh was genuine, her voice bubbly, and her eyes shone bright with mirth as she teased Arkkadian.

Arkkadian laughed. "Hey now!"

The ease with which they joked with each other suggested strong ties. There was a friendship there. And the love of family. Sara trusted him and thought well of him. It went a long way toward easing my reservations about him.

"Oh, shush, you know it's true," she teased him. "Please come in and make yourself at home. Gideon's at work, so it's just me and you. Gives us a chance to get to know each other."

I followed her into the house, blushing at the mention of her husband. I'd seen Gideon in his birthday suit last night, and he had an excellent physique, much like his brother.

With that thought, the image of a very naked Arkkadian popped into my head, and the room suddenly felt overwhelmingly hot. Neither man had seemed bothered by their nudity, which I found odd, especially in front of a strange woman. And Gideon was married. Did Sara know I'd seen her husband naked? Would she care? Even so, there was no way I would admit that little tidbit.

Sara gave Arkkadian a hug as he walked in behind me. "Gideon said to tell you he's over at the canteen with Madigan. Go. I'll look after Aislin." She patted him on the shoulder and turned him toward the door like she couldn't wait to get rid of him.

"If you need anything before I return, Sara will see to it."

And then Sara was shooing Arkkadian out the door. I stifled a giggle. She was sassy. I liked her already. A brief pang hit me in my heart at how much like Paige she was, and the thought of never seeing my best friend again hurt more than anything.

Sara tugging on my hand pulled me out of my reverie. "Girl time!"

I smiled in return, glad at having something else to think about. Breaking down in front of a stranger was not high on my to-do list.

"Come on! I've got a kettle on for tea, and the cookies are almost done baking," she said as I watched Arkkadian out the window as he disappeared from sight. "Trust me, you'll be glad you stayed here. The guardhouse is about as entertaining as a pet rock."

Sara's smile put me at ease as I followed her into the kitchen. The dining table sat in front of a huge picture window with a crystal-clear view of the entire vale and the mountains in the distance. The snowy peaks glinted like diamonds in the late afternoon sun. It was even more beautiful than the view from Arkkadian's bedroom window. From his room, I'd only seen but a small portion of the scene laid out before me.

"Wow! This is magnificent!" It captivated me. Cabins dotted the surrounding landscape in all directions. In the center of the vale sat a large grassy lawn and the community garden I'd noticed earlier. There was also a wooden platform on the big green lawn. A stage, maybe? On top of it stood two upright beams, and I idly wondered what they were for.

"Isn't it spectacular?" Sara beamed. "It's my favorite thing about this house. Gideon put that window in for me a few years ago. I couldn't keep staring at that amazing view through a tiny window frame any longer."

"It's stunning."

"Oh, the baby kicked! Do you want to feel it?" Sara excitedly placed my hand on her belly. I felt tiny little pokes and jabs, and I wondered at the little miracle.

"That's amazing. Does it feel weird?" I asked. I'd only been here a few short minutes, and already I felt more comfortable. Sara seemed so genuine. I could picture us getting along well.

"It's weird and beautiful at the same time. I can't wait until the wee babe is here. I feel like this pregnancy is taking forever," she explained, smiling from ear to ear. The love she already had for her unborn child was clear.

I pictured little Arkkadians running around, and my heart flipped in my chest at the possibility.

When the kettle whistled, she brought a tray laden with teacups, tea bags, milk, and honey to the table. "Please, help yourself."

I made myself a cup of peppermint tea and quickly fell into an easy conversation with Gideon's lovely wife. The next couple of hours flew by as we talked about the baby, dancing, books, and more. I found out she loved a good paranormal romance just as much as I did.

She'd even told me a little about Arkkadian. How he was a kind and honorable man and always had the best interest of others in mind. She told me that while he was fierce and dominant, he was also fair and just, and safety had always been his biggest priority. I knew her words to be true, as I'd witnessed some of those things myself.

By the time Arkkadian returned to collect me, I was in better spirits and much happier to see him.

13

ARKKADIAN

I met Gideon and the rest of my security team at the guardhouse. The four of them were in charge of security for the entire Eagle Ridge compound. I needed to inform them of our new arrival and follow up on any updates since I'd been away. Security around territory lands would increase with Aislin living here now.

Madigan, James, and Corbin were three of our best. The five of us had grown up together, and the three of them had proven themselves time and again. They weren't blood-related, but they were brothers just the same. Gideon was waiting out front when I arrived. The rest were inside, and I had dismissed the handful of men and women on duty until the meeting was over.

As we gathered around the conference table, all eyes were on me. Desks, chairs, and four rows of monitors lined the opposite wall. Each monitor rotated through a set of cameras placed in specific areas of our territory. We covered every square acre of our border, making it difficult for anyone to enter Pack land without us knowing about it. That said, the trail cameras needed updates anyway, and Aislin being here just gave us an excuse to do it sooner than originally planned.

As I pulled up a chair, my men filled me in on recent activity. Some poachers were turned over to Randall, over at Fish and Game, and my men had helped rescue four lost hikers. Randall, the area game warden, was a friend to the Pack despite being human. He was one of the few we trusted with the knowledge of our existence. In return for keeping our secret, our trackers helped him with poachers and searches for lost hikers and missing children. Our Pack has lived on this land for several centuries, long before humans encroached. Long before they designated the surrounding land a national park.

"Other than that, it's been relatively quiet," Corbin added. "Unless you count that blasted woodchuck that's been stealing vegetables from the garden again."

Everyone laughed. That obnoxious rodent had evaded every live trap they'd set.

"Thank you, men. Job well done. Listen, I'd like to tighten security. I want extra cameras placed around the borders, throughout the woods, and the compound. Whatever equipment you need to make it happen, do it. I don't care what it costs."

"Is there something we should know?" James asked. "Other than the increased poaching lately?"

"Yes. You've all heard the news about the fire down in Whitewater." My men all nodded. "Gideon and I were there last night. We saved a woman, and she's staying with me. With any luck, she'll be staying permanently." I gave the men a moment to comprehend my meaning.

"So, you finally found—" James excitedly attempted before I cut him off.

"Yes, she's my Aeternus." I grinned.

A hush filled the room as I waited for the words I'd just spoken to sink in. I'd never bonded with anyone in my four hundred years of existence, and every man in this room knew it. Of the five of us, only Corbin and I were unmated. They all looked at each other in shock before erupting into a barrage of questions before James shushed them.

"So what does your Aeternus have to do with increased security?" James asked, his head cocked in question, getting back to the business at hand.

"Kane West tried to kidnap her last night, and it isn't the first time he's tried to harm her. I suspect he's already tried to force a bond, but she escaped."

A string of curses flew around the room. They all knew what a sick bastard Kane was. All three of them had been present the night we'd found him with the teenage girl he'd taken. They'd also born witness to the challenge for Alpha that had resulted in Kane's exile from Pack.

Once again, my men bombarded me with questions. Who was she? Why wasn't she with the Pack? What was she doing in Whitewater all alone? What caused the fire?

I raised a hand for silence, and the talking ceased immediately.

"A few weeks ago, I'd stopped in at the Black Horse on my way back from rounds. I scented her, but she wasn't there. I've been searching for her ever since, and it turns out she worked there. I finally found her a few days ago, and while I was there, Kane showed up. Put his hands all over her and threatened her. I put a stop to it. Yesterday, Gideon and I returned to Whitewater and discovered Kane had taken her and her roommate captive."

More curses filled the air. When silence returned, I continued once again. "They planned to take both of them until we intervened. The apartment caught fire during the fight. We killed one, one fled, and we left Kane for dead. The apartment was burning much too fast. Escaping the flames took priority, so we're working under the assumption he survived. They murdered her roommate before we could get them both out. My mate, however, doesn't know who or what she is."

I gave my men just enough detail without alerting them to her true identity. That information would stay between Gideon and me for the time being. At some point, I would have to tell them, but for now, I felt it prudent to keep her information as close to home as possible. The more people who knew, the more they were in danger.

Gideon was the first to speak. "If Kane is still alive, he'll want revenge."

"Fuck. We'll start on upgrades immediately," James spoke. He was a pro with computers and entirely responsible for programming our entire security system.

"James, is there a way to set up the cameras to detect motion?" I asked.

"Yes, I can program that easily enough. I can also program it to alert for body heat. Would that work?" he answered.

"Yes. If Kane tries to enter Pack land, I want to know. I also want alerts sent in real time to our phones, complete with live feed. Can that be done?"

"Yes, Alpha."

I dismissed the team, and Gideon and I returned to his cabin together, where Sara invited Aislin and me to stay for dinner. I'd wanted to spend dinner alone with my mate, but once I saw the smile on Aislin's face, I agreed. Apparently, she and Sara had become fast friends. I was thrilled and took it as a sign that my mate would be okay here.

Even though Aislin was quiet through most of the meal, she looked like she was enjoying the conversation. Before we said our goodbyes, Sara hugged her and begged her to come back. Aislin assured her she would.

14

AISLIN

The heavenly scent of bacon woke me up. I sat upright in bed and stretched, trying to work out the kinks. Despite the enticing aroma of breakfast wafting upstairs, I felt awful. We'd stayed late at Gideon's place, and then I'd not slept well at all last night. Nightmares had plagued me all night long, as usual. Sleeping in a strange bed hadn't helped, either. I was starving, though, so I climbed out of bed, determined to have a good day.

Little did I know, it wouldn't be.

Arkkadian had slept on the couch in the den last night, his attempt at giving me some privacy. I'd offered to sleep on the couch since I was a guest, but he'd insisted I take the bed. It was the gentlemanly thing to do, but I suspected it was his way of monitoring me in case I tried to run. I wouldn't lie, that very thought had crossed my mind several times, but I still didn't know my way around, and his warning about predators in the woods was enough to slow my roll for the time being.

After a quick shower, I found Arkkadian in the kitchen. He was at the stove, scrambling eggs in a skillet.

"That smells lovely," I told him.

He laughed when my stomach grumbled. It seemed to do a lot of that lately. Food was in abundance here, something I hadn't really had in a long time. Paige and I squeaked by on the bare minimum most of the time.

"Good morning. Breakfast is almost ready if you'd like to set the table."

I quickly busied myself with the task while he carried food over. All the tantalizing smells made my stomach rumble again, which left us both laughing. Arkkadian and I enjoyed easy banter as we ate, passing the time quickly. Honestly, I could get used to this. But near the end of the meal, my food turned to ash as uneasiness filled me. It shocked me at how easily I'd become comfortable here, but did I really want to stay here with a stranger?

"Is everything okay? I can get you something else if you're still hungry."

"No, I'm fine. It was wonderful, thank you. It's just... what happens now? I can't stay here forever. I have a life. I need to go home. Not that I have one anymore." I would have to find a new apartment. A new job. A new town. I wrapped my arms around myself, despair filling my gut faster than a thousand-pound anchor plummeting to the bottom of the sea.

"We'll work it all out. You just need to have patience."

"But I can't stay here. This isn't my home, Arkkadian. I appreciate everything you've done for me, but I don't know anyone here. I don't even know where here is, and I barely know you." I let out a long, frustrated sigh, the last words barely spoken above a whisper.

Those mesmerizing eyes studied me. "Listen. I know this is upsetting, but your place is here. Your safety is of the utmost importance, as is the safety of this community. Your safety is tied to every single man, woman, and child outside my front door right now. I not only have a duty to keep you safe, but a duty to keep my people safe. Your presence here presents a substantial danger to my people. You won't like some things I have to say, so Gideon and Sara are coming over shortly so I can explain everything. I want them here for support because upsetting you is the last thing I want to do."

I shook my head, confused. "I don't understand. What does my safety have to do with anything?"

"It's best we wait for Gideon and Sara. Trust me."

"Trust what? Am I just supposed to take your word?" His

evasiveness was frustrating, as was the fact that every time I felt comfortable, the rug was yanked out from under me. This roller-coaster of never-ending fuck with my emotions tug of war was maddening.

Arkkadian stood up from the table, dirty plate in hand, and reached for mine. I pushed it across the table toward him, refusing to look him in the eye. Anger seeped through my pores like black tar, sticky and foul, mucking up my ability to keep my emotions in check as usual, and I hated it. I was literally a poster child for the phrase "hot mess."

"Are you still hungry?" he asked, picking up my plate.

"No. Thanks. I just want you to tell me what's going on," I demanded. "Whatever game you're playing, please just stop."

"It's not a game, it's your life. And mine. It's the life of everyone in this entire community." There was a dark, heated edge to his voice. I knew that tone. I was treading on dangerous waters, but I was too furious to care at this point.

"Trust me, you'll want the support. You won't like what I have to say. In the short time that I've known you, I've discovered you're prone to angry outbursts and panic attacks, and I don't want that to happen."

"I'm angry now!" I shouted. The longer he delayed, the more irate I became. I burst out of my chair so fast, it clattered to the floor behind me. "Please, just tell me what the fuck is going on!"

I glared at Arkkadian, and he carefully set both plates back down on the table. I was fired up. The angel on one shoulder told me to back down, but the devil on the other egged me on as I continued to shoot daggers at him with my eyes. I was unprepared when he stalked toward me; I backed up until I hit the wall. Arkkadian didn't stop until we were inches apart, his imposing form towering above me, pinning me in place. I felt every ounce of power without him even touching me.

"Stop." The command was savage on his lips. Lethal. The irises of his eyes flared to life, little blue bolts of static swirling around, charging the air as a storm brewed between us. Every instinct told me to back down. Told me to kneel and submit to my Alpha before the lightning struck. But did I listen to those instincts? Nope, I listened to the devil and issued a challenge.

"Fuck. You." Two words, succinct and unapologetic.

"Watch. Your. Tone. Need I remind you that behavior will not be tolerated? I will take you over my knee." Arkkadian glared back. I watched the lightning swirl in his cerulean eyes, and I knew I should shut up. Instead, I continued to run my stupid mouth like a runaway freight train. Take me over his knee? I'd like to see him try.

"Excuse me? Watch my tone? You dangle a carrot in front of me without telling me anything at all and expect me to just trust you blindly! You took me from my home and planted me in the middle of nowhere! And you want me to watch my fucking tone? I don't fucking believe this! I'm going home, even if I have to walk! You can't keep me here!"

I stormed off toward the stairs, and that's when the lightning finally struck. I didn't make it three steps before Arkkadian flipped me upside down over his shoulder. I had a direct view of his delicious backside, and for a moment, I forgot why I was angry until a harsh swat on my backside caught my attention.

What the fuck? Did he actually spank me just now?

I lost my shit.

"Let me go!" I screamed, kicking and flailing for all I was worth. Stupid, stupid girl. I just couldn't shut my mouth, could I?

"No. You listen. I explained yesterday what happens when you misbehave, did I not? I warned you again just now." His voice was low and dangerous, which should have been my final cue to stop. It wasn't.

"Punishment? You're fucking kidding me! I thought you were joking!" I yelped when a second swat landed on my backside.

"I don't joke about things like that."

"Put me down!"

"No. And watch your mouth or I'll wash it out with soap," he warned. I bounced over his shoulder with every step up the stairs. "I will not tolerate your blatant disrespect. I won't hurt you, but I will punish you. Maybe then you'll stop acting like an insolent child. You're lucky your punishment will be a spanking in the privacy of my bedroom and not out on the green in front of everyone."

What? He couldn't be serious. The platform flashed in my mind and I knew. I knew exactly what they used it for.

The bedroom door squeaked as it swung open, and then I was unceremoniously tossed onto the bed. I bounced when my backside hit the mattress. Jaw clenched, I glared daggers at the sexy, beautiful, angry man towering above me. How could he be so hot, yet make me so furious?

"Don't you dare touch me," I seethed, but his face was deadly calm. Dangerous. I'd intentionally sparked his ire, and now I would pay. Play stupid games, win stupid prizes. He cricked his finger at me and pointed to the floor beside him. I shook my head and refused to move.

"Fine. We do this the hard way."

Arkkadian sat down at the foot of the bed, grabbed my leg, and pulled me toward him. In the blink of an eye, I was face down on the mattress with my hips across his lap, butt in the air. From beneath me, he released the button on my jeans. I tried to squirm away, but a firm hand planted in the middle of my back, effortlessly pinning me in place. Then my jeans and panties were tugged halfway down my thighs.

"What in the hell are you doing?"

The answer came in the form of a smack across my bare bottom, and I screeched at the resounding sting across my skin. It shocked me more than it hurt.

"Count. We'll start with five. And you will call me sir."

"What the fuck?"

"Stop talking and count," he ordered, softly rubbing the spot where he spanked me. "For every spank you don't count, you'll receive five more. I'll forgive the first one."

"I am *not* a child! You can't spank me!" Before I could speak another word, his land landed where the curve of my cheeks met the top of my thighs, and I jerked. This one stung a little more. "Ow! Stop it!"

"I said, count! I gave you every chance. We'll stop at ten," he said, massaging the spot where his hand had landed again, soothing the sting.

"Stop! Let me up!" I kicked my legs out, trying to slide off his lap, but he wrapped a leg over both of mine. I swung my fist back in retaliation, catching him on the arm, but Arkkadian grabbed both of my fists and pinned them uncomfortably behind me.

A third smack came down across my bottom, and again, Arkkadian soothed the spot. He leaned down close to my ear and whispered, "Count. I won't tell you again. You're lucky I'm not adding another ten for that punch you just threw."

"Okay! Three!"

"One. We're starting at the beginning. The first two didn't count. No more talking. Understood?"

I nodded, floating somewhere between anger and humiliation.

"Say it."

"Okay! One!"

"One what?"

"One, sir!"

Another smack rained down.

"Two, sir!" Another. His hand soothed the spot again.

"Ouch! Three, sir!" Smack!

"Four, sir!" I ground out. Again, he rubbed soothing circles, but my backside was on fire now, the sting of each slap starting to spread. Mixed with the sensual caress of his hand upon my flesh, it was a heady feeling I unexpectedly found myself enjoying. I didn't want to enjoy it.

"Five!" I wailed as his hand landed again. "Please stop! I'm sorry!"

I didn't know how much more I could take. Though my backside burned, a wetness grew between my legs. I'd become aroused despite the shame I felt, and tears of embarrassment pricked my eyes. It wasn't the spanking I couldn't take. It was the betrayal of my body I couldn't handle.

"No, you're not, keep counting," he said, ignoring my pleas.

And so it went, Arkkadian's fingers kneading my hot and achy flesh after every expertly placed swat on my tender bottom and me counting until he stopped at last.

By the tenth, my voice cracked and no other sounds came forth as I openly sobbed through ragged breaths. Arkkadian rubbed slow, sensuous circles across my skin, easing the pain. Then I felt a finger graze across my moist nether lips, sparking desire deep down in my core.

Shocked by my body's traitorous reaction to the spanking, I buried my face in the bedspread. Arkkadian pulled his hand away, and then my panties were being tugged back up. He lifted me into his arms and carried me around the side of the bed, where he gently laid me down on the pillows.

"Stay there, I'll be back," he ordered.

I didn't respond. Instead, I buried my face in the pillow and cried, wondering what just happened. I'd just become fully aroused by a spanking. A punishment. I was mortified, but mostly, I was angry with myself for provoking him. He'd warned me, given me chances, and I just couldn't shut my stupid mouth. I was so busy wallowing in my misery that I didn't hear him return to the bedside.

"Aislin, roll onto your belly, please. I brought some arnica. It will help," he said gently.

"Go away," I whimpered into the pillow.

"No. I punished you, and now it's my job to take care of you. That's how this works. Please do as you're told," he softly said, though his voice still pricked with authority. "I'd rather not have a repeat, would you?"

He waited patiently for me to comply, and then I felt the mattress give as his weight pressed down beside me. I squirmed as he lowered my panties, the fabric scraping painfully across sensitive skin, stoking the coals back to life. This was even more embarrassing than the spanking. The heat radiating off my backside was nearly unbearable.

"This will help, I promise."

I flinched at the first touch, but it didn't take long for the salve to take effect. The burn eventually abated, and I found the kneading of my soft flesh relaxing. Ever so slowly, though, the familiar warm feeling of arousal enveloped my body again, spiking higher and higher. Strangely, I also felt a sense of relief. The anger. The frustration. The stress. I'd been wound tighter than a two dollar watch, but now, I felt like it had all floated away on a cloud.

Arkkadian's gentle voice interrupted my thoughts. "How do you feel?"

How did I feel? Confused mostly, but yes, relieved. Like I'd given the anger away. I'd given it up to him. I'd ceded control, if only for a moment, and it had felt so good. I told him as much.

"That's good. Your body recognized your need to submit." I wanted to pretend I didn't know what he meant by that, but it would have been a lie.

Once again, fingers dipped low enough to glide across my sweet center. No one had ever touched me there before. Not until now. Instinctively, I tilted my hips back, granting him easier access. The longer Arkkadian massaged my tender skin, the more aroused I became. Fingers slid between my wet folds. I moaned at the sensation, and a whole new kind of fire stoked deep in my belly as he slid a finger inside. I felt a sense of loss when he pulled his finger away before pushing inside me again. It wasn't long before I ground myself on his hand as he slid a second inside, instantly setting every nerve ending alight with desire.

Then I heard him inhale. Deeply. I froze. Oh, my God! Could he smell me? Flustered, I jerked away from Arkkadian's ministrations and pulled my pants back up. I tried to sit up, but my sore bottom screamed and made me hiss, so instead, I jumped out of bed and stormed into the bathroom. Then I slammed the door shut and locked it behind me.

"Aislin?" Arkkadian called out from the other side.

"Go away." I'd just let the man who spanked me touch me in an intensely intimate manner. What did I just do? What just happened? I spun wildly around, unable to think.

"I'm not leaving until I know you're okay. Come out and let's talk about this," he said. "I know you're confused. Let me help."

"How would you know what I'm feeling right now?" Just the sound of his voice rankled. I just wanted him to leave. I needed space to process everything.

"Aislin, I can smell it," he said.

Wait. What? Oh, God. Was he serious? Did he know ab—?

I yanked the door open. "What the hell does that mean? Smell what?" I asked, feeling my face suffuse with heat, even though I knew exactly what he meant. I was losing my mind. My chest heaved with every intake of breath.

Arkkadian smirked and looked me straight in the eye as he

leaned against the door jamb. "You have no reason to be embarrassed. It's natural."

"No, it's not. A spanking should not arouse me!" I slammed the door again before yanking it open a second later. "You didn't answer my question. What did you smell?"

God, I wanted to slap that smug grin right off his gorgeous face. Wipe the amusement in his eyes away. I ground my teeth while I waited for his answer, thinking how much I wanted to taste those smug lips.

"We're not human. I can smell lots of things, including your arousal."

"Oh, my God! This is ridiculous!" I slammed the door again and locked it.

Not human. Right. Uncontrollable laughter bubbled up. I was losing my mind. So why did I suddenly want to wrap myself around him and kiss him as if my life depended on it? And then, like a battering ram to the castle gate, it hit me. My laughter ceased instantly. We. Not he. He'd said, "We're not human." What did that even mean? Then Gideon's wolf flashed in my mind, and I slid down to the floor, yelping when I landed on my sore ass.

"Aislin, please come out," Arkkadian begged.

"No. Go away." I was on the express train to crazy town with a one-way ticket.

"Aislin, please."

"You're crazy. Or maybe I'm the crazy one." I laughed. "Please, just go. I can't do this right now."

"Fine. Gideon and Sara will be here in an hour. I expect you downstairs when they arrive." The command was clear in his tone, but the sound of silence was deafening when he turned and walked away.

15

ARKKADIAN

I sat in the old wooden rocker out on the front porch and fumed. My wolf prowled, begging for freedom, something he was doing a lot of lately now that I had found our mate. What I wanted was to go back upstairs and give Aislin a piece of my mind again for acting like a spoiled brat. She'd continued to push me, eventually landing herself in a compromising position over my knee with my hand on her sweet little ass. I had cautioned her more than once. I hoped the spanking would serve as a warning to keep her mouth in check from now on.

It was a pleasant surprise, however, to see my mate had a tough side. It was a sharp contrast to the anxiety she had previously exhibited. If she wasn't afraid to fight, I could work with that. I could help her rebuild her confidence. I waited outside my bedroom door, but when it became clear she wasn't coming out, I'd come down to the porch to calm down. Maybe the fresh air would clear my head.

A short while later, Gideon and Sara walked up the drive, hand in hand. Judging by what had happened upstairs, asking for their help had been one of my better ideas. They followed me inside, and I sent them to the den while I fetched Aislin. I knocked on the bedroom door as a courtesy, but received no answer. She was sound asleep on my bed when I entered.

She was sleeping so peacefully, unlike last night. Lycan hearing was excellent, and throughout the night, I'd heard every whimper and shriek as she dreamed. I gazed down upon her sleeping form, hating that I had to wake her, but we were long past due for a discussion about her past and our future.

I sat down on the bed beside her and tucked a loose strand of hair behind her ear. She lay on her side, facing the wall, knees pulled up and the blanket tucked under her chin. Her cheeks were tear-stained, and her eyes were puffy. Dammit. A small part of me felt guilty for making her cry, but she also needed to understand how things worked around here. At my gentle touch, she stirred and opened her silver eyes. She didn't move, didn't speak, but her eyes moved from me to the wall where they stayed.

"Hey," I said softly. "Listen, about earlier..."

She cut me off. "There's nothing to talk about."

I caught the subtle clench of her jaw. She was still angry. I couldn't blame her, but I wouldn't put up with the attitude either.

"Look. I'm sorry I upset you, but I'm not sorry I punished you. I warned you twice, but you didn't listen. I told you I don't condone that kind of display. Had you been anyone else, your punishment would have taken place publicly. In front of everyone," I explained. "Is that what you want?"

Her eyes widened a fraction. I had her attention now. She squirmed under the bedspread. Not so tough now, are we?

"Do we have an understanding?" I asked.

"Yes," she answered, her voice barely above a whisper.

"Embarrassment was not my intention. I know you're confused. It's completely normal to feel those things. But as part of this community, there are some things I can't let slide," I said. "Got it?"

"Yes, but I'm not part of this community."

"From now on, you are. You'll understand more shortly. But before we go, is there anything you want to talk about?" I looked directly into her dazzling silver eyes.

She clenched her jaw again and looked away, but I reached out and tilted her head back, holding her chin and forcing her to look at me. "I want you to know those things you felt... it's okay."

"I don't know what you're talking about." The lie clung to her lips, and she pulled away, scooting up toward the headboard. She tried to school her face, but the blush that crept into her cheeks betrayed everything she was feeling.

"Fine. Gideon and Sara are waiting, so I'd like you to come down and join us. Take a moment to collect yourself. Wash your face. You've got five minutes." I got up and left the room, not giving her a chance to respond.

In the den, Sara had set out coffee and tea, and Gideon was watching news coverage of the fire. There was still nothing new to report. He shut the television off when I entered and plopped down on the end of the sofa next to his mate.

"How's she doing?" he asked.

"Frustrated. She was asleep. But she'll be down in a minute," I told him. "She's a bit out of sorts after getting a little mouthy with me earlier."

Sara rolled her eyes. "Arkkadian Rime, please tell me you didn't. That poor woman." She only used my full name when she thought I was being an ass, which, if I were honest, happened a lot.

"I warned her twice for screaming and cursing at me in anger, and she chose not to listen. I made it clear I won't tolerate any disrespect," I said.

"Arkken, you need to remember she's not familiar with Pack life and she's just been through something traumatic. I swear, for a man who's been alive as long as you have, you can be such a daft fool. She probably feels like a prisoner. Explains her defensiveness," Sara scolded me. She was right, but I wouldn't be doing my job as Alpha if I let that kind of behavior slide.

I scented my mate just before she appeared around the corner. She stood in the doorway with a wary look on her face, arms crossed defensively.

"Who's Arkken?" she asked.

"Me. Only close friends and family call me Arkken. Everyone else uses my first name or refers to me as Alpha," I explained.

"Arkken." She tested it on her tongue, then shook her head. "I like Arkkadian better."

"You may use either, I don't mind."

"So, what's a Pack?" She took a cautious step forward and stopped. She'd been listening in on our conversation.

All eyes were on Aislin as Sara embraced her in a hug and then led her over to the leather sofa next to the fireplace. Sara sat in the middle, Gideon and Aislin on either side of her. When she shivered, Sara wrapped a blanket around her.

"Please tell me this isn't some crazy cult or something," she said.

Gideon laughed, and Sara cuffed him on the back of the head. "Shut up, Gideon."

I turned to Aislin and saw the quizzical look on her face, but Sara beat me to it. "Ignore my mate. Sometimes he can be a royal pain in the butt. Just like his brother." Sara rolled her eyes with a grin.

"Hey, I resent that!" I laughed.

"All joking aside, you're about to hear some bizarre things, except that every bit is true. I promise you'll receive nothing but the truth, Aislin. Remember that there are good people here. Honest, hardworking people. Families. Children. We're a community that shares a special bond because of who and what we are. What you are," Sara emphasized. "I want you to listen to what Arkkadian has to say with an open mind. I encourage you to ask questions. You may feel confused or even angry, and that's fine, but know that you have nothing to fear here."

"What do you mean? What am I?" She looked to each of us, confusion mixed with concern darkening her face.

"You're one of us, you just never knew. Listen to Arkkadian, okay?" Sara said as she squeezed Aislin's hand in support.

"O—okay."

I pulled my chair out from behind the desk and pushed it over to sit in front of Aislin. "Do you remember upstairs when I said we're not human?"

Her face flushed with embarrassment. I said nothing, but I knew exactly what she was thinking as I waited for her to answer.

"Wait. Did you really mean that? I thought you were joking."

I shook my head. "Yes. And, no, I wasn't joking."

"Then if you aren't human, what are you?" Aislin pulled the blanket snug around her, almost using it as a shield between us.

"Not I, we. We are immortal," I said, gesturing to include everyone in the room, including her. "Specifically, Gideon and I are Lycans. Shapeshifters. As are all the men here in Eagle Ridge. You and Sara are Aeternus."

Aislin steepled her fingers under her chin and tilted her eyes toward the ceiling in thought. Then she busted out laughing. That wasn't the reaction I was expecting.

"I'm losing my mind. You're telling me you're a freaking were-wolf and that I'm sitting here in the middle of an entire compound full of werewolves," she answered back in complete disbelief. "Fucking hell. This has to be a dream. I'm gonna wake up any moment now, nice and cozy in my bed, and none of the last few days will have happened."

"We aren't werewolves," Gideon spat. "Those made up abomi-nations from storybooks don't exist. Please don't insult us."

The inference pissed off my brother, and my mate sobered at Gideon's rebuke. Very few things pissed my brother off, but comparing him to a werewolf? That put you on a fast track to his shit list. Gideon didn't take kindly to being compared to storybook frauds.

"Gideon, stop," I chided, shooting him a look. "No, we're not werewolves. The werewolf, as you know it, is a violent beast controlled by the cycles of the moon. It attacks people, turning them into werewolves with either a bite or a scratch. They are naught but a storybook legend created centuries ago by humans as a scare tactic."

"I still don't understand."

"Lycans are shapeshifters. We don't howl at the moon, we don't attack people, and we can't turn anyone. We're born this way and we're all male. Most of the Glacier Mountain Pack are dire wolves, but there are other shifters here. We live in a peaceful society away from humans and we have rules that keep our community running smoothly and safely." I gave her a knowing look. Her cheeks flushed at the reminder and a frown formed on her lips before I continued.

"We do nothing that draws attention to our existence, and we don't harm others as a general rule, except in self-defense. We will, however, defend ourselves to the death."

She rubbed her temples as she struggled to make sense of the information given. It was a lot to process. "Back up a minute. You said all Lycan are male, but you said 'we' aren't human. What did you call me again?"

Her breathing quickened, and I could sense the anxiety building up as she clenched and unclenched her fists, fidgeting in her seat.

"Let's take a break," I offered. "I can tell you're stressed."

"No, I don't want to stop. Just get it over with."

"You're breathing is erratic. I don't want you to have another panic attack," I said, reaching for her hand. She didn't pull away when I touched her and rubbed her palm with my thumb. "Here. Will you let me try something?"

She hesitated, closing her eyes for a moment, and nodded. I let go of her hand and carefully pulled the blanket off her. In an instant, her anxiety spiked, rolling off her like violent waves crashing upon the shoreline in the middle of a thunderstorm. I didn't let it deter me from what I was about to do.

"Sit up straight, knees together."

She did as I bid her, despite the instinct I felt through the bond telling her to flee. She flinched when I placed my hands on her knees. "Relax. You're safe."

She clenched and unclenched her jaw several times before answering with an okay. It tore me and my wolf up that Aislin was so easily upset and untrusting. I vowed from this moment to do everything in my power to remedy that.

"I tried this the other night at the bar, and I've done it a few times since. I know you've felt it, but you probably didn't recognize it for what it was. Do you remember?" I asked.

She nodded. "I felt warm and calm. Like a tranquil ripple of energy flowing through me." Her eyes grew big. "That was you?"

"Yes, it's an ability I have. I'd like to try it again."

"Okay." Nodding, she reached for Sara's hand and gripped it tightly.

"Close your eyes and take slow, deep breaths. I can feel what you're feeling so try to relax. Picture your feet. Imagine all those tiny little muscles going lax. When you feel the tension leave, work your way upward until you feel every muscle, every nerve, every joint releasing all tension they're holding."

With my hands resting on her knees, I pushed heat out of my

body and into hers. I followed its path with my mind as it worked its way from her knees and up to her center and then outward into her limbs. Next, I pushed a quiet stillness into her, and followed it along the same path, directing it toward her center as well. I felt her racing heartbeat slow and her anxiety beginning to subside. Her breathing soon followed and the tension in her body disappeared as she visibly relaxed.

"Whoa." Aislin's eyes snapped open with a gasp, and she looked directly into mine. "I feel woozy."

I thought it strange how the colored parts of her eyes swirled like ominous thunderclouds. Something tickled the back of my mind, like I should know why. Like I should remember something, but it was all forgotten when she swayed in her seat, and I reached out to steady her.

"I'm sorry. I used a little more energy this time because I wanted you to recognize what you're feeling. It's normal to have a reaction when you're not bonded. Put your head between your knees and keep breathing." I shouldn't have pushed so hard.

Several minutes passed before she finally sat up. She rubbed her temples, and when she finished, Sara handed her a cup of tea, which she sipped slowly. "That's really weird. I'm not sure I like it."

"It won't always be like that. You'll get used to it," Sara promised.

"What's a bond?"

"When we find our mate, we form a bond. Every one of us has a match out there somewhere. Someone we're fated to be with, and when we meet him or her, we feel an inexplicable pull toward each other. We're drawn to them. Familiar. And when we bond, we bond for life," I cautiously explained. "Some of us don't wait for our fated mates and some of us wait forever if we have to."

"Oh." She looked anywhere and everywhere except at me. I knew this subject still made her uncomfortable, but eventually, instinct would win no matter how hard she fought it. Her reaction told me what I already knew.

"You've felt it, haven't you?" I coaxed. Her cheeks flushed again. "And you don't feel it with anyone else, either." She shook her head, still avoiding eye contact, and I sensed her becoming overwhelmed again. "That pull you feel, it's because you and I... we're mates."

At that, she laughed and returned her gaze to mine. "Mates? I barely know you, yet you think you have some claim on me? No." That last word was a lie upon her lips, and she knew that I knew.

"I don't think. I know. As time progresses, the pull will become increasingly harder to resist until the bond is complete. You won't be able to deny it."

"No. No way," she argued. "This is some freaky shit."

"Let me ask you something. When you first met me, you could smell something. Do you smell it now?"

Recognition lit across her face. "Cinnamon. And cloves. Maybe a slight hint of vanilla. Oh, and musk."

I nodded. "And Gideon?"

She cocked her head to the side in thought, then inhaled deeply. "Teakwood. Cardamom. And bourbon." Her eyes widened in surprise. "But it's different. I'm not drawn to him."

"We all have our own unique scent. Our bond mates have a slightly different, but similar scent that complements our own. You scent of cinnamon and spice with hints of vanilla and citrus. That magnetic pull I described? Only fated mates feel that. That's how we identify our mate when we meet them. The tug is instantaneous, but you wouldn't have known without being raised in the Pack. I'm sorry," I apologized. "Your parents would have taught you this."

Aislin's mixed emotions swirled around us in the atmosphere. My wolf whined under the surface, unhappy at causing her discomfort.

"Is that why Kane... why he sniffed me? He's one of you, isn't he?" she asked.

"Yes. Any Lycan could scent you and know by your essence that you're an Aeternus, but the difference between Kane and me is that he wouldn't have felt the connection. You're not his mate," I continued explaining.

"So, I'm what again? I'm sorry I keep asking. I'm just having a hard time wrapping my head around all of this."

"You're an Aeternus," I answered. "It's Latin for forever. Eternal. In our world, it means 'life mate' or 'soulmate.' All females are born Aeternus. The difference between us is that I can shift into my animal and you cannot. An Aeternus is bound to her human form."

I'd be lying if I said the possibility of my mate being an Immortalle hadn't crossed my mind. She descended from both Vamphyre and Lycan lines, just as all Aeternus used to be, but that was impossible. The last known Immortalle died centuries ago after Aislin's grandfather instituted First Law and forbade all members of the Covenant to mate with Lycans. And dying with them? Their ability to share in their mate's gifts. But... what if? It would be an incredible thing if that were the case. And just as dangerous.

Sara caught the knowing look I shared with my brother and covered her open mouth. Gideon frowned. Aislin puked.

16

ARKKADIAN

I replaced the bowl of cold water on the nightstand for the second time. Aislin rested on my bed with a cool cloth across her forehead. I took it and dipped it in the bowl, squeezed out the excess, and replaced it.

"I'm sorry. This is my fault," I said. "There isn't much to do, except rest. It'll pass with a little time."

"Let's not do that again." She groaned before leaning over and retching into the bucket. "It's a cool trick, but my stomach does not agree."

"Just rest. I'll come back and check on you shortly. I'm sending Gideon and Sara home for now. We'll talk more when you're feeling better."

"Not going anywhere." Moaning, she leaned over and vomited into the bucket again.

I closed the door behind me, kicking myself for being so reckless. Even so, that wasn't a lot of energy. Not by a long shot. That much of a reaction wasn't normal. I suspected someone had tampered with the memory block. It wasn't unheard of. If someone wanted to suppress dangerous information, adding that devious little trick would make gaining access to certain memories a hell of a lot harder.

If I couldn't even pass a small amount of energy into her without causing such discomfort, then probing into her mind would have much worse consequences. There were only a handful of Soul Shadows in existence, and fewer still who had the power that afforded that extra ability. I was one of them. That drastically narrowed the playing field. By the time I made it back downstairs, Sara and Gideon had everything cleaned up.

"I'm sorry for being a jackass earlier," Gideon apologized, sheepishly rubbing the back of his neck.

"Don't apologize to me. Apologize to my mate the next time you see her," I told him. "You forget she didn't grow up in our world. Hell, I have to keep reminding myself. She knows virtually nothing of her ancestry, and until recently, monsters didn't exist in her world."

"The hard part is over, at least," Sara said as she returned from the kitchen. She stood with both hands on her lower back, belly protruding, and winced as the baby kicked. Without a doubt, the little one was strong. "I'm sure none of this is easy, but imagine witnessing your best friend being murdered right in front of you and then finding out your whole life is a lie. I'd say she took it rather well, considering. She'll have a tough time, Arkken. Be gentle with her. Be patient. She's grieving the only family she had. Give her a chance to learn our ways before you go full Alpha on her again or you'll scare her away." Sara turned to her mate. "I'm tired, and I'm going home to take a nap. Are you coming with me?"

"Go ahead. I'll be home shortly, my love. I need to talk to my brother about a few things first." He hugged her and kissed her belly. While Gideon walked her out, I put another pot of coffee on to brew.

"You've got your work cut out for you, brother. She's got a lot of demons to deal with. I don't envy you," he said solemnly as he rejoined me in the kitchen. He leaned against the counter next to me and clapped me on the shoulder. "What I'd like to know, though, is who planted that little nausea trick in her head? She shouldn't have reacted so strongly. Whatever they're hiding, it must be pretty damaging."

"I know." I ran a hand through my hair and sighed. "I could break the block now, but I'd rather wait until she's mentally and physically ready. I have to take my time and get to know her better. Get her to trust me. It would be much easier if the bond was complete. Lord knows my damn wolf is aching to fulfill the need, but she's nowhere near prepared for that. It's taking every ounce of restraint to keep him in check."

Gideon drummed his fingers on the counter, staring out the window at the children playing outdoors. The look of concern etched on his face was disconcerting. "Who do you think is responsible?"

"There's only a handful of Soul Shadows with that level of skill. I've been thinking about it for a while now. Besides me and you, there are the Vanes; Arden, Rafe, and Rhett. Alaric and Mathias, Malcolm Fisher, and Weston Knight. I'm not sure anyone else has lived long enough to have obtained that much skill."

"As far as I know, that's it," Gideon agreed.

"Arden and Rafe would have killed her outright. Malcolm and his Caribou River bears rarely step foot outside of Canada, except for the annual conclave of Lycan Nine. They mostly keep to themselves."

"Weston and Alaric were close. Alaric spent a lot of time between the Pacific Rim and Yellowstone packs. The rumor was Weston was one of the shifters who helped Alaric rescue Wren after her father imprisoned her. One of them could have done it, but Weston told me once that Alaric had cut off all ties with everyone when they went into hiding. Weston said he'd tried numerous times to find them, but every trail was a dead end. Does Mathias know he has a granddaughter?" Gideon asked.

"Honestly, I doubt it," I replied. "If he did, he would have hidden her somewhere among the Lycan Nine. Mathias would never have left his own flesh and blood unprotected like that, but on the offhand that he did, then he sure concealed one hell of a secret."

"That only leaves Rhett. He doted on his little sister, and everyone knows he detests his father. It's entirely plausible he and Wren kept in contact all those years she and Alaric were in hiding. Rhett wouldn't have hesitated to kill Ryker Slade if given the chance, either," Gideon suggested. "Hell, maybe he did. Everyone knows there was no love lost between those two."

"It makes sense, but until we break the block, we won't know for sure," I remarked.

17

AISLIN

Ugh. I felt like death warmed over. Twice. Maybe three times for good measure. I'd spent the better part of the last several hours lurching up the non-existent contents of my stomach into a plastic bucket. Breakfast had long since departed, and my stomach was as empty as my wallet. My mouth tasted sour, my teeth were fuzzy, and I had the worst headache I'd ever felt in my life. That loathsome little woodpecker was once again pounding out Morse code in my skull. Even small bits of light made my whole head scream in protest. I'd finally given in a few hours ago, turned off the lamp, shut the curtains, and surrounded myself in a pitch-black cocoon. I only poked my head out from under the covers long enough to puke.

Arkkadian had come in a few times to check on me and bring me water, giving me a lecture about staying hydrated. He'd also brought some heavier pain meds since the others he'd previously given me hadn't even touched the incessant boom boom boom stomping around in my head.

My stomach was finally waving the white flag of surrender, ending its assault on the poor bucket. My headache hadn't raised the flag yet, but it was getting there. At the sound of a knock on the door, I peeked my head out from under the covers. The light from the hallway blasted my retinas, and I scrunched my eyes shut, wincing in pain. I yanked the covers back over my head with a whimper.

"Sorry about that," Arkkadian apologized and shut the door quickly behind him, once again blanketing the room in darkness.

He carried a tray to the bedside, and I sat up, leaning against the headboard. He clicked on the lamp, and I squinted as my eyes adjusted to the dim light. The smell of warm toast made my stomach rumble. I didn't think I'd be this hungry after spending the last several hours paying homage to the bucket gods, but I'll be damned if that toast didn't smell like the finest home-cooked meal I'd ever had.

"Feeling any better?" He brushed a stray lock of hair out of my face and tucked it behind my ear.

I noticed the fire had been stoked. I must have been pretty out of it because I didn't remember him even lighting the fire. The warmth was soothing.

"A little. I'm kind of hungry. The toast smells good."

"Good, but we'll keep it bland to start. I also brought some saltines. If you can keep those down, then maybe you'll be up for some of Sara's chicken soup later." Arkkadian sat down on the bed next to me. Then he reached up and took my chin, gently examining my face. I was sure I looked as bad as I felt, but he didn't seem too worried. Apologetic maybe, but not worried. Or maybe that was just his Alpha façade.

Interestingly enough, I didn't feel the need to pull away from him. Instead, I felt that strange little tug way deep down again. The more time we spent together, the more I recognized the sensation. Maybe Arkkadian wasn't so bad. Despite the spanking he'd given me earlier, one I'd unquestionably deserved, he'd been very kind to me from the moment we'd first met. He'd saved my life, and not once had he ever tried to take advantage of or hurt me.

It didn't help that he had the body of a god, one that shouted *fuck me now!* from the rooftops. Or that every time we were in a room together, I constantly caught him adjusting himself when he thought I wasn't looking. The reaction in his pants hadn't escaped my attention, and the sexual tension revolving around him was thick. The feeling was definitely mutual.

When I saw him in his birthday suit yesterday, I'd gotten way more than I'd bargained for. Just thinking about it sent searing heat straight to my core, and my cheeks flushed. Not that I had any experience in that department. None, to be exact. Shaking my head, I pushed all such thoughts from my mind.

"Thank you. I'm sure this will help," I said, and then took a bite of the toast. It was still warm, the butter fresh. Homemade. It was heavenly, and I groaned with pleasure. I ate slowly, though, worried my stomach might opt for an instant replay. "You make great toast."

He laughed. "Thanks. So, I was thinking, if you're up for it, we could go downstairs and watch a movie. You've been cooped up in this room for hours."

"That sounds fun, actually. I can't even remember the last time I watched a movie."

"Really?"

"I've been so busy with work that I barely have time for anything else. Not that I can afford it, anyway. Oh, crap." The diner. Dammit! My stomach dropped, and I buried my face in my hands. I'd completely forgotten about my other job.

"What's wrong?"

"I have a second job. Or did. Hell, I don't know. Things just keep getting better and better."

I jumped out of bed, intending to search for my phone, but when I stood up, the room swam around me, and I almost toppled over.

"Easy. Not so fast." Arkkadian caught me and eased me back down onto the bed. "There's no rush. Tell me what you need and I'll get it for you."

"My phone. I need to call the diner. They're probably wondering why I haven't shown up for my last two shifts. Dammit. Now I've probably lost that job, too."

God, how dismal could my life get? I buried my face in my palms again. The last thing I needed right now was a lack of income, not with the mounting bills I owed. Life sure knew how to kick a woman when she was already down, and I was sure down.

"You work two jobs?" Arkkadian almost sounded incredulous. Yeah, well, not everyone could afford the finer things in life, wolf boy. I didn't say it aloud in case he took offense like his brother did when I'd called them werewolves earlier.

"Yeah. I've got a bunch of bills to pay," I admitted. "I'm so screwed."

"Tell me." He seemed genuinely concerned.

I suddenly felt uncomfortable. I never enjoyed talking about myself much, but with recent revelations, I answered him honestly. There wasn't a lot to tell, but I could feel the compassion emanating from him. I was so used to being on my own and doing things for myself, but this—here with him—felt different somehow.

"I grew up in foster care and bounced from home to home. I never fit in anywhere. Some of the kids were bullies, sometimes the parents were. I was never in a home for long before they were moving me somewhere else. As soon as I aged out of the system, I left Seattle with nothing but a backpack full of clothes and a couple of credit cards. I moved several times, taking any waitressing or bartending job I could get, but I never stayed in one town for long. None of them ever felt like home, at least not until I came to Whitewater three years ago. Carter and Paige quickly became family, giving me a job and a place to stay where I truly felt welcome for the first time in my life. But that's how I racked up all the credit card bills... all that moving from town to town, working two, sometimes three jobs just to survive. Trying to find a place of my own. Trying to find a home."

"What about your family? How did you end up in foster care?"

Arkkadian sat quietly and waited. He reached for my hand and squeezed, reassuring me. I pulled my knees up to my chest and wrapped my arms around my legs, hesitating to say more.

"You can tell me anything. Really. No judgment," he offered.

Nervously twirling a finger in my hair, I let out a long sigh. Maybe it was time I stopped bottling it up. Arkkadian seemed like he wanted to help, and it wasn't like I had anyone else I could confide in anymore. Not with my previous life gone.

"I don't like to talk about that part of my life very much. I don't remember some of it. Some of it I don't want to remember. I still have nightmares. You've already seen me at my worst. The fear. The anxiety. Quick to anger," I explained. "You've seen how easy it is for me to lose myself. Not even therapy has helped."

Arkkadian listened silently and nodded in reassurance when I paused my story. The next part was the worst. I hated those memories more than anything, but I steeled myself and continued anyway, and before I knew what was happening, the words tumbled out.

"When I was seven, I woke up in a hospital waiting room. I didn't understand how I got there. My clothes were ruined and bloody. I knew my name, but I couldn't recall the names of my parents or what had happened to me. When a nurse found me in the waiting room, I freaked out. They had to sedate me, and when I woke up, I had bandages all down the side of my body, from my hip all the way to my neck. They said someone had cut me and then sewn me back up."

It didn't escape my attention that Arkkadian stiffened beside me. I didn't blame him. It was a story straight out of some deranged killer's police file. Who does that to a child? Someone insane, that's who.

I wiped away a tear as it slipped from the corner of my eye. The lump in my throat felt ten times bigger than it actually was. "I have the letter R carved into my hip. I don't know what it stands for. They said I just kept screaming over and over about a fire. I've had the same nightmare about it my entire life. I dream about fire and I hear a child screaming, but I can't see any faces or hear any voices. I have nightmares about Kane, too, but at least I know what happened with him. I don't have any memory of the fire or how I got all those scars."

"I'm sorry. I can't imagine how terrifying that must have been," he told me. By the gravel in his voice, I knew the things I said were upsetting to him. "Maybe over the coming days, I'll be able to answer some of those questions for you when you're feeling better."

I swallowed hard. "Thank you. This is hard. My life did a one-eighty in the last couple of days. The only friends I've ever known are both dead. My home is gone. The bar is gone. My job at the diner is probably gone. Not like it matters, we both know I can't go home, anyway."

"The good news is you aren't alone. You have me. And Sara and Gideon. We're not going anywhere. Give us a chance, please. Trust us. I promise it will be worth it," he said.

"Thank you."

Arkkadian reached up to brush another tear away with his thumb. I leaned into his touch, letting the warmth of his skin comfort me. I couldn't remember a time I'd ever let myself be so vulnerable with someone. I hadn't even told Paige all the things I'd shared with him. Somehow, with Arkkadian here beside me, it just felt right. It felt freeing. Like the weight pressing me down into the ground had finally lifted.

"Truthfully, I'm sure I know who are you are and what happened. There are stories, but they can wait for now. I think you're where you're meant to be, though."

He was right. Somehow, I knew in my heart I was where I was meant to be as well. Even if my brain hadn't caught up with the idea.

"I never did thank you."

"For what?"

"For saving me."

"You're welcome. I'd do it all over again. I hope you know the last thing I want to do is make your life any harder." He squeezed my hand gently and interlaced his fingers with mine. I didn't pull away, finding comfort in his touch. I took that as a positive sign that maybe things would be okay.

"So, what do you say about that movie?" he asked.

"I think I'd like that, but I still have to call the diner." I had a feeling, however, that it wouldn't matter. No show... no job. Those were Marcy's rules. One strike and you were out.

"Okay. Make your call and then we'll go downstairs." Arkkadian produced his own cell phone from his pocket and handed it to me.

"Thanks." I stared down at our interlaced fingers and a few more tears streaked down my face. Once again, Arkkadian wiped them away, the pads of his thumbs soft against my skin. For the first time since waking in his bed yesterday morning, I felt truly safe. It made me smile.

I dialed the diner, and a new waitress, one I didn't recognize, answered the phone. That wasn't a good sign. I asked for the owner and waited for Marcy to pick up. Unfortunately, she didn't take too kindly to my unexplained absence and confirmed what I already knew. My home being burned to the ground hadn't mattered one bit to her. I was well and truly screwed. I owed a lot of money, and now I had no way to pay it off.

"Well, that's that I guess." I had expected it, but now that it had happened, I felt numb. I never liked the diner job, but the tips had been worth it. Now, that was no longer an option.

"I'm sorry," Arkkadian said. "I'll make it right. Tomorrow, we'll take care of whatever bills you owe. It's the least I can do."

I bristled at the thought. Why would he pay my debt? We were nearly strangers. Acquaintances. I couldn't ask him for that kind of money. It wouldn't be right.

"No, really. It's okay. You don't have to do that. I'll find a way to pay them off."

"Aislin, let me do this for you. Please," he pressed.

"Arkkadian, it's a lot of money. I don't feel right taking it." I gripped his phone in my hands, rubbing my thumbs across the surface like a worry stone. I stared at it, willing it to wipe all the awful away, all the while knowing it was pointless.

"You're not taking it. I'm giving it to you. Now, how much do you owe?" When I hesitated, he asked again. Fuck.

"Twelve thousand. Please, I don't want you to think less of me," I said, hanging my head in shame. I was so used to relying on myself most of my life. I hated needing his help. I hated needing any help at all. I'd gotten myself into debt, and I needed to get myself out.

"Stop. I don't think any less of you. You did what you had to do to survive on your own. That's commendable. I want to help. Please let me."

"I'll pay you back. Every cent. I'll work for it if I have to."

"It's a gift. Let me do this for you," he said. "Let me take care of you."

I wasn't getting out of this. Me and my big fat mouth. I let out a huff, resigned to his generosity. Accepting all that money went against every fiber of my being, but I didn't have much of a choice at this point. My bills wouldn't pay themselves.

"I... thank you. That's really generous of you."

"No need to thank me. That's what mates are for."

"I really appreciate it." I did my best to ignore the mate comment, not on board with that part of my new reality just yet.

"Now what do you say we finally enjoy that movie?"

Arkkadian helped me up off the bed, making sure I was stable on my feet. So far, so good. I still felt a little dizzy but remained steady as he helped me across the room and down the steps. Halfway down, I stopped him when a thought crossed my mind.

"Can I ask you something? It's probably silly."

"Shoot."

"Should I be calling you 'sir' or something? You are the Alpha."

"I only like to be called 'sir' in the bedroom," he said with a laugh and a wink. Heat crept up my cheeks. I walked headfirst into that one.

"And... I'll just stop talking now." I was suddenly very aroused and very embarrassed. And then I remembered him mentioning he could smell such things. Oh, my God! Mortified, I descended the steps quickly, leaving him to trail behind.

"Relax." He followed me into the den with a chuckle. "We'll save that for later, after we've gotten to know each other better. A lot better."

Changing the subject to something where I wouldn't shove my foot in my mouth, I asked him where the nickname Arkken came from.

"It's a childhood nickname. Only my family really uses it, though. Gideon had trouble saying my name when we were little, so it got shortened and it just kind of stuck. Sara, however, likes to use my full name when she thinks I'm being an ass. You'll find she uses it often." He wiggled both eyebrows, and the twinkle in his eye made me laugh. "Most everyone else refers to me as Arkkadian or Alpha, though. But you are my mate, which also makes you my family."

Family? The idea warmed my heart, and I wanted to know more about who I really was. I tried to remember what he'd said before I'd vomited all over his shoes. Aeterna? Aeternus? I just couldn't recall, but for now, I put it aside. I still had a slight headache and just wanted to relax. I'd already experienced information overload once today, and for now, that was enough.

18

ARKKADIAN

I could barely contain myself during the movie. We relaxed together on the big leather sofa in the den, Aislin snuggled under a cozy blanket on the cushion next to me. The fire crackled in the hearth, lending a warm ambiance to the room and amplifying my desire for the woman beside me. She picked a romantic comedy, and within minutes, she'd nestled comfortably into my side, our bond ultimately working its magic. This knowledge made my wolf increasingly happy. It also made me increasingly and desperately randy.

I wrapped my arm around her shoulder and gently stroked her arm, and she relaxed into me. The feel of her body up against mine drove me wild, and for the entire length of the movie, the only thing I could think about was her delectably naked body splayed out on my bed. Or her long legs wrapped around me as I delved into her heavenly essence and kissed my way around her body. I wanted to taste every single inch of her. Feel her soft body beneath mine. Feel her heat wrapped around me like a tight glove. Listen to her beg for more while I ravished her and drove her over the edge of ecstasy.

Thankfully, she didn't notice the heat I packed in my pants. Or at least I'd hoped not. I was painfully hard almost the entire movie, and I would have to take care of that or take a very long, very cold shower. Possibly both.

Gideon walked in the front door just as the credits were rolling.

I met him in the other room, leaving Aislin to cozy up under the blanket and pick another movie. He handed over the day's security report and then left just as quickly as he'd come, but not before he noticed the tent in my pants. I could hear him laughing as he made his way back down the path outside. Ass. When I returned to the den, Aislin was watching the news.

"Anything new?" I asked, placing the folder in a drawer to look at later. It wasn't unusual for Gideon to drop off regular reports.

"None," she answered sadly. "Just the same old 'robbery gone bad' spiel. They still haven't mentioned the names of the deceased or any upcoming services."

"I'm sorry. I wish I knew more. Either way, attending the service is out of the question. Not while Kane's whereabouts are unknown. If he's still alive, that's exactly where he'd come looking for you."

"I know." She sighed. "I just... I don't know."

I sat back down beside her, putting my arm around her again, and kissed the top of her head as she leaned into me.

"Maybe I can pay my respects another time. I really miss them, Arkkadian. It hurts so much."

I hugged her to me, recognizing the longing in her voice and her need to grieve as she fell apart in my arms. "Shh... I'm right here." I held her close, comforting her as best as I could. "Everything will be okay."

I wished with all my might that I could fix everything for her. That I could make all the bad things go away. If I could bring her family back to life, I would. It hurt that I couldn't, but what I could do was be there for her. However she needed me to be. Whatever she needed me to be. Her eyes were red and swollen by the time she stopped crying.

"All right, beautiful. Buck up. Let's get our minds off all this sadness. Are you hungry?"

"Starving."

"I'll warm up some of Sara's homemade chicken soup. It's so good." I smiled, patting my stomach and releasing her to stand.

"That sounds wonderful."

"How's your headache? Any better?"

"Much. Thank you."

"Good." I was glad to hear it. I still felt fairly guilty for making her sick earlier.

She pushed her hair behind her ears. "Why are you being so nice? I'm such a mess."

"Because I'm a nice guy? And you're not a mess. You've just been through a lot. Every woman deserves to be treated with kindness and respect."

"You're chivalrous, too, I see." The corner of her lips quirked upward in a half-grin.

"Yes, yes I am." I winked. "Plus, you're my Aeternus. It's my duty to cherish you."

"Whoa, whoa, whoa. I hardly know you. Slow down, speed racer." She laughed, a small bit of humor poking through the sadness. So I played on it.

"I'll win you over. You'll see." I grinned, taking it as a good sign that she was in a playful mood.

"Yeah, yeah, so you say." She grinned. "Anyway, I'm starving, remember?"

"I know. Your stomach's been growling for an hour," I teased, and she tossed a throw pillow at me. I laughed. "Uncle! Uncle!"

Just then, her stomach grumbled so loud, her face flushed in embarrassment. It was adorable.

"Why don't you look for another movie, and I'll go warm up dinner."

"Sounds good."

"Your wish is my command, milady." And then I bowed with a flourish, enjoying the fact that I could make her smile and laugh.

She giggled like a schoolgirl. She was definitely more comfortable in my presence. I loved it. So did my wolf. Maybe it wouldn't take her so long to come around. And just maybe, this new life could help her heal.

"I shall return momentarily." With that, I gave her a swift swat on the butt and was out the door to the other room.

"Hey!"

My laughter filled the air.

19

AISLIN

I snuggled up under the blanket with the remote. For a while, I just stared blankly at the television, my mind still on what I'd seen on the news. The smell of chicken soup drifting into the room broke me out of my reverie, and my stomach growled again in response. Turning my attention back to the television, I searched for another romantic comedy, but a short while later, I realized Arkkadian hadn't come back into the room yet. Longing for his company, I went to look for him when I heard his voice in the kitchen.

Arkkadian was listening intently to someone on the phone. He held a finger to his lips and reached a hand out for me to join him. When I reached his side, Arkkadian pulled me close and wrapped an arm around my waist. I instinctively leaned into his warmth and inhaled, taking in not just the delicious aroma emanating from the stove, but his scent.

Hints of cinnamon and clove tickled my senses, and a feeling of rightness wrapped itself around me. The apprehension I'd felt for so long faded. Arkkadian rubbed a hand up and down my arm in a soothing motion as if he understood exactly how I felt, which really didn't surprise me. He always seemed to have a sixth sense when it came to my emotions. Maybe it was the bond. I didn't know. I still had a hard time believing we were somehow linked, despite feeling connected.

"Good. Make sure you turn him over to Randall, along with the evidence, and then finish the security updates as quick as possible. The fool didn't learn his lesson last time. We don't want any of our people to get hurt or killed by mistake, especially the children. Thanks, James."

When he hung up, Arkkadian gave me a squeeze and kissed the top of my head. I wanted to stay wrapped in the comfort of his embrace, the feeling of rightness settling somewhere deep down inside me.

"Is everything okay?" I asked.

"Yes, everything's fine. We just have a poacher who seems to think he can encroach on our land any time he wants. This is the second time we've caught him crossing into our territory. James will see that he's turned over to Fish and Game," he explained.

"Is this why you're updating security?"

"Partly. Until we know Kane's whereabouts, we need to take all necessary precautions to keep you safe. Our security system is state-of-the-art, but it's not foolproof. So, I'm having my team install additional cameras around our land and add a few other upgrades. Kane's come after you twice already. I expect he won't give up."

I shivered, leaning further into Arkkadian's strong arms and buried my face in his chest. He tightened his arms around me in response and stroked the back of my head, fingers curling gently through my hair. The thought of Kane coming back terrified me. I inhaled, and his warm scent of cinnamon and clove washed over me again, soothing away that fear, making me feel safe. At least for the time being.

"Hey, aren't you supposed to be finding us another movie to watch?" he asked, rubbing my back. I knew he sensed my uneasiness over Kane.

I looked up and gave him a half-smile. "I got distracted. I smelled the soup and then wondered why you hadn't returned. And now I'm wicked hungry." I leaned over the stockpot and took a whiff.

"Yeah. I heard your stomach grumbling all the way from the den. Again," he teased.

I laughed. "I can't help it. It smells so good. Besides, you're the one responsible for my stomach turning inside out," I teased back. I liked this playful side of Arkkadian.

He winced. "I'm so sorry about that. Really. But I'm glad to see you got your appetite back. It makes me feel a lot better."

"Don't worry about it." I shrugged.

When the soup was ready, Arkkadian ladled the delicious smelling concoction into my bowl. I wondered if my stomach could handle it and the thought reminded me of our earlier conversation before I'd so ungracefully deposited my breakfast on his boots.

"Hey. What was that thing you called me earlier? Aeterna? Aeteru?" I stumbled over the word as Arkkadian looked up from filling his bowl.

"Aeternus. I wasn't sure if you remembered, considering." He inclined his head to the side with a wink, and I flushed with embarrassment all over again.

"I'm so sorry! Truly. Please tell me I didn't ruin your boots? I'll buy you a new pair. I swear." With what money, though?

Arkkadian just laughed. "You worry too much. It's okay. Sara took them with her, she'll clean them and they'll be good as new." He smiled warmly and tugged on a lock of my hair. "It's not a big deal. Those boots have seen much dirtier days than that."

He led me back to the table, and we sat down, the movie all but forgotten. I took a bite of my soup and moaned with delight. My stomach rumbled in appreciation.

"Oh, this is so good." I reveled in all the flavors dancing across my tongue. Sara's soup was perfect.

"So how much do you remember?"

I shook my head. "Not much. I know you explained it, but I just don't remember."

"Well, Aeternus literally means eternal. For life. Or soul mate, as I said before. All females are born Aeternus and bound to their human form. Centuries ago, however, all Aeternus could take the form of their mates. They were called Immortalle, but their ability died out and there hasn't been an Immortalle in several centuries," he explained while I devoured my meal.

"I still don't understand. How do you know I'm an Aeternus? Or that I'm yours?"

"Do you remember what I explained about scents?" he asked. I nodded. That, I remembered.

"That's one way. The rest is kind of hard to explain. Think of it like a guitar string connecting two points, and when it's plucked, both ends feel the ripple. We feel it. Our animals feel it. It's an instinct we feel soul-deep. It's stronger for the male because we have this innate need to protect what's ours. We're possessive and dominant by nature. You've felt the pull, your body knows. The more time we spend together, the stronger it gets. Even now, you're already more comfortable around me, aren't you?"

I knew exactly what he meant with the guitar string analogy. That explained almost perfectly what I felt every time Arkkadian was near. Every time he touched me. And when we weren't in the same room, it felt like something was missing.

"It's weird. Somehow, I know I should trust you, even though I don't really know you. I'm having trouble reconciling the two," I told him. "It's really confusing."

"I get it. If you'd been raised with Pack instead, this all would have made so much more sense."

I sat silently for a moment, processing the information when something he said caught my attention. "You said Immortalle could shift."

"Yes, but only when the bond between mates is complete."

"But I'm not an Immortalle, right?" I questioned, still confused.

"Not as far as I know. It would be a miracle if you were, though."

"And what's the difference between the two?"

"They're basically the same. Or used to be until their Immortalle gifts died out."

"Oh." I wasn't sure what to say after that. Much of this was still so unbelievable. I needed time to digest this bit of information.

"I promised you another movie and you should be resting, anyway. Not up and about. Go. Find something good, and I'll clean up. We'll talk later."

"Party pooper." I laughed and handed him my empty bowl. I'd eaten every drop. "Just when it was getting good." He was right, though. I was tired.

"Careful now, that'll earn you another swat on the butt," he teased.

"You wouldn't!" I faked outrage but failed in my sincerity when I couldn't deny the grin creeping across my face. Arkkadian was thinking the same thing I was—my lust-filled reaction to his hand on my backside. It was written all over his face as I slowly approached him.

"I would." His smoldering gaze lit my insides on fire, and heat pooled low in my center.

"I dare you," I teased breathlessly, staring up at him as I splayed my fingers across his belly and licked my lips.

Wait. No. Where did that come from? What was I thinking? I wasn't bold, and this was bold. I tugged on the collar of my shirt as if doing so would release the steam building up in my engine.

"You're playing with fire, Aislin." His voice was so deep. So sultry. And very, very intense. I watched as his tongue snaked across his bottom lip, and then my gaze wandered up to his eyes. They were glowing bright blue, but instead of fear, my insides burned with desire as I looked upon those two cerulean orbs staring right back into my soul.

Suddenly, I wanted to devour him.

My heart pounded in my chest and the heat rising in my core snaked its way throughout my body. I was lost in the moment until Arkkadian broke the stare. I shook myself with a huff. Reality beckoned once again, the sexual tension broken.

With that, he turned me toward the den, swatted my butt, and sent me back to the couch to rest. "Park it. Doctor's orders."

"Y... yes, sir," I stammered, giving him a bit of side-eye and a grin. I couldn't help myself. I giggled as walked out of the room. Good heavens! What had come over me just now?

20

ARKKADIAN

That little vixen! I watched my mate's sassy little backside as she sauntered out of the kitchen. My dick was instantly hard. Again. Like that was a surprise. I'd spent the last several days in a near constant state of arousal, giving the term blue balls a whole new meaning. I needed to take care of this or I'd be spending the next few hours in agony.

Poking my head into the den, I apologized and told Aislin I needed to return a quick phone call and excused myself upstairs, leaving her to pick another movie. I locked my bedroom door behind me and padded barefoot to the bathroom, also locking that door behind me.

My wolf needed a hard and fast release, and I couldn't unzip my pants fast enough. I yanked them down and let them fall around my ankles. Planting one hand on the edge of the counter to brace myself, I wrapped my fingers around my hard length with the other.

I quickly stroked up and down, not wasting any time. I imagined walking right up to my mate, pulling her up off the couch, and delving my tongue into her delectable mouth as I wrapped my hands in her hair. I thought about how I wanted to tear her shirt off and suckle at her breasts before laying her back on my desk so I could have my way with her.

As the imaginary images flashed through my mind, I squeezed and stroked faster. Harder. Slapping sounds echoed through the bathroom as I jacked my hand up and down in a hurried frenzy, seeking the warm rush of pleasure that would be my reward.

In my mind, Aislin lay before me on the desk, knees bent, her bare feet resting on the edge. I leaned forward and kissed her belly, slowly inching my way down to that sweet spot at the apex of her luscious thighs. Thighs I wanted wrapped around my head. I could almost hear her gasp as my tongue swirled around and around her clitoris, making her writhe and moan. I imagined probing into her wetness, tasting every single drop and letting the magic flow over my tongue.

I stroked harder and faster, wanting to taste her so badly. I was almost tempted to go find her. Almost. A tingling began in my balls, and they tightened. Lightning-quick sparks of electric ecstasy shot up my spine, and flashes of light danced in my vision as my body jerked. I clenched my mouth shut in an effort not to howl, and I nearly collapsed to my knees, panting hard, as my orgasm spread through me like liquid fire.

I desperately wanted to show my mate just what her "sir" could really do. Maybe I'd spank her again later for that bit of sass. My beast sated, at least for now, I tucked myself back into my pants and joined her downstairs.

21

AISLIN

After Arkkadian left to go make his phone call, I curled up on the sofa with the remote and flipped through the channels one more time. By the time he appeared in the doorway, I still hadn't found anything interesting, but my headache was barely a blip on my radar. He carried a glass of water and set it down next to me.

"Thank you."

"Find anything?"

"Nope." I sighed. "Nothing that sounds good. Maybe you can find something."

I handed him the remote when he sat down next to me. I sidled up beside him, and he wrapped his arm around me. As we sat there quietly flipping channels, I realized I truly enjoyed his presence and quiet strength. I finally trusted Arkkadian, that trust pouring forth like a fountain. The dam I'd built to protect my heart was finally crumbling.

When I looked up and smiled at the realization, he pulled me onto his lap, almost as if he knew exactly what I was thinking. His arms cocooned me, and I leaned into him, resting my head on his chest and relaxing into him. *Safe.* The thought disappeared just as suddenly as it had appeared, and unfortunately, the feeling didn't last long.

Minutes passed in silence as we watched whatever movie he had finally picked out. I had been too distracted cuddling up to this beautiful man to even notice. I listened to the slow and steady beat of his heart. Ba-dum. Ba-dum. Ba-dum. Before long, my breathing matched his breath for breath, and our hearts synced together in perfect rhythm. When Arkkadian reached a hand up and rubbed my back, an overwhelming sense of ken zipped through me with a shock.

The intimacy was suddenly too much. I knew it was our souls recognizing one another. It should have been comforting, but the sound of Kane's dark laughter echoed in my head instead, tormenting me and filling my mind with terrible things, like the memory of his hands all over me. Or the feel of his body on top of mine. His hot, stale breath making my skin crawl.

I jerked upright out of Arkkadian's lap and crossed the room. My whole body felt squirmy, as if a million little ants were tunneling just below the surface. I tensed, hunching my shoulders around my neck. My skin itched everywhere, and I wanted to scratch it all off. Tear at it and suck all the little six-legged creepies out. Breathing hard and fast, I spun in circles around the room, and my vision swam. I raked both hands through my hair, pulling at it in fistfuls. I couldn't breathe. All the oxygen in the room taunted me. Called my name. But I couldn't pull it into my lungs no matter how much I struggled.

One flashback was all it took to destroy a beautiful moment. No, not just the moment. Everything. In an instant, I was the frightened woman I'd been that night. I was the traumatized and terrified little girl in that hospital waiting room. Anyone else I tried to be was just a façade. A fraud. I hadn't moved on. That person was just an imposter teasing me, living in my skin, filling my head with the idea that I could be a normal person. No, I was a fragile little flower wilting at the first sign of drought.

"No. No, no, no, no."

"Aislin?" Arkkadian stood, but wisely didn't come any closer. "Aislin, what's wrong?"

"I..." The walls closed in around me. I couldn't speak. I couldn't think. *Run*, my brain screamed.

I spun toward the door and bolted from the room. Yanking the front door of the cabin open, I took off barefoot down the gravel path. I ignored Arkkadian's worried shouts behind me. I didn't stop running until I collapsed on the big open lawn in front of the strange wooden platform, my body giving out as outright fear and loathing—the demons that possessed me—took over my body.

I crashed to my knees, gulping air like my life depended on it, hands fisting the soft grass. I choked on sobs that wracked my body. Twilight enveloped me as fireflies flitted inches from my face, but I was too frantic to take in the serenity surrounding me. I swatted at the tiny little lights floating in the air, slapping them away, hating the beauty they represented. The beauty I was not and would never be. At that moment, it was all so ugly. The grass. The sky. The air. Life. But I—I was the ugliest thing of all. I was a weak thing. A pathetic thing.

Like brittle glass under the stress of thermal shock, I shattered into a million tiny pieces.

Footsteps sounded on the gravel behind me, and I bowed my head in shame. Hot tears trailed down my face, leaving little salty paths in their wake. All these months later and I still felt so ugly. Dirty. Ashamed. And I'd just ruined a wonderful moment with Arkkadian. Completely. What a fool. How could anyone want a sniveling disaster like me? Because that's what I was. A walking, talking disaster. I shrunk in on myself as if doing so would somehow make me invisible.

"Aislin?" The higher pitch of Arkkadian's voice revealed his concern. I couldn't answer him. I didn't want his concern. I didn't deserve it. I felt his presence behind me just before his gentle hands covered my arms, and I jerked away.

"Don't. Don't touch me," I cried, my body trembling with deep-seated anguish. I never hated myself as much as I did in this moment.

I couldn't bear to have anyone touching me right now. Arkkadian circled around and knelt down in front of me, but I scrambled backward, putting some distance between us. Uncontrollable tears dropped onto the blades of green beneath me. Hot, angry tears. Ugly tears. Sad tears. Tears of torment and weakness. Tear for all the things I had lost and would never get back. Tears for all the things I was not and would never be.

"Aislin, what happened? Tell me what's wrong." He spoke

barely above a whisper. I still couldn't find my words, and the silent void between us expanded until it drowned out the world.

"Come on, talk to me, love," he soothed but he didn't move closer, and I blessed him for it. The sad light in his eyes echoed the anguish in my tight chest. Had I hurt him? Or was it the link between us that allowed him to feel all of my hurt? Guilt filled me. It was too much. Way too much. I couldn't do this.

"Please. Just go. I need a few moments." I barely choked out the words as I waited for his rejection. How could he still want me like this?

"I'm not going anywhere. We'll sit here as long as you need."

I tried to stand and put more distance between us, but I stumbled, hissing at the stinging pain in my feet. They felt like I'd stepped on shards of broken glass. Arkkadian caught me, and I struggled in his arms, but he refused to let me go. His refusal shattered something in me, and the last vestiges of the dam I'd built finally and entirely collapsed. Instead of rejection, Arkkadian shrouded me in patient strength and gently lowered us back to the ground. He just held me close while I shed every tear I could. He held me after the tears stopped. He held me until the last shudder shook me, and I finally fell silent.

"Dear God, what happened to you?" Arkkadian spoke softly into the air. It wasn't a question for me. It was a question for the fates. It was a question spoken by a man so consumed with emotion, he felt every ounce of my heartache. He felt rage. Grief. Remorse. Determination.

He was so consumed with my pain that the connection we shared sent all of it spiraling back into me, and I knew. I knew we were inexplicably linked. I knew the storming rage he felt was for every wrong ever done to me. I knew the grief was for all of my suffering. I knew the remorse was for not being there to stop it. And I knew he was determined to make it right. That he would pick up all those tiny pieces and put them back together if I let him.

22

ARKKADIAN

I held Aislin as she wept, my wolf seething just under the surface. For every hurt. For every ounce of pain. For all the trauma and the torment. For all the times she was alone. I couldn't let the rage, or the grief, or the remorse consume me. No. I would fix this. I knew then that if I ever laid eyes upon the bastards who'd hurt her, I would tear them limb from limb. She was my mate. The other half of my soul. And no one would ever hurt her again if I had anything to say about it.

As the evening sun slowly set in the distance, the fireflies faded into the shadows, making way for the dark of night falling around us. When her tears finally stopped, Aislin released a heavy sigh and sat upright. She tried to stand and winced in pain. I pulled her back down to sit and reached for her feet. Bloody cuts on the soles of her feet glinted in the pale moonlight, revealing where sharp bits of gravel had sliced through her skin. Dammit. I'd been so distracted by her pain, I hadn't noticed the injuries.

"Come on, love, let's go home. You've had a long day."

She wrapped her arms around me, and I carried her back to the cabin where I went to work cleaning her wounds.

She didn't flinch, she didn't speak, and I didn't push. She'd talk when she was ready. I grabbed one of my t-shirts and a warm pair of sweats and set them on the bed beside her. Then I set to work stoking the fire back to life before returning to her side.

"Why don't you try to get some sleep? I'll be downstairs in the den if you need me. Do you need anything before I go?" My wolf whined, not enjoying leaving her alone, but also understanding the need for space. She didn't reply, but just as I turned toward the door, her hand snaked out and grabbed mine.

"Please don't leave me alone," she begged.

The desperation in her voice tore at my heart, and I sank down beside her on the mattress and pulled her to me. She held on to me like I was her last lifeline. I traced circles on her back as I focused my energy, and then I sent small waves of it into her. Small enough to hopefully not cause the same trouble as before. I tucked her head under my chin, and I tilted my face just enough to kiss the top of her head.

"I won't go anywhere. Not if you don't want me to," I promised, breathing in her scent and letting it ease away the stress of earlier.

"Okay."

"Are you sure?" My mate looked entirely lost. The ground beneath her had collapsed, and she'd finally hit rock bottom. I would be here to help lift her back up, but I couldn't do it all myself. She had to fight. She had to find her own strength, the strength I knew hid way down deep behind her broken and crumbling walls. I could help her find it, but ultimately, it was up to her to grab ahold of it and never let it go.

"Please," she said, just barely above a whisper. When she didn't move, I picked up the sweats and handed them to her. "What's this?"

"I thought you'd like something a little more comfortable to wear. Why don't you go change and I'll be right here when you return?"

When she wandered off to the bathroom, I quickly changed into sweats and a t-shirt myself. Exiting the closet, I saw the bathroom door was ajar, so I poked my head inside. Aislin was just standing there in the middle of the room, holding the clothes, staring blankly at them in her hands. Damn that bastard, Kane. Just what had he done? The urge to destroy crept under my skin, but I pushed it away. All that anger, that hatred, none of that was important right now. But she was.

"Hey," I said quietly, and she jumped. "Can I come in?"

She nodded, and I took the clothes from her and set them on

the counter. "Come on, love. You can't wear these to bed. You've got grass stains on your jeans and mud on your shirt. Lift your arms for me."

She did as she was told, and I lifted the pink blouse over her head. Then I undid the button on her pants and lowered them so she could step out. Aislin wrapped her arms around her torso and cast her eyes to the floor, obvious shame and embarrassment over the disfiguring marks on her body flooding through our shared connection. I pretended not to notice, not wanting to make her any more self-conscious than she already was. She didn't need words right now. She needed quiet comfort. Tenderness. I held up the sweats so she could slide her legs into them and ignored the racing thoughts in my head.

"Turn around," I coaxed.

I undid the clasp on her bra and slipped it down over her arms, letting it fall to the floor with the rest of her soiled clothes. Then I handed her the t-shirt so she could slip it over her head before turning back. Aislin kept her eyes downcast, the shame she felt still visible on her face. She hadn't looked at me once since I carried her home.

"It's okay," I quietly told her when she bent to pick up her clothes off the floor. "Leave them."

Grabbing her hand, I led Aislin back to the bed. Then I folded down the covers and climbed in after her. She lay silently on her left side facing away, but moments later, she scooted up against me, her back to my front. Her smaller frame fit perfectly next to mine.

I shut the bedside lamp off, tucked one arm under my head, and lay there watching flickers of firelight dancing across the ceiling. When Aislin didn't move away, I wrapped my other arm around her and pulled her closer. For the first time in a long while, my wolf was subdued. Quiet. And I was grateful for it. The constant stress of a high-strung wolf was exhausting, both mentally and physically. As a shapeshifter, my wolf and I were one in the same, but in times of stress and trouble, with heightened instincts, it felt like another being lived beneath the surface of my skin. Invading my body. And if the wolf was stressed, so was I.

I lay awake for a while, just listening to the sounds of her breathing as she cuddled up against me. It destroyed me knowing she was hurting this much, and I didn't understand how bad it truly was until this evening. Earlier on the sofa, I'd felt the connection spark between us, a sign that the bond was strengthening. I hadn't expected it to startle her, or for her to fly out the door like a frightened bird.

Her fingers unexpectedly interlacing with mine pulled me from my thoughts.

"You want to talk about it?" I propped my head up to peer over her shoulder and waited, giving her the choice to open up or not. This was her hurt. Her pain. Only she could decide when she was ready.

"I…"

"It's okay. You don't have to, but I'm here if you want to." I wanted her to trust me. To be open with me. But I also didn't want to push her if she wasn't ready.

"No. I want to. It's just… it's bad, Arkkadian. It's really bad."

"Take your time, love. Take your time."

Control, I told myself. I needed to keep absolute control. I had an inkling, but I would let her lead the way. It was Aislin's story to tell. Her pain to reveal. And no matter what she told me, no matter how angry it made me, I couldn't lose myself to the anger. I couldn't lose myself to the wolf. I would be the rock. The foundation. The support and the love she needed to find her footing and rebuild her life.

23

AISLIN

I took a deep breath and tried to steel myself against the emotions bubbling to the surface. If I didn't tell him now, I didn't know if I would ever have the courage. What happened downstairs had set my anxiety off like a rocket, and then the flare of the flashback had sent me running out into the night, unable to tell the difference between memories and reality. Arkkadian just being here, listening, giving me the time I needed to work through my thoughts meant everything.

"I'm sorry I ran off like that. I freaked out." I could feel Arkkadian nod behind me, but he stayed quiet. His only answer was to brush the hair off my neck and twirl his fingers in slow, gentle circles upon my skin. I let it comfort me. Even now, I could feel the familiar tingle that connected us, and I let it fill me until my entire body buzzed with energy. Only this time, it wasn't such a shock to my system. Instead, it brought me peace and, with it, the beginnings of the healing I so desperately needed.

When Arkkadian still didn't speak, I continued. "Did you feel it? What was it?"

"I did," he answered calmly. "I think you know."

I did know. The surface of my skin prickled with awareness everywhere our bodies touched, like two atoms bonding at an atomic level.

I couldn't make myself admit it out loud, though. I wanted him to say it. Until this moment, I hadn't truly believed anything

Arkkadian had told me. Mates? Being able to "sense" each other? That weird calming thing he did when he touched me? It had made me sick. Literally. I'd spent hours puking in a bucket because of it. And even then, I hadn't believed. Hell, I was still reeling from the knowledge that he and his brother could turn into wolves. Big, scary wolves. That alone, seeing Gideon's wolf surrounded by flames in my apartment... that should have convinced me, but it hadn't.

I'd thought I was going crazy. I had believed none of it. Not until that moment, when the tiny trace of electricity that had been there all along suddenly shot off like a bolt of lightning through my being, striking me right in the epicenter of my soul. That was when I knew it to be true, and it had scared the ever-living shit out of me. That fear lit the match that sparked the flashback to life.

"That was the connection. That was your instinct finally accepting what had been there all along. It was telling you you were finally accepting that here was where you were meant to be, Aislin. Instinct always knows, just as our souls always recognize their other halves."

I knew he was right. It felt right. I just didn't know how I felt about it. All of this was too heavy. Arkkadian placed a soft kiss on my neck. My skin tingled where his lips touched me.

"My entire life has been a lie, hasn't it?" I whispered.

"Not a lie. Just... different. That's all," he said. "What's important is that you're here now and that you treasure the good parts. Learn from the hard parts. Remember the loved ones you lost. They may be gone, but they will always be a part of you."

I let go of his hand with a sigh and traced circles on the pillow next to me. He was right. Again. That still didn't make any of this easier. I mean, I could devour a paranormal romance easily, but to find out the characters from my books were real? And the odds I was part of that immortal world? It was surreal.

"Want to tell me what happened tonight?" He continued gently stroking my skin, his fingers soft and soothing as they moved up and down my arm with feather-light touches.

And we were back to the heart of the matter just like that. The thing that, months later, still plagued me. That would probably forever plague me, just like my childhood dreams always had. You don't forget things like that. I couldn't avoid it forever, and I'd already resigned myself to be open and honest with Arkkadian. If he had gone to the trouble of saving me and keeping me safe, then he deserved to know the truth.

"It's just... everything is moving so fast. When I felt the connection, it startled me. It's been there from the start, always growing stronger, but this time, it felt like lightning zipping through me, down into my very soul. It was the moment I knew everything you'd told me was true. It was the moment I knew you were mine, and I was yours, but the very idea of it frightened me. I've spent months being afraid of men, and yet, here I am connected to one I hardly know, unable to deny it. Then I had a flashback and all these memories of Kane came flooding back. I couldn't handle everything all at once. I couldn't breathe. I felt like the walls were closing in and I had to get out of here before I suffocated."

"Did he hurt you?" Arkkadian stopped stroking my arm and wrapped it around my waist, pulling me tighter against him. I needed that closeness. The warmth. The comfort. The strength. I didn't know how much I needed that strength until now. I thought I'd been strong all along, doing things on my own and not relying on anyone when all I'd been doing was running. That wasn't strength. That was me refusing to face my demons.

"He tried," I answered. I would not cry. I would not. This time, I would hold it together. I would draw on Arkkadian's strength. I could do this. I took a deep breath and let it all out.

"At first, he'd been charming and kind. Always dressed nice. Clean cut. We dated a handful of times, nothing remotely serious. Then, on the last date, he asked me back to his place. I stupidly went with him. I learned what a creep he truly was that night. He was nothing like the person he'd presented himself to be. We were halfway through a movie when, out of nowhere, he pushed me down and tried to shove his tongue in my mouth. I pushed him off me and told him I wasn't ready for that.

"The next thing I know, I'm pinned to the wall, and he's in my face and he's so angry. He told me I 'owed' him for taking me out on nice dates, and that one way or another, he would get what he wanted. I tried to push him off, but he dragged me back to the bedroom. I fought. I kicked and screamed, but I wasn't strong enough. He hit me so hard I saw stars. By the time I realized what was happening, he'd ripped my clothes off and pinned me face down on the bed. And then he... he tried..." I buried my face in the pillow. I couldn't say it. Not out loud.

"Ash, love, it's okay. You don't have to," Arkkadian soothed.

"No. You need to know what he tried to do, and I need to be strong enough to say this. I need to be strong for myself. Kane had me pinned. I felt his hands. Back there."

I clenched my butt involuntarily, and I could have sworn Arkkadian growled behind me. I could feel the anger rolling off him, but I couldn't stop. I had to tell him the rest. To get it out of me and get rid of the fear. I had to get rid of the shame and find my strength. I couldn't let it eat away at me any longer.

"I couldn't move. He was saying something about making me his forever and I didn't understand what he meant." At that, Arkkadian swore. "The laughter. God. I can't forget how evil he sounded. He just... kept... laughing. Then my head went all fuzzy, and I felt like I wanted to puke. Kind of like that thing you did, but I didn't know. I thought it was because he'd hit me in the head. I took the first opportunity when he let go of my hands to grab the lamp on the nightstand, and I slammed it into his head. When he reared back, I rolled over and kicked his balls, and I ran. Kane disappeared after that; the police never found him. When he showed up the other night, that was the first time I'd seen him since that night."

"I'm so sorry that happened. So sorry." He hugged me tighter. I wrapped my arms around his and held on tight. Being in his arms, it felt good. It felt safe.

"It's my fault. I was stupid. I still feel dirty and ashamed every time I'm reminded of him, even though he didn't..."

"Stop. Never say that about yourself. It's not your fault, and you are *not* stupid. Kane is a creep. He always has been, always will be. If I find the son of a bitch again..." He let the sentence trail off, but I knew what he meant. There was no doubt in my mind Arkkadian would kill him. I hoped he did.

"Do you know how brave you are? How strong you are? You fought. You got away. And you had the courage to tell me about it. You are stronger than you realize, love."

I shook my head. "No, I'm not. I shouldn't have gone with him. If I hadn't..."

"Yes, you are. He didn't get what he wanted from you. It took courage for you to fight. I am so proud of you. And you should be proud of you, too," he said, his tone turning serious. "Aislin, I mean it. If you hadn't fought him, you wouldn't have escaped. When he said he would make you his, he meant it. When your head went all fuzzy, that was Kane attempting to force a bond on you. Had he succeeded, you would have become his plaything, and there would have been almost nothing you could do about it. Forced bonds are vile, and they're not permitted among the Pack. The only way to force a bond, well, it's what Kane tried to do to you. The only ways to break a bond are death, forcing a new bond, or having a Soul Shadow shatter the bond. And they're all horrible things to experience."

Arkkadian's words sat heavily on my chest. The realization that I could have been stuck with that bastard forever terrified me, and I shuddered at the thought. If I hadn't been able to get away.... No, I didn't want to think about it.

"Come here, love. Look at me." He tugged on my arm until I rolled to face him. I was met with the most gorgeous steel-blue eyes. Eyes that revealed the truth of who and what we were to each other. Eyes that promised I'd never be alone again. "I mean it when I say you're stronger than you realize and that I'm proud of you. It not only took the courage to fight him, but it took courage to confide in me. What you endured, those are hard things to talk about, but you did it. Be proud of that."

"But I still shouldn't..."

Arkkadian took my face in his hands. "Stop blaming yourself. I'll keep saying it until you get it through your head. It's not your fault, Aislin."

He was right. I let his words fill me with love and light. The weight lifted off my chest, and at that moment, I realized I was no longer afraid. Not of Arkkadian, not of Kane. Kane had no power. Not anymore. I was no longer beholden to that fear.

"Thank you." I snuggled closer to him, and he wrapped his arms around me and held me tight. "Thank you for saving me."

"You're welcome," he whispered, and then he leaned in and kissed my forehead, his hand gently cupping my chin.

That familiar little spark zipped through me again, sending every little synapse into overdrive, and I sighed. I tilted my head up and met Arkkadian's smoldering gaze. His cerulean eyes bored into me, and my heart leaped into my throat. I swallowed, instantly becoming a bundle of nervous energy, and just like that, the evening's drama was all but forgotten. Right then, I wanted Arkkadian to kiss me. I stared and waited, too nervous and inexperienced to know how to make a move. I parted my lips and licked them in anticipation.

"Do you trust me?" he asked.

"Yes," I replied without hesitation. Butterflies took flight in my stomach, and I forced out a clipped breath.

And then he leaned in, brushing his lips ever so lightly across mine. I'd been waiting for this moment. I opened for him, and his tongue slowly dipped into my mouth, tasting me, exploring me. As he pulled his tongue back, I chased it with mine, unsure of what I should do. It wasn't like I had any experience to rely on.

I lay back on the pillows as Arkkadian kissed me from above, his hand still cupping my chin, his thumb stroking my cheek ever so gently. I tasted him as he had tasted me, our tongues playing a slow, sensuous game of tag. Then Arkkadian pulled away, leaving me breathless as he smiled down at me. Embarrassed by my inexperience, I tucked my head under his chin. I sucked on my bottom lip, trying to gather any trace left of his taste, wishing he would do that again.

"Hey," he said, tilting my chin up, so we were eye to eye again. His sultry smile made my toes curl. "You okay?"

"I... yes... I..." I stammered, my cheeks aflame with rising heat. Damn. That kiss was amazing. And I was messing this up. I let out a puff of air. "I'm okay. Better than okay, really. That was amazing. I just don't know what I'm doing."

Arkkadian let out a small chuckle. "You could have fooled me, love."

"I've never done that before. Not like that."

"Mm." And then he leaned in again, kissing me, teasing me. The tantalizing dance of his tongue lit my body on fire and made my toes curl again. His teeth scraped across my lower lip, nipping, and then Arkkadian slowly kissed down my chin and neck, and back up to the base of my ear. Little electric sparks rippled through me when he suckled on my earlobe, and I gasped at the sensation. My panties were instantly soaked, and I flushed at Arkkadian's slight chuckle. He could probably smell my arousal. Again. But this time, I wasn't embarrassed.

Excruciatingly slow, Arkkadian kissed his way back to my mouth and dipped his tongue in again. Instinctively, I sucked on the tip before he slid back out. Too soon, Arkkadian broke the connection between us. Catching my breath, I lay there staring at the ceiling as I basked in the afterglow of my first real kiss.

Wow. I didn't know a kiss could feel this incredible. If a kiss could make me feel like that, what would it feel like to make love? I didn't want to stop kissing him. I ran my hands up under his shirt, feeling the strength of his body above mine, but Arkkadian rolled back onto his side and stopped my hands from wandering.

I froze. "Did I do something wrong?"

"No, love. Not at all. You're perfect. As much as I would love to keep kissing you, I have to slow down or I may not stop. My wolf is bursting at the seams to claim you, but you're nowhere near ready for that. Not yet," he explained. "I would love to ravish you. To make love to you all night. But we should take this slow. Okay?"

"But what if I don't want to take this slow?" Whoa. Down, girl. Where did that come from?

"Trust me, love. This is about you. And making sure your needs are taken care of first. Like a lady should be taken care of, the right way. Not rushed. I'm trying to be a gentleman and you've had another long emotional day." A smile played across his face. "You are, however, are an excellent kisser."

Then he took my chin and planted one last kiss on my lips. "All right, love. Time for bed."

"But…"

He grinned. "Nope. Bed."

I could see I was getting nowhere. Fine. Plan B. I rolled over, climbed out of bed, and padded to the bathroom as seductively as I dared, shutting the door behind me. When I finished with what I needed to do, I slipped off the sweatpants he had given me and tossed them on the floor. The t-shirt Arkkadian had given me hung down to mid-thigh, leaving just enough leg showing to slake his thirst.

When I opened the bathroom door, Arkkadian was standing on the other side, a wicked grin on his face. Desire raced through my body, and my pulse quickened. My heart beat frantically with excitement.

I looked directly into his eyes and intentionally licked my lips. I wasn't sure what had gotten into me, but I wasn't giving up. A woman wants what a woman wants.

Arkkadian broke the stare and slowly lowered his gaze down my body. At the sight of my bare legs, a low, sexy growl escaped his throat. I bit my lip in anticipation as I gazed over the muscles emphasized by his tight shirt. And the very obvious, very large bulge in his pants.

He was all Alpha. And I... I wanted to surrender.

"I know what you're doing, Aislin."

I played coy, trying to keep my expression as innocent as possible. "I'm not doing anything."

Arkkadian's voice was husky. "You have a naughty streak, I see."

Moisture pooled between my legs at that smooth whiskey sound, the one that sent delicious shivers rippling down my spine. My knees went weak and almost buckled, and I gripped the doorjamb for support. Oh, God! How could he do that to me with just his voice?

"Damn." I hadn't realized I'd spoken the word aloud until Arkkadian's eyes zipped back up to mine. The sound of his voice and the view before me had sent my libido through the roof.

"We should remedy that potty mouth, shouldn't we?" A sly grin crossed his face.

"Sorry," I said unabashedly, letting my eyes roam up and down before meeting his again. "It's just when you talk like that, and you look like that..."

"Don't worry, you can make it up to me. Now's a good time, I think."

"Now?" I squeaked. "But didn't you say it was bedtime?"

My little act hadn't fooled him one bit. Arkkadian knew exactly what I wanted.

"Come now, love. You tease me like that and think you'll get away with it? Nah, I think we'll handle this bit of mischief right now. How many swats do you think should suffice?" Arkkadian grinned, and it made me want to bite his lip. This time, though, I knew it wouldn't be like the other spanking. I trembled with anticipation. I was horny as fuck, but my inexperience made me nervous.

I took a deep breath and let it out slowly. "What is it with you and spankings?"

"Mm. Just you wait." His eyes flashed a brilliant blue, promising something darker in their depths.

Arkkadian turned me toward the bed and pointed. When I didn't move just to push his buttons, he growled and gave me a quick swat on the butt.

"Go." A hint of Alpha graced the edge of that one word. I couldn't help but obey.

I sashayed over to the bed and sat down on the edge. Like a predator on the hunt, Arkkadian stalked toward me, his eyes locked on mine. They promised a fierce hunger. Beautiful danger. A dark desire waiting to consume me. I craved him as much as he craved me.

The closer he got, the farther back I had to tilt my head to look up at him. Towering above me, Arkkadian parted his lips and slowly, sensuously slid his tongue from side to side. And then, in the space of but one single heartbeat, he stripped his shirt and tossed it away.

I gasped, feeling every bit of his dominance race across the link and wrap around me like a soft, supple leather glove. It clung to me like a second skin, and at this moment, Arkkadian was pure, unadulterated Alpha. I reached a hand out to trace the lines defining his perfect abs, but a single shake of his head was enough to make me freeze. He was the predator, and I was his prize.

He loomed over me for a moment, letting the sexual tension soak into me before he finally sat down beside me. "Stand and face me."

I did as Arkkadian demanded, responding without hesitation.

"Take your shirt off," he ordered, his voice low and firm, yet smooth as velvet. My knees shook at the sound as I reached for the hem and slowly lifted the shirt. "Panties, too."

Holy shit. I was really doing this. Arkkadian never took his eyes off mine, and I couldn't look away.

I stood naked, silent under his appraisal, the cool air teasing my nipples. Then his eyes slid from mine to the scars marked upon my body, and I instinctively tried to cover them as all my insecurities bubbled up. I cast my eyes to the side, unable to meet his gaze.

Warm hands tugged at my own, and Arkkadian slowly pulled them away from my body. I tried to pull them back and cover myself again, but he wouldn't release me.

"Hey. Aislin. Look at me."

"Don't look at them. Please," I begged, closing my eyes as if doing so could block out the shame I felt at my disfigurement.

"Why not?"

"They're hideous. They make me ugly."

"Aislin, you are beautiful. Scars and all. They may be hard to look at, but every scar tells a story. Every single one of those scars tells us you fought a battle. That you lived. There is no shame in that. Now say it. You are beautiful."

"I am beautiful," I whispered.

"Louder."

"I am beautiful," I said, this time with more drive and I opened my eyes. It was empowering, and for the first time in my life, I truly felt beautiful.

"One more time. Louder," he commanded.

"I am beautiful." I stood tall and proud, feeling every bit of truth in those three simple words. Arkkadian didn't look at me like I was damaged or ugly. He looked at me like I was the most gorgeous woman he'd ever seen.

"Good. Don't you forget it. Now, where were we?"

Without warning, he grabbed my hand and tugged me down over his lap, my torso angled over the bed with my legs dangling down, my toes barely touching the floor. My center instantly blazed, my scars forgotten. I felt a gentle hand at the small of my back and another come to rest on my backside. The hand on my bottom began to move in slow delicious circles.

"Teasing me isn't very nice, now is it?" he asked. "Nor is cursing."

"No." I giggled. I couldn't help myself. I was giddy with lust.

"No, what?" he asked, continuing to rub sensuous circles over my skin.

"No, sir."

"I think five will do. Don't forget to count."

"Yes, sir." I sighed. The anticipation drove me crazy.

A slap came down across my right cheek. I barely felt the sting as Arkkadian rubbed the spot where he'd swatted me.

"One, sir." I giggled more.

"No giggling. This is a punishment." The seriousness of his words belied the lust in his tone.

Another slap, this time on my left cheek, a little harder, followed by his hand massaging the area. Like the first, it stung a little but didn't hurt.

"Two, sir."

I stifled my smile as best I could, and then another strike landed back on my right cheek. It ignited the sting from the first swat, and exquisite heat spread out across my backside. This time, a moan escaped my lips as he kneaded my soft flesh. I could barely get the words out as arousal spiked through me.

"Th-three, sir."

"Good girl." Arkkadian rained down another on my left cheek, the sting of the slap making me jump. Even while it stung slightly, liquid pooled between my legs.

"Four, sir."

This time, Arkkadian slid his fingers lower, and my legs parted of their own accord. I felt a finger slide between my folds, and I gasped, excited by the spark that soon followed. This was nothing like the first spanking. This was so much more.

The feeling disappeared as Arkkadian pulled away, leaving me ravenous, but then I felt a quick tug of my clitoris. I bucked my hips in response and begged for more.

Instead, Arkkadian pulled away. "Uh uh. Not so fast."

He rained one last slap down on my backside, catching both of my cheeks at the same time. The final blow stung the worst, but wasn't nearly enough to cause any pain. No, it sparked more desire. More heat. More lust.

"Five, sir!" I moaned, my body jerking upward in response.

The hand on my lower back pushed me back onto the bed ever so gently, and fingers returned to my wet folds, sliding and teasing, pressing upon my sweet little nub. Snippets of fire danced across my skin, sending the heat in my core racing all the way to my toes. My toes curled into the plush carpet, and I relished in the delicious sensation between my legs. I didn't know how else to describe it, but it was like tiny little shocks firing milliseconds apart, making all my nerve endings explode.

I wanted more.

Arkkadian slid a finger inside, torturously slow, and began working it in and out of my wet sheath. I shivered with wanton lust as he invaded my most private space. A second finger soon followed, gliding smoothly in and out as my juices flowed around them. When he hooked his fingers in a come-hither motion, sliding the tips across that little ridge of hidden magic deep inside, I nearly came undone.

Then his thumb found my clitoris again, circling in slow, tantalizing circles. Round and round. Back and forth. My hips bucked. Little sighs and moans of pleasure slipped from my throat. I scrunched the sheets in my fists, undulating my hips just enough to match the cosmic rhythm set by Arkkadian as he ground his fingers into me.

"That's it. Come for me, love." The command in Arkkadian's deep velvety voice set me off like a rocket, shooting straight into the stratosphere.

I let slip a cry of sinful rapture as every neuron, every synapse, every fiber of my being exploded into brilliant bits of golden light that filled my vision and showered down around me as I came down the other side.

Mind blank, breathing heavy, I collapsed onto the bed in a state of heady euphoria. I lay with my eyes closed and a grin across my lips as Arkkadian slipped out from underneath me. I was too tired to move or even speak. The orgasm had pulled every last vestige of energy from me. Then Arkkadian picked me up, shifted my limp body up onto the pillow, and pulled the covers over me. He placed a kiss upon my temple.

"Where are you going?" I asked, unable to stifle a yawn. I watched him stoke the fire beneath half-lidded eyes that threatened to close. "Aren't you coming to bed?"

He grinned. "Of course. You think I'd miss sleeping next to you?"

With that, the darkness pulled me under.

24

ARKKADIAN

S tanding by the hearth, staring at the flickers of firelight, I listened to Aislin's even breathing while she slept. She was exhausted, both mentally and physically. I hadn't planned for that to happen, feeling sex was the last thing she needed after an emotionally draining night like tonight. It wouldn't have been right to rush straight into something that intimate so soon, but I'd let the urge temporarily get the better of me.

In the end, though, my mate had needed the release. She'd needed our connection to prove the one thing she'd been seeking since her arrival here, and that was the truth of our bond. Afterward, it had taken every ounce of willpower to stop there, despite my wolf begging for his own release. Thankfully, Aislin had quickly fallen into slumber, giving me the excuse I needed to end it. I tossed a couple more logs onto the coals, climbed into bed, pulled her up against me, and wrapped my arms around her.

"Sleep, love," I whispered, even though my mate wouldn't hear the words.

I lay there next to her, enjoying the feel of her body against mine while I listened to the crackle of the flames in the fireplace. My wolf, somewhat content for now, finally settled. Sleep would not come for me though, not for a while. There was just too much going on in my head, and I lost track of time. I hadn't expected her to trust me so quickly. Despite her earlier reservations, the walls surrounding Aislin were crumbling faster than I could have ever imagined.

OVER THE NEXT TWO WEEKS, a comfortable routine developed between us. Most of my time was spent keeping the compound running smoothly, updating security, and filtering through Pack complaints.

Aislin spent her afternoons visiting Sara, and the rest of her time reading some of the books in my personal collection. Seeing her smile so brightly when she got herself lost between the pages was a balm to my wolf. So when I discovered how much she loved to read, I reminded myself I'd have to take her to the library one day soon.

We spent all our meals and spare time together, stealing glances or small touches here or there, and occasionally a quick kiss when I'd come home for lunch or dinner. Every night, she slept peacefully beside me, wrapped in my arms, but we hadn't shared another intimate moment since that night. My wolf champed at the bit constantly, but I was doing my best not to rush Aislin even though she now knew the truth of our connection.

When the time was right, I would make her mine, but not until I was sure she was ready and not just lust-drunk. I'd spent many mornings and nights in the shower easing the beast or taking runs with Gideon to help curb the need. My wolf wasn't happy being denied.

Aislin had been relatively quiet and reserved most of the time. I knew she was spending much of her time reflecting on every-thing that had happened over previous days, and she was still grieving the loss of her dearest friends. We still hadn't finished our discussion, and there was so much more she needed to know, but I was determined to let her take the lead and come to me when she was ready to learn more.

I woke early Sunday morning and let Aislin sleep. Once dressed, I made my way to the kitchen and put on a pot of coffee. When it was ready, I took my mug to the den and turned on the morning news, only to discover the authorities had finally identi-fied the two bodies. It'd taken them long enough. They listed one

Edgar Taggert, and Paige, Aislin's best friend and roommate. There was no mention of Kane West.

Preoccupied with the news, I hadn't heard Aislin come down the stairs, and she'd picked that exact moment to walk through the door.

The mug she held dropped to the hardwood and shattered on impact. Steaming coffee splattered in every direction. She jerked with a hiss of pain when the hot liquid streaked across her bare legs. She was wearing a pink camisole and shorts, not the t-shirt she had slept in last night, and her hair was damp. Tears rolled down her cheeks.

I jumped up from my chair and pulled her over to the couch and then grabbed a towel from the kitchen to dry her legs and clean up the mess on the floor. Her skin was red but otherwise unharmed. Her tears weren't from the coffee.

Aislin sat in complete silence, her silver eyes glued to the screen and swirling with sadness. I grabbed the remote to turn it off, but she stayed my hand. I sat down beside her, and she leaned into me, seeking support. The authorities were still calling the situation a robbery. They didn't know if there had been any accomplices since the fire had burned everything beyond recognition, but they'd at least identified the bodies and announced when their services would be. We both knew better.

When the story was over, I shut it off. The two of us sat silently together, Aislin wrapped in my arms with her head tucked under my chin. I held her, giving her the time she needed to process everything.

"Arkkadian? I...." she started but stopped. I waited. "I really want to go. Please?" Her voice was small. Timid. And her messy hair drifted down over her shoulders as she dropped her head, looking at the floor. She hid her face from me, already knowing the answer.

"I'm sorry, but the answer is still no," I told her. "We still don't know where Kane is. It's not safe right now."

Aislin pulled away. "Arkkadian, please?" she begged. Her silver eyes darkened, and I sensed her anger bubbling up. "I just want to say goodbye. I n-need to say goodbye. Besides, I need more clothes. I only have a few days' worth. I can't keep washing laundry every couple of days. We can kill two birds with one stone while we're in town."

"Aislin, I said no. My job is to keep you safe. And if you need clothes, you can borrow some from Sara or some of the other women here. They won't mind."

She stood up, breathing slow and heavy, and I sensed the ire she was about to unleash upon me. If I didn't curb the anger now, she'd end up over my knee again. Not that I minded, but I wouldn't put up with a tantrum.

"But you have a security team. Can't you bring them?"

"Aislin. Stop. I said no, and that's the end," I ground out.

"Gah!" she screamed. "This is so unfair! I hate my life!"

"Careful," I told her, letting the Alpha warning fill the air.

She stopped in her tracks and glared at me. "You wouldn't."

I crossed to where she stood and put a finger to her lips in warning. I would. And she damn well knew it. Her eyes burned with pure fury at being denied.

"Unless you want to find yourself over my knee, I suggest you settle down," I warned again, deadly calm.

Her eyes grew round and her face flushed before she shot daggers my way. With her breathing loud and ragged, I could feel her anger swirling around us, like Hades about to open the floodgates of hell.

Aislin turned on her heel and stormed out of the den. She stomped her feet as she ran up the stairs, and then she slammed the bedroom door. Another scream echoed through the air. I didn't blame her for being upset, but she also needed to understand the danger of the situation she was in. I'd thought she had as the days had passed, but apparently not.

I let her be for now. We both needed to cool off, and I'd rather she excused herself than throw a fit.

I busied myself making breakfast instead, and soon, the delicious aroma of sizzling bacon, potatoes, and eggs filled the air. I took two place settings from the cupboard and set them on the counter. Just as I turned off the burners, the door upstairs opened, as I suspected it would. I could hear Aislin's bare feet slowly pad down the stairs and then she appeared in the doorway, fully dressed, hair braided.

"Hi," I greeted. "Feeling any better?"

She nodded, keeping her eyes downcast. My mate couldn't look any more sheepish if she tried.

"Good. Let's eat."

Without being asked, she set the table. We ate most of our meal in silence, Aislin preferring to spend most of her time staring out the window. Children played with a soccer ball out on the green, and occasionally, she let slip a half-smile while she watched. I waited until our stomachs were full to speak.

"Listen. Let me talk to Gideon and my team," I said. Honestly, with a security team on standby, there wasn't a reason to keep her from the memorial service. Her ears perked up, but she continued to stare out the window. "I won't make any promises, but if we can come up with a plan, then maybe we can make a trip to town. But don't get your hopes up."

Her head turned, and her eyes drifted up to mine. "Okay. I can live with that."

"Like I said, no promises. I need you to understand how dangerous your situation is. In fact, we've put everything off long enough."

25

AISLIN

An hour later, I waited in the den, pacing in front of the fireplace with my stomach full of knots. What else was there to talk about? Hadn't I been through enough already? The past two weeks had only been a passing lull in the inevitable storm that was now my life.

I stopped pacing when the front door opened. Sara's head poked around the corner with a smile, and then she rushed in to greet me with a hug. Gideon and Arkkadian followed behind her. Gideon nodded hello, and I half-smiled in return. I was glad to see Sara again, but the trepidation I felt overshadowed seeing her. I knew Arkkadian had called them here for my benefit, which probably meant shit was about to hit the fan. Again.

Great. I sat next to Sara on the couch. Gideon parked in the window seat overlooking the valley. All eyes were on Arkkadian. I steeled myself for what may come and gripped Sara's hand. Arkkadian didn't even ease into the conversation; he went straight for the kill. My family. The one thing I knew nothing about.

"I know we've gone over this, but is there anything else at all you remember prior to the accident? Anything about your family?" he asked.

I shook my head. "No. Nothing."

"I've been doing some research, and this arrived yesterday. It affirms what I've long since suspected." Arkkadian pulled two files from his desk and handed them to me.

I opened the first one to find a printed copy of a birth record and a certified birth certificate I'd never seen before. I scanned both pages, finding my name and birth date easily enough. Listed at the bottom of the birth certificate were two names. Wren and Alaric Barrington. Like a dagger straight to the heart, a fierce ache struck me right in the chest.

Both pieces of paper slipped from my hands and drifted to the floor where I continued to stare at them, frozen in place. Words escaped me. I knew those names. I'd never heard them before, but I knew, beyond any shadow of a doubt, they were my parents. I scrubbed both hands over my face. I didn't know whether I was elated at finding out their names, or angry they'd been taken from me.

Sara picked the slips of paper up and placed them back in the folder. The movement snapped me out of my head, and I opened the second to find a copy of an old news article. According to the date printed in the corner, I'd have been just seven years old. My stomach flip-flopped as I read. I remembered it like it was yesterday. I read halfway before I had to shove the page back into the folder, unable to finish. I let out a breath I hadn't realized I was holding.

The dagger in my chest twisted this way and that, slicing my heart in half. My hand went to my side, brushing against the scars that marked my torso. I trembled as the memory of a fair-skinned woman with raven hair flashed through my mind. She was my mother.

Arkkadian reached into his desk drawer one more time and pulled out a photograph. He handed it to me, face down. My hands shook as I took the photo from him. I stared at the back of it with apprehension, afraid of what I'd see.

"When you're ready," he said.

With hands still shaking, I flipped it over and saw the woman I'd just imagined, and a brown-haired man next to her. Except for my hair, I looked like her, but I had his eyes. Silver eyes rimmed in black.

My parents.

"Yes," Arkkadian answered. I hadn't realized I'd spoken aloud.

"What happened to them?" I asked, anxiously tapping my foot on the floor.

He bowed his head, and I tried to swallow the lump in my throat. I'd sought answers my entire life, and now, sitting right here on the precipice, I feared everything I was about to hear. But I feared the unknown even more.

"They were murdered. Presumably by the same man who did that to you." He nodded at my hand, still upon my side.

I pulled my hand away, thinking of what lay beneath the fabric. I listened with rapt attention as Arkkadian told the story and how the man thought to have killed them disappeared. How my grandfather, a Vamphyre, had ordered their execution. How they believed my existence was kept secret to keep me safe.

"Wait. So not only are there shapeshifters, but now you're telling me there are vampires? Like bump in the night, suck your blood, rip your throat out vampires?" I asked, unable to hide my skepticism. Wolves I could believe, but vampires? Fate was seriously fucking with me.

"Vamphyre is their true name, but yes," Gideon answered. He pronounced it like "vam-fear," correcting my pronunciation, surprisingly without sarcasm this time. "But most of them aren't the killers you think they are."

"Do I have any other family?"

"Yes. You've two uncles, Rhett and Rafe Vane. Rhett is a lot like your mother. The two of them were very close. We suspect he's the one who saved your life. Rafe is much like your grandfather. Neither he nor Arden will hesitate to kill you. To the two of them, you're an abomination. Your existence directly violates First Law as the descendant of both Lycan and Vamphyre lines. Fortunately for you, we don't think they know about you. Alaric's father, your other grandfather, is Mathias Barrington. He's the current Alpha of the Pacific Rim Pack out of Vancouver. Rain wolves," Arkkadian explained.

"Does Mathias know?" I asked.

Arkkadian shook his head. "No. At least we don't believe so. If he does, then he's hidden the secret well, but I can't foresee him having left you in foster care. It's not his style. My security team knows you're here, but we're keeping this on the down-low for the time being. Arden Vane will kill you just for existing. He'll see your existence as a failure to stamp out his daughter's betrayal of the Coven. Others could seek to use you against us and you already know what Kane is capable of."

I pulled my braids out and ran my hands through my hair, scratching my scalp. Staring at the floor, I rested my elbows on my knees and let my hair fall down around me, hiding my face from everyone in the room while I tried to make sense of everything I'd just heard.

This was too much. How did my life come to this? A few weeks ago, I was just a girl working two jobs, eking through life as best I could. Now I was being thrust into a supernatural world I never knew existed, a world where my own flesh and blood wanted to see me dead and buried simply for being born. All I could do was sit there and shake my head. Just when I thought things were finally returning to normal, my world came crashing down again.

"What now?" I asked.

"That's what Arkkadian and I have been trying to work out," Gideon said from the window seat. "We can't keep you a secret forever."

"I can't stay here. I can't. I need to go." Saying the words killed me. This place had become my home. Arkkadian was home. But me being here... I was putting everyone in danger.

"Aislin, you know you can't leave."

"I know, I know. It's not safe." Fidgeted in my seat, I ran my hands through my hair, flexing my fingers before curling them into fists. "Well, it's not safe for me to stay either! What about all these people? If my grandfather's as dangerous as you say, what's stopping him from hurting everyone here? It's already my fault Paige and Carter are dead. I won't be responsible for more deaths. I can't do this, Arkkadian. I can't deal with any more death!" I let out a scream through clenched teeth and stomped a foot on the floor, willing myself not to cry.

Arkkadian came around the desk and pulled me up to face him. He pulled my hands down from my face and tipped my chin up. His glowing eyes, no longer shocking, showed a warm resolve and the desire to protect me.

"Stop. None of this is your fault, Aislin."

"But—"

He stopped me with one look. That Alpha look he was so good at. God! Why wouldn't he listen to me?

"Listen. At some point, we'll have to break the block in your memory. It won't be pretty. In fact, it'll probably be pretty horrifying, but it's the only way I know to find the truth of what actually happened to your parents. We need to know what we're dealing with," he said.

"No. The last time you did your weird shadow trick thing, I spent hours vomiting up my insides. I'm not doing that again," I told him vehemently, shaking my head forcefully. Just the thought of it made my stomach want to retch.

"Relax. I don't mean right now. You'll need the strength of the bond for that," he said. "Fewer side effects. And I won't mate with you until you decide you're ready."

I let out a small sarcastic laugh. I couldn't stay, and I couldn't leave. I was an unwilling prisoner to the fates. Then a thought occurred to me.

I could run. Leave the state. Go east. Canada. Mexico. Anywhere but here. Shapeshifters. Vamphyre. Immortals. Mates. No, no, and no! The next time I was alone, I was packing my bag and getting the hell out of Dodge. Though Arkkadian had paid off my credit cards, I was reluctant to use them. I had enough emergency cash in savings to get by for a month or two, at least until I found a new job somewhere. I couldn't stay here.

"Mates," I said, shaking my head. "Arkkadian, your people aren't safe with me here. Don't you get it?" I had to leave. I needed him to listen. I needed him to understand.

"You know it's true, Aislin. Instinct doesn't lie. You feel it every time we're together. Every time we touch. You can fight it all you want, but eventually, the fates will have their way," he told me. "I will protect you, and I will protect my people just as I've always done."

"How are you so sure?" I asked, even though I knew he was right, despite my misgivings.

"Because you and I, we weren't written in the sand. We were written in the stars."

Why did he have to say such beautiful things? The words cut

through my already torn heart. It only made it that much harder for me to do what I needed to do. Fuck the fates. I would not cause more innocent deaths.

Tears stung my eyes. I couldn't sit here any longer. I couldn't let my desire or my feelings for Arkkadian get in the way, so I left everyone in the den and went upstairs. I needed time to think and time to plan. I knew full well it would break his heart. And mine. But two broken hearts were better than a few hundred dead.

26

ARKKADIAN

L ater that night, a small whimper pulled me from sleep. Aislin's body trembled in my arms. I watched and waited, hoping it would pass, but the trembling and whimpering continued. She was dripping in sweat. I laid a hand on her forehead and was shocked to find her burning up. As immortals, we never got sick. We didn't get viruses or catch diseases. We didn't get cancer. This was highly unusual.

I barely had any time to ponder what could be wrong, when unexpectedly, a mass of images flooded into my mind the moment our skin touched. Aislin was in the midst of a dream so vivid, I felt like I'd been sucked through a time warp. Instantly, I was there, seeing everything through her eyes. Through the eyes of a small, terrified child.

A raging inferno filled my vision, and terror flooded me. Everywhere I looked, flames roared around me, destroying everything in sight. The curtains shriveled under the onslaught. Paint bubbled and peeled off the walls, crackling as it split. Windows shattered from the searing heat. Snarls and growls leaked through the wall of fire, but I couldn't see through to the other side.

"Mommy! Daddy!" I screamed, but no one answered. It was so hot. I didn't know what to do. Sweat dripped down my face and neck. My hair and clothes stuck to my skin and made me itch.

A shout sounded over the crackle of flames. "Run! Aislin, run!" And then the voice was gone.

I spun around to flee and smacked into a giant of a man looming over me, a wicked smile lighting up his face. No, not a man. A monster. His glowing eyes were as red as the blood dripping down his arms and hands. He grabbed a handful of my hair and dragged me kicking and screaming down the hall, leaving the fire behind as he kicked a door open and threw me onto the floor. Large hands tore at my clothes, shredding them to pieces. A knife flashed, and I knew excruciating pain. Felt the biting sting as it sliced through my tender skin. Slice. Slice. Slice. Over and over it cut. I begged for help, but none came. The monster laughed sadistically as he cut away at me. He was pure evil, wretched and unfettered.

I lay there bleeding while he stood over me, laughing and licking my blood off the knife. Out of nowhere, a fist burst through his chest. Blood sprayed, raining down upon me. In its grip, a bloody heart still pumping, the red viscous liquid squirting out of it in pulsing spurts. His glowing eyes widened in shock.

Then the hand pulled away, taking the fist-sized organ of life with it. The monster's scarlet eyes went dark, and he crumpled to the ground, his mouth ajar in a silent scream. Uncle Rhett stood in his place, and the still-beating, bloody heart dropped from his hand, landing with a sickening squelch on the carpet. I watched it, unable to take my eyes off the bloody muscle until its uneven pumping slowed to a stop.

I blinked, and I was instantly back in the comfort of my bed beside Aislin, my skin dripping with sweat. My t-shirt was soaked. Aislin thrashed beside me, eyes open and unseeing, screaming into the night. What had started as a dream had now become a full-blown night terror. Was this what she saw every time she dreamed?

Fuck! What have I done? Had I unwittingly caused this? I racked my brain, trying to understand what had happened, but I didn't have an explanation. Nor had I ever heard of something similar happening. Usually, mental blocks had to be broken, but somehow, Aislin's dream had been strong enough to project itself into my mind. Or suck me into hers. I wasn't sure which, and I was confused as hell.

I backed out of the bed as slowly as I could without disturbing her and went to clean myself up. There was nothing I could do for her in that state except wait it out. I returned with a bowl of cold water and a damp cloth, which I set on the nightstand, and then I sat by the fire and waited, feeling guilt ridden and utterly helpless.

Mostly, Aislin's nights had been uneventful, but an occasional nightmare or terror would crop up. Tonight's was worse than usual, like the one she'd had her first night here. I watched for nearly an hour as Aislin writhed in the sheets. When she finally stopped, I placed the cool, damp cloth on her forehead, breathing a sigh of relief when she didn't stir. I wanted to disturb what sleep she got as little as possible.

By now, it was nearly five in the morning. After what I'd just witnessed, I didn't think I'd be going back to sleep any time soon. I rinsed and cooled the cloth several more times, replacing it every time it warmed up. Half an hour later, she still hadn't moved, so I set the cloth aside and let her be while I took a shower.

I rested my head against the tile, letting the hot water run over me. The images from Aislin's nightmare bombarded me, and before I could stop it, my stomach heaved. I dropped to my knees and retched repeatedly. The bile from my empty stomach left my mouth feeling fuzzy and acidic.

I could still hear the terrified screams in my ears. I could still feel the piercing pain of the knife slicing across my skin as if I'd actually been there. I could still hear the maniacal laughter of Ryker Slade as he tortured Aislin's tiny body. I could still picture the pulsing, bleeding heart where Rhett Vane had dropped it on the floor.

My inner beast was awake and enraged. Uncontrollable wrath bubbled up and threatened to boil over. I shut the water off, the urge to kill feeding that wrath even more. I didn't even bother to dry off before I took off down the stairs at a dead run, jumped off the porch, and shifted in mid-air.

I raced up one of the trails leading into the surrounding mountains. The cold morning air ruffled my black fur, but instead of finding it soothing, it rankled. I circled around the Eagle Ridge territory three times before the compulsion to rip Ryker Slade's head off cooled enough to let me think rationally. The Vamphyre leader's second was dead, but that didn't stop me from wanting to murder him all over again for what he'd done. He was lucky he wasn't alive or I would hunt him to the ends of the earth. I guess I had Rhett Vane to thank for that. If I ever met the man, I'd shake his hand.

I approached the lake just as the sun peeked over the horizon, and I lapped at the water's edge, letting the cool water slake my thirst. I took a few peaceful moments to watch the sunrise before racing back home. It wouldn't be long before Aislin would awaken, and I didn't want my mate to wake up alone. Not after a dream like that.

She was still asleep when I entered the master bedroom, so I hopped in the shower once again to wash the sweat off my body. It occurred to me that her dream had given me exactly what I needed to know. Gideon and I both assumed we'd need to break the block. Maybe we wouldn't need to, but I sure as hell needed a better understanding of what had happened. And knowing what I know now, it changed my whole perspective. Did I really want to subject my mate to memories that horrific?

When I emerged from the closet fully dressed, Aislin was sitting up in bed. Her skin was pale and one hand covered her eyes as she cradled her head.

"You okay, love?" I asked, padding over to sit beside her. I felt her forehead with the back of my hand. She was a little warm, but nothing like earlier, the dream fever having receded. Black circles had formed under her eyes, denoting her lack of proper rest. I worried I had caused her this discomfort when I'd inadvertently gotten sucked into her dream.

"My head is killing me."

I offered her pain meds and ushered her into the bathroom, thinking a shower might do her some good. I left her there to wash up. I was just setting the table for breakfast when she came down the stairs. She was wearing a pair of my sweats and one of my t-shirts again, and her hair was damp, hanging limply over her shoulders. Her face was still fairly pale.

"Feeling any better?" I asked, feeling her forehead again before taking her face in my hands and looking her over.

"Not really. I think maybe I just need a little something to eat. I'll be fine."

"Breakfast is on the table. Do you remember anything from last night?"

She nodded as she sat. "I had that stupid dream again. It's always the same. Fire and the sound of a child screaming."

I watched her fill her plate before sitting down across from her. I was still overcome with guilt, even though I'd had no control over what had happened.

"Do you remember anything else?" I wanted to know if she'd had any recollection of the vision I'd witnessed.

"No. Just fire and screams. It's always the same. You'd think after so many years the dream would evolve, but that's all I ever remember," she explained, sounding exhausted. Her head was slumped to the side, propped up on her hand where she rested her elbow on the table. "Why do you ask?"

"Because something strange happened last night."

Aislin froze, mouth open, fork in mid-air.

"It's okay," I assured her. "You were trembling in your sleep and drenched in sweat. I think your headache is because of me, and I'm sorry. I placed my hand on your forehead, thinking maybe you were sick, which is unusual because we don't get sick. I don't know what happened, but it's like I was pulled straight into your dream. There was nothing I could do, and I was stuck there until it ended."

"You were in my head? You should have asked!" Her breathing quickened, and she pushed away from the table but remained in her seat. The look of betrayal on her face made my heart sink. I'd violated her. Not intentionally, but it was still a violation. That it wasn't intentional didn't make the guilt I felt any better, though.

"I apologize. It just happened. It wasn't intentional. I just got sucked in. I didn't know something like that was even possible, Aislin. That's not how it's supposed to work, but I saw everything. Enough that I don't think we need to break the memory block. Not unless you want me to." I kept my voice low and soft, hoping to allay her fears. The last thing I wanted to do was send her into a downward spiral of angry panic, but things didn't always play out the way we wanted.

"What did you see?" she asked, her back rigid and anger etched into her flushed face. She was right to be mad.

"Aislin...." I stopped and looked away, unable to meet her eyes.

What I'd seen had been distressing. Was she ready for it? I couldn't swallow past the elephant-sized lump in my throat.

"Tell me," she demanded. The ire burning within her stung as it filtered through our connection. I wanted to protect her from the things I saw, but doing so wouldn't earn me any trust at this moment. Any trust I'd previously built back up between us was probably gone for good this time.

My stomach rolled as I thought about the dream. I turned back toward her and huffed. "Aislin, what I saw, it's the stuff of nightmares. It makes me sick just thinking about it. Are you sure you want to know?"

"Please don't make me ask again." Her jaw ticked as she angrily ground out the words.

"Your dream, it pulled me in. It was like I was living it through you. I saw the fire, heard voices telling you to run. And then I saw the man who hurt you. I saw... I saw what he did to you. And then I saw your uncle Rhett kill him," I explained. I couldn't relay the gory details. As much as it sickened me, I couldn't let it destroy my resolve. I was an Alpha, and I would handle this.

Aislin ran a hand through her hair as the other went to her side. "Who?"

The lone word hung in the air for a moment before I answered. She stared straight at the wall in front of her, refusing to look at me while she waited for an answer.

"Ryker Slade. He was your grandfather's right hand. They called him the Blade because he liked to torture his victims by slicing up their skin before he killed them. Arden Vane sent him to kill your parents, and he must have found you there. Rhett, your uncle, found you and killed him before he could finish. The dream ended there. I won't tell you the bloody details. I can't bear it again," I said. The bile rose in my throat again just thinking about it. Instead, I walked to the sink and rinsed my mouth while I tried not to retch.

"Why don't I remember this? Why do I just see fire and hear screaming?"

"It's the memory block. They're not perfect. They're meant to block everything, but sometimes little bits sneak past." I gave her a moment to process that bit of information. "Come on, you should eat something. It will make you feel better. I really am sorry."

I watched as she pulled her chair back up to the table and slowly ate. Satisfied, I dug into my own meal, forcing myself to eat despite my lack of appetite. We ate most of the meal in silence again, and when we finished, she excused herself to go lie down. She'd at least gotten some color back, but she still looked exhausted.

I needed to meet with my security team for updates, so I went upstairs to let Aislin know I'd return in a few short hours. She was sound asleep in my bed, so I left a note on the nightstand telling her to help herself to lunch if I wasn't back by then and left. I hated leaving her, but duty called.

27

AISLIN

As soon as I heard the door shut downstairs, I listened for any other sounds. When I heard nothing, I peeked my head out of the bedroom door. The house was silent. I slipped down the stairs and poked around, but Arkkadian had left. My ruse had worked. I had at least a two-hour head start if I hurried.

Back upstairs, I quickly dressed, then shoved as much of my stuff into my backpack as I could. What didn't fit, I stuffed into the paper bag I'd saved from Paige's shopping trip.

I snagged a few snacks from the kitchen, and then frantically searched the house for car keys. I finally found a set in Arkkadian's desk.

The sky had darkened drastically since breakfast. Rolling gray storm clouds blocked out the sun. It smelled like rain, and the heavy static in the air made the hair on the back of my neck and arms stand up. In the distance, dry lightning ripped across the horizon.

Thunder cracked and bellowed as the clouds roiled above. Not long and the storm would drench the compound. I needed to leave now if I wanted to make good time before the rain fell. An urgent sense of foreboding filled me, but I pushed it back down. If I listened to it, I'd never leave.

I unlocked the black SUV and climbed in, tossing my bags in the passenger seat. I hoped the tinted windows were dark enough to hide my identity as I drove away. I started the vehicle and waited, watching to see if anyone came running, but no one did. All was quiet, so I slowly pulled out onto the main road.

I wasn't sure which way to go, so I picked the direction of the valley since it sat at the southern end of the compound. Arkkadian had said it was nearly a three-hour drive south to Whitewater, and the closest road out of here was in that direction. I prayed it would lead me to the way out. I drove slowly, so as not to draw attention to myself. I didn't pass anyone on the road through the valley, but I unexpectedly came upon a guardhouse on the other side. A young man poked his head out with a friendly smile and signaled for me to stop. Fuck! I pretended not to see him and drove on past.

When I looked in the rearview mirror, the young man ran after me as he yelled into a handheld radio. Shit! I hit the gas and tore off down the dirt road as fast as I dared. Just up ahead, the road curved to the right around a hillside, and I came upon a fork. I picked the branch leading south and sped off again. I had no idea where I was, but heading that direction had seemed like the best plan overall.

Giant raindrops began pelting the windshield, and before long, visibility dwindled. I couldn't see more than thirty feet ahead, but I didn't dare let up on the gas. It was stupid in this weather, but I didn't have a choice. I had to get away. I wasn't safe here, and neither was anyone else until I left. I would never forgive myself if anything happened to Arkkadian's Pack. I had to keep them safe. Mate or not, I wouldn't endanger them any longer.

I kept my foot on the gas, speeding down the bumpy mountain road. Potholes made the vehicle jerk and swerve on the dirt. I didn't dare let my white-knuckle grip on the wheel slip. Every time I came to a fork, I always took the path leading south. The scenery blurred as I sped by. Eventually, hail slapped down from above and cracked the windshield. Ignoring it, I continued to push on the gas.

An hour down the road, I came upon a curve much too fast. The SUV slid to the left on the muddy track. I slammed on the brakes and yanked the wheel, trying to avoid a boulder sitting just off the shoulder on the left side of the road. Just beyond it, a steep embankment gave way at the bottom to a swatch of trees. I hit a puddle and lost control as the vehicle hydroplaned across the murky water.

I wasn't quick enough to crank the wheel, and the front driver's side hit the boulder square on. My window shattered and bits of glass sprayed all around me, nicking my skin as it flew every which way. The vehicle flipped sideways over the boulder and tumbled down the hillside. Over and over I flipped, my head bouncing between the window and the steering wheel. The skin on my face and arms stung as pieces of glass sliced into me.

The vehicle crashed into a tree at the bottom, its descent halting abruptly and leaving me suspended upside down. My hand came away from my face covered in blood. My head throbbed. Everything hurt. Before I could unlatch my seat belt, my vision swam and then the world went black.

28

ARKKADIAN

The radio crackled to life and Eric, the young shifter on guard duty, shouted through the speakers. He was one of the newest members of Pack security, barely twenty years old and still in training.

"Anyone know what's going on? The Alpha just drove by the guardhouse without stopping. I tried to flag him down, but he just took off!"

"Fuck!" I shouted, and all eyes turned to me. Gideon was out of his seat before I could blink. "She's running. We need to go. Now!"

Gideon grabbed a radio and told the gate guard we were on the way.

"Alpha, what's going on?" James asked.

"My mate. We need to find her," I yelled as I burst toward the door, my security team following close behind. Shit. I stopped in my tracks, my men nearly crashing into me from behind. This wasn't how I expected them to find out, but they needed to know what they were up against.

"Wait. Before we leave, there's something all of you need to know. This doesn't leave this room under any circumstances. Do you understand?"

"Alpha, what's go—"

"Let me finish," I said, cutting James off. I closed my eyes and huffed. "My mate is the granddaughter of Arden Vane."

One by one, my men looked me in the eye, stood tall, and

nodded in understanding. They knew the story, and being my mate, they would protect Aislin with their lives.

"We'll find her, Alpha. Tell us the rest later," Corbin said, and we piled into the SUVs parked in front of the security building. Gideon and I climbed into the first, James and Madigan in the second, and Corbin in the last. They knew the plan. Each vehicle would take a different route, searching until they found her and brought her back.

Gideon hit the gas, and the vehicle roared down the road. Off in the distance, lightning blazed across the sky. Rain pelted our vehicles. It wouldn't be long before the heavy rain made the winding mountain roads too treacherous to travel. We stopped at the guardhouse, only giving Eric an abbreviated version and telling him not to speak to anyone about it. The others followed behind, and at the first fork, I told Gideon to take the southern route knowing she'd head straight back to Whitewater.

James followed behind us while Corbin took the other fork in the road, and we continued south. If I was Aislin, that's what I'd do. I hoped she wouldn't take a wrong turn and get lost. If that happened, it could take us hours or even days to find her.

At the second fork, James veered off while Gideon and I again continued south.

About an hour later, Gideon rounded a curve and slammed on the breaks. Skid marks in the mud disappeared down the embankment. A swipe of black paint marred the surface of a boulder on the side of the road, and my wolf scrambled to get free. Where was she? Where was my mate? Like salt in a wound, dread burned in my gut. Something was very wrong.

We couldn't have been but fifteen minutes behind her. I jumped out and ran over to the shoulder. Tiny pellets of hail slammed into me, but I barely felt the sting in my rush to find my mate. The SUV lay upside down at the bottom of the embankment. The wreckage leaned at an awkward angle against a tree with its wheels in the air. All the windows were shattered, and the body dented to hell and back.

I stopped short at the sight before me, not believing what I was seeing, only running again when Gideon zipped past me down the hill. Fear coiled around me, strangling my heart like a python devouring its latest meal.

"Aislin!" I screamed. "Aislin!"

Please be alive!

I screamed her name repeatedly as I ran. There was no answer. At the bottom, we climbed around to the other side and found her suspended upside down, unconscious. Blood smeared her face, dripping down onto the ceiling of the SUV, where it pooled in the fabric beneath her.

"Aislin! Wake up! Come on, love, wake up!" She didn't move.

Gideon used a knife to cut the straps free as I held her, trying to keep her from falling down onto her head. We slowly pulled her from the wreckage, keeping her head and neck as stable as possible, and laid her down on a soft patch of grass. Gideon ran back up to the SUV and radioed for a medic. The minutes dragged by as we waited.

Her pulse was strong, but the gash on her forehead continued to bleed. Blood covered both arms, tacky in its half-dried state as the bleeding slowed from all the tiny cuts where the shattered glass had cut her. I ripped my shirt off, rolled it into a ball, and held it to the gash on her forehead to staunch the free flow of blood. Unlike the cuts on her arms, the small head wound showed no signs of slowing down.

The world around me receded to nothing. My mate lay broken and bloody on the ground before me. Her left wrist twisted at an awkward angle. I saw and heard nothing but her. Hell, I couldn't put a coherent thought together if I tried.

I felt a hand on my shoulder pulling me back, and a snarl tore through me. "Don't touch her!" I bellowed, the madness of desperation creeping in.

"Arkken, it's me. It's Gideon," my brother soothed. I almost didn't recognize him.

"Get away from her! Don't touch her!" Fury consumed me, tearing through me like a raging hellfire of chaos and destruction.

"Arkken, I won't hurt her. Let me look at her," he said, not kowtowing to the Alpha order in my voice. Gideon was the only one who could get away with that usually. But without warning, the wolf ripped out of me with a ferocious roar.

I stood over Aislin's body, snarling and gnashing my teeth. No one would touch her! She was mine! The dangerous combination of desperation and rage had turned me into more beast than wolf, willing to do anything to protect my mate from further harm.

I saw red, and then a snarling body slammed into me. Before I knew what had hit me, teeth wrapped around my throat, and I was pinned to the ground. My own brother took me down. Reality hit me, and I was suddenly very aware I'd lost control, something I'd never done before as Alpha. Not like this. Never like this.

I forced myself to stop thrashing under Gideon's grasp and breathe, willing my wolf to calm down and realize it was not an Alpha challenge. Only once I fully submitted to my brother and shifted back to my human skin did Gideon release me and back away. I sat up, panting, and watched angrily as he shifted back into human form.

"Arkken, she's hurt. You need to calm down. I can't help her if you won't let me near her." Gideon was right.

I bowed my head in shame and slowly backed away. Then Gideon tossed me a pair of sweats. At that moment, I was very grateful we kept an emergency stash in the back of all our vehicles. We'd both shredded our clothes when we'd shifted.

"Look, I know you need to protect her, but we need to assess her injuries while we wait for the others to get here," he said. "Go back up to the road and wait for the others. I'll look after her."

I turned on my brother with a growl, still walking a fine line between man and beast. I knew Aislin was safe with him, but my wolf refused to see reason where my injured mate was concerned. It was nearly impossible to ignore my baser instincts. "I'm not leaving her alone!"

"Arkken, go. You're too volatile. I won't hurt her, I promise. But if you lose yourself again, you could hurt her. Go. Now."

Another growl tore through me, and it was all I could do to contain the wolf. I nearly launched myself at my brother. "I said I'm not leaving her!"

"Fine. Stay. But you need to calm down," Gideon warned.

"Don't fucking tell me what to do! My mate is lying there bleeding and unconscious!"

Gideon sighed. "I know, but I can't help her if you won't let me near her. We're wasting time standing here arguing."

Wheels ground on the gravel up above us. Doors slammed, and my security team and two medics climbed down the embankment. Stefan and Jorah set a stretcher down beside Aislin. I growled, planting myself between them and my mate, blocking their way. Damn this instinct to protect.

Stefan and Jorah kneeled before me, necks bared in deference to their Alpha, acknowledging my need to protect her. I slowly moved out of the way, though my wolf could barely stand anyone else touching her.

I paced around impatiently as the medics checked her over. Time slowed to a crawl. Every second eked by excruciatingly slow. I knew they were there to help, but it became increasingly difficult to maintain control.

Gideon put a hand on my shoulder, and I slapped him away. He was only trying to offer support, but it only angered me more.

"Don't. Touch. Me. I don't want to hurt anyone," I growled. "Why isn't she waking up?"

Gideon stepped in front of me and blocked my path, making me stop short in my attempt to get closer to my mate again. "Arkken, Aislin will be okay. Stefan and Jorah know what they're doing. Come on, let's give them some space to do their job."

He was right. I moved off to the side and sat on a small boulder, watching helplessly as they worked. I couldn't protect her by preventing them from helping her. I had to let them work. My men surrounded me in quiet solidarity, lending me their strength when I needed it most. Ever so carefully, the medics placed a neck brace on her, and then Gideon helped them slide the stretcher underneath her.

Corbin and Madigan stepped up to help them carry her back up the hillside. The rain hadn't let up, and we were all soaked to the bone by the time we made it to the top. I tried to climb inside the medical van, but my men pulled me back. A whimper slipped out of me as I was separated from her. I couldn't bear to let her out of my sight, but there was no room for all of us in the back of the van, so instead, I rode with Gideon, and we followed it back to the infirmary.

I was beside myself the entire trip home. With the torrential downpour, it had taken us an extra half an hour to get home as we navigated through a few flooded areas. My mind raced. How bad were her injuries? Why wouldn't she wake up? What made her leave in the first place?

I racked my brain, trying to figure out what could have scared her off. The dream. That had to be it. Dammit! I should have known by the look on her face when I'd told her what had happened. I'd broken her trust. Not intentionally, but I'd still done it.

"I'm sorry, brother. I lost my cool back there." I said with a rough sigh, guilt weighing me down.

"Don't sweat it."

"No. I'm the Alpha. I shouldn't have lost control like that," I told him.

"Look, I get it. She's your mate. I'd have done the same if it was Sara and you know it," he told me. "Instinct is both a boon and a curse. The most important thing right now is your mate. She needs you, but you can't be there for her if you're losing your shit."

I swallowed hard. "I can't lose her, Gid. I love her."

"I know."

29

ARKKADIAN

From the chair next to Aislin's bed, I listened to the beep of the machines surrounding her small frame. Her hand rested in mine, and I willed it to move. To twitch. To show any sign that she would wake soon. I'd been here since yesterday, ever since she'd been brought into the room. When we'd arrived, she'd been whisked away for testing. X-rays determined she'd broken her left wrist, so it had been reset and cast. There were no internal injuries, but she'd taken a pretty good knock to the head. My mate was damned lucky. The accident could have been much worse.

Emmaline Gray, our head physician, said it would just take time for her to wake up. She couldn't give me an estimate as to how long that would take. So, here I sat. Waiting. Listening. Watching. And kicking myself in the ass.

A knock on the door pulled me from my sullen reverie, and when I opened the door, Sara stood on the other side. She immediately wrapped me in a hug.

"How are you holding up?" she asked, releasing me and moving to Aislin's side. I grunted in response, not really in the mood to talk. "Really, Arkken, you can do better than that. Talk to me."

"Where's Gideon?" I asked, turning the conversation away from me. I really wasn't in the mood for company, and my wolf, well, he wasn't interested in anything other than standing sentinel over Aislin.

"He's with the guys. He said something about working on some security upgrades you asked for."

"Good." I sighed as I looked back at Aislin lying on the hospital bed. I hated feeling helpless. It made me feel inadequate. Weak. Something I was entirely not used to feeling as an Alpha, and I hated it. More than hated it. Nothing could have ever prepared me for all the emotional turmoil having a mate entailed. I'd gone from steadfast to stressed-the-hell-out literally overnight, and it had only gotten worse over the passing weeks.

"Any changes?" Sara asked.

I paced back to the bedside and sat down with my head buried in my hands. "No. Emmaline said it's just a waiting game until she wakes."

"And you? How are you doing, Arkken? Besides wallowing in your own self-pity?"

"I am not wallowing," I snarked.

"Don't lie to me, Arkken. I know you."

I huffed. If I knew anything about Sara, it was that she wouldn't leave me alone until I talked. Fine. "Honestly, I'm a wreck. My wolf wants to bond and his incessant prowling and hard desire to do so are tearing away at me piece by piece. It's getting harder to manage. And my mate? I'm angry she's hurt. I'm angry she left without a word. Mostly, I'm angry with myself, and I feel all too helpless to fix it."

Sara rolled her eyes. "Please tell me you didn't punish her again. Tell me that's not why she ran off."

"No, but I should," I told her. "She stole a vehicle, and then she wrecked it."

"Arkken, don't you dare. You know she's not well-versed in our ways. Her entire life was turned upside down. At least give her a chance to explain."

"I suppose you're right. Doesn't mean I shouldn't."

Sara rolled her eyes. "I am right. Don't be a stubborn ass."

I rolled my eyes back at her, and she cuffed me on the back of the head. As much as Sara was a pain in my ass sometimes, I loved her like a sister, and I even loved our easy banter. She had an easy way of pulling me back into the light when something bothered me.

"How does Gideon put up with you? You're exasperating," I teased.

She laughed. "Someone has to keep the Rime boys in check. Have you told anyone else yet?"

I shook my head. "James, Madigan, and Corbin know. And the medics and Emmaline. But otherwise, no."

"Probably wise for the time being," she agreed. "In all seriousness, though, do you want to punish her or does the Alpha in you need to punish her?"

"She stole a vehicle. There must be consequences."

"That's not what I asked."

I blew out a breath. "Well, that's my answer."

"Fine, but I urge you to think about it," Sara lectured. At her words, a little niggle of doubt settled firmly in the pit of my stomach. If I were honest with myself, fear was the root cause of all this chaos. Fear wasn't punishable.

"Fuck," I ground out. Sara simply raised her eyebrow. Damn her.

"Why do you think she left?" she asked.

"That's my fault."

I hung my head as I told her about the dream. Gideon knew everything already, including the attempted rape. I'd filled him in earlier on the drive home. So, I may as well tell his mate because my brother would tell her eventually, anyway.

"I can't forget the look on her face. I violated her all over again, just in a different way. I would have done the same thing in her situation."

"If you'd have done the same thing," she paused, "then you can't really punish her for that, can you? Fear makes a person do things they wouldn't usually, Arkken."

"Mm." I couldn't argue with that logic, especially after I'd already come to the same conclusion.

Sara sat in the chair next to me and gripped my hand. We sat together quietly for a bit before she spoke again. "I think you have a lot to think about, and you're exhausted. Go home. Eat something. Take a shower, change your clothes, and for heaven's sake, take a nap so we don't have to put up with your grumpy ass. I'll stay and watch her for a few hours."

"No." Like hell, I was leaving my mate.

"Arkken, you need a break."

I shook my head, refusing to budge. "I'm not leaving her."

"Don't you dare play Alpha with me, Arkkadian Rime. I'm not giving you a choice. Go home. Don't make me call your brother and have him come and drag your ass out of here because I will."

Didn't I say she was exasperating? Family can be such a pain in the ass.

"What if she wakes and I'm not here?"

She shot me a look. "Arkken, for the last time, go home."

"Fine," I relented. "But I won't be gone long."

Sara rolled her eyes.

30

ARKKADIAN

Though I needed a break, my instinct was to rush right back to that hospital room and never leave my mate's side again. Every inch of my skin chafed as the wolf yearned for freedom. To go to her. To protect my mate. No. I needed to collect myself first. I couldn't help her if I couldn't help myself.

Back at the cabin, I traipsed despondently up the stairs and headed straight for the shower. I didn't even wait for the water to warm up before I stepped behind the curtain. I let the chilly spray of water rain down over me as I stood there, breathing slow and deep. I stared blankly at the rivulets of water swiveling down the drain and thought of nothing and everything at the same time.

Only once the water ran cold again did I wash up and climb out. My reflection stared back at me with little flickers of blue fire-light, the churning flashes within the depths of those cerulean orbs mirroring the unrest deep in my soul. The wolf still lurked just under the surface, a turbulent storm of rage and remorse.

Steady, Arkkadian. Steady. Don't let the beast loose.

In my closet, I stood somewhere between half lost and half thinking about Aislin's bags on the floor. Someone had collected her belongings from the wreckage and brought them back here. Everything was just shoved in the bags haphazardly, reminding me of the way the saplings and plants had been crushed beneath the

SUV as it plummeted down the hillside. What if the vehicle had thrown her? I shuddered at the thought.

Stop it, Arkkadian. Pull yourself together. She was safe. Nothing positive would come from dwelling on the what-ifs.

Unable to leave her things in a mess like that, I busied myself with making space in my closet, needing something—anything—to occupy my mind. I should have done it weeks ago, but I'd felt that Aislin didn't need the added pressure. At the bottom of the bag, I found an old book. The cover fairly worn. I flipped it over, surprised to see a man and a wolf gracing the cover. Much to my amusement, it was a book about a shapeshifter. He was tall, dark-haired, and well-muscled, much like me. I chuckled at the irony. Well, I'll be damned. There was also a cheap laptop, but the hinge was busted and the screen shattered. It would be easy to replace, preferably with something more reliable and much sturdier.

My stomach grumbled then, so I went in search of food. I hadn't eaten breakfast yet, since I'd spent most of yesterday and all of last night sitting beside Aislin's hospital bed. My meal, however, tasted like ash as I stewed with worry.

I wanted so badly to return to the infirmary, but I knew if I returned too soon, Sara would just kick me out again, anyway. Sometimes, even the Alpha had to know when to back down and let others help. And if anything changed, she'd be the first to call. So instead, I checked in with my security team and then went for a run to ease the beast.

I FINALLY RETURNED to the infirmary and sent Sara home after my run. The rest of the evening dragged on as I listened to the incessant beeping of the machines monitoring Aislin's vitals. The nurse came and went discreetly every few hours. For a while, I read the book I'd found in Aislin's bag aloud to her, internally laughing at the disparities between the characters and actual Lycans. When the night grew late, I nodded off in the chair.

THE NEXT MORNING, I awoke to Gideon perched in the chair next to me with breakfast, but I wasn't hungry. I barely grunted a good morning as it was. Aislin was still unconscious, the machines droning on and on with their relentless beeping.

"Have you been here all night?"

"Where else would I be?" I growled in warning. The waiting became more unbearable by the hour, and my wolf was becoming increasingly desperate with worry. Even knowing she would heal and be okay didn't ease the protective instinct.

"Dammit, Arkken. Have you slept much at all? When was the last time you ate something?"

"I'm not leaving her again."

Gideon gave a frustrated sigh. "You're as stubborn as a damned mule. You may be my Alpha, but I'm still your brother. Stop acting like I'm a threat."

"Dammit, Gideon! She's my mate. It's my job to protect her. It's my fault she's in this mess." I was so angry with myself, and nothing would make it better until she woke up.

"You don't know that. Stop blaming yourself. Besides, there's nothing you can do for her right now anyway, but what you can do is take care of yourself. You're no good to her in this state. Come on. Let's go eat and then we'll go for a run. Sara's on her way, she'll look after Aislin. Don't make me drag your sorry ass out of here." Gideon stood up and headed for the door.

I sighed. "Fine."

I kissed Aislin's hand and then released it. "I'll be back later, love," I told her, and then I begrudgingly followed my brother outside.

THE LANDSCAPE FLASHED by as I hurtled through the forest, chasing my brother. We ran the territory circuit over and over. Pine needles crunched underneath my paws with every step as we raced down the north trail. Sunlight dappled the path ahead, and a light breeze ruffled the fur along my back. I followed Gideon around the bend toward the lake, coming to a stop at the shoreline. A golden eagle soared above, the clear blue sky a perfect backdrop for its magnificent display of flight. Fresh mountain air filled my lungs, cleared my head, and sated my soul as we rested on the small beach at water's edge.

I needed this. The beast beneath my skin needed this. I leaned down to lap at the water's edge, and all at once, the bone-deep strain tearing away at me disappeared when a tiny tickle of awareness rippled through the connection I shared with my mate. I shifted and dove into the cold, crisp, clear water, letting it absolve me of the guilt and anger that had been strangling me for the past few days. It was time to return to my mate.

Wading back to shore, I nodded at my brother, still in wolf form, and he tipped his head in answer. Then together, we raced off toward home.

31

AISLIN

B eep. Beep. Beep. Would someone please shut that thing up? I reached for the alarm clock, and a sharp pain jolted up my arm, jerking me awake.

When I opened my eyes, light rushed in, and I let out a painful moan. It stung, and I quickly scrunched them shut. A wrecking ball pounded around inside my skull with every movement of my head. Why do I feel like a truck ran over me? A truck. No, wait... an SUV. Images of upside-down trees and broken glass flashed through my mind, and I sat up with a jerk.

I was in a hospital room.

"Aislin? Don't get up, love. Come on, lie back." At once, Arkkadian was by my side, ushering me back down onto the pillows. "I'll get the doctor."

I took in my surroundings. The room was clean and new and the smell of antiseptic tickled my nose. A machine beside the bed let out a long, obnoxious beep, and the blood pressure cuff around my right arm puffed up. An IV stuck out of my right hand, and a purple plaster cast adorned my left arm to my elbow. It throbbed, and my fingers were puffy and swollen where they stuck out of the cast.

Just as I laid my head back on the pillow, utterly exhausted, the door opened, and an older, gray-haired woman entered the room with Arkkadian right behind her. I tried to speak, but I choked on the words. He was back at my side in an instant.

"Here. Small sips now," he said, holding the straw up to my mouth. The cold water soothed my parched mouth and throat as I sipped. I was so thirsty.

"Not too much, love." I was disappointed when he pulled the cup away. I wanted more.

"My arm. It hurts. And my head." Groaning, I reached up to touch my forehead and winced at the bandage there. I didn't remember hitting it.

Arkkadian pulled my hand away. "Don't mess with it, they'll change the bandage again soon. Just relax."

"You broke your wrist, and you received a nasty little gash on your head." The doctor. She shined a small penlight in my face, and I jerked my head to the side as the light stung my sensitive eyes. "We'll get you something for the pain."

She continued speaking to Arkkadian, but I barely heard a word of the conversation. I rested my head back on the pillows. I was so tired. Before I knew it, I'd slipped back into the realm of unconsciousness.

32

ARKKADIAN

"I want the gate installed as soon as possible. The cameras can wait a day or two. Just get it done," I barked into the phone before ending the call.

Movement caught my eye. Aislin groaned, and her eyes opened. She'd woken briefly this morning for a few minutes, but had slept most of the rest of the day away. To bide the time, I'd spent much of the afternoon and evening on the phone with my men discussing more upgrades to our systems. Gideon and Sara had stopped in twice more to check in on her and give me a break when I needed one. Emmaline had also been in to check on her a few times.

I went to my mate's side. "Hey there," I said, carefully smoothing her hair back. At least some color had returned to her face. "Welcome back."

When Aislin tried to speak and choked, I grabbed the cup of water and held the straw to her lips. "That's it, small sips. Slowly."

"What... what happened?" she asked through a cough.

I sighed. "I thought I lost you. How are you feeling?"

"Ugh."

"How's your pain? I can call the doctor," I told her.

"I'm okay, but I really have to pee," she said, trying to sit up.

I laughed. "I think we can manage that. Let me call the nurse, just stay there."

"No, it's fine. You can help me. I really need to go."

"Are you sure?" I asked with a touch of hesitation.

She nodded. My mate was trusting me to help her. A small step, but a step nonetheless. I'd take it. I'd take anything that got us back to where we were before.

I helped her swing her legs over the edge of the bed and then to stand. She wobbled on her feet, falling back to sit on the bed, her hand going to her temple.

"Dizzy?"

"Yeah."

"Here, let me." I gently picked her up and carried her to the bathroom, setting her down on her feet in front of the toilet. "Can you manage from here? I'll wait just outside the door."

She tilted a little, and I caught her. "Maybe you'd better stay. I'm not very steady."

"All right. Here, hold on to the safety rail."

Kneeling in front of her, I reached under the gown to slide her panties down and turned my head to the side so as not to make her uncomfortable in such a vulnerable situation. I held onto her arms and helped lower her to the seat before stepping outside to give her some privacy.

When I carried her back to the bed, she wrapped both arms around my neck and snuggled into me, letting out a soft sigh. I realized at that moment that she still trusted me. Maybe the reason she left wasn't what I thought.

I gently placed her on the bed and fluffed up the pillows so she could sit up more comfortably. I pushed the call button and then held up the cup so Aislin could take another sip of water.

She groaned into the straw. "That's so good. My throat was so dry."

"Take it slow, you don't want to make yourself sick. You've been out for three days," I told her.

The side-eye she gave me told me she knew she was in trouble. We had some things to talk about, but she didn't need to know I'd already decided about not punishing her. I'd let her stew a little instead, just because I could. Nina, one of the nurses, chose that moment to walk into the room.

When I stood to leave, Aislin looked at me with worry in her eyes. "I'm not going far, just stepping outside the door for a few minutes to give you and the nurse some privacy." I leaned down to kiss her on the cheek. "I'll come back in a few minutes."

I shut the door behind me as I stepped out of the room and pulled my phone from my pocket. I sought Gideon, but Sara answered on the first ring.

Before I could speak, she peppered me with questions. "How is she? Is she okay? Do you need anything?"

I laughed. "Sara, slow down. Everything's fine. Aislin's awake. The nurse is in with her now. Besides the broken wrist and a minor concussion, she's fine."

Sara breathed a sigh of relief into the phone. She had taken an instant liking to my mate from the moment they'd met, and it warmed my heart to know Aislin had others here she could rely on. Sara had been cool, calm, and collected at first, but over the past couple of days, she fretted. All the pregnancy hormones didn't help.

"Okay, good. I've been worrying like a mother hen. It's the pregnancy. I can't help it. I know it's late, but do either of you need anything? I can have Gideon stop by on his way back from security."

I chuckled at her rapid response and the large intake of air at the end. "No, we're good. I just wanted to give you a quick update. The nurse is coming back out. I'll speak to you in the morning. Goodnight," I told her, hanging up before she could babble on.

The nurse stopped me on her way out, letting me know they were keeping her another night and would reevaluate in the morning. I nodded my thanks before opening the door.

Aislin was sitting reclined in the bed, a smile on her face despite the bags under her eyes. She looked haggard.

"Are you hungry? I can have someone bring you something."

"I'm starving actually, but the nurse already called for some broth." She closed her eyes and laid her head back on the pillow for a moment.

I approached the side of her bed and leaned down to kiss her on the forehead. "I'm glad you're okay, but don't scare me like that again."

Aislin fidgeted with the sheets, twisting them in her hands. "I'm sorry," she whispered.

"What possessed you to take off like that?" She stared at her hands, still twisting the sheets in her grip. I continued when she didn't answer. "Was it me? Did I do something?"

She shook her head side to side. "Yes. Well, no. Not really. I mean, I was angry with you, but that wasn't why I left. I know you didn't do the dream thing on purpose. I left because as long as I'm here, your people aren't safe. There are families here. Children. If someone got hurt because of me... I would never, ever forgive myself. I was trying to do the right thing by removing the one thing that endangered all of them."

When she teared up, I cupped her face with both hands and brushed her tears away with my thumbs. I leaned in, pressing my forehead to hers, and looked her straight in the eye.

"Yes, you being here puts everyone here in danger, but what you fail to realize is that we are a community. They aren't just my people, they're your people now. And when one of us is in trouble, we band together. We take care of each other. We fight for each other. We live, and we die for each other, and we don't leave anyone behind. That includes you, love."

"But...."

"Shh. Let me finish. Our lives are fraught with danger from the moment we're born because of what we are. Living on the fringes of human existence is how we maintain at least some safety and peace. You being here puts our community at risk, but you being here also keeps you safe. You've been alone for so long, I think you've forgotten what it's like to have someone take care of you," I imparted. "Please let me."

"Okay."

Upon her agreement, I tilted her chin and placed a chaste kiss upon her lips before pulling away and breathing a sigh of relief. "Thank you."

Dr. Emmaline Gray chose that moment to enter the room. She placed a small bowl, crackers, a spoon, and a container of apple juice on the bedside table.

"I heard you were awake, dear. Nina filled me in, but I insisted on coming to see you myself. I'm Dr. Gray, but you may call me Emmaline. Everyone else does." I watched as she busied herself with my mate and smiled at the tender, motherly vibe. One thing about Emmaline, she worried over all of her patients as if they were her own children.

"I brought you some soup. Try to eat something, then I'd like it if you'd try to get more rest. I'll be back in the morning to check on you." She squeezed Aislin's hand in farewell, and then I walked Emmaline to the door and shut it behind her.

As Aislin dug into her soup, I lamented the dark circles under her eyes. They looked terrible. Dr. Gray was right. Aislin needed rest. As soon as she finished, I helped her fluff her pillows and lower the bed so she could lie down. I resigned myself to sleeping in the most uncomfortable chair for one more night and sat down with a sigh.

"Arkkadian?"

"Yes?"

She reached a hand toward me. "Will you lie with me tonight?"

I smiled. "Of course, love."

She scooted to one side of the bed and rolled to her side, making room for me behind her. I wrapped an arm around her waist and pulled her close. Within seconds, sleep claimed her. I stayed with her all night, the wolf inside me savoring her nearness, relieved she was once again safe beside me.

33

AISLIN

I squinted at the bright sunlight peeking in through the blinds, cursed the morning, and wished for another couple hours of sleep. I had a slight headache and my wrist ached, but mostly, I felt weak and fatigued. I rolled onto my back and scooted up on the hospital bed, pushing the button until it shifted into a reclined position. I stretched my arms and back and yawned.

Arkkadian was no longer beside me, but a miniature carton of milk and a small brown paper bag sat on the rolling table beside the bed. Curious, I opened it and squealed excitedly at the contents. Inside were two eclairs frosted with a dark chocolate ganache. Oh, my gosh. My stomach didn't just rumble, it thundered like a hungry lion presiding over its kill, exhaustion forgotten. I couldn't pull an eclair out of the bag fast enough. I bit into it, and smooth, rich cream leaked out of the middle. Groaning with delight, I devoured both in record time, licking every bit of decadent, gooey chocolate off my sticky fingers. I had just taken a sip of milk to wash it all down when the door opened, and Arkkadian walked in with a small duffle bag in hand.

My soul sang with instant recognition, dancing on the precipice of forever. His familiar scent of cinnamon and cloves wafted across the room and I inhaled deeply, letting it wrap around me like a warm blanket. Three words immediately flashed through my mind. *Safe. Home. Mine.* Arkkadian Rime was mine. My mate. My... *love.* Was that right? Did I truly love him? Yes, and I knew it to be true. With him was where I needed to be. Not out there alone and on the run. I wouldn't survive without him. He was home.

Yesterday's stubble was gone from his chin, and his hair was still damp. He must have gone home for a shower. I took in the magnificent sight before me, afraid to look away in case it wasn't real. This beautiful Adonis of a man, all dark and handsome, unmistakably strong and fierce. Dominant. All Alpha. *My* Alpha. My real-life fairy tale come true. I would never let him go.

"Good morning, beautiful," he said with a smile. "How are you feeling?"

I leaned into his hand as he cupped my face and placed a gentle kiss on my forehead. The touch of his skin against mine sent delicious little flickers of desire crackling through every nerve ending, lighting my body on fire. I stared into his eyes, wondering what thoughts lay behind their deep blue depths, and smiled in return.

"Better this morning, but I'm still tired."

"I'm sure. Did you eat yet?" He eyed the brown bag that lay crumpled on the table. "I figured you might like something better than hospital food this morning."

"I did. They were delicious. Thank you very much."

"You're welcome."

I smiled inwardly, knowing that while Arkkadian was a true Alpha male, he was also tender and loving. He was hard and tough, but he was also kind and warm. He was dominant without being domineering. I knew I need never fear him. And true to Arkkadian's word, the more time we spent together, the stronger the tether between us became. I'd felt it the instant he'd touched me. Even now I could feel the connection vibrating through every fiber of my being, and it sang all the way to my heart.

Dr. Gray entered just then, cheery and warm, nodding to each of us in greeting. "Good morning, Alpha. Aislin. I see you've eaten something this morning already. That's great! We'll check your vitals one last time, and then I don't see any reason you can't go home this morning."

I brightened at the thought. I wanted out of this hospital bed as soon as possible. Dr. Gray continued on in conversation with

Arkkadian while she checked me out, and I only half paid attention, too busy thinking about going home with my mate.

"Aislin?" My name caught my attention.

"Sorry?"

Dr. Gray studied me with her kind eyes. "I'm letting you go home, but I want you to take it easy for the next few days. Get lots of rest and try not to do anything too strenuous. If you feel tired, you rest. Do you understand?"

I nodded. "Yes, ma'am."

We said our goodbyes, and she made me promise to return in a couple of weeks for a check-up.

Arkkadian set the duffel bag on the bed next to me. "I brought you some clean clothes. I'll give you some privacy so you can change."

"Please stay. I could use your help." I'd caused Arkkadian enough trouble the last few days, it was time I showed him I trusted him. That I accepted him. That I loved him. He'd saved me twice, after all. Surprise flashed across his face at my words before he grinned.

This time, I didn't shy away from his gaze as he helped me remove my gown. This time, I let him look upon my nakedness, feeling confident, cherished, loved.

34

ARKKADIAN

"Please. Stay. I could use your help."

I hadn't expected those words to come from her, and the thought of what it meant thrilled me to the core. Brick by brick, the defensive walls Aislin had built around herself had come crumbling down until eventually, the last stone had finally fallen. My wolf was beyond exhilarated.

She stood confidently before me in her nakedness, hands at her sides, light and love in her eyes. This was her accepting her new life. Accepting herself, scars and all. Accepting me. Accepting us. I reached up and gently stroked her cheek, and she leaned into the embrace.

"You are so beautiful." I leaned in and placed a sweet kiss upon her lips before pulling back to gaze into her eyes. Then I wrapped both arms around her, tugged her close and held her to me, burying my face in her neck, inhaling her sweet essence of cinnamon and spice.

"Arkkadian?"

"Hmm?"

"I... I think... I mean... I love you." Aislin's voice was low, almost as if she was afraid to admit it.

Did I hear that right? She loved me? My heart skipped a beat inside my chest and swelled with happiness. I took her face in my hands and tilted her up to look at me. Vulnerability shown in her eyes, and it made the moment that much more intimate.

Aislin wrapped her arms around my neck and leaned up to kiss me back. I let her set the pace. This was her moment, and I wouldn't deny her the chance to open herself up to me if she was willing. Her lips were soft and pliable against mine, slow and tender in their ministrations, but as I parted my lips and let our tongues tangle, the passion between us ignited, and her kisses quickly became urgent. Her pert breasts grazed against my flannel shirt, her nipples peaking in response. The scent of her arousal filled the room. My wolf went on instant alert, awakened by the fervent desire pulsing through Aislin's body.

My erection sprang to life, but as much as I wanted to continue kissing her, now was not the time or place. Anyone could enter the room unexpectedly, and my inner beast bristled at the thought of someone other than myself seeing my mate naked.

When I broke the kiss, a look of confusion crossed her face, and she moved to cover herself. "Did I do something wrong?"

"No. You did nothing wrong. Trust me, you did everything right," I said, pulling her to me again. "This just isn't the place, love. Anyone could walk in, and you're still naked." I lifted my eyebrows, emphasizing that last word with a chuckle.

She bit her lip. "Oh. I thought maybe...."

When she didn't finish the thought, I gently placed a kiss upon her forehead, comforting her. "I love you, too, Aislin. I've loved you for a while now."

"You have?"

"I have. I've just been patiently waiting for you to come to the same realization." I grinned, trying to put her at ease.

She wrapped her arms around me once more and buried her face in my chest. I held her to me, the admission of her love filling me with immense joy. We stood there for another moment, just basking in each other's embrace until Aislin shivered and goosebumps peppered her skin.

"All right, love. As much as I'm enjoying this, it's time to go home."

"Yes... please."

Just as I finished helping her dress, the door opened, and a nurse entered with a wheelchair. Aislin frowned at the chair, instantly on the defensive. "I can walk."

"It's just to the car, love. That's all."

"No." A look of dread, mixed with a little anxiety, crossed her face as she stared at the chair, rubbing at her wrists. She took a step backward, away from the chair, and faltered. I caught her before she tripped and steadied her against me. When she looked up at me, her eyes were glossy, and she shook her head side to side.

I looked at the nurse and shook my head. "I've got this," I mouthed silently.

She took the chair and left, leaving us alone.

"Come on, I've got you," I assured. I picked up the bag and tossed it over my shoulder, and then I took Aislin's hand and put an arm around her. Together, we made our way to the black SUV waiting out front and then we were on our way home. Together.

35

AISLIN

On the short drive home from the infirmary, the guilt over what I'd done parked center spotlight right in my gut. As Arkkadian came around to my side of the SUV, I stared out the window at the cabin and wondered what would happen once I walked through that door again. Would he punish me for leaving? For wrecking the SUV in my haste to escape?

Honorable as my intentions were, I'd knowingly put myself in danger in my attempt to save Arkkadian's people from the threat of my existence. I knew he was still upset with me, despite our affirmations of love for one another just this morning. That neither of us had spoken on the way home was telling. Best get it over with. I would accept whatever punishment Arkkadian decided with my chin held high.

Arkkadian opened my door, and I stepped out onto the gravel drive, sighing with apprehension. He took my hand and led me up the steps and into the cabin. Inside, he dropped the duffle by the door, and then led me to the sofa in the den. I sunk down onto the cushions, fatigue quickly taking hold. I hadn't realized how much this morning's activities had worn me out.

"Tired?"

"Much," I said, unable to stifle a yawn.

At my admission, Arkkadian propped up some pillows, and I laid down. Then he took the afghan from the back of the couch and tucked it around me. He knelt in front of me and tucked a stray lock of hair behind my ear. Our eyes locked, and guilt once again consumed me.

"I'm sorry." I blanched, waiting for the lecture that never came.

"It's all right, love."

"Are you mad?"

"No, I'm not mad."

"Are you going to punish me?" I asked.

"We'll talk about that later. I want you to rest." He smiled as he cupped my chin before pulling away.

Within seconds, my eyes drifted shut as sleep claimed me, and down I tumbled into the dark abyss of sleep once again.

36

ARKKADIAN

There was something about watching Aislin and listening to the light sounds of her easy breathing that brought me peace and steadied my wolf. She was here, and she was safe. After four hundred years on this earth, I'd finally found my Aeternus, then almost lost her. I paled at the thought, remembering when my brother and I found her unconscious and bloody in the wreckage mere days ago. Seeing her there had nearly destroyed me. I'd temporarily lost control of the wolf, and if it hadn't been for Gideon knocking some sense into me, I'm not sure what would have happened. I needed to complete the bond. And soon because my control of the wolf was waning.

I slipped into the kitchen, needing to make a call while she slept. Aislin had begged to attend the memorial service, and I'd told her I'd think about it. So, my team and I needed to work something out. A security detail wasn't optional. On that, I wouldn't compromise.

With coffee brewing, I dialed Gideon's cell first, but the call went straight to voicemail. He and Sara must be at the infirmary. She had mentioned she had an appointment for an ultrasound today. Instead, I called the security building, and James answered.

"Good morning, Alpha."

"Good morning, James. Dr. Gray released Aislin this morning. I wanted to let you know I'll be home for the rest of the day and see if there are any updates."

"We finished the new gate installation yesterday afternoon. Madigan and Corbin are on their way back. They've finished installing the last of the new cameras up on the north ridge, so we should be all set."

"Good. Thank you."

"How is she?" James asked.

"She's tough, but she's got a lot of emotional trauma. Listen, she'll probably be asleep for a while. If you're available in the next hour, I'd like you to come to my place. I've got some things I still want to discuss."

"I can be there in thirty."

"Good. Bring the team."

"See you soon."

I stuffed the phone back in my pocket, then poured a mug of coffee and sat down at the table. As I sat there sipping the hot drink, watching the steam swirl up and disappear, my thoughts turned to my mate. Much to my wolf's chagrin, I'd already decided I wouldn't punish her. The more I thought about it, the more I knew I'd made the right decision. Aislin hadn't run to defy me. She ran out of fear. Out of guilt. She thought it would protect a community of people she didn't even know. And in her haste to sacrifice her own safety for theirs, she'd gotten hurt. Was it stupid? Of course. But she hadn't done it with ill intent.

No, Sara was right. Aislin was already suffering the consequences of her actions. Exacting punishment at this point might ruin any progress I'd made in convincing her she was my mate. I may wield the Alpha position of the Pack and Lycan Nine with an iron fist, but I wasn't a tyrant, and my mate didn't deserve punishment. It didn't matter what the wolf inside of me wanted.

Finally, James pulled up the drive, and all four members of my team climbed out. Gideon's face was beaming as he walked in the door. I closed the door to the den before leading them into the kitchen where we would have less of a chance of disturbing my mate. Gideon wrapped me in a bear hug, his excitement clear as I slapped him on the back.

"How did it go?" I asked.

"Twins! We're having twins!" His excitement was palpable, and I couldn't help but hug him again.

I grinned. "Two? Do you know what you're having?"

"They're both boys!" Gideon was beside himself with excitement.

"That's amazing, brother. Congratulations!" I was genuinely happy for my brother and his mate. They would make excellent parents.

"Thanks. Sara is over the moon. When I dropped her at home, she went straight to the nursery. I'm sure she's nesting already." He laughed.

I smiled as an image of a pregnant Aislin popped into my head. I hoped that would one day be a reality.

I looked around the room at my men, the energy turning from elation to serious as I explained why they were all gathered there. Gideon knew everything already, but the others still had more to learn about my mate. I'd only told them enough to get them out the door as quickly as possible in my haste to find my mate when she'd taken off the other day.

I worried about Corbin, particularly, and how he'd take this information. He'd lost an older sister when he was a teenager. She had been sexually assaulted and stabbed, her body dumped in the woods. She was only twenty. They never found her killer. It happened long ago, but some wounds never healed. I warned them that what they were about to hear might be difficult to process and urged them to keep themselves in check. I eyed each of my men, lingering on Corbin last, trying to convey my meaning. He nodded in clear understanding.

I recounted everything in vivid detail, about how I'd first stumbled upon her scent at the Black Horse Saloon, and how I'd returned over and over until I'd finally found her. I told them more about the incident with Kane in the bar, her subsequent rescue, and the murders of her friends. I filled them in on her childhood, passing around the files confirming her true identity I'd collected in my research. I told them of the nightmares and anxiety that continued to plague her. I told them about the previous assault and how I thought Kane had tried to force the bond. And lastly, I told them about the dream I'd been witness to, of the savage horrors Ryker Slade had committed upon her when she was just a child.

213

That last bit had their faces lighting up in a storm of pure fury. Every pair of eyes but mine sparked even as I tried to rein in my anger. James paced back and forth across the floor. Madigan stood quietly, seething as he stared out the window, arms crossed defensively in front of him. Corbin pushed up from his seat at the table and stomped outside. I caught the door before it slammed shut behind him.

I followed him out to the front porch. Standing just behind him, I reached up, placed a hand on his shoulder, and waited for him to speak. He stood there, hands on his hips, taking deep angry breaths as he glared up at a cloudless blue sky. Then, shrugging my hand off, Corbin stepped away and ripped his shirt off.

"Corbin, wait."

He turned to face me, his normally brown eyes glowing orange. "Please don't, Alpha. Not now."

"I'm not done. I know this is difficult, but please come back inside." Honestly, I didn't have the heart to enforce my authority, though. He was hurting, and rightly so. The death of his sister had never stopped plaguing him. Her death was one reason he'd done his best to avoid finding a mate. Losing one loved one had been difficult enough, and he didn't want to risk losing another.

"Fill me in later." And with that, a gray wolf ripped out of his skin, jeans flying in shreds around him. He bounded down the drive, rounded the corner, and was gone. This morning's discussion had ripped the scab off that wound once again.

I let him go for now, picked up the shreds of fabric, and walked back into the house with a heavy heart.

"Is he okay?" my brother asked.

"He will be," I answered, gripping my brother's shoulder for a moment before crossing my arms. "He'll come back when he's blown off some steam."

"How is she?" Madigan asked, turning back from the window with a grimace. His eyes were red as if he'd been crying. I couldn't blame him for being upset, nor could I blame the others. We cherished our women, and the things my mate had suffered at the hands of others were difficult to process with our naturally protective nature.

"She'll be back up to speed in no time. She just needs some rest."

"I'm glad to hear it, Alpha." Madigan's voice was slightly hoarse.

"Listen. The memorial service for her friends is on Monday evening, and she's been asking to go. I told her I wouldn't make any promises, but considering all she's been through, it might be good for her to have some closure."

James spoke up. "Are you sure that's wise? Kane is still unaccounted for."

I inclined my head. "I'm aware. She also needs clothing and some other things. So, I thought we'd travel down in the morning, get what she needs, and then take her to the service."

James stepped away from the wall he was leaning against and crossed his arms. His movements were stiff and wary. "What does she need that she can't borrow from someone here?"

"Nothing, but that's not the point. She's lost virtually everything. If your life was turned on its head and you were stuck with people you didn't know, would you want to rely on strangers to provide for you?" I replied, leaning on the back of the kitchen chair in front of me and tapping my fingers on the chair back.

"True," James answered. He ran a hand through his hair, letting his unease show. "It's still not wise, though, Alpha."

"I'm just as wary. That's why I intend to take all of you with us. I refuse to compromise on security, so I'd like to brainstorm," I replied, crossing the room to stand next to him.

It was Madigan's turn to speak. He turned away from the window and faced the room. "James is right. If Kane is alive, he'll seek retribution. He's already gone after her three times. He won't stop."

"Then we end him. For good," I spoke, my voice deadly calm. I wouldn't hesitate to tear the bastard's head off.

"Alpha." I turned my head toward James as he spoke. "It didn't take you that long to determine Aislin's true identity. Surely, he's figured it out by now. What's stopping him from going straight to the Vanes? It's no secret he wants you dead."

I nodded. "It's a possibility, but I think he wants her for himself. If he turns her over, they'll kill her. Kane knows that. At some point, we must notify the rest of the Pack. We'll need the added support and security."

Gideon cleared his throat when Aislin shuffled through in the doorway. Her hair hung limply around her shoulders, and purple bags still circled under her eyes. There was a pained look upon her face, and she cradled her broken wrist in her good hand.

"I'm sorry, love, we didn't mean to wake you." I crossed over to her and hugged her to me, cradling the back of her head in my hand.

"You didn't. My arm hurts."

"I'll get you something for that and then you can go lie back down. It's quieter upstairs. You won't be disturbed up there." I attempted to lead her toward the stairs, but she stopped me.

"I'm not really that tired. I'm actually kind of hungry."

I looked at the clock on the wall. It was nearly two in the afternoon. My men and I had talked long past lunch, and she hadn't eaten since breakfast. Those two eclairs wouldn't have tided her over for long.

"Right. Well, let's go. I'm sure the two of you could use some privacy," Gideon announced.

Aislin pulled away from me and turned toward my men. "Wait. Please?" They all looked at her in question. "Are you the ones who helped me?"

"Aye," Madigan answered.

She took a tentative step toward my men. "Thank you for saving me. I want to apologize for scaring everyone."

As one, Madigan, James, and Gideon knelt down on one knee before her, palms flat on the hardwood, their heads bowed. Aislin looked at me with confusion. She was still unaware of many of our customs.

I came up beside her and wrapped my arm around her waist. "They're recognizing you as my mate, love. They're pledging their allegiance. They'll protect you."

"But I—" She faltered, looking back and forth between me and my men. She was uncomfortable. "Why me? I'm no one special."

"But you are special. You're my Aeternus. That makes you an Alpha female. You will rule by my side once the bond is complete," I told her.

A look of shock crossed her face as she processed this new bit of information. I introduced James and Madigan, each nodding at their name. She would meet Corbin later.

"Oh." Then her eyes widened in recognition of what I'd just said a moment ago. "Oh!" It was finally sinking in that she was well and truly something special.

I exchanged a few more words with my men and then they were on their way. Gideon held back a moment.

"I'm glad you're okay," he told my mate before giving her a brotherly hug. For once, my wolf didn't get upset. "Sara will be delighted to know you're okay. She's got some exciting things to share with you. I won't spoil the surprise."

He smiled down at her and then hugged her one more time before taking his leave.

"All right. Food, medicine, and rest. No arguments. Go sit down at the table and I'll bring it to you."

She did as she was told, and I busied myself with warming up some chicken soup. Sara had once again come to the rescue and brought over another pot last night. Aislin smiled as I set a steaming bowl in front of her.

I sat across from her, happily watching her eat, glad to see she had a decent appetite. I was elated to know my men accepted her as my mate. Their submission was proof enough. When she finished, I handed her a glass of water and the pain pills Emmaline had sent home. She took them without question. Hopefully, the pain in her wrist would be short-lived as her healing abilities worked their magic.

"Have you thought any more about letting me attend the memorial?" she asked, nervousness clear in her voice as if she expected my usual response.

"That's why my men were here. They will provide us a security detail." She looked at me with a mix of excitement and apprehension, as if what I was saying was too good to be true. "Going without isn't an option, Aislin."

"But..."

"No. It's not up for discussion. We go with security, or not at all. Understand?"

"Yes." She wasn't too happy, but she resigned herself to my decision. It was just the way it had to be.

"Good. We'll head down Monday morning, and then you'll have the afternoon to pick up anything you need before the evening service." I picked up the bowl, pleased to see it empty, and set it in the sink. "All right, love, time to rest."

"I'm fine. I mean, I'm tired, but not sleepy tired." I could see she was pushing herself, testing limits, and I worried about her doing too much.

"How about a movie? Your choice." I knew it was probably the only way I could get her to relax.

"Actually, I was kind of thinking maybe we could go for a walk. Outside?"

Warning bells rang in my head, and my wolf bristled. On one hand, I wasn't sure she was up for it. On the other, the fresh air would do her some good. And maybe it would be good to finally introduce her to everyone. I couldn't keep her a secret forever. Honestly, I wasn't sure how I'd kept the secret this long to begin with. It would mean added security for Aislin, and as an Alpha female—my female—they would also want to show their allegiance just as my security team had done. Yes, maybe we should take a walk.

"Are you sure you're up for it? Dr. Gray wants you to rest."

After a moment's hesitation, she finally answered. "I think so. Yes."

I helped her up from the table. "All right. But we take it easy. And the moment you feel it's too much, we come home. Promise?"

"Promise."

I placed an arm around her waist, and together, we walked out into the afternoon sunshine, but before we left, I sent a quick text to Gideon. *Taking Aislin for a walk. Security detail now. It's time to meet the family.*

I didn't wait for Gideon's response. He would know what I meant.

37

AISLIN

I couldn't stay cooped up inside any longer. I'd been sleeping for days, and my body yearned for a good stretch. Standing in the gravel drive in front of Arkkadian's cabin, I basked in the warm sun, letting it all soak in. The soft heat upon my skin and the clean, clear, crisp air in my lungs filled me with a burst of energy.

"Where to?" I asked. In the few short weeks I'd been here, I hadn't really gone anywhere besides Gideon and Sara's. So, I really didn't know which way to go.

"Well, let's see where your feet lead us," he said. I knew he was placating me, but still, the thought of him letting me take the lead made me feel like his equal, and I appreciated that.

I spotted the community garden off in the distance and noted the small group of people diligently working to gather vegetables and dispose of the weeds. A few children played a game of tag on the big lawn next to the garden. I supposed that was as good a destination as any. It wasn't far from Arkkadian's cabin and would afford me a chance to stretch without becoming too worn out.

I interlaced my fingers with his, and together, we strolled toward the garden. As we neared, the group of men and women stopped working and watched us approach. I noticed one man stiffen with awareness, though the movement was almost imperceptible. Another waved at Arkkadian in greeting as we approached.

"Good afternoon," he greeted them.

"Alpha," a gruff male voice said. The big man had long, dark brown hair pulled back into a single braid, a thick reddish-brown beard, and icy blue eyes. He was easily six inches taller than Arkkadian and somewhat Viking-like in appearance. Broad. Stocky. Built like a brick shithouse, if you asked me. He was mending the fence while the others worked the garden.

The women all smiled, but the men eyed me warily, and I wondered if they could scent me just as Arkkadian had. My question was soon answered when he introduced me to the group as his Aeternus, and the men began openly sniffing the air. It was bizarre. Almost as one, the entire group knelt on one knee, hands flat to the ground, bowing their heads just like Arkkadian's men had done in the cabin earlier.

I took a step back, entirely unprepared for the display before me. I wasn't used to this much attention. Arkkadian squeezed my hand, and a gentle wave of comfort passed into me, calming me. I internally thanked him for it.

Movement from the corner of my eye caught my attention, and when I turned to look, I noticed a larger group of people congregating around us. Men, women, and children were exiting their cabins and joining the quickly gathering crowd. If I ventured to guess, I'd say there were nearly four hundred individuals. Quiet murmurs filled the air, and I picked up on the words "mate" and "Aeternus" spreading like wildfire through the group. The cat was out of the bag now. And here I'd only meant to go for a walk. I don't know what I had been expecting, but it sure wasn't this.

"Ladies. Gentlemen. Please." Whispers flew through the crowd until Arkkadian held up a hand, and they ceased immediately. In an instant, he'd commanded their attention.

I felt the eyes of every single individual upon me, and it made me slightly uncomfortable. A few weeks ago, I was just a girl. In a bar. Working two jobs to make ends meet. Now I was some sort of werewolf royalty? Wow, had my life taken a turn. For better or worse, I wasn't sure yet.

"I see the questions in your eyes. I hear them on your lips. I would like you all to meet my Aeternus, Aislin." More murmurs filled the crowd, and again, Arkkadian held up a hand for silence.

Like before, the response was immediate. "Yes, the woman who stands before you is, in fact, my mate."

You could have heard a pin drop as the words he'd spoken were digested by everyone in the crowd. And then the rest of the congregation joined the others, kneeling before us. Even the children knelt down. Not a soul was standing except Arkkadian and me. This couldn't possibly be for me. Except it was. I stood in awe, not knowing what to make of this outright display of fealty.

And then Arkkadian divulged the biggest secret of all.

38

ARKKADIAN

I noted Gideon, Madigan, James, and even Corbin on the outskirts of the crowd, and nodded to each of them. I was glad to see Corbin had returned. If he hadn't been told everything already, he would soon learn what he'd missed earlier.

"Please, rise." I waited for everyone to get back on their feet and for my men to join Aislin and me before continuing. Everyone looked around at each other with curiosity, but no one spoke. "There are some things you should be aware of. Some of you may have noticed the increased security in the last few days. Aislin's presence here presents a risk to our community. Most of you know the story about Wren Vane and Alaric Barrington. Aislin," I said, indicating my mate with a nod, "is their daughter. She isn't safe outside our territory."

The crowd erupted into questions as all eyes landed on the woman beside me. She shifted to stand behind me. I could feel her fear vibrating through me and did my best to soothe her through our connection. She didn't know these people, nor did she know if she could trust them. With her history, she didn't trust easily, anyway.

"Silence. Please." I spoke without raising my voice, the authority blatantly clear. Everyone ceased speaking immediately. "Until recently, no one knew of her existence, and until she came here, Aislin herself didn't even know who she was until I figured it out. She was raised in foster care, and she knows very little of our ways. It is up to us to teach her. However, if Arden Vane finds out, he will kill her. I can't let that happen. As Alpha, I call upon the Pack to fulfill its duty. To protect one of its own."

Shouts of "Aye!" and "Yes, Alpha!" sprang up from our audience. I pulled Aislin back around to my side and wrapped an arm around her. She trembled in my arms, and I could feel the tension in her muscles. I leaned in and kissed her cheek, hoping to reassure her.

"It's okay, love," I whispered in her ear. "These are good people. You're safe."

One by one, folks lined up single file in front of us. As they approached Aislin, they knelt before her and bowed their head just like before, this time individually pledging their loyalty. Aislin watched silently until the last of the crowd had finally dispersed. It had taken nearly an hour for the last person to reach her.

It was nearing dinnertime by the time we walked back to the cabin, and Aislin looked much more fatigued. The unexpected events of this afternoon had taken a lot out of her. I regretted my decision to let her explore and tire herself out, but it had been necessary for gaining Pack support, and now that it was done, she could rest.

After a quick meal, we headed upstairs to bed early. Aislin was asleep just moments after her head hit the pillow.

39

AISLIN

The sound of running water woke me. I opened my eyes to bright sunshine filtering in through the window, the open curtains revealing the lightly snow-capped mountains in the distance. With the weather warming, the snowcaps were slowly receding, but the sight was still as majestic as ever. I could get used to this.

I felt much more refreshed this morning than I had yesterday. My wrist still ached a little, but the headache and dizziness were gone. I lay in bed a moment longer and stretched, working out the kinks from a long night's sleep. It surprised me when I couldn't recall having even a single nightmare.

The water in the bathroom shut off, and just as I sat up in bed, the door opened, and Arkkadian appeared. Like the first morning I'd woken up in his bed, he was nude. It was the first time I'd seen him naked since. My heart did a little pitter-patter in my chest, and when I swung my eyes up, a grin lit up his face. Suddenly, the room got very, very hot, and I blew out a puff of air, lost for words. My libido had gone from zero to sixty in the blink of an eye. Arkkadian lifted an eyebrow in amusement, and an involuntary shiver shook my entire body from head to toe.

"Like what you see?" His voice did that deep, velvety, smooth-as-whiskey thing that made my insides go flippity flop.

I looked away, embarrassed at having been caught gawking at

this fine specimen of masculinity. He was my personal nectar, and I thanked whichever of the fates had sent him my way.

"Mm," was all I could muster in response.

I closed my eyes, inhaled deeply through my nose, and then let it out slowly through my mouth. I continued to breathe deeply, finding it nearly impossible to control the hunger I felt for Arkkadian. I wanted to launch myself at him. I wanted to taste and feel every bit of sweet ambrosia he offered, but I couldn't make myself move from this bed, not with my affliction of inexperience outweighing my wanton appetite. I heard footsteps padding across the carpet, and I silently wished they were headed in the closet's direction so I could catch my breath.

They weren't.

The duvet tightened around my legs, pinning me in place as strong hands planted on either side of my lap. I opened my eyes to find Arkkadian's strikingly beautiful eyes just inches from my own, sparkling with vivid blue fire. Their glow lit up the space between us and stole my breath away. The smile on his face made my toes curl and my heart hammered away inside my chest. One hand reached up to tuck yet another stray lock of hair behind my ear. He was always doing that, playing with my hair. I tried to keep my eyes on his, but a quick glance downward divulged just how happy Arkkadian was to see me this morning. Oh, boy. Breathe, Aislin, breathe!

"Good morning," he said, before gently placing a kiss upon my forehead.

I opened my mouth to speak and quickly shut it again when the words wouldn't come. Then, just as quickly as he appeared before me, he disappeared into the closet, leaving me bereft and wondering what just happened. He reappeared dressed in his usual black t-shirt and dark blue denim jeans that hugged his muscular form in all the right places. I was so hot and bothered, I couldn't decide if I was relieved or disappointed at him having covered up that exquisite body of his. The smile on his face told me just how much he was enjoying this.

"I'll be in the kitchen making breakfast. When you're ready, come and join me," he said, and then promptly turned on his heel and headed out the door with a smirk on his face and a mischievous glint in his eyes. I swallowed. Hard. He did that on purpose! What the...?

It took a couple minutes to clear my head and get my libido in check before I could even climb out of bed. I was still reeling from the sexual tension that I couldn't make heads or tails of what came next. It took a few rounds of walking back and forth between the bedroom and the closet before the spell was broken and I could finally think. Clothes. I needed clothes... and a shower.

My bags were empty, but my broken laptop and the book I had been reading sat atop a large dresser. I opened a few drawers and found the rest of my belongings. I was so tired yesterday, I hadn't noticed Arkkadian had taken time to unpack my stuff. All of my clothes were washed, neatly folded, and organized. My heart swelled at the notion of him making room in his life for me. I may have lost my family when Paige and Carter died, but I wasn't alone, I realized. I had a new family here in Eagle Ridge.

I quickly picked out everything I needed and headed for the bathroom. The warm shower felt heavenly on my skin, leaving me feeling clear and energized. I had expected to be tired over the coming days, so it surprised me at how good I felt compared to even a day ago. That didn't mean I could do anything too crazy, though. Dr. Gray had said I'd need to take it easy, and I knew if I didn't behave myself, I'd have to answer to Arkkadian. Not that I minded those consequences... I blushed at the thought.

I joined Arkkadian in the kitchen, and the smell of bacon and eggs cooking made my stomach rumble in hunger. I was starving this morning. On the way down the stairs, the realization that Arkkadian had seen the book hit me. How ironic that I'd been reading a paranormal romance about a werewolf right before everything happened, and here I was now, the potential new mate of one. What was once legend had become truth, though technically he wasn't actually a werewolf. I couldn't make this stuff up, though. I just hoped he wouldn't mention it.

"You look well," Arkkadian greeted me, all traces of earlier mischief gone. "How are you feeling this morning?"

"Much better, thank you. I expected to still be fairly tired. I'm surprised I'm not."

When I reached his side at the stove, he wrapped an arm

around me and kissed the top of my head. I wrapped both arms around his waist and snuggled up, feeling warm and safe in his presence.

"That would be the bond between us. It's a happy side effect of being mates. Though we haven't yet completed the bond, you'll still feel some of its effects, healing quickly being one of them. Don't be surprised if that cast comes off early."

"Oh," I said, liking the possibility.

Then Arkkadian's voice turned serious for a moment. "Your scars will fade also," he said, rubbing a hand up and down my left side where they lay hidden beneath my shirt. "They're much older and more extensive, but they could fade entirely."

This bit of news shocked me. The scars on my torso were a constant reminder of the horrors I'd experienced as a child, even though I had no memory of how I'd gotten them. Did he really mean I could be relieved of their burden once and for all? No longer ashamed of their presence upon my body? I wanted to believe him, but how was that even possible?

I pulled back to look at him, half expecting to see him laughing as if making a joke. He wasn't. His face was dead serious. Still, I questioned the truth of his statement. But after everything that had happened, why would he lie?

"You're joking, right?" I asked, my eyebrows pulling together in consternation.

"No, I'm not joking. It'll take time, and they may never go away completely, but they will fade," he answered. "I promise."

Wow. If this were indeed true—and judging by Arkkadian's face, it was—this was huge. I'd never known a life without them. What would it be like to actually wear a swimsuit or even a tank top, and not have to worry about others staring at my broken body? This could be life-changing.

"I don't know what to say. I mean, that's amazing, but I worry it's too good to be true," I told him.

"You also thought shapeshifters weren't real. And look what happened there," he said with a laugh and a wink.

"True."

I really had thought the entire idea insane in the beginning. I knew it to be real, but Arkkadian had yet to show me his wolf.

40

ARKKADIAN

reakfast was filled with light banter and feeding Aislin's curiosity. She had a lot of questions about our little community of Eagle Ridge and the people here, other Packs, her family, and more. I filled her in as best as I could, but when it came to her parents, I'd never known them very well so I could only tell her bits and pieces. Her disappointment was palpable, but I assured her that when the time was right, I would take her to meet her grandfather, Mathias. Satisfied with that answer, we moved on to other topics.

"I never asked you how old you are," she said.

"Take a guess," I hedged. She'd never believe me.

"Thirty."

I pointed upward.

"Forty?"

I kept pointing.

"Fifty-five?"

I pointed upward again, and her eyes grew as round as saucers. "Remember, we're immortal. Think bigger."

"One hundred? Two hundred?"

"Four hundred," I answered. She rolled her eyes and laughed in doubt. "Honest truth."

"You're yanking my chain. You barely look thirty." She laughed again.

"I was eight years old when King James VI of Scotland died,

love. I witnessed the Great Plague kill thousands in London. I fought in the American Revolution. Saw the invention of the first airplane. Even met Charles Darwin once."

She stared at me in awe. "Okay. Wow. So, you're immortal, but can you be killed?"

"Yes. No one really knows how long we can live, though there are some immortals who have reached a thousand years. We age almost imperceptibly. Most injuries heal quickly. As for death, well, the only ways to kill us include an injury to the heart or brain, beheading, burning in fire, or excessive blood loss from severe injuries."

She paled. "And that's not gruesome or anything."

"You asked." Not that I wanted to discuss such morbid things, but I wouldn't avoid her line of questions either. If Aislin was going to be my mate, she would learn these things, anyway.

"So, if you live so long, why aren't there more of you?"

"There could be, but we often take decades or even centuries to find our Aeternus. And, we like to keep our existence private."

"Can you mate with someone who isn't your Aeternus?"

"Yes, but it isn't common. Most of us would rather wait for fate, and when we find our true mates, the connection is instantaneous. We're not attracted to others in that way usually. We may sow some wild oats once in a while, but once we find the one, that's it for life. Also, Aeternus are infertile until the bond is complete, and after that, they're only fertile for three days surrounding the full moon. So we don't have to worry about unexpected pregnancies."

She digested that with a quiet sound of interest. "What about humans?"

"No. There has never been a human mate. Nor can we impregnate them."

"What happens if a human finds out about you then?"

"Ah. That's where certain skills come into play. You know that trick I do you love so much?" I asked. She rolled her eyes in disgust, surely remembering the afternoon she spent holed up in the bedroom with a bucket. "Well, some of us can plant memory blocks in someone's mind, like the one that prevents you from remembering certain things. There are few of us who can do it though, me being one. We're called Soul Shadows."

"Okay," she answered, pondering the information I had imparted. My mate was much more open to information than she had been in the beginning, and I was glad for it. None of this had been easy for her. "What's next?"

"Well, I thought maybe, if you're up for it, that you might like a tour of the compound. Then this evening, I'd like to take you up to the lake for a picnic dinner. Tomorrow, we'll go into town for the service. What do you think?"

Her eyes lit up at the suggestion of the tour, but dampened when I mentioned the service. Sensing reservations, I reached across the table and took her hand in mine.

"If you're not ready, we don't have to go."

"No, it's not that. I'm just sad is all. I want to go. I never got to say goodbye." A single tear rolled down her cheek, and I reached up to brush it away, my thumb lingering on her cheek for a moment.

"If you change your mind, all you have to do is say so. Okay?" When she nodded in answer, I smiled. "All right, let's go. It's a gorgeous day outside."

We headed down the driveway to the main walking path. Ahead of us lay the community garden and the green. Past that, the guardhouse and the road south out of Eagle Ridge. To either side and behind were cabins. A left would take us east toward the security building and the canteen. A right would lead us west to the library and the infirmary. The path leading up behind my cabin and into the mountains would take us north to the lake, but I was saving that for later.

"Left, or right?" I asked, giving her the choice.

She chose left. As we passed between some cabins, Aislin took them in, commenting on how cozy they all looked. Occasionally, we'd catch someone in a window waving hello as we passed. A few people passed us on the path, stopping to introduce themselves to my mate. Aislin surprised me by taking the time to speak with each individual, getting to know them.

Rounding a corner, we came upon the canteen. It sat parked between two cabins, overlooking the green. We entered, and I explained to Aislin that this was where the community took many of its meals. Community meetings and celebratory events were held here, and it also doubled as a shelter should the weather turn dangerous. On the other side of the canteen, I showed her where the little store sat attached. This was where we stocked any groceries we didn't make, grow, or hunt ourselves.

From there, I led her to the security building behind the canteen. Corbin and Gideon were inside. Madigan and James, whom Aislin had already met, were out on rounds this morning. Corbin stood up slowly, a pained expression on his face. He was still bothered by the information I'd shared with him the day before, but he quickly hid his discomfort and crossed the room to introduce himself to my mate.

"I didn't get to thank you yesterday. For helping me," she told him.

"It's no bother, just doing my job." His face was unreadable, his voice slightly brusque. He was uncomfortable. She smiled, and eventually, he offered one in return before returning to his seat in front of the monitors. Aislin cocked her head as he walked away from her. His abruptness caught her off guard. I whispered in her ear not to let it bother her, that I'd explain later.

"This is where we monitor all the cameras that surround our territory," I explained. She looked around in awe at the vast system of monitors, keyboards, and various computer equipment. "We take our safety seriously."

"I see that."

I purposely brought her here so she could see the measures we took to keep our community and everyone in it safe. I needed her to know this. I needed her to know she was safe.

As lunchtime approached, I led Aislin back to the canteen. Isabelle, Camille, and Nora had just finished setting out the meal, and Pack members were lining up to fill their plates. A simple beef stew, fresh bread, sliced cheeses, and grapes had been set out along with various beverages. Aislin and I helped ourselves and then picked a table away from the main crowd. Occasionally, others came up to introduce themselves but thankfully kept their interruptions to a minimum so as not to disturb our meal too much. Aislin took everything in stride, seeming to enjoy herself.

After lunch, we headed past the community garden, across the green, and toward the other side of the compound. As we passed the garden, she asked a few questions about how the community thrived, and I explained how we did almost everything off the grid. We relied on growing and hunting most of our own food and using solar energy. We piped fresh water in from a nearby spring.

When we reached the wooden platform, she stopped and stared silently. "Is that what I think it is?"

"That depends on what you think it is," I answered. Aislin was smart. She could figure it out if she hadn't already. I suspected she had, and her next statement proved it.

She eyed me cautiously. "Public punishments?"

"Yes, and no. Generally speaking, it's only used for serious infractions. Usually, punishments involve things like community service or hard labor. Otherwise, it's normally used for outdoor weddings and other community events."

"I stole a vehicle, Arkkadian. That's fairly serious." She clenched and unclenched her jaw as she continued staring at the platform.

"Is that what's bugging you?" I asked, taking her hand.

"Yes."

Only then did I realize we'd never talked about her punishment. Truth be told, since I'd decided not to punish her, I'd kind of forgotten about it. "You have nothing to be worried about, love. Under normal circumstances, maybe some community service, but your situation is anything but normal. You weren't being defiant; you were running out of fear. I think you suffered enough with a concussion and a broken wrist."

"Oh." She looked at me and then acknowledged the platform again. "When was the last time you used it? For punishment, I mean."

"You really want to know?"

"Yes."

"Kane," I answered honestly.

Aislin looked at me with shock. "Kane West?" she asked, her voice pitching high.

"He was exiled." I launched into the story about how he had taken the young girl and later challenged me after he was caught and punished.

Her face paled. "You said you grew up together."

"I may have hedged a little on that, but only that. We'd only just met, and you didn't know you weren't human. I couldn't exactly explain that."

"Makes sense. I'd have probably thought you were insane," she admitted. "Hell, I thought I was going insane."

"I'm over three hundred years his senior. He's always been trouble, though, even from the time he was a child. His father was an alcoholic and murdered his mother in a drunken rage. He used to beat on Kane a lot. Even as a kid, Kane was always breaking into someone's home, stealing or vandalizing something. His father's frequent drunken behavior exacerbated the already troubled child. He even started harassing teenage girls, which ultimately led to his banishment. Damn shame, but it's better he's gone from here."

It would be even better if he were dead.

From there, we continued on our path toward the rest of the cabins, with the library and infirmary beyond. As we passed by more homes, men and women came out to greet Aislin, and she once again invited them into a conversation, getting to know each one. I beamed with pride at the sight of her fitting in so well with the Pack. Her integration into our society was going so much better than I ever could have hoped. The nervousness she'd exhibited yesterday was nowhere to be found.

Once the last had said their goodbyes, we continued toward the library. It also housed several classrooms and an entire computer lab. Since we lived so far from the nearest town, the children here needed a place to learn, and our library provided everything they could need.

I followed Aislin as she wandered through the aisles of books and smiled at the joy written all over her face. Her love for books was clear, and it made me happy knowing I could provide her with something she loved so much.

"See anything you like?" Watching her peruse the stacks was like watching a child in a candy store. Pure joy.

"I love books. Ever since I was a kid. The stories, the characters, all their adventures. Books were the one place I could escape the real world. There are so many choices here."

"Well, the library is at your disposal. We even have a paranormal romance section." I smirked, letting out a little laugh when her eyes went wide and her face turned bright red. Oh, yes, I'd seen the book.

"I can't believe you saw that," she replied.

"Oh, yes. I even read it aloud to you in the hospital."

The mortified look she gave me was priceless.

A glance at my watch told me it was nearly four o'clock, so we meandered back home to prepare for our picnic, much to my mate's delight. I think she was happy not to be discussing her choice in reading material any longer. At least not with her own personal "werewolf."

As we worked side-by-side packing everything we needed, I kept thinking about this evening. The more time Aislin and I spent together, the more strung up my wolf became in his desire to bond. The last few weeks had been nothing short of torture, and I'd spent plenty of extra time in the bathroom taking care of every urge. I knew I couldn't hold the beast off much longer.

It didn't help that every time we passed each other in the kitchen, one of us brushed up against the other, sneaking touches here or there. By the time we left the cabin, my wolf was clamoring to sate its craving.

41

AISLIN

Following Arkkadian, I rounded a bend in the trail, and like a technicolor dream, the glorious view of a clear mountain lake surrounded by towering peaks in the distance opened up before me. I gasped at the sight, trying to take it all in, but there was so much to see. Every color, every sound, they were like a fine-tuned melody playing nature's song.

The trail ended at the edge of a clean sandy beach on the shoreline. Great silver firs and ponderosa pines lined the lakeshore, interspersed with the occasional larch, spruce, or hemlock. Purple forget-me-nots and yellow buttercups dotted the serene landscape while little fat bumblebees flitted bloom to bloom, their tiny wings defying everything nature said they couldn't do. Smooth as glass, the lake's surface perfectly mirrored the sky, giving everything an otherworldly feel. All was quiet, except for a few songbirds singing in the trees and the buzzing of those busy little bees.

Never had I seen such beauty. This hidden paradise was a boon to my damaged soul, healing me from within. Giddy with excitement, I kicked off my shoes and socks and dug my toes into the soft sand. Over my shoulder, Arkkadian watched me, his smile genuine, his eyes burning bright with love.

"It's so beautiful," I told him, wandering to the water's edge and splashing my feet around. The water was cold and sobering, and I quickly jumped back out. "Oh, my God, it's freezing!"

Arkkadian laughed from somewhere behind me, his joy and passion bleeding into the connection we shared.

Together, we set out the blanket and the basket of food. We sat in silence for a time, enjoying the food and being in each other's company. We watched the sky fill with brilliant pinks and purples as the sun slowly sank toward the horizon. It was so relaxing just being present in the moment and not having the weight of the world on my shoulders for a little while.

Nearing the end of the meal, I summoned the courage to ask Arkkadian the one burning question that had plagued me for weeks. The one I was too scared to ask before now. "Will you show me your wolf?"

As if he'd been waiting for this moment, Arkkadian let loose with a small whoop, and his face lit up with excitement. "I was wondering when you might ask. I've been dying to show you, but I was afraid of scaring you."

"You're not dangerous, are you?" I eyed him.

"No. Not to you, but be forewarned, he may be a bit—how do I say this—enthusiastic. My wolf has been craving the bond since the day we met, and it's been difficult to keep him in check."

I tensed at his admission. "Oh."

"He won't hurt you, love. I promise. Do you still want to see?"

"Yes." I so desperately wanted to see. More than anything.

Arkkadian stood and stripped, removing every article of clothing until he stood before me in all his glory. I couldn't help but stare in awe. His body was a magnificent sight. He was a solid wall of well-defined muscle, lean and strong. Like the first night I'd met him, he radiated power and mystery, but this time, I felt no intimidation. Instead, I felt love. Pure, radiant love.

Arkkadian knelt down on the ground, and the air suddenly shimmered. In the next instant, a very large, very black wolf with a silvery-white star upon its chest stood in his place. His eyes were still the same bright blue that had bewitched my soul the night we met. My eyes went back to the star, noticing its similarity to my own silver eyes. Was it a coincidence? Or was it truly fate? My gut told me it was the latter.

I sat up on my knees, legs bent beneath me, and beckoned the wolf closer, despite my heart pounding a tattoo into my ribs. Most normal people wouldn't dare approach a wild wolf, let alone a wolf this size. Had I been standing up, his head would have reached mid-chest. The black wolf in front of me easily dwarfed a wild wolf three times over. He was splendid. Majestic. Regal. Proud.

The wolf approached slowly, surely sensing my unease at his unnatural size. I reached out a cautious hand, and his nose met my fingers. I leaned closer, eased my hand up and around the back of his ears, and gave a scratch. He tilted his head into my hand in response. His dark fur was sleek and soft as silk as it slid through my fingers.

Then, out of nowhere, I was on my back on the blanket, staring up at black fur and sharp canines. The wolf—Arkkadian—had knocked me over. I almost panicked until I realized his tongue was playfully hanging out of his mouth in a lopsided grin. Then he leaned down and licked my face. I giggled, and his reaction was to nuzzle me all over. His attempt at tickling me, I supposed. I tried to roll away, hysterical with laughter as he dug his nose into my ribs first, then my armpit, and even the side of my neck. I was severely ticklish, and somehow Arkkadian had found all my most sensitive spots, making me shriek with uncontrollable mirth.

Without warning, Arkkadian jolted upright, instantly on alert, ears cocked. His head jerked toward the forest, picking up on some distant sound I couldn't hear. Placing himself between me and the trees, he let loose with a low growl, baring teeth that could probably shred through the hide of an alligator. I never wanted to be on the receiving end of those.

Turning my attention back to the situation, I looked around us but didn't see or hear anything unusual. Until I realized there were no birds happily twittering. No bees buzzing. It was eerie. Arkkadian's hackles were up, and he continued to growl in warning.

"Arkkadian? What's going on? You're scaring me."

Arkkadian kept his eye on the woods, but our connection rippled with a feeling I could only liken to danger. Then the air shimmered again, and Arkkadian reappeared next to me. "Something's wrong. Listen to me. I'm shifting back. I'm not going anywhere, but if something happens, you run. You take the trail and run straight to Gideon's. You know the way."

"But—"

"No. You run and you don't stop until you get there. Do you understand?"

"Yes," I replied, suddenly terrified.

The silence surrounding us was deafening. The air shimmered once more, and Arkkadian's wolf stood before me again. He wandered a few steps forward, and I waited behind him, trembling where I stood. I hadn't realized I was holding my breath until a gunshot rang out, shattering the silence around us, scattering the birds to the four winds.

Arkkadian jolted to the side, letting out a whimper, but he continued to stand his ground. I ducked as low to the ground as I could, while still keeping watch of my surroundings. Blood splashed on the ground, and I tracked the steadily flowing path upward to the wolf's shoulder. Arkkadian had been shot! Fear tore through me, and I did everything in my power to will it back down. Now wasn't the time to lose myself. I needed to keep my head about me.

The phone! Arkkadian had a phone in his pocket. Before I could grab it, a second shot rang out, quickly followed by third, and then a fourth. Down the wolf went, landing on his side, and I screamed.

"Arkkadian! Oh, God! Oh, God! Arkkadian!" I quickly crawled toward him. He didn't move. He didn't whine in pain. I gave a giant shove, trying to roll him on his back, but he was too heavy.

My hands slipped in blood. There were three holes in his chest, but not knowing anything about wolf anatomy, all I could do was pray the bullets hadn't hit his heart. Arkkadian said they couldn't die unless they took a hit to the heart or... or... what else did he say? Fuck! I couldn't remember.

I kept shouting his name, trying to shake him awake, but there was no response. My chest felt like it was caving in. Please don't be dead! Please don't be dead!

I went for the phone again, but a pair of legs stopped me in my tracks. I tipped my head up and found the last man I ever wanted to see again. Kane leered down at me, nothing but murderous rage written on his face. Ugly scars marred the entire left side of his head, neck, and arm. Burn scars. I scrambled backward through the sand on my hands and feet, stumbling over the lifeless body of Arkkadian's wolf.

Where was security? How had Kane found me? Arkkadian told me to run and in my panic, I hadn't listened. Stupid! How could I be so stupid?

Kane just stood there, gloating above me.

"Arkkadian!" I screamed again, one hand reaching back to push on his body, but there was still no response. I willed him to wake up, but my pleas went unanswered.

Climbing to my feet, I stepped over his body, slowly walking backward toward the trail and away from Kane, never taking my eyes off him. He just smiled wickedly, as if he carried a secret. Why wasn't he following me? Something was wrong. Very wrong.

I continued backing up, preparing to tuck tail and run back down the trail as Arkkadian had instructed. Step by step, back I went until I bumped into something hard. Turning, I came face to face with glowing red eyes and fangs.

I screamed and stepped back as the terrifying man in front of me sneered in disgust. His features seemed oddly familiar, and my mind flashed back to the picture of my mother. Oh, fuck! Fuck! Fuck! Fuck!

Behind the creep with the fangs, the young guard from the gatehouse cowered on the ground. Blood covered his face and chest, and one foot was bent at an odd angle. The shame on his face said it all. Hadn't he sworn his loyalty to me just yesterday? The fucking traitor! That his hands were bound and he was beaten and bloody didn't matter to me. He'd still betrayed us.

I ran for the trail, but before I could take two steps, an arm clamped hard around my waist. A white cloth pressed down over my face and a sickly sweet smell filled my nose as I flailed, trying to wrench myself free. My nose and throat burned, and I struggled to breathe, unable to avoid inhaling whatever chemical soaked the cloth.

Then the blue sky above disappeared.

42

AISLIN

Something wet landed on my cheek, pulling me from a deep, uncomfortable slumber. Drip. Drip. Drip. I wiped the wetness away and my tired eyes landed on the ceiling above me. Tiny droplets of stale water dangled from the edges of a moldy crack in the plaster, waiting for gravity to set them free.

I wrinkled my nose at the damp smell of mold and mildew in the air. A single, dim lightbulb hung by a chain from the ceiling, providing the bare minimum of light while leaving the corners of the dank room obscured in shadow. I sat on a smelly a mattress stained with God knows what, the springs creaking beneath my weight as I sat up. My movements were sluggish at first, probably from whatever they'd drugged me with.

A heavy shackle wrapped around my left ankle. The other end connected to a wooden post in the center of the floor by a long, heavy chain. The post had several metal rings mounted to it, and I knew without a doubt I wasn't the first woman locked down here. I tried to stave off the panic creeping up my spine, the thought of other women being chained in this room making me nauseous.

Taking of my surroundings, I looked for anything I could use to my advantage. The floor and the walls were made of thick concrete blocks. It was cold and unforgiving, the chill soaking into my bare feet still gritty with sand. A dirty old plastic bucket sat next to the mattress. It smelled of piss. And other things. Gross. A row of steel bars formed one wall. I might have been able to kick through a wooden door if I tried, but there was no escape through those bars. I made my way toward the cell door, limping as I dragged the heavy chain behind me. It wouldn't open. There was another cell straight across from mine, two more to my right, and a wall to the left. I called out, but no one answered.

I was alone in this dark and dirty prison.

I leaned against the bars and looked around one more time. A tiny red light in a back corner caught my eye. A camera. I was being watched. The fear that had settled in my spine earlier slithered through me like a serpent stalking wounded prey and striking just as it reached the base of my skull. I tried to remember what had happened.

I was at the lake with Arkkadian. And then he'd been shot. Kane was there. Then the memory of red eyes and fangs slammed into my mind, and I gasped, one hand coming to rest over my mouth, covering a silent scream.

Only one word came to mind. Vamphyre. That's what Gideon had called them. I quickly felt around my neck, relieved when I didn't find any marks on my skin. The face in my mind bore a striking resemblance to the image of my mother. Same raven hair. Same ivory skin. There was no doubt in my mind that I'd come face to face with one of her siblings, none other than Rafe Vane. But how? A million questions raced through my mind. Had Kane somehow figured out who I was? Were they working together? Did my grandfather know?

My mind swam. My chest caved further in with every exhale. I scrunched my eyes shut and tried telling myself it was all just a dream, but when I opened my eyes, I was still in the same dark cell. I had to keep my wits about me. Panicking now wouldn't do me any good. I thought of Arkkadian and let the sound of his voice filled my ears, telling me to slow down my breathing. I inhaled deeply through my nose and counted as I exhaled through my mouth, repeating the process several times until I felt calmer. It surprised me when it worked.

"Well, if it isn't my long-lost niece," a voice behind me said. The tone was eerie, almost macabre, with a slight English accent, and the hairs on the back of my neck stood up.

I jerked away from the bars with a shout and turned around as slow clapping and dark laughter filled the air. The man with the red eyes stood just on the other side of the bars. I'd never even heard him arrive. Amusement lit up his face as I limped away, dragging the heavy chain across the floor again. His eyes radiated pure insanity, and his lips turned upward in a smirk, revealing razor-sharp fangs.

An icy, putrid fear like I'd never felt before spread through me as he stuck a key in the door and unlocked it. This scary son of a bitch made Kane West seem about as vicious as a bunny rabbit on a carrot binge. The cell door swung open just as my back hit the wall. I scanned the room again, hoping to find a weapon or anything I could use, but there was nothing but the mattress, the bucket, and the chain. The chain!

But I realized my mistake too late. I hadn't left enough slack in it to do anything, but I couldn't win a fight against Rafe, anyway. He was a wall of solid muscle and at least a full head taller than I was. He could snap my skinny frame like a toothpick without even breaking a sweat.

"Who are you?" I asked pointlessly, already knowing.

Rafe stalked ever so slowly in my direction. Chained to the floor like I was, I was easy prey for the deadliest predator of all. He came to a stop right in front of me, our noses mere inches apart. The heat from his breath warmed my face as he spoke, making me feel ill.

"What's the matter? No hug for your dear Uncle Rafe? But then, I suppose this wasn't exactly the family reunion you expecting, was it, my dear, sweet Aislin?" He laughed and clapped his hands again, enjoying the discomforting effect he had on me.

I turned my face away, squirming into the wall, wishing I could sink into it, all the while knowing there was no escape.

"No, I suppose not. I admit I was rather skeptical at first when Mr. West reached out, claiming there was a girl I just had to meet. Imagine my surprise at finding you, every bit your traitorous mother's daughter, waiting right here. All chained up and nowhere to go."

Rafe placed a hand on the wall on either side of my head and leaned in, his nose just under my ear as he inhaled. Garnering a small ounce of courage, I stomped on his foot and pushed out with my hands. But like a giant oak tree, he stood rooted to the spot. I couldn't break him. I couldn't even make him bend. Instead, he just stared at me silently, his eyes lighting up brighter than a ruby splashed in sunlight.

"You smell like a dog," he sneered with disgust. "Don't you know? That's how my lovely sister died, little one. No one violates First Law and gets away with it. Seems your whore of a mother did a lot more than mate with a dog, though, didn't she? Because here you are. Where have you been hiding all these years? Hm?" Like a spider weaving its web around me, the demonic lilt in his voice made my skin crawl.

"Don't you talk about my mother!" I yelled, spittle flying out of my mouth and landing on his face.

He wiped it away, and then suddenly his hand was on my throat, squeezing off my air supply. He hauled me up the wall. My feet dangled as I pushed at him, kicking and struggling to draw in air.

"You are an abomination, you little slut. Not only were you born of a forbidden coupling, but you're consorting with mongrels yourself! My father will be so delighted to learn about you. He already had your mother and that wretched mutt taken care of. Soon he'll take care of their rotten little cur, too. You know what? Maybe I'll ask him if I can do it myself."

I wanted to slap the vile grin off of his face as my fear quickly turned to hatred.

Without warning, he let go, and I dropped to the floor. My windpipe burned with every breath returning to my lungs. I coughed and hacked as I tried to sit up and catch my breath. When I looked up again, my cell was empty, the door locked tight. He'd disappeared just as quickly and quietly as he'd arrived.

I thought of Arkkadian and his lifeless body lying on the beach. He couldn't be dead. He just couldn't! He would come for me. I couldn't give up. He wasn't dead. I refused to believe it. Arkkadian would save me. As long as I had hope, it had to be true.

Feeling defeated, I curled up in the corner, thinking there was nothing else to do. No, there was something I could do. I could fight. Arkkadian told me I was strong, and dammit, I wouldn't let him down.

I grabbed the bucket and made my way to the post in the middle of the room, gathering the chain as I went. I struggled to lift it and had to settle for dragging some of it behind me. I sat down next to the post with the cell door to my left and leaned against it. I tugged and pulled on the rest of the chain, gathering it to me, piling it inside the bucket to my right to hide it. If I could lift it, I could swing it.

And then... I waited.

43

ARKKADIAN

A crisp breeze rippled across my skin, and I cracked my eyes open. It was dark, the stars having filled the night sky hours ago. Brilliant blues, greens, pinks, and purples flashed above as the aurora borealis lit up the sky.

Dazed, I tried to make sense of where I was. Still naked on the beach. My hand touched something cool and metallic in the sand. A bullet. The realization that I'd been shot slammed into me. There were three more bullets lying atop the bloody sand. The remnants of three bullet holes in my chest were still knitting themselves closed. Dried blood covered my chest; the wounds had stopped bleeding hours ago. If one of those bullets had been even half an inch the other way, I would be dead. Fuck!

Confusion gave way to anger as the memory of what happened filled my mind. I'd just introduced Aislin to my wolf. And then gunshots had sounded, sending an explosion of pain throughout my body. The last thing I remembered was collapsing to the ground.

"Aislin!" I screamed.

Where was she?

"Aislin!" I scrambled to my feet, spinning all around, shouting her name over and over.

Fear and anger flooded through me, and a great angry howl erupted into the night sky. Hours had passed. My mate could be anywhere. I would kill Kane when I found him. No, not just kill him. I would tear him apart piece by piece and make him beg for death. Then again, maybe I shouldn't kill him. Maybe I should let him heal and then torture him all over again. And again. He deserved nothing less.

I ran straight for the water to wash off the blood, checking for other wounds and finding none. I yanked my phone out of my shirt pocket. It was just after midnight. Nearly five hours passed since I went down. I dialed my brother, pacing back and forth in the sand.

The moment he answered, I barked into the phone, "Aislin's missing. I want everyone to report to the security building now!"

"What the fuck is going on?"

"I'll tell you when I get there! Just go!"

If there were tracks, I couldn't find any. So, I shifted back into wolf form and sniffed around. Where the sand met grass at the edge of the woods, I picked up two distinct scent trails. One I identified instantly as Kane's. The other called forth a murderous wrath once I recognized it for what it was. Vamphyre. What the fuck was a blood leech doing on Pack land? And how in the bloody hell did they get through our security?

The urge to follow the scent trail plagued me, but if I was going after the assholes who took Aislin, I needed my team. My wolf howled beneath the surface, imploring me to run after her, but I couldn't. Not yet. I needed to think. To plan. Jumping straight into battle without backup was a fool's errand.

I picked my phone, tucked it carefully between my teeth, and raced back toward home as fast as I could. I didn't stop or shift back until I reached my cabin, where I quickly dressed and then filled a bag with a pair of sweats, one for myself and one for Aislin. She might need clothes when we found her. I realized too late that I'd left her shoes at the lake.

By the time I made it to security, my lead team was already there, along with nearly every other member of Pack security. Except for Elijah, who was at the gate, and one other. Eric, the new trainee, was missing. Dammit! If that little shit was involved, I'd kill him myself!

"Where's Eric?" I demanded.

"We can't find him," James answered. "We've accounted for everyone else."

I ground my teeth. "If I find out he has anything to do with this..."

"Arkken, let's focus on Aislin," my brother said, reminding me of what was important. He was right. Finding Aislin was more important right now. "Tell us what happened."

"We were up at the lake having a picnic and watching the sunset. The birds went silent, and I knew something was wrong. Then I took three bullets to the chest and one in the shoulder. When I came to, it was dark, and she was missing. I picked up two distinct scents, Kane's and a fucking Vamphyre. How the fuck did they get in without setting off alarms? I want answers and I want them yesterday!" I screamed that last.

Like a torrential flood, fury engulfed my entire being, over-flowing into every other individual in the room. As one, they all tilted their heads to the side, baring their necks in deference to their Alpha.

Elijah's voice sounded on the radio, static punctuating his words. "Someone better get the Alpha. And a medic. Eric's here, he's torn up bad. Says he's got a message."

Wrath boiled beneath my skin, the beast inside me a ticking time bomb. Detonation was imminent. The veins in my neck throbbed, and an angry heat crept up my face. I was known for my steadfast control even in the worst of situations, but ever since finding my mate, that control was slipping entirely out of my grasp. This wasn't like Aislin's accident. It was so much worse. This wasn't how the Alpha of Lycan Nine behaved, but since Aislin had come into my life, I was finding it more and more difficult to overrule my baser instincts.

Gideon placed a hand on my chest. "Calm down."

It was everything I could do to keep from ripping my brother's hand off at the moment. He was right, but anger didn't see reason. Rage could make even the most rational person lose control.

While I tried to calm myself enough to think, Gideon addressed the team. "Madigan, I want every experienced tracker at the lake in thirty minutes. Find the trail. James, I want you to go through all the security footage for the last twenty-four hours.

Find out what we're missing. I want to know how, where, and when they got in. Corbin, retrieve Eric and take him to the infirmary. We'll meet you there."

This was why my brother held the title of Beta. I could trust him to lead in my place and get things done. I wasn't graceful under fire when my mate's safety was threatened.

Corbin's face was grim as he met us at the entrance of the infirmary and led us to Eric's room, where he was still being attended to by Emmaline. The younger ones didn't heal as quickly as older shifters. Time was of the essence, though, if we were to find my mate, and Eric had the information we needed. His face paled when he spotted me, and he bared his neck in submission.

Blood covered Eric's body from head to waist. Large cuts and purple bruises on his face, neck, arms, and torso still seeped as the wounds tried to knit themselves shut. One eye was swollen shut, and his nose was broken. One leg was propped on the bed, his foot twisted at an odd angle.

Emmaline was working to stitch the worst wounds and stem the bleeding. Still, I had no sympathy for the young shifter. Not when my mate was in danger. I'd somewhat regained my composure on the way over, but I still seethed, knowing he was responsible for this shitstorm. How I wanted to beat the shit out of the kid. That was mild compared to what my wolf wanted to do to him.

"Tell me everything that happened. Leave nothing out." My voice was dangerously lethal. I felt murderous, and Eric was skating on a treacherously thin line.

"I was standing watch. The phone rang in the gatehouse, but when I answered it, no one was there and I thought nothing of it until I turned around and caught a punch to the face. Next thing I know, I'm on the ground staring up at a fucking blood leech threatening to rip my throat out if I didn't do what he wanted. Kane was there, too. The leech made me call and inquire about your whereabouts and wanted to know what time my relief showed up. When I told him you were at the lake, he threatened to kill me if I didn't disable a few of the cameras," he explained, his voice growing more pitchy as he spoke.

I fumed as he continued on.

"You know, the ones by that gnarled old tree that sits on the north edge of the territory. So, I waited for Elijah to show up for his shift, and then I made my way up to the north ridge, the whole time thinking you'd take them out. As soon as I chucked the cameras, they attacked me. The leech busted my ankle. Then they gagged me and tied me up and dragged me through the woods. They made me watch while the leech shot you. Then they dragged us both to their van and tossed me out down on the main road. I made for the gatehouse as fast as I could. I'm so sorry."

The more he shared, the angrier I became. The room brightened around me as my eyes lit up with blue fire.

"Why didn't you alert anyone?" I growled, and Eric cowered away in fear. Good. Let the little shit cower.

"I didn't have time. They only gave me five minutes to make the north ridge from the gate once Elijah relieved me. Said if I didn't make it there in time, they'd kill you both. Said if I told anyone, they'd kill you. I swear, I didn't know what they were planning!"

I lunged for him, but Gideon blocked my way and shoved me back with a snarl. "Not now. We'll deal with him later. We need to find Aislin." He turned toward the kid. "Did they mention where they were going?"

"Kane mentioned a cabin. Said he took a girl there once before. That was all he said."

Gideon and I eyed each other, nodding in agreement. They'd gone east, toward parklands. Though there hadn't been a cabin there all those years ago. That gave us a basic idea of where to canvas, at least. We'd start at the lake, though, in case the trail led elsewhere.

"What was the message?" I growled.

"If you lived, Kane said to tell you that you couldn't save this one. Not this time. He said that Rafe Vane would see all the mongrels dead, including you, before that happened."

Just like that, I saw red, and the world crashed down around me. My worst fear had come true. Kane West had figured out everything. And he'd gone straight to the Vanes.

I picked up the plastic pitcher of water on the table in front of me and threw it. It bounced off the wall with a clatter. Water rained down and formed a puddle on the floor. A feral growl escaped me and reverberated throughout the room so loudly, everyone in the room froze.

Forget a woman scorned. Hell hath no fury like the savage creature I was about to unleash.

I stormed out of the infirmary and didn't stop until I reached the lake with Gideon and Corbin by my side. There were thirty trackers, along with Madigan, waiting for us when we got there.

"We found a trail. It leads north through the woods, out of Pack territory, but dead ends in a small meadow. The tire tracks in the grass lead north to road forty-seven," Madigan announced.

Road forty-seven was an old farm road that skirted around Pack territory to the east and back around south again. It marked the boundary between our land and Glacier Mountain National Park. If the kid was right, Kane hadn't given up old habits. We knew exactly where to look, and Kane knew we were coming for him.

44

AISLIN

I waited. And waited. And waited more, for what felt like hours. I must have nodded off at some point because the sound of a slamming door startled me. I jerked my head upright, listening as footsteps sounded outside my cell, coming closer and closer. My heart pounded when both Kane and Rafe appeared on the other side of the bars. A third man joined them, and I recognized him as one of Kane's asshole friends.

This was it. They were probably here to kill me just as they had killed Arkkadian, though I still refused to believe he was dead. Despite my penchant for panic attacks, I remained calm, remembering Arkkadian's words. Breathe. Count. Breathe again. If he were here with me now, I know that's what he'd tell me to do. He'd tell me I was stronger than I gave myself credit for. Anxiety be damned. If they were here to kill me, I would fight them tooth and nail to the very end. I would stand tall to the very end. I would *not* give up.

My uncle stood just behind and to the side of Kane, his eyes glowing ruby red, Kane's a stunning emerald that contradicted his repulsive nature. The longer they watched me, the more I questioned their true purpose for me.

I studied Kane's disfigured face while I waited. The gnarly scar covered the entire left side of his face, drifting up into his hairline and down below the collar of his ratty shirt. It looked years old rather than weeks. Whatever wounds he'd suffered in the fire that had destroyed my home and family a few weeks ago had been severe, but with his enhanced healing abilities, I didn't doubt those scars would disappear in a few more weeks. I hoped the flames burned like hell that day. Too bad he hadn't died in that fire.

"That's the deal, right, Vane? We have a little fun, you pay me the money, and then she's all yours," Kane said, already undressing me with his eyes.

Bile rose in my throat and made me gag. How had I ever let this man near me? How had I not seen from the beginning what a disgusting creature he truly was? Good God, I'd been so naïve all those weeks ago.

A subtle movement behind Kane caught my eye. Rafe cocked his head to the side, eyeing Kane from behind before shifting just his eyes toward me and smirking. Kane hadn't seen it. My uncle was playing at something. Instinct told me to get up and move. Now. The bucket full of chain by my side completely forgotten, I shuffled back toward the corner as quick as I could, the heavy chain toppling the bucket, making my movements slow and awkward as it dragged along the floor.

Kane jingled the keys in his hand before unlocking the door and stepping inside. His buddy followed him in, leaving the door open behind them. Not that it mattered, since I was shackled to the post, anyway. I pressed myself up against the wall as the two men ambled toward me, taking their sweet time. Breathe. Stay calm.

Kane stopped a few inches in front of me. When he reached a hand toward my face, I slapped it away. "Don't touch me," I grated.

He leaned forward, his lips nearly touching my ear, and whispered, "Oh, we'll do more than touch, honey. And this time, you aren't going anywhere. My only regret is that I don't get to keep you, but it's worth it knowing the anguish it'll cause that Alpha prick you love so much."

"You don't scare me," I retorted. "Fuck you!"

Could he hurt me? Absolutely. Could I fight him off? Probably not. It didn't mean I wouldn't try. Did he scare me? Nope. Not anymore. I knew Kane for the weak coward he was. Only cowards hurt women the way he did.

My uncle, however, was a different evil altogether.

Once again, Kane reached up to touch my face, and I slapped it away again. I brought my knee up, attempting to jam it into his groin, but he was too quick and shoved my leg out to the side. In one swift move, he jerked me around and pinned me face-first into the wall with his body. His hardness pressed into my backside, and a memory from that night popped into my head. This time, I didn't panic. I let that memory fill me with strength, and when Kane leaned in, I threw my head back into his face and connected squarely with his nose. A sharp crack resounded, and he jerked backward with a shout of pain.

"You fucking cunt!" Blood leaked out of his nose, the small bone cockeyed on his face. Wide-eyed, I watched as Kane snapped the end of his nose back into alignment. The blood instantly stopped, and he used his shirt to wipe his face before peeling it off and tossing it to the floor.

My eyes immediately went to his chest. It, too, was greatly scarred.

I managed all of three steps before Kane grabbed me by the arm and dragged me back toward the mattress on the floor. I poured every ounce of wrath I could into each punch and kick I threw at him. His partner laughed as he watched me struggle. I knew I wouldn't win this fight, but I refused to give up.

Kane threw me down and climbed on top of me. He straddled my hips, grabbed my hands and pinned them above my head. I glared at him, intentionally breathing hard and loud through my nose, letting my anger show. Letting him know he would never get the best of me again, despite being pinned and unable to move. The other man knelt beside my head and took my hands from Kane. He squeezed so hard, pain radiated through my good wrist and I did the best I could not to give them the satisfaction of hearing me scream. Thankfully, my cast protected the other. Without it, my injured wrist would have snapped under the pressure.

Kane tore at the front of my blouse and the buttons flew every which way as it fell open. He continued to rip and tear until there was nothing left of the fabric. My chest heaved as I continued to breathe angrily. Kane slid down my body and did the same with my pants. He tossed the shredded remnants to the side, leaving my body exposed with nothing but my undergarments to shield me from their leering eyes. Kane crawled back toward me, and I lifted both legs and kicked, catching him off guard as my feet connected with his chest. He toppled backward onto the floor with a growl.

Just then, the man pinning my hands flew backward and slammed into the wall. His head hit the cement with a resounding crunch, his skull caving in, killing him on impact and leaving blood spatter on the cement. Before Kane could react, my uncle appeared behind him and hauled him into the air by his throat. I crawled away, reaching for the tattered remains of my clothes, and tried to cover myself as I backed into a corner.

Kane flailed in Rafe's grip, unable to break free. His eyes bulged, and his face turned scarlet. My uncle tossed him into the iron bars as if he weighed no more than a rag doll. He bounced off the bars and landed on the floor with a thud. The moment Kane reached his feet, he shifted into a giant gray wolf, teeth gnashing and snarling, hackles raised. His tattered clothing fell to the floor.

My heart pounded in my chest. I hadn't panicked yet, but this —watching two monsters fight—this was so beyond any scope of fear I'd ever felt. I froze in place, unable to do anything but watch as the two immortals battled in front of me.

The wolf lunged for Rafe, but my uncle simply sidestepped at the last second. He lashed out with a boot, landing squarely on Kane's side. The move sent the wolf flying across the room, where he crashed into the opposite wall. The wolf rose to his feet again and raced for the Vamphyre, pure hatred emanating from his glowing eyes.

Halfway across the cell, he jumped into the air and flew at my uncle, who once again side-stepped, causing Kane to fly face-first into the bars. Kane was letting his anger dictate his every move, rushing blindly into battle when he should have studied his opponent better. Given the choice of two evils, I preferred Kane. I had a better chance of surviving him than the creature with fangs and sanguine eyes, but even I could see Kane's anger would get him killed.

Barely missing a beat, the wolf turned on his heel and lunged for Rafe again. My uncle tried to side-step a third time but wasn't quick enough. He and the wolf crashed to the ground, the wolf pinning the red-eyed bastard down as he lashed out with his teeth just inches from Rafe's throat. The Vamphyre just smiled as he held Kane at bay, and before I could blink, Rafe dug his claws into the belly of the wolf, shredding flesh. Blood sprayed as he sliced, the wolf's entrails bursting out of his belly. Kane howled in anguish before collapsing atop my uncle.

Rafe shoved him off and climbed to his feet. His clothes were drenched in blood. Pieces of flesh fell off onto the cold floor, and he didn't even bat an eye. I retched on the floor at the grisly sight before me.

The Vamphyre bent over the injured wolf and addressed him, voice low and murderous. The wolf's breaths came in rapid huffs as he stared up at Rafe through dimming eyes, too injured to move. "Did you really believe I would conspire with a fucking mongrel? Or that I'd stand here and let you violate First Law in my presence? You're more pathetic than I thought, dog. Her death belongs to the Vanes!"

And then, in the blink of an eye, Rafe shoved his fist into Kane's chest and ripped out his beating heart. I watched, petrified, as my uncle crushed the still-pulsing heart in his grip, and it exploded, painting the walls and my skin with a fine mist of crimson. Rafe dropped the bloody mess without another thought. When it hit the floor, my stomach heaved again.

"Worthless mutt," he said, turning his scarlet eyes toward where I huddled in the corner. Rafe paid no heed to the blood covering him from head to toe. Tendrils of dark terror ruthlessly weaved their way through every fiber of my body as my worst nightmare came to life in the form of my mother's brother.

"My death belongs to no one. Least of all some blood-sucking vampire."

Goading him was dangerous, but I had nothing left to lose. The only way out of this cell was death, unless my mate somehow miraculously showed up to save me. I was a sitting duck, but I'd be damned if I was giving up.

"Oh, that's where you're wrong, little one. You're a hybrid wretch, and neither my father nor I will stand for it. First Law is absolute in our world and I guarantee the moment my father finds out about you, he will come for you. Do you even know what First Law is?" he asked menacingly.

I shook my head. I knew my grandfather had a law about Vamphyre and Lycan not being allowed to interbreed, but I didn't know the entire story.

"Why don't you tell me? I could use a history lesson," I snapped sarcastically. Instinct told me to keep him talking.

"Watch your tone in the presence of your elders!" he roared. When I didn't flinch and continued to glare at him, he went on. "Centuries ago, when my grandfather ruled, Vamphyre and Lycans lived in peace. In fact, all Aeternus often intermixed between the two. But my father coveted an Aeternus who did not love him. Emilia was the true Aeternus of his best friend. Your precious Arkkadian Rime's grandfather, Tiberius, to be exact.

"When he found out that Emilia and Tiberius were to bond, my father flew into a jealous fit of rage and stole her. Then he killed his own father, taking over the Covenant. War broke out. Lives were lost. But no one succeeded in saving Emilia from my father. He forced the bond, dooming my mother to a life of misery. Once my siblings and I were grown, she took her own life. She was weak and pathetic, but my father was never the same after that. I'd only ever known him to be cruel and vicious, but he was even more so after my mother's death."

"It's a shame you turned out just like him then," I said, disdain dripping from my lips like rancid fat.

His eyes flared brighter than ever. Rafe barely took a step in my direction before the rumble of engines somewhere above caught our attention. He cocked his head to the side with a frown, listening for something I couldn't hear.

"Well, little mutt, it seems your knight in shining armor has finally arrived. That didn't take him as long as I expected. Seems our little visit is over. For now. Just so you know, I could have killed him earlier, but where would the fun in that be? No, I think we still have some games to play, you and I. Until we meet again, dear niece." His voice was heavily laced with venom, and I could easily say I felt the same. And then he was gone.

I huddled in the corner, trying to process everything I'd just witnessed and questioning what my uncle had admitted. Was Arkkadian alive? Please let it be true!

Kane, at least, was dead. The mutilated remains of his body lay on the ground only a few feet away. I could barely stomach looking, and even though I knew he was dead, I worried that if I took my eyes off him, he'd come back to hurt me. The air shimmered around him, and his body shifted back into its human form. His eyes were vacant and glossy as they stared into the ether.

Somewhere above, doors slammed and men shouted. I wanted to shout for help, but fear of the unknown paralyzed me. What if it wasn't Arkkadian? What if my uncle had lied? I backed up into the dark corner as far as I could, silencing my breathing as much as possible, and stared at the ceiling, listening to the muffled voices coming from above. I thought I heard Arkkadian's voice, but I couldn't be sure.

Then two men I recognized, Corbin and Gideon, appeared in the doorway. Arkkadian! I covered my mouth with my hands and burst into tears at the realization that I was safe. Neither of them approached me, wisely opting to call for my mate instead. If I knew Arkkadian as well as I thought, his wolf wouldn't want another male anywhere near me. They were right to remain where they were.

"Arkkadian! She's down here!"

"Arkkadian!"

I buried my head in my knees and fell to the floor, curling into a ball, listening to the shouts of men gathering outside my cell. Arkkadian had literally brought an army to rescue me. Relief poured out of me as I wept and waited for him to come to me.

Warm, familiar hands gripped mine, pulling them away from my face. Then Arkkadian's beautiful face filled my vision. I jumped into his arms, and he held me tight against him as tears of relief leaked from my eyes. I let his body heat soak into me, and with it came the familiar healing waves he released. Despite knowing I was safe, I couldn't stop crying. Arkkadian was here. My mate was alive!

"Shh, love. You're okay. Everything will be okay," he soothed, petting my hair and kissing the top of my head as his voice cracked. "I was so afraid we wouldn't make it in time. I thought I'd lost you forever this time."

"I thought you were dead!" I cried.

"I'm right here, love. And I'm not going anywhere. I promise."

"I love you," I sobbed, burying my head in his neck, clinging onto him for dear life. I inhaled his scent, letting it heal me from within as I relaxed into his embrace. This man—this fierce, dominant, protective man—I was never, ever going to let him go. Never again.

"I love you, too. Come on, let's go home."

45

ARKKADIAN

"Get me a blanket and a bolt cutter!" I shouted to no one in particular.

Aislin's clothes were ruined, leaving her in nothing but her bra and panties. She had since given up covering herself with the scraps of clothing piled on the floor in front of her. Her auburn locks were a stringy, dingy mess, and dirt and blood streaked her face and body. Fortunately, none of it was hers.

I used my t-shirt and a bottle of water to wipe the blood away. Then Gideon appeared at my side and handed over a wool blanket. I wrapped it around my mate while my brother removed the shackle, and then I carried her out to one of the waiting vehicles.

The relief that washed over me upon finding her was a boon to my wolf. The rage within had died down quickly, finally allowing me to think again. I hesitated to think what might have happened had we never found her.

We were only about half an hour east of Eagle Ridge, in the spot where Kane had taken the young girl many years ago. Back then, this cabin hadn't existed, and this place had been a small meadow. It's exact location long forgotten until now. It seemed Kane had been very busy since his exile, somehow slipping under our radar all this time, reminding me once again of my stupid decision not to kill him all those years ago.

It had still taken our trackers nearly eight hours to track Aislin here, though, as the Vamphyre's scent trail had crisscrossed all over the woods. Fake trails had led several of our trackers in the wrong direction. Those eight hours of searching were sheer hell. The beast beneath my skin continued to rage, and I'd nearly lost control several times. Twice, I'd almost attacked one of my own. The longer it took to find Aislin, the angrier I became. The angrier I became, the harder my wolf fought to break free. I had my brother to thank for keeping a tight rein, or I'd have probably torn apart anyone who stood in the way of finding my mate, even if they were helping to find her.

The cells in the basement left little to the imagination. How many women had Kane brought here? How many had he hurt? What happened to them? The mere thought of what might have taken place here sickened me. I should have killed Kane the day he took Aislin hostage. Hell, I should have killed him decades ago. Back then, I hadn't realized how unhinged he truly was, though. At least he wouldn't be harming anyone else from now on, though I regretted not being the one to finish him. Regardless, seeing his dead body brought me satisfaction all the same.

"Are you hurt anywhere?" I asked her after she dressed, tilting her head this way and that so I could get a better look. Aislin had a few new bruises, but overall, she looked okay. The way she sat with her knees up and arms wrapped around her legs concerned me. "Are you sure? Talk to me."

"Can we just go home?" she whispered, burying her face in her knees.

"Of course, love. But I need to speak to my men before we go. Stay in the vehicle, I'll be right back." I reached for the door to close it when her hand shot out and grabbed mine.

"No! Please don't go!" She looked around wildly at the surrounding trees, terrified of whatever lurked there and pulled the blanket tighter. "Don't leave me! Please don't leave me!"

"It's okay. I'm not going anywhere. Tell me what's wrong, love."

Gideon joined us at that exact moment. "We've identified the other body in the cell. He's the one who escaped the night of the fire. The entire cabin also reeks of the blood leech."

I had scented the creature the moment I'd entered the empty cabin, but I had been too preoccupied with finding my mate to pay it much heed since the cabin appeared empty, at least until Corbin found the secret passage in the wall that led to the dungeon—for lack of a better word—where we found Aislin. At the mention of the Vamphyre, Aislin cowered under the blanket.

"There's more," Gideon added grimly, with hands on his hips. "There's a hidden door in the basement leading to a tunnel, and the blood leech's scent leads that way. Two trackers followed the tunnel, and it leads back to a small gravel patch hidden by trees just off the main road. The scent ends there and tire tracks lead back out to the road. He's gone now, but at least the son of a bitch did us the favor of killing Kane before he split. By the looks of it, we just missed him."

Aislin scanned the trees again before uttering a single word. "Rafe."

So, she knew who he was.

"You saw him?" I questioned. Jesus. My mate had come in contact with one of the very people who would kill her just for existing. If we hadn't gotten here in time.... I thanked my lucky stars we did.

"Yes. Can we please go now? I don't want to be here anymore," she begged.

"Of course," I answered, cupping the side of her face. I turned to my brother. "Collect anything that looks suspicious, and then I want this monstrosity torn down. Destroy everything. I want this blight and everything that happened here wiped from existence. And when that's done, fix those broken cameras. I'm taking my mate home."

As the two of us drove back to the compound, I listened in horror as my mate described everything that had taken place in that cell. Not once did she cry. Not once did she shy away from uncomfortable details. She shared it all, every last bit, and I marveled proudly at the strength she exhibited.

Though Aislin's uncle had done us a favor and put a stop to Kane's attempts to harm my mate, Rafe Vane was still as dangerous as ever, which meant this war was only just beginning.

But for now, my mate was safe and that was all I could ask for.

46

ARKKADIAN

One month later

My mate lay next to me, curled against my side, sound asleep, and I knew exactly how I wanted to wake her up. Raised up on my elbow, I leaned down and placed slow, gentle kisses upon her shoulder. As I worked my way across her skin, up to that sensitive little spot just below her ear, she stirred to life.

Aislin grinned. "I could get used to waking up like this."

I laughed. "Could you now?"

With that, I began to pepper her neck with more kisses, moving my lips over her skin with a slow, sensuous passion. When she rolled to face me, I covered her lips with mine and she immediately opened, accepting me into her mouth. Our tongues collided, tangling and dancing as my mate melted in my arms with a moan.

The scent of her arousal instantly filled the air between us. I had her exactly where I wanted her. Hot. Burning. Lusting for more. My hands wandered her body, the pads of my fingers teasing as they grazed across a nipple, down to just above where her panties covered her center, and back up across her breasts one more time.

When my fingers grazed across her nipples, she let out a lust-filled moan. Just as she tried to pull me closer, I pulled away, tugging her out of bed with me. I wrapped my arms around her, holding her flush against me, and once more delved my tongue into her mouth. With a whimper, her legs nearly buckled. I chose that moment to slam on the breaks, leaving Aislin standing breathless and dazed before me.

"That's enough for now," I told her, my voice husky. As much as I wanted to continue, we had a special day planned. And I wanted her thinking about this kiss all day, anxiously waiting for what would come later.

"What are you doing? Don't stop!"

"Nope," I said, grinning mischievously.

Unbelieving of my little trick, my mate wrapped her arms around my neck and tried to kiss me again. Instead, I pulled her arms free, spun her around and swatted her on the butt.

"Get dressed. We've got things to do."

"But—"

"Closet. Go. Now." I laughed as she pouted all the way to the closet.

"ARKKADIAN, HURRY UP!" My brother laughed, pulling me from my replay of this morning's events as I stared in the mirror, adjusting my fly plaid over my left shoulder once more. "You look great. You're gonna make us late and you know Sara will give me the what for later if we keep your mate waiting. Although, she'll probably enjoy the fact I've gone commando under this blasted kilt you've made us all wear."

I laughed in return. "It's a tradition! And you love it!"

"Touché."

Centuries ago, our ancestors had called Scotland home, and there were still some traditions we hadn't given up, like wearing kilts during weddings.

With one last look in the mirror, I turned to my brother and grinned. "It's happening, isn't it? Four hundred years I've longed for this day, and now that it's finally happening, I've got the damned collywobbles."

"Come on, big brother. Relax. Just think how happy your wolf will finally be when it's all said and done." He clapped me on the back, and I followed him out of the cabin and down to the commons to wait for my beloved.

Gideon, as my Beta and brother, would officiate our hand-fasting ceremony. His mate, Sara, would stand in as Aislin's matron of honor. She and some of the other ladies had worked diligently on the flowers decorating the stage and had put together an entire buffet over at the canteen to celebrate afterward.

Unbeknownst to Aislin, I'd reached out to her grandfather, Mathias. He'd been ecstatic to learn about his granddaughter, though he'd been pretty pissed I hadn't contacted him sooner. Fortunately, he'd understood Aislin's safety had been my top prior-ity, and he'd easily forgiven me. He and several members of his Pack, including Aislin's Uncle Gryphon and Aunt Kendle, and their sons, Brendan and Rowan, would be in attendance. Her grandfather would have the honor of walking her down the aisle, and I couldn't wait to see her reaction.

On the walk down toward the commons, my thoughts turned to the past four weeks. My near-death experience and Aislin's subsequent abduction a month ago had given us a lot to think about. Though things had been relatively quiet since Rafe Vane's escape, she and I both knew the lull wouldn't last forever. Another storm was brewing on the horizon, and together, we would weather it as best as we could. Until then, I vowed to maintain a life as normal as possible for my mate. Nearly losing her—twice—had shaken me to the core, and I would do everything in my power to prevent it from happening again.

Listening to her describe the horrors of her abduction on the ride home that day had made my blood run stone cold. I'd entered that cabin intending to kill Kane West, only to discover him dead and disemboweled, my work already done for me by Aislin's Vamphyre uncle. I was grateful Kane could no longer haunt my mate, but I was still angry I hadn't been the one to avenge her. Everyone knew Rafe hadn't saved his niece out of the goodness of his heart. No, that bastard didn't have a heart. Unlike his siblings, Rafe was as cunning and wicked as his father, Arden.

Eric, the young guard partially responsible for Aislin's kidnap-ping, was relieved of his position on the security team. I'd sentenced him to twenty-five lashes and three months in the brig. I would have made it longer, but the young wolf had apologized endlessly to me and my mate. No punishment given would make him suffer more than the remorse he already felt. Once his three months were up, Eric would have to spend the next year doing community service before he would be eligible to reapply for a spot on the security team. And because of Eric's flagrant misstep, we were revamping our entire training program.

Despite the abduction, Aislin still insisted on attending the memorial for her loved ones later that same day. I'd relented, but only on the condition that we took not one, but two security teams as a precautionary. The memorial had been difficult for her, but my mate had handled everything with grace as she said her final goodbyes to those she had lost. Finally having that closure was a blessing to her troubled soul after everything that had happened.

Aislin had also surprised me greatly over the past month. Since Kane's death, the nightmares that had plagued her had mostly disappeared. Though one would crop up here or there, they were relatively mild and nowhere near as disturbing as they used to be. She was no longer prone to panic at the drop of a hat and had instead shown a quiet strength and confidence she didn't know she had. She'd come a long way from the easily frightened young woman she was when I first found her. Truth be told, I believed the magic that worked to strengthen our bond was partly responsible. Whether or not it was, I was just thrilled at the improvement.

When I wasn't working with my security team or attending to the needs of the community, I spent every waking moment with my mate, determined to give her the home and love she deserved and craved. I worried she would struggle with the transition from a human life to one among immortals, but she took it all in stride. Not a day went by where she didn't make it a personal mission to meet someone new and get to know them, and so far, everyone she met had become quite taken with her. Especially the children. I was proud of her. She was an Alpha through and through.

All of that aside, the little minx had driven my wolf crazier than a mad hatter over the past few weeks, stealing kisses and tender touches, slinking around in skimpy nighties. To be fair, I bought them for her, but she delighted in teasing me. I had wanted to complete the bond much sooner, and she probably would have let me, but when Aislin confirmed something I'd long suspected—that she was still a virgin—I slammed on the brakes as fast as I could, much to my wolf's chagrin. She wasn't thrilled when I told her I wanted to wait until we were hand-fasted, so she'd spent weeks teasing me on purpose. As difficult as it was, I never gave in.

For the past couple of months, the instinct to bond had been a driving force, albeit a force I couldn't follow through with because of the circumstances. Aislin needed to come to terms with her new life first. So, I'd spent the last month behaving myself as much as possible, though I admit I did my fair share of teasing back, such as that kiss this morning.

Now, with the hour finally upon us, I stood on the stage with joy in my heart, watching as members of the Pack found their seats. I waited impatiently for the ceremony to begin, thanking the heavens for clear blue skies. We couldn't have asked for a more gorgeous day.

A hush fell over the crowd when my beautiful mate appeared at the end of the aisle. My heart swelled at the sight of her. She was positively stunning.

Aislin wore a vintage Celtic, floor-length, off the shoulder dress made of white crushed velvet with long flowing sleeves in pale blue chiffon. Matching blue ribbons laced up the front and back of the form-fitting bodice. The neckline and waist were trimmed with traditional gold Celtic braiding. Her sun-kissed auburn hair was styled in a Dutch braid with a low bun, and a wreath of white daisies, sweet alyssum, bluebells, and purple heather sat atop of her head like a crown. She carried a matching bouquet of daisies and heather.

Aislin's face lit up when she saw me, but before she could take her first step down the aisle, Mathias appeared beside her with his arm out. She was taken aback by the big, bearded, barrel-chested man with silver eyes just like hers. He looked just like her father. She looked from him to me, and back again.

"Grandfather?" she asked, her voice cracking with emotion.

"Yes, my darling." He reached forward and cupped her chin. "You're just as beautiful as your mother was, but you have your father's eyes."

"But why? How?" My mate smiled at me, though shock clearly showed on her face even as happy tears pricked her eyes. I stood there grinning like a Cheshire cat as she jumped into his arms. Mathias wrapped his arms around her, holding her tight. Despite his big-bellied laugh, his eyes were watery with emotion.

"Your mate. I guess he wanted to surprise us both. Don't cry, darling. This is a joyous day! May I have the honor of walking you down the aisle?" he asked, wiping a tear from Aislin's eye. "Your beloved is waiting."

She quickly nodded and took his arm as the harpist played a delicate version of Pachelbel's "Canon in D." Together, my mate and her grandfather made their way down the aisle. Every step she took personified the grace and beauty that she was, and I watched with bated breath, impatiently waiting for the moment she would join me.

When they reached me, Mathias passed her hand to mine, gave her a kiss on her temple, and then turned to me with a tear in his own eye as he shook my hand.

"Thank you. Thank you for finding her. For saving her. And thank you for bringing a part of my son back into my life. I thought I'd lost him forever, but with Aislin, I know he's still here. I can never repay you for what you have done, Arkkadian. Please, go forth with my blessing. Take care of her. Cherish her. And love her."

"I will," I said, looking him in the eye, man to man, before he returned to his seat. "Ready?" I whispered to my mate.

"Yes," she whispered in return, beaming with great pride as she gazed upon her grandfather sitting in the front row. "Thank you, Arkkadian. This means the world to me."

"You're welcome," I replied, and when she returned her gaze to me, I continued. "You're so beautiful, my love." Seeing her so happy right here at this moment made my heart swell with pride.

Gideon cleared his throat, ready to begin.

"Friends. Family. Welcome! We are gathered here today to witness the joining of Aislin, daughter of Alaric and Wren, and Arkkadian, son of Bastien and Seraphine. Today is a celebration of commitment, friendship, family, and, most of all, love. We are here to rejoice with them at the beginning of their new life together.

Aislin and Arkkadian, may your bond be anchored in the strength of your love and faith in each other. Trust each other. Learn and grow together. Laugh with each other. May you always remember that love is patient, and it is kind. Love does not envy, nor does it boast. Love does not dishonor but rejoices in the truth. Love will protect you and guide you all of your days. And... like all the stars in the sky, love will always persevere."

Gideon stepped forward with a braided cord. He wrapped it around our joined hands as he spoke. "As this knot is bound, your lives are so bound. You are bound to your best friend, your confidant, your soul mate as you promise to love each other today, tomorrow, and for eternity. With these hands, you will cherish one another and comfort each other in times of fear and sadness. These are the hands that will wipe away tears of sorrow and joy. These are the hands that will not only give you strength but tenderness when you need it. Aislin and Arkkadian, please turn toward each other and recite your vows."

Aislin's face lit up with joy at my brother's words, her smile as bright as the sun above us. "Arkkadian, I promise to love you and cherish you. I promise to trust you and respect you, honor you and be honest with you in good times and bad. I give you all that I am, from this day forward." As she made her promises, a single tear slid down her cheek.

Aislin's words wrapped around my heart like sweet sunshine, filling me with immense happiness. It was like ambrosia for the soul. She was the nectar that gave me life, and in that moment, I wanted to forget everything and just kiss her, but I had to reign in my desire just a little longer.

"Aislin, I promise to love you and cherish you. I promise to be yours in times of want and times of plenty. I promise to be yours in times of sickness and in health, in times of joy and in times of sorrow. I promise to respect you, care for you, and protect you. I promise to comfort you and encourage you, and I give you all that I am, from this day forward."

Gideon grinned before speaking the words we were anxiously waiting for. "Arkkadian, you may kiss your mate."

I took Aislin's face in my hands and leaned in close as she tilted her face up to mine, our foreheads touching. "I love you, Aislin. With all my heart," I whispered so only she could hear.

Her eyes sparkled as she whispered the same. Then, cupping her chin, I kissed her. Her soft lips parted, and our tongues entangled in a slow dance of passion, fire consuming us from within as we shared our love. Aislin gripped my waist with both hands. I slowly slid mine from her face, down her shoulders and arms, to her backside and pulled her closer against me.

I was so distracted by the kiss, I'd nearly forgotten we were still standing in front of gathered witnesses until Gideon cleared his throat and the guests all cheered. When I pulled away from my mate, her cheeks were flushed with heat and my skin itched as the wolf begged for release.

"We'll save that for later," I whispered into her ear, letting the warmth of my breath heat the soft, delicate skin just below it. She shivered, and I loved the effect I had.

"By the power vested in me, Gideon Rime, as Beta of the Glacier Mountain Pack, it is my honor to present to all of you the Alpha and his Aeternus, Arkkadian and Aislin Rime!"

47

AISLIN

I touched my fingers to my lips, my tongue darting out to taste them as I thought about the kiss this morning that had nearly knocked me off my feet. My knees had gone weak, and my libido had shot through the roof like a rocket. I'd practically begged Arkkadian to seal the deal, only to find myself sent on my merry way with lust as the only reward for my efforts. The past month had been nothing short of sexual torture, with the two of us teasing each other and my mate refusing to give in. No, after I'd confided in him about my virginity, Arkkadian had decided he would do things the traditional way and wait until we were handfasted, proving even a hard-ass Alpha could still be a chivalrous gentleman.

I loved him all the more for it, but damn if it wasn't pure agony on my sex drive. The more we were together, the more the bond pushed and pulled in its appetite for completion. I don't know where Arkkadian got the willpower to hold off his wolf for so long, but somehow, he'd managed. If he could do it, so could I.

The time had finally arrived, though, and tonight, Arkkadian and I would complete the bond. I was nervous, especially being so inexperienced. Kane's attacks still haunted me, but Arkkadian had assured me everything would be okay, and if I wanted him to stop, he would. The power belonged to me. Throughout everything that had happened over the past few months, he had proven to be an amazing man, and I knew he would follow through on his word.

Spending the day in wedding preparations with Sara had given me plenty of time to think back on the past few months. I'd gone from human woman to immortal mate literally overnight, and now here I was about to marry that tall, dark, handsome, and mysterious man who had come to my rescue all those weeks ago. Little did I know then, a maelstrom would follow, uprooting my life and turning it upside down. I shuddered to think what could have happened had he not been there that night in the bar, the night of the fire, or saved me from my uncle. Because of Arkkadian, I was alive and safe. Because of him, I was reunited with the family I never knew I had. And because of him, I knew I was strong enough to take on the devils that wanted me dead.

The hand-fasting ceremony went off without a hitch. I'd never felt more beautiful than I did in that dress, and Arkkadian, he was handsome in his traditional Prince Charles jacket and tartan kilt, with the matching fly plaid and gleaming pewter brooch on his shoulder. Throughout the entire ceremony, his eyes gleamed with more love than I ever thought could exist.

He never took his eyes off me even once. And that kiss... That kiss had spiked my libido, curled my toes, and nearly melted my insides. Though I'd wanted to run off with him right then and there, we'd still had the reception to attend, so we'd had to put our lust-filled desires temporarily on the back burner.

The reception was filled with love, light, and laughter. Friends and family showered us with well-wishes, and Arkkadian's Pack once again pledged their loyalty to me. Actually, they were no longer his Pack, but our Pack. I found it overwhelming, but with time, I knew I would get used to it. Arkkadian even led me around the dance floor a few times, something we hadn't been able to do since that night in the Black Horse Saloon, and I loved every single minute of it.

I also spent some of that time getting to know my grandfather, Mathias, and my uncle, aunt, and both of my cousins. For so long, I'd believed myself alone in the world until Paige and Carter had come along. Losing them had nearly destroyed me, but with Arkkadian and my newfound family, my heart was mending quickly.

My grandfather couldn't stop looking at me or hugging me. It was like he was afraid I'd disappear. It was the same with my Uncle Gryphon. A few times I caught them both wiping a tear from their eye when they thought no one was looking, and I knew they still missed my father dearly.

"Are you okay?" I asked them.

My grandfather smiled, his teeth showing through. "I'm more than okay, my darling girl. I have you." He took my chin between his thumb and finger, and let out a large sigh before pulling me into a hug. "I just never thought I'd see the day when a piece of my son came back into my life. I miss your father so. And you, my precious girl, are a miracle."

When I pulled away, there was sadness in his eyes. And pain. But it was sadness and pain I understood. Though a part of us was forever lost, a part of us had also been found in each other. A part that would lead to new beginnings, new memories, and new traditions. That part was infinite love.

I turned toward my uncle and reached out a hand. Instead of taking it, he pulled me into a hug. "I'm so glad you came," I told him. Before I could continue, a painful lump formed in my throat at the thought of how much time with each other we had all missed out on. My uncle shared a knowing look with me, one that told me he understood.

"Wouldn't have missed it for the world, kiddo. Your father—," Gryphon paused, and I could see he was struggling with words. "Your father would be so proud of you."

I let out a rough sigh as I hugged him once again and bid them all goodnight. I looked forward to spending more time with them, but as the evening grew late, my loving mate whisked me away, leaving the partygoers to continue in their celebrations long into the night without us.

With the stars beginning to pop out from wherever they'd been hiding, the last of the evening's warmth was waning. Arkkadian led me up the trail toward the lake, and I was grateful we'd already changed into more comfortable clothes. The hike through the woods would have ruined my gown. We hadn't returned since the night Kane and Rafe had taken me, but tonight, I put those thoughts entirely out of mind. Tonight was about Arkkadian and me. Tonight was for love. Tonight was our night.

Already set up on the sandy beach when we arrived were two large blankets, a few pillows, a lantern, a bottle of white wine chilling in a bucket of ice, two wine glasses, and a small platter of fresh grapes and cheese. A small campfire crackled next to the set-up, keeping the late evening chill away. We tossed our shoes aside and sat down on a blanket together, Arkkadian behind me with legs on either side, me leaning back against his chest as we sipped wine together. I rested my head on his shoulder, trying to quell the anticipation that had been building for weeks. We watched the night sky fill up with twinkling lights a million miles away. The moon was full, giving off its own pale light.

"Thank you for bringing my family here. It means everything." I tipped my head up and kissed him on the edge of his jaw just as a shooting star shot across the horizon. As I watched it, I secretly wished for tonight to be extra special.

"You're welcome, love. It's important you get to know them. I may be your mate, but there are some voids I can't fill on my own. You need your family. And with everything that's going on, we'll have the additional support of another Pack." He plucked a grape off the platter and held it to my lips.

I took it from him, letting my teeth graze his fingertips. Arkkadian's eyes lit up with that familiar blue fire, and his nostrils flared. Suddenly, all the pent-up sexual frustration I'd been holding in for days burst free. Like a moth to a flame, I pushed him down onto the blanket and straddled him, planting my lips on his. I sucked his bottom lip into my mouth and gave it a light nibble as I ran my fingers through his hair. Arkkadian let slip a light growl, and my insides dissolved into liquid desire.

Moving away from his mouth, I placed light, feathery kisses along his jawline, working my way up to that small sensitive spot just behind his ear, lingering there before tracing my way down along his neck. Cinnamon and cloves—Arkkadian's personal brand of pheromones—permeated the air between us, growing more potent with every kiss I sowed across his skin. With every intake of breath, the intoxicating scent worked its way into my system, winding me up while also soothing the nervous energy I felt about my first time.

I skimmed my hands down the front of Arkkadian's shirt,

releasing one button at a time. I gazed at his broad, muscular chest, taking in the tight, washboard abs and those delectable little muscles just above his waistband that pointed toward the obvious bulge in his pants. Just as I was about to lean in and kiss his stomach, I was suddenly flipped onto my back. Arkkadian towered above me. His eyes were still bright with blue fire, and a devilish grin crossed his face.

"That's enough topping the Alpha," he growled, his voice laced with that smooth, deep whiskey tone I loved.

Heat pooled down low in my core, and I felt wetness slip from my center. My mate closed his eyes and inhaled deeply as the scent of my arousal drifted up between us. When he opened them again, the hunger I saw there suffused my body with lust. I wanted him to do wicked things to me.

A moan slipped from my lips as Arkkadian laved the sensitive spot just below my ear, sending electric tingles racing through my body. His hot breath teased across my skin, and I arched below him, shameless and wanton in my desire, but left wanting when he pulled away. He removed his shirt and tossed it to the ground before standing up. I took his hand when he reached for me, and then he pulled me up to stand in front of him.

He reached for the hem of my shirt, and I lifted my arms so he could pull it over my head. Then he knelt in front of me and deftly unbuttoned my jeans before sensuously peeling them down my bare legs. When I stepped out of them, Arkkadian traced his way back up my body, his fingers gently gliding along my skin on their path upward until they came to rest on my hips. He stood there a moment, drinking me in, eyes devouring me.

Feeling vulnerable, I attempted to cover the scars on my side, but he pulled my hands away and slowly shook his head from side to side.

"Do you know how beautiful you are?" he asked, cupping my chin. I tilted my head down, feeling self-conscious again, but he tipped my face back up to meet his and then gently touched the scars on my body. "Don't turn away, love. I mean it. You are gorgeous. Scars and all. I want to look at you."

I sighed as I looked him in the eye and dropped my hands back to my sides, reveling in the love and warmth I felt there.

Arkkadian pulled me into his arms, nuzzling my neck, placing soft kisses upon my shoulder. His hands inched their way around my body, finding the clasp of my bra and undoing it. Then he slid the straps off my shoulders and gazed tenderly at my breasts bared before him. Goosebumps prickled my flesh and made me shiver.

After he stepped back and removed his pants and boxers in one swift motion, he carefully laid me back down on the blanket. By now, my panties were soaked, my breathing heavy with lust. Arkkadian climbed over me, settling between my thighs as I spread for him, the thin fabric of my panties the only barrier left between us. The full length of his hardness pressed into me, and I blushed when he swiveled his hips. I shivered at the thought of his hard length filling me, finally sating long-awaited desires.

I slid my hands up his torso, surprised when Arkkadian sent a pulsing wave of energy through his skin and into mine. With it came the sheer sense of Alpha power, his wolf telling me I belonged to him. My body answered by arching up into his with a slow moan. My nipples peaked as they rubbed against his chest, sending explosive little sparks all the way to my clit.

"Love me, please?" I whined.

I'd never been so turned on in my life. If Arkkadian wound me any tighter, I wasn't sure how long I could last. Moisture collected on my skin as lust warmed me from the inside. Every kiss, every touch, every whisper—they were a tease. A prelude to what came next as I writhed impatiently beneath him.

"Relax," he growled. The richness in his deep voice taunted my libido. "All in good time, love. All in good time."

Arkkadian trailed kisses down my neck, across my shoulder, and then down to my breasts. He lingered on one nipple, nibbling lightly with his teeth before teasing with his tongue. I gasped when he sucked it into his hot mouth, every touch and every taste of my body a pure calculation of sinful delight.

I gasped again as he drove a hand under the hem of my panties, his fingers finding my silky folds and dipping inside while he continued to suckle at my breast. I writhed with hungry desire as his fingers expertly and skillfully brought wave after wave of pleasure. I greedily bucked my hips, urging Arkkadian to drive deeper, my body yearning to be filled. The sensation began with a small tickle, quickly turning to a heart-stopping tingle, and I rode the crescendo into exquisite ecstasy as he worked his fingers in and out of me.

Panting, I grabbed Arkkadian's body, holding on for dear life, a lustful moan ripping from my throat as the orgasm tore through me. I collapsed back down onto the blanket, consumed by bliss. Only then did Arkkadian slip his thumbs under the waistband of my panties and pull, shredding the fabric like it was nothing. He tossed them to the side and settled between my legs once more.

I watched him through half-lidded eyes, the fire inside me still scorching hot. His erection pressed into me, and I tilted my hips instinctively, relishing the friction. He slid back and forth between my moist folds, teasing, but never slipping inside.

"Arkkadian, please," I begged. "Please! I need you!"

Our mouths met in a gentle kiss and I parted my lips as he slid his tongue out to meet mine. My tongue curled around his, tasting, dipping in and out before he once again trailed kisses down my body and back up again. I felt him reach down between us, taking himself in hand, and rub the tip of his cock between my folds. I held my breath as he teased in, inch by aching inch.

When he was fully seated, he stopped, allowing me to get used to the feeling of being so full. Arkkadian fed me a slow, sultry kiss, and I forgot the odd sensation as my body surrendered to his completely, and soon, our movements melded in perfect synchrony.

Every masterful thrust, every swirl of his hips, every ounce of friction between our bodies conjured a vortex of delicious pleasure. The harder he thrust, the higher I rose. As I neared the peak, about to crest over the top for a second time, Arkkadian slowed his rhythm and tipped my face up to meet his.

"Aislin, love," he paused, "it's time."

I nodded my okay, and we locked eyes as he had previously explained last night when we'd discussed the bond and what would happen. The intensity of his glowing eyes increased, brighter than I'd ever seen. Continuing to move above me, Arkkadian projected energy, wildly potent and stronger than ever, from his body into mine.

"Focus on it. Gather every tendril of electric current. Let it fill you. Let it ignite your very soul with its raw, magnetic power," he'd said to me last night. His voice had been hypnotic. Seductive. Bewitching in all its deep, velvety splendor. And now I took his words and did that very thing.

The energy swelled in my chest, radiating outward throughout my body, relaxing every muscle and nerve along the way. Arkkadian continued to thrust above me, and I basked in the unbridled splendor of his dominance as that power soaked into my marrow.

Instinctively, my body sent the energy back into Arkkadian, where it traversed a path through his body and back into mine once again. The connection of our souls was complete, and with it, my core throbbed as it danced upon the precipice of another impending climax. Arkkadian buried himself with one final thrust, and together, we crashed over the edge. My vision blanked to bright white as our two heartbeats became one under the moonlight, and then the stars above twinkled once again.

Breathless and spent, I lay upon the soft blanket, savoring the afterglow of our bond as Arkkadian placed gentle kisses upon my shoulder. My vision seemed strangely sharper than usual, but I paid it no heed, assuming it was because of the amazing sex I'd just had and the completion of the bond. I lay on my side, watching the water lap at the shoreline, with Arkkadian spooned against my back, our fingers entwined and our legs in a tangle.

Joy filled my heart to the brim, so much so I couldn't hold it in. A single tear of happiness escaped, and I quickly wiped it away, hoping Arkkadian wouldn't notice, but he caught my hand and pulled it up to his lips, where he placed a chaste kiss upon my knuckles. Then he leaned up on one elbow and looked down at me with the concern only one's beloved could show.

"Aislin? Is everything all right, love?"

Arkkadian had told me it would happen, but I still wasn't prepared to hear his voice in my head. Having completed the bond, we now had the ability to converse telepathically, and it was an odd feeling hearing him speak that way. I still wasn't sure how I felt about it, but I supposed, with time, I would get used to it.

"I'm good," I answered. *"Just... happy. I never knew it could be like this."*

"Never knew what could be like this?"

"*Sex. Love. Life*," I answered in my mind.

I released his hand and rolled over to face him. When Arkkadian jerked upright, I jumped and sat up at the look of shock on his face. The blanket he had covered us with earlier slipped down to my waist, and I shivered as the cool night air danced across my bare skin.

"What's wrong?" I asked.

"Your eyes. They're glowing."

"Wait... what?" I was sure I hadn't heard him correctly. "Is this a joke?"

"They're glowing, like bright silver starlight." He grinned and pulled me up to stand in front of him.

"What does that mean?" This shouldn't be possible. Arkkadian said Aeternus no longer took on their mate's gifts.

"Aislin, you're not just an Aeternus. You're something very, very rare."

"Arkkadian, you're worrying me. Please tell me what's going on?"

"You are an Immortalle! This means you can shift! You can shift!" Before I could respond, he lifted me in the air and twirled me around, our naked bodies entwined as he laughed merrily. Then he set me back down on the ground, cupped my face, and kissed me with the fire of a thousand burning suns.

When he pulled back, leaving me breathless and once more full of lust, I asked him the question I'd asked him so long ago. "How are you so sure?"

"Because, love, I told you once. We're not written in the sand. We were written in the stars."

With his words, my earlier wish came back to me and I laughed. Then Arkkadian kissed me again, and we fell into ecstasy once more while the magic of the aurora borealis lit up the night sky above.

ACKNOWLEDGMENTS

To my readers, thank you for reading my first book, Aeternus, and taking a chance on this newbie author. I am beyond grateful. This book was a long-awaited journey. A dream eleven years in the making, that all started with Arkkadian, before I finally found the courage to sit down and write the story. Along the way, I fell in love with Aislin and Arkkadian and I hope that you, dear readers, love them as much as I do. I can't wait to share the rest of their journey with you.

To my beta readers, I appreciate you more than you know. Your awesome feedback and advice helped me turn this book into something I'm so very proud of.

To my editor, Sara, at Telltail Editing and my cover designer, Melony, at Paradise Cover Design, thank you. There are no words to adequately describe how grateful I am for the both of you, and how amazing you are. You took this newbie author and patiently answered countless questions about the process of editing and cover design, and helped me create something truly extraordinary. You are both, quite simply, magic. I can't wait to work with you again!

ABOUT THE AUTHOR

D.M. Shane is a mom to two amazing kids, is married to her high school sweet heart, and was a military spouse for over twenty years. She loves animals, collects butterflies, enjoys the outdoors, and her favorite color is purple. D.M. enjoys country line dancing and reading every single day. Not a day goes by without a book in hand. She can often be found enjoying an epic story and a good cup of coffee in the quiet moments before dawn when the rest of the world is still fast asleep. She writes urban fantasy and paranormal romance.

Visit www.dmshane.com for more
information on future books!

Love the book? Leave a review and let me know!

 facebook.com/DMShaneAuthor
instagram.com/dmshaneauthor

COMING SOON

Immortalle

The Immortalle Series Book Two

Imperium

The Immortalle Series Book Three